Olivia heard a sharp report. A gunshot?

She scooped her sleeping son into her arms and went inside the bathroom within the motel suite.

"Mommy?" Aaron raised his head.

"Shh. We have to be quiet. We don't want the bad guys to find us." She hated scaring him but was more worried about what would happen if he cried loud enough to draw attention.

"Olivia? Are you in there?" Ryker's familiar voice made her knees go weak.

She opened the door, grateful to see Ryker standing there. "What happened? Is everyone all right?"

"Yeah, but we need to hit the road. Now."

She stepped into the suite but stopped abruptly when she saw the two men unmoving on the floor.

"Thankfully, they must not have realized I had Duncan and Mike with me. I'm sure if they'd known, they would have come with more men."

More men. It was horrifying to think that there would be more men coming after them.

Forever, or at least until they'd gotten what they'd wanted.

AN HONORABLE MISSION

MISSION

USA TODAY BESTSELLING AUTHOR
LAURA SCOTT
AND
NEW YORK TIMES BESTSELLING AUTHOR
SHIRLEE McCOY

2 Thrilling Stories

Guarded by the Soldier and *Undercover Bodyguard*

LOVE INSPIRED
INSPIRATIONAL ROMANCE

LOVE INSPIRED®

INSPIRATIONAL ROMANCE

Recycling programs
for this product may
not exist in your area.

ISBN-13: 978-1-335-43063-2

An Honorable Mission

Copyright © 2022 by Harlequin Enterprises ULC

Guarded by the Soldier
First published in 2020. This edition published in 2022.
Copyright © 2020 by Laura Iding

Undercover Bodyguard
First published in 2012. This edition published in 2022.
Copyright © 2012 by Shirlee McCoy

For questions and comments about the quality of this book, please contact us at CustomerService@Harlequin.com.

Love Inspired
22 Adelaide St. West, 41st Floor
Toronto, Ontario M5H 4E3, Canada
www.LoveInspired.com

Printed in U.S.A.

CONTENTS

GUARDED BY THE SOLDIER   7
Laura Scott

UNDERCOVER BODYGUARD   231
Shirlee McCoy

Laura Scott has always loved romance and read faith-based books by Grace Livingston Hill in her teenage years. She's thrilled to have been given the opportunity to retire from thirty-eight years of nursing to become a full-time author. Laura has published over thirty books for Love Inspired Suspense. She has two adult children and lives in Milwaukee, Wisconsin, with her husband of thirty-five years. Please visit Laura at laurascottbooks.com, as she loves to hear from her readers.

Books by Laura Scott

Love Inspired Suspense

Justice Seekers

Soldier's Christmas Secrets
Guarded by the Soldier
Wyoming Mountain Escape
Hiding His Holiday Witness
Rocky Mountain Standoff
Fugitive Hunt

Callahan Confidential

Shielding His Christmas Witness
The Only Witness
Christmas Amnesia
Shattered Lullaby
Primary Suspect
Protecting His Secret Son

Visit the Author Profile page at LoveInspired.com for more titles.

GUARDED BY THE SOLDIER

Laura Scott

Help us, O God of our salvation,
for the glory of thy name: and deliver us,
and purge away our sins, for thy name's sake.
—*Psalm* 79:9

This book is dedicated to my niece
Taylour Rose Iding, DPT.
Welcome to health care. I'm so proud of you!

ONE

Olivia Habush closed and locked the office door, then shouldered her large zebra-striped bag before heading out the back door of the church. The early June evening was warm, and she resisted the urge to fan herself. Early summer in the quaint town of Harrisburg, Illinois, was much warmer than what she was used to when she'd lived in Madison, Wisconsin.

The edges of her oversize blouse flapped around her large pregnant belly as she made her way across the street. Mrs. Willa Bentley was watching over Olivia's three-year-old son Aaron while Liv did her weekly Thursday-night bookkeeping job for the We Are One Church. As an accountant, she enjoyed working with numbers and it was the least she could do for the nice people who'd welcomed her with open arms.

Upon turning the corner, the hairs on the back of her neck rose in alarm. For the second time this week she had the distinct feeling she was being watched.

The Blake-Moore Group.

Was it possible the organization her late husband worked for had found her again, after all this time? Having overheard details about what the former soldiers belonging to the Blake-Moore Group had gotten involved in, she knew they were not to be trusted.

Resisting the urge to glance over her shoulder, she began to run, her movements awkward and clumsy because of her pregnant belly. Her oversize purse/diaper bag banged against her hip as she moved. The run didn't last long, and she slowed to a fast walk while frantically looking for someone nearby.

But there wasn't anyone around. For whatever reason, the streets of the Garden Ridge neighborhood were unusually vacant and quiet.

Liv pulled her phone from the front pocket of her bag, intending to call 911 despite her determination to avoid the police, but before she could push a button, large, strong hands roughly grabbed her from behind.

"No! Let me go!" She managed to get most of the words out mere seconds before a firm, calloused hand clamped hard over her mouth. Her phone fell uselessly to the ground with a loud clatter.

She couldn't breathe!

Panic flared, paralyzing her with fear. They'd found her. After all this time, the men employed by the Blake-Moore Group, the men who'd turned her husband into a monster, had found her!

Dear Lord, help me!

Desperate to save herself and her unborn baby, she lashed out against her attacker with all her strength, kicking backward with her feet and scratching at every exposed inch of skin on his face and hands.

"Knock it off," her attacker growled, his voice low and rough in her ear as his arm tightened painfully around her. "Or I'll kill you right here and now."

Kill her? No! This couldn't be happening! She

thought about her son, Aaron, and her unborn baby. Her eyes burned with helpless tears as her attacker easily subdued her feeble struggles and began to pull her backward, away from the streetlights and deeper into the shadows.

She stopped struggling, in an attempt to preserve her strength while reminding herself that she'd escaped once before and could do so again. Granted, that was six months ago, when she'd only just discovered she was six weeks pregnant instead of thirty-four.

How had they found her?

"Oomph." The man holding her in his iron grasp abruptly let go. Still off-balance, Liv felt herself falling backward, even as she flailed her arms in an attempt to stay upright.

A pair of strong hands caught her before she could hit the ground, gently pushing her upright so that she was back on her own two feet. Her bag was somehow still on her shoulder and she hitched it higher, feeling relieved for a brief moment before realizing this could be another guy from the Blake-Moore Group.

"Let me go!" She shouted as loudly as she could, but the words came out like a weak croak. "Help! Police! Help me!"

"Olivia, please be quiet. We need to get out of here and pick up your son before this guy regains consciousness."

The stranger's use of her first name pulled her up short. She twisted out of his grasp and stared at his face, but he didn't look familiar. She noted he was dressed from head to toe in black, making it easy for him to blend into the night. Then her gaze dropped to the body of a man lying on the ground, also dressed in black, apparently unconscious. The silver glint of a knife blade lying on the asphalt beside him caught her eye, making her swallow hard.

What was going on? Who were these men?

"Olivia, I'm not with the Blake-Moore Group," the stranger continued in a tone she was sure he meant to be reassuring. "I'm here to keep you and your son safe."

He knew about the Blake-Moore Group? And her son? Had he known her late husband, too? Questions flashed through her mind like laser beams, but she managed to pull out of his grasp, hitching her bag more securely over her shoulder then clutching the edges of her long blouse together like a shield over her belly.

She tucked a chin-length strand of dark hair behind her ear and bravely faced him. "I don't know who you are, but I'm fine on my own."

"You *were* fine on your own, until now," the stranger agreed. The fact that he didn't try to strong-arm her was confusing. She rubbed her hand over her belly, hoping he wouldn't notice her nervous gesture. "But there are likely others on the way. We need to leave immediately. We're running out of time."

She instinctively shook her head, not wanting to go, yet deep down she knew he was right. She and Aaron couldn't stay in Harrisburg any longer. Oddly enough, while they'd only been here for a little over two months, it already had begun to feel like home. Regret swelled in the back of her throat and it was all she could do to keep from bursting into tears.

Stupid hormones.

"My name is Ryker Tillman." In the darkness she couldn't see the stranger's facial features clearly, but noted he was taller than Tim had been, with broad shoulders and short dark hair. He cupped a hand beneath her elbow. "Come on—we need to hurry."

The name didn't mean anything to her and frankly she wasn't sure if that was good or bad. Ryker knew about the Blake-Moore Group, but claimed he wasn't one of them. But he hadn't said he was a cop, either.

Not that hearing he was a cop would have helped her relax. She'd trusted a cop once, but when he'd called the Blake-Moore Group, instead of backup, she'd realized he was in with them. Thankfully, she'd gotten away in time, and gone back on the run.

Nope, she wasn't doing that again.

"I don't know you and I don't trust you." She forced the words past her constricted throat. "Please leave me alone."

"I can't do that. They're obviously coming for you." Ryker urged her forward. "That guy was only the first. There will be more. Your son's nanny is this way, correct?"

Wait, he knew where Willa Bentley lived? Where she and Aaron lived? As much as she wanted to pull out of his grasp, she knew there was no possible way she could outrun him. For a moment she glanced back at the man lying on the sidewalk.

The assailant had threatened to kill her. Ryker Tillman claimed he wanted to protect her.

Why? What was this all about? She didn't know who or what to believe.

When she could see Willa's duplex up ahead, she began to doubt the wisdom of going along with this stranger. "You knew my husband, then? Timothy Habush?"

There was a momentary hesitation before Ryker

spoke. "No, not personally. I knew of him, as we both served in Afghanistan. But he joined the Blake-Moore Group when we returned stateside while I decided to go in another direction."

To hear Ryker was former military wasn't surprising, and far from reassuring. She didn't want to be associated with another soldier. Her husband had once served with honor, but after his last tour of duty had ended, he'd decided to work for the Blake-Moore Group. After the first year, she'd known it was a mistake. The missions Tim had talked about were motivated by greed, not by doing what was right. When she'd overheard something about selling guns to the enemy, she'd felt sick at the realization Tim had sold out his country.

He'd sold out her, too. He'd been more interested in making money than having a family.

It had happened gradually, not all in one fell swoop. But one day, about a month before his death, she'd looked into his eyes and had seen nothing but a dull, flat emptiness.

His cold, dead eyes had scared her in a way nothing else ever had. Even now, the memory made her shiver.

She glanced up at the man at her side. It was too dark to see Ryker Tillman's eyes. Did they look the same way? Had being in combat changed him, the way it seemed to have changed her husband?

Tim was dead and so was her brother, Colin. It was all so surreal, especially when Colin had dragged her and Aaron out of the house during breakfast shortly before Christmas, insisting Tim wanted them to go into hiding. But it wasn't until she realized she and Aaron were locked in a small motel room that she understood they were being held prisoner under the guise of being safe.

Upon hearing the news that Tim was dead, she'd managed to escape Jeff, the guy Colin had ordered to watch over her. Oddly enough, the past several months being on her own with Aaron had felt liberating. Tim had become a coldhearted stranger to her, and when she'd discovered she was pregnant she'd worried about what her future, and the baby's future, would hold. As she left the Madison area, she told herself that it was better to be on her own. If Tim had lived, she felt certain he would have treated the new baby with the same indifference that he'd displayed toward Aaron.

On her own, she'd managed to drive Jeff's car to the closest town, then had been able to withdraw enough money from several ATMs. Her plan was to make her way south, seeking warmer weather. But her progress was slow. She'd stayed in one town for two weeks, the next town for three, the following one for two and so on. When she'd reached the charming town of Harrisburg, she'd liked it so much she'd decided to stay.

The two months she'd been here were wonderful. But now that the Blake-Moore Group had found her, the town was no longer safe.

She and Aaron would need to go on the run again.

As she walked down the street toward Willa's house, the feeling of dread became suffocating.

How in the world would she manage to keep running once her baby was born?

Ryker could tell Olivia's nerves were frayed and she was nearing her breaking point. There wasn't much time. They needed to get out of town. Maybe head into the Shawnee National Forest. It wouldn't be easy to hide off-grid considering Olivia's advanced pregnancy and her three-year-old son, but there wasn't another option.

The sooner they hit the road, the better.

He mentally kicked himself for letting that idiot get his hands on her in the first place. If he'd been quicker, he could have taken the guy out before he'd hurt her.

"I'm sorry." The words came out of his mouth before he could stop them. "I should have gotten to you sooner."

"You were following me?" The edge to her tone made him wince. But he wouldn't lie to her.

"Yes. But only because I'd noticed the guy from Blake-Moore following you." He'd been here for about two weeks, watching Olivia and her son from afar, shocked at first to discover she was very pregnant. He'd kept his distance, but then had gotten a glimpse of the mercenary following her.

The Blake-Moore Group was a team of former soldiers turned mercenaries who were highly paid to take on secret missions for anyone willing to fork up the asking price. In his opinion, they were motivated solely by greed, and that was enough to raise his suspicions.

About six months ago, he'd helped former army buddy Hawk Jacobson, his wife, Jillian, and their young daughter escape from the powerful man who'd hired the Blake-Moore Group to find and kill Hawk. Ryker had gladly helped arrest the man in charge and had assumed the group would have been disbanded.

But it seemed they were still afloat.

While helping Hawk with the investigation, he'd come across a scene at Tim Habush's house that had concerned him. A half-eaten breakfast, and the mysterious and obviously rushed disappearance of Olivia and Aaron.

His first priority was to help Hawk, but once that was finished, Ryker hadn't been able to get Olivia and Aaron out of his mind. It had bothered him that they were out there somewhere, likely scared and alone.

Vulnerable.

It hadn't been easy to find her; she'd done well staying under the radar. It had been frustrating to discover she'd disappeared without a trace. He'd backtracked, trying to ascertain what he'd missed, when he'd finally stumbled upon a clue. One of the last ATMs she'd used had been located near a small used-car lot outside Chicago. When he'd questioned the owner, the older guy denied knowing anything, but later that night, Ryker had entered the unlocked office and found paperwork that showed Olivia's car had been exchanged for an older model.

It was the break he'd been waiting for. With renewed vigor he'd gone back on the hunt, determined to find her. It had taken time, but that clue had finally led him here to Harrisburg, Illinois.

When he'd gotten his first glimpse of Olivia and Aaron, he'd felt a huge sense of relief to discover they were safe and unharmed. Yet he couldn't seem to simply walk away.

Especially once he'd realized Olivia was pregnant.

"Listen, Mr. Tillman," Olivia said as they walked up the short sidewalk toward the two-story house. "I really don't think—"

"Ryker. Please call me Ryker."

She let out an exasperated sound. "Ryker, then. I appreciate your willingness to help but Aaron and I can disappear easier on our own."

He didn't agree, but waited as she dug her key from the depths of a giant bag and inserted it into the lock. She opened the front door, and he followed her inside.

"Willa? I'm home," she called.

The interior of the house seemed unusually quiet. From the little interaction he'd had with Hawk's daughter Lizzie, he knew young kids tended to make noise.

"Willa?" There was a note of worry in Olivia's tone.

He pulled his weapon, just in case. "What is it?" he asked in a low voice.

"She usually waits up for me."

There was a light on in the kitchen, but the rest of the lower-level apartment was dark.

Every one of his senses went on full alert.

Something was very wrong.

"Stay behind me." Ryker gently but firmly pushed Olivia behind him. He debated whether or not to tell Olivia to call the police, but decided to find out what they were dealing with first.

"Where is Aaron's room?" he asked in a whisper.

"His room is upstairs next to mine," she whispered back.

He nodded and made his way down the short hallway to the two bedrooms separated by a tiny bathroom. One bedroom door was open, the other was closed.

With his foot, he shoved the door hanging ajar all the way open. The room was apparently used as a guest room and appeared empty.

Behind him, Olivia sucked in a harsh breath and he knew she hadn't expected the room to be vacant. He took a moment to check the closet and beneath the bed, before deeming the room clear.

He checked the bathroom next, but found nothing.

Testing the knob of the closed bedroom door, he found it wasn't locked. Keeping Olivia behind him, he abruptly shoved the door open, then stepped back to wait.

Nothing happened. Leading with his weapon, Ryker cautiously crossed the threshold, then stopped abruptly when he saw the older woman lying on the bed.

After checking in the closet and beneath the bed to make sure there wasn't anyone hiding in wait, he crossed over to feel for a pulse.

The nanny was dead.

"Willa!" Olivia's horrified gasp indicated she knew the woman was gone. "Oh no! Where's Aaron?"

"Olivia, please," he tried but then he heard the sound of someone coming down the stairs. "Run away and call for help."

"Not without my son!" She had her phone in her hand, but he knew any chance of help arriving would be too late.

"Go!" He pushed Olivia toward the door then quickly but silently crossed the living room into the kitchen, flipping the light off as he went. There was a side door-way that he felt certain led up to the second-story apart-ment.

He took up a defensive position behind the door, and waited, hoping the guy who likely had Aaron didn't know that his cohort in crime had failed at kidnap-ping Olivia.

"Mommy! Mommy! I want my Mommy!" Aaron's

cries echoed high and shrill above the thumping footsteps coming down the stairs.

"Aaron! I'm here, baby, don't worry!" Olivia's voice rang out loudly and Ryker momentarily closed his eyes, wishing he'd handled things differently.

He should have gotten Olivia and Aaron out of the city the moment he'd found them.

Instead he may cause the very thing he'd been trying to avoid.

Getting them both killed.

The footsteps came closer and he instantly felt all his emotions drain away, a sense of cool calmness washing over him. Every one of his senses was keenly focused on the threat and what needed to be done.

The same eerie sense of control had always come over him when he faced death. Back in Afghanistan and back in December while he'd been helping Hawk.

From his position he could see that Olivia hadn't left the duplex as ordered. He speared her with a stern look, but she ignored him. At least she was hovering near the doorway leading into the kitchen, somewhat protected behind the wall.

Except for her pregnant belly which was too large to hide.

He waved her back, but Olivia didn't see him. Her eyes were glued to the doorway.

Steeling his resolve to get her and the boy out of this mess, he waited.

"Mommy, Mommy!" Aaron cried again. "Lemme go!"

Ryker sensed the man holding Olivia's son was standing on the other side of the doorway, planning his next move. Ryker believed the perp was cowardly enough to use the child as a shield.

Which meant he'd have to find a way to take the guy out without harming the little boy.

His gut knotted with tension, but he kept his ears and eyes focused on the door. Ignoring the child's cries wasn't easy, but then he heard the barest whisper of sound.

He dropped his gaze to the doorknob and watched it slowly and silently turn. He mentally counted the seconds.

The door flew open. There was a long pause but Ryker was ready. He shot out from behind the door, bringing his gun hand down hard on the back of the perp's head.

"No! Aaron!" Olivia cried.

The guy stumbled, but didn't go down or let go of the child. Ryker grabbed his shoulder and hit him again just as Olivia rushed forward and grabbed for Aaron.

On some level he was aware of Olivia wrenching Aaron out of the perp's grasp, even as the big guy groaned and turned toward Ryker. In a nanosecond Ryker saw the gun and fired.

The sound of twin gunshots echoed loudly through the kitchen, and a flash of pain along the upper part of his left leg made Ryker realize he'd been hit.

But he forced himself to ignore it. They had to move! Keeping Olivia and her son safe was all that mattered.

TWO

"Ryker!" Poised near the front doorway, Liv hesitated. She wasn't sure why she was suddenly so worried about the stranger she hadn't trusted a few minutes ago, but she couldn't bear to leave him behind.

The man who'd had Aaron collapsed on the floor at Ryker's feet. He groaned but didn't move. Bright red blood began to pool beside him on the floor.

"Go! I'm right behind you." Ryker staggered forward, carefully stepping around the man. "We need to get out of here before the cops arrive."

Logically she knew they shouldn't leave the scene of a crime. They should wait for the police. But she'd been on the run for so long, she couldn't do it. Hiking Aaron higher in her arms, she followed Ryker outside. Willa was dead and two men had almost succeeded in grabbing her and Aaron.

Every fiber of her being longed to get far away from the quaint town she'd once thought could be her new home.

"This way." Ryker once again cupped his hand beneath her elbow, guiding her to the left.

"Wait." She dug in her heels. "I have a car here."

"No good. That's how they tracked you. I have a vehicle stashed on the next block."

They'd tracked her here through her car? How was that possible? She'd exchanged her newer car for an older model and asked the owner of the used-car lot to keep the transaction off the books.

"How do you know that?" she asked, already feeling breathless. Aaron wasn't overly big for his age, but she was carrying her unborn baby, as well. She'd tried to keep in shape, but obviously she wasn't going to be able to continue going at this pace for long.

"Because that's how I found you." Ryker glanced down at her. "Will Aaron cry if I hold him? We need to hurry."

"Yes, he's likely to cry, since the man on the stairs scared him." The little boy was calmer now, but was sucking his thumb, a habit he'd broken six months ago. He was also, thankfully, wearing a Pull-Ups diaper as she could tell he'd wet himself.

The poor child had been scared to death.

She tried to match Ryker's long-legged stride to avoid slowing them down. But seconds later, she could hear the wail of sirens.

"Almost there," Ryker said encouragingly as he continued urging her forward. "See the black SUV?"

"Yes." She was breathless with exertion, but pushed herself to keep going. It wasn't until they reached his car that she realized they didn't have a car seat for Aaron.

"Wait! We need a car seat," she protested when Ryker opened the passenger door for her.

"I already have one in the back, see? Let me strap him in." Without asking permission, he plucked Aaron from her arms and opened the back door to place the toddler in his safety seat.

Amazingly, Aaron didn't cry. She wondered if her son sensed they were safe with Ryker.

It wasn't until she'd climbed in and buckled her seat belt and Ryker slid in behind the wheel that the significance of the child safety seat hit her.

"You were planning to take me and Aaron all along!" Betrayal hit hard and she fumbled for the door handle. "You're one of them! I can't believe I fell for your act and—"

"Don't, Olivia." Ryker's voice wasn't harsh, but firm. "I have never lied to you. I don't work for the Blake-Moore Group, in fact I helped bring some of their men down. However, I have been trying to find you and Aaron to make sure you were safe. That's why I have a car seat. I wanted to be ready if they came for you."

He'd already pulled away from the curb and was driving slowly away from Willa's home. Liv glanced at her purse/diaper bag, thinking about the clothing and toys she'd left behind, and bit down on her lower lip to keep from crying.

Were they really safe with Ryker? She wanted to trust her instincts, but too much had happened in such a short time. Her life as she'd known it was over.

It had first ended six months ago, and now for a second time, as well. How many new starts could she handle?

How many could Aaron handle?

"Listen, I know you have no reason to trust me," Ryker said calmly. "But I've been worried about you and Aaron for months. Since a few days before Christmas when I was at your house and realized you and your son had been removed in a hurry."

She glanced over at him, wishing she could see his eyes. But the interior of the car was too dark.

"I'm sorry your husband and brother are dead," he continued. "But you need to know they were attempting to kill a friend of mine, leaving us no choice but to stop them."

She stiffened in her seat as the realization sank deep. "You killed Tim and Colin?"

"Technically, my buddy killed your husband in self-defense," he corrected. "But yes, I'm sorry to say I had a part in killing your brother. Just know, I only did it to save my friend Hawk's life."

He wasn't telling her anything she hadn't suspected, but the news sent her reeling all the same.

Ryker had killed her brother. The older brother she'd once looked up to. She and Colin had been close once, but that was before he'd done a tour overseas.

Before he'd joined the Blake-Moore Group.

Before he'd turned into a killer.

On some level she was surprised Ryker was being so bluntly honest with her. He easily could have kept that information to himself.

"Why?" The word came out low and strained.

"I told you, to save my friend's life. And I only fired in self-defense."

"No, why were my husband and brother going after your friend?"

There was a long pause before Ryker answered. "The Blake-Moore Group was hired by a man high up in the government to silence Hawk because he knew too much about the guy's role in illegal arms dealing. They sold American guns to the enemy."

She closed her eyes as shame washed over her. To have her own flesh and blood and the father of her children involved in what was little more than a murder-for-hire scheme made her sick. She had to take several deep breaths to keep from throwing up in Ryker's car.

Wishing she'd brought some crackers along, she waited for the nausea to pass. When she opened her eyes, she was startled to realize they were already outside the city limits.

"Where are we going?"

"South." Ryker's answer wasn't helpful.

"Where, south? What city?"

This time he didn't respond for several long moments. She was about to ask again, when he said, "I thought we'd hide out in the Shawnee National Forest for what's left of the night and decide where to go from there in the morning."

Liv glanced over her shoulder at Aaron, who'd fallen asleep. "I can't stay in the forest with Aaron. It's too remote. He's never camped outside."

"They have hotels," Ryker said dryly. "There are cabins for rent, too."

"Oh." She felt foolish for assuming the worst. Rubbing a hand over her belly, she did her best to remain calm. Being upset and anxious wasn't good for the baby.

"How far along are you?" Ryker asked.

"Thirty-four weeks. I'm due in six weeks." She frowned. "I'll need to establish care with a new obstetrician soon, though. Since I can't go back to the one I was seeing in Harrisburg."

"Of course."

She felt an odd comfort in knowing that if anything did happen to her, Ryker seemed to be the kind of guy to get her and the baby the help they'd need.

Maybe between God and Ryker, she and Aaron would be okay.

Ryker thought about calling his buddy Duncan O'Hare for help. He'd have called Hawk, but knew Hawk had taken his family on a honeymoon/vacation to Florida. Duncan would help, but Ryker decided to wait. No doubt he would soon need the assistance of others, but for now he just wanted to get Olivia and Aaron settled somewhere safe.

The side of his left leg burned like crazy, but he knew the bullet had only grazed him. The wound wasn't bad enough to slow him down. He figured there would be time later to examine the injury.

His instinct was to use one of the cabin motels. From the research he'd done online, the cabins in the Shawnee forest were spread out from each other creating a better sense of isolation than what he and Hawk had experienced before Christmas.

He cast a sidelong look at Olivia. She appeared to be resting, her palms spread protectively over her belly. He had a picture of Olivia and Aaron that he'd taken from her home tucked deep in his pocket, but the photo didn't do her justice.

She was heart-stoppingly beautiful. Her dark hair was cut shorter than what she'd worn in the photo, but he liked the way the ends curved along the edge of her jaw.

Wait a minute. He gave himself a mental shake. There was no point in thinking about how pretty she was, or how cute Aaron looked sucking his thumb. The last thing he wanted was a relationship. Not after the way he'd lost his girlfriend and her young daughter in a senseless carjacking while he'd been deployed overseas. He never wanted to feel that kind of sorrow again, yet couldn't help but reach out to help women and children in danger.

The way he'd wished others had helped his girlfriend and her daughter.

Besides, Olivia was mourning the loss of her husband and brother, and he'd been personally involved in their deaths, in a big way.

He hadn't shied away from telling her about his role in their deaths. He didn't want to lie to her, yet he hadn't exactly told her the entire truth. There was no good reason for her to know that her brother had held a gun to Jillian's head while threatening to kill her and her four-year-old daughter, Lizzie.

Ryker always felt remorse when he was forced to shoot someone, even knowing that the deed had been done to save the lives of innocents. It was the main reason he had only done one tour in the army. Being deployed in Afghanistan had been difficult. For one thing he'd left his girlfriend and her daughter behind, along with his foster parents. But more so because of the seemingly endless violence.

And here he was tangled up with another case that forced him to use skills he'd rather forget he possessed.

The close call at the nanny's house had sent a cold chill down the back of his neck. He and the perp had both fired their weapons at nearly the exact same time but thankfully Ryker had had the advantage.

If not, the outcome would have been much different.

He rubbed a weary hand over his face and focused on taking less-traveled highways to reach the Shawnee National Forest. When he came up to the gate, he pulled out his wallet and rolled down his window.

"Good evening," he greeted the guy at the gate. He sensed Olivia was awake, but she kept her eyes closed. "We'd like a week-long pass. We're spending some time at the Cedar Rock Cabins."

The guy nodded and took the cash Ryker offered in exchange for a seven-day pass. He slid it in the lower-left-hand corner of the windshield so it was visible to the rangers, and then drove through the gate.

When they'd cleared the area, Olivia straightened. "You have this all planned out, don't you?" Her accusatory tone caught him off guard.

"Not exactly. I mean I know about the Cedar Rock Cabins, but we don't have a reservation. I'm hoping they aren't booked."

"And if they are?"

"Then we'll keep going until we find a place to stay." He glanced over at her. "I won't make you and Aaron sleep in the car. We'll find something."

She let out a sigh and relaxed. "Okay, sorry. All of this seems so crazy. I keep thinking of Willa. She didn't deserve this. I hate knowing her death is my fault. I just don't understand why the Blake-Moore Group is going to such lengths to get me back."

The idea had bothered him, too. He'd been focused on finding Olivia and Aaron, but he didn't really understand why she was in danger. His instincts had been right, but he had no idea why they wanted her.

"You really don't know why they're after you?" He

tried to sound nonchalant, even though he'd always suspected she knew why she was in danger.

"No. I've thought back over those last few months
before things got so crazy." She grimaced and rubbed
her stomach again. "I hadn't seen much of Tim during
that time, and when Colin showed up that day, dragging me and Aaron out of the house, I knew something
was wrong."

He found that information rather curious. "Your
brother didn't tell you why you had to leave in such
a rush?"

"He only said that we were in danger." Her tone was
defensive. "But after twenty-four hours I could tell the
guy watching over us was getting nervous. I heard him
talking on the phone, that's how I learned Tim had
been killed. That concerned me, but when I asked about
Colin, the guy told me he'd be there soon, but I felt certain he was lying. That Colin was dead, just like Tim.
Then I discovered the door was locked from the outside,
which only heightened my feeling that something was
wrong. The guy was basically keeping us prisoners in
that dive of a motel room and I started to think that it
might be on orders from someone higher up at Blake-
Moore. At that moment, I decided that it might be best
to go off on our own."

"You escaped?"

"Yep. Told Jeff I was pregnant and bleeding. He panicked and when he turned to call his boss, I hit him over
the head with a lamp and took his car keys." There was
a note of pride in her voice.

His lips curved in a smile. "Good for you."

"I thought I did a good job of getting away without

leaving a trail." The confidence in her tone faded. "But I was wrong."

"Hey." He reached over to take her hand. "Don't sell yourself short. It's not every woman who could escape former military special ops guys for six months. If it wasn't for the paperwork I found at the used-car lot, I wouldn't have found you. And neither would anyone from the Blake-Moore Group."

"I told that guy not to keep the paperwork!" She sounded angry now. "He promised he'd shred it. Claimed he knew someone who'd take the car off his hands even without the title."

"You should have made him shred the documents while you watched." Ryker wasn't sure why he was giving her advice on how to stay under the radar. She didn't need it now that he was there to watch over her. "But it doesn't matter now. You, Aaron and the baby are safe."

"For now." He hated hearing the faint note of hopelessness in her tone.

"For as long as I'm alive," he swiftly corrected. "And I have friends who will help us if needed. You'll never be alone."

He could feel her gaze on him, but kept his eyes on the winding road weaving through the dense foliage.

A faint rumbling from her stomach caught his attention. "You hungry?"

She looked embarrassed as she rubbed her belly.

The corner of his mouth kicked up in a reluctant smile. Ryker knew he should have thought of food earlier. "There are plenty of places to get food around here. Just let me know what you're in the mood for."

As the words left his mouth, they came upon a sign advertising Torra Tacos one mile ahead.

"Maybe something less spicy," she said. "Heartburn has been my constant companion over the past few weeks."

"There's a burger joint in five miles. Will that work?"

Her answer was another rumble coming from her stomach which made his smile widen.

Ryker had to respect the way she'd taken everything in stride. The sign for the Cedar Rock Cabins indicated they were located about twelve miles away, so stopping for food wasn't a problem. He thought about getting breakfast, too, something they could easily heat up for Aaron in the morning.

He pulled up to the drive-through window and looked expectantly at Olivia. She was intently scanning the menu before placing her order for a cheeseburger and a bottle of water.

The restaurant didn't offer breakfast at this hour, so he settled for getting several burgers to go, knowing that having some food was better than nothing at all.

"You're going to eat four burgers all by yourself?"

"No, just one. The others can be warmed up in the morning." He paid for the food, then handed the bag to Olivia.

Thankfully, they got a cabin, one that was located in a secluded area off the main road. Ryker was glad to have four-wheel drive as he headed up the rugged hill.

He was relieved to find the cabin was clean and had indoor plumbing. Olivia brought the bag of food in, then went back out to get Aaron. The little boy didn't wake up as she carried him inside.

While she was busy, Ryker quickly ducked into the bathroom to examine his thigh wound, grateful to realize it wasn't bad. When he emerged, he found Olivia pulling a fresh diaper from the bag. She went back and changed Aaron, before gently placing him on one of the twin beds and pulling the covers up over his pajamas.

She was a good mother. Not like his who'd abandoned him at the age of ten. Ryker pushed the unwelcome thoughts away. He unpacked her cheeseburger and his Quarter Pounder at the kitchen table. When Olivia returned she washed her hands, then removed her large purse from her shoulder and set it on the table. Then she surprised him by crossing over to where he was seated. She stood over him and cupped her hands on either side of his face.

The soft touch of her fingers made him go still. Her blue eyes, clear as the sea, stared into his.

"What's wrong?" He barely recognized his own voice.

She stared down at him intently for a long moment before releasing him. "Nothing. I just wanted to see your eyes."

"My eyes?" He missed the warmth of her hands, wondering if she had something against hazel-colored eyes.

"Yes." She pulled a chair from the table and sat down. "I needed to see for myself."

"See what?" He couldn't hide his bafflement.

"I needed to see exactly who I am about to trust with my life, my son's life and that of my unborn child." She avoided his gaze now as she picked up her cheeseburger and took a bite.

He shook his head, battling confusion. What had she seen in his eyes? He had no idea, but decided to let it go.

Mostly because he'd liked the brush of her fingers on his skin a little too much. He had to resist the urge to touch the same spot her fingers had been.

Idiot. Olivia wasn't Cheri, and Aaron was hardly little Cyndi. He wasn't going down the path of caring too much. He sternly reminded himself that his role was only to keep Olivia, her baby and Aaron safe.

Getting emotionally and personally involved wasn't an option.

THREE

Ryker's hazel eyes were alive, full of caring, compassion and concern.

He wasn't the type of man her husband and brother had turned into and for that she was grateful.

Yet it was pretty clear he was a soldier. The way he'd taken out the bad guy holding Aaron had left no doubt about that. She was touched by the fact that he hadn't outright killed him, firing only because the other guy had. And she was especially grateful that he hadn't been injured in the struggle.

The cheeseburger congealed in her stomach. She took a deep breath. Those minutes inside Willa's house had been the scariest of her entire life.

Worse than being attacked on the street by that guy from Blake-Moore. Hearing Aaron's cries, seeing that stranger gripping her son with that harsh look in his eyes, had been heart-wrenching. And poor Willa. Her eyes filled. Willa had never hurt anyone and hadn't deserved to die.

"Olivia, don't." Ryker reached out and lightly touched the back of her hand. "Don't dwell on what nearly happened back there. Concentrate on your future. Reliving that fear and worry can't be good for the baby, right?"

His kindness only made her eyes burn with more tears as she tried to smile. "Right."

Ryker gestured to her meal. "Eat up. I'm sure the baby is hungry."

Taking another bite of her burger, she did her best to ignore the weird awareness that had come out of nowhere when she'd held Ryker's face and looked deep into his hazel eyes.

Ridiculous to be attracted to a man who was only trying to help her out of a dangerous situation. She was as big as an ox and would only get bigger as the baby grew. No man would be interested in someone who probably not only outweighed him but waddled when she walked.

Besides, she wasn't about to become involved with him. With any man, but especially not another soldier. The last few weeks of her marriage to Tim had been difficult. She'd known Tim since high school; he'd always been Colin's best friend. Tim was a man she'd known for ten years, yet somehow her husband of five years had turned into a complete stranger.

If that sort of personality change could happen to Tim, it could happen to anyone. She was better off alone, especially since she would have her hands full with a new baby to care for.

These feelings stirring deep within must be gratitude toward Ryker, nothing more. Not only had he saved her life, but he'd helped rescue Aaron. Despite her earlier misgivings, she was thankful that he'd come to find her.

She risked another glance at him from beneath her lashes. Ryker was handsome. His chiseled features belonged on billboards selling anything that women might want to buy. Even something they didn't want to buy, but would anyway once they saw him. Yet she still found it odd that he'd come all this way to find her and Aaron just because he'd feared they were in danger.

Who did that? Who jumped at the chance to get involved in a perilous situation to protect strangers? She had no idea.

It wasn't until she finished her meal that she remembered she'd forgotten to pray. Attending church with Willa these past few weeks had been amazing, but she still wasn't used to doing the simple things like thanking God for her food. She sent up a quick, silent, guilty prayer then crumpled up her empty wrapper and pushed to her feet.

"I'll take that." Ryker plucked the garbage from her hand while pressing on her arm. "Just sit and relax, okay?"

She sank back down into her seat, eyeing him warily. "Don't worry, I don't think all of this excitement will send me into early labor."

The flash of frank fear in his gaze was oddly reassuring. "Don't joke about that."

Her smile faded and she rubbed her hands over her belly. "You're right—it's not a laughing matter. I want this baby to keep growing inside for as long as possible. My doctor says the baby shouldn't come much before forty weeks."

Ryker scrubbed his palms over his face for a moment and she could tell the responsibility of keeping her, Aaron and the baby safe had overwhelmed him.

She liked that he cared about her, and about the baby

she carried. Her instincts told her Ryker was a man she could trust.

Of course, she'd once felt that way about Tim and look where that had gotten her.

She tried not to remember the way their marriage had slowly unraveled over time. Like a sweater, first the hem, then the sleeves then finally the entire garment until there was nothing left but a pile of yarn.

"Would you like some herbal tea?" He held up a box of chamomile tea that must have been left behind by previous occupants of the cabin. "There isn't a microwave but I can heat some water on the stove."

"That would be nice." Liv knew that she'd need to sit and relax for a while before trying to sleep. She pulled her purse toward her and rummaged for the bottle of antacids she kept with her at all times. No matter how dull and bland the food was, the baby pushed up on her stomach in a way that caused endless heartburn.

"Are you certain you don't know why the men of the Blake-Moore Group are after you?"

She glanced up at Ryker, who was leaning against the counter with his arms crossed over his chest. A small pan of water was heating on the stove, but he looked anything but domestic standing there. The gun on his hip and the muscles straining at his shirtsleeves made her mouth go dry.

Stop it! She gave herself a mental shake and did her best to concentrate on what was important. "I've been thinking about that since I first went on the run," she admitted. "But honestly, I can't think of anything that would make anyone within the organization upset with me."

Ryker's gaze was steady. "Have you met the owners? Harper Moore or Kevin Blake?"

She frowned, thinking back to when Tim had first talked about his new job. He'd spoken of the two men, but had she met them? There had been a welcome-to-the-group party early on with other members of the Blake-Moore organization, and she thought maybe Kevin Blake and Harper Moore had been there. But for the life of her, she couldn't bring either man's face into focus.

"About four years ago," she admitted. "But I met a lot of guys Tim worked with back then, and I can't say for sure who was who. I vaguely remember being introduced to the owners during the Fourth of July barbecue."

"Nothing more recent?" Ryker pressed.

"No. Those gatherings didn't last. Things changed within the first year Tim was with them. I originally thought it was because of Aaron and the fact that Tim hadn't adjusted well to having a baby disrupting our lives. But over time, I got the sense that the camaraderie between the men had changed. At least as far as Tim was concerned. It seemed to be more competitive. He slowly became someone I could barely recognize." She felt a little guilty for speaking poorly of her husband. Of Aaron's and the baby's father. She smoothed her hand over her abdomen, trying not to imagine how incredibly difficult it would be to raise two children on her own.

If Willa was here, she'd remind Liv that she would never be alone as long as she had faith in God. She clung to the memory of the woman who'd loved her like a mother. Who'd treated Aaron like a grandmother would.

A sense of fierceness washed over her. She wanted the men who'd killed Willa to pay for their crimes.

Ryker set a steaming cup of tea before her and she thankfully cupped her hands around it, savoring the warmth.

"It just doesn't make sense." She shook her head, feeling helpless. "I've tried to think of what could have happened to cause Tim's bosses to come after me, but I can't think of anything."

"It's okay." Ryker offered a lopsided smile. "I don't want you to stress about it. For now, all that matters is that you and Aaron are safe."

She took a sip of her tea, enjoying the calming scent. "Thanks to you, Ryker."

A shadow crossed his features. "No reason to thank me," he said in a low voice. "I should have acted sooner."

She tipped her head, regarding him thoughtfully. "You were the one who told me not to dwell on what happened back there, but to focus on the future. Maybe you should consider taking your own advice."

A ghost of a smile flitted across his features. "Maybe."

Liv finished the rest of her tea and set the mug aside. "Thanks again, Ryker. For everything."

This time he accepted her gratitude. He tipped his head in a nod. "Get some rest. We'll likely have to find a new place to stay in the morning."

The idea of leaving so soon bothered her, but she didn't argue. Pushing up from her seat, she winced at the sore muscles in her legs. Running was not a normal activity for her these days. She carried her mug to the sink then turned and glanced back over her shoulder.

"Good night."

"Good night, Olivia."

She used the bathroom first, chewed another antacid, then slipped silently into the room she shared with Aaron.

A wave of exhaustion hit hard. Moments before she fell asleep, she found herself secretly wishing that Tim could have been half the man Ryker seemed to be.

Ryker waited until Olivia was safely tucked in with her son before heading into the bathroom to further tend to his wound. He was glad that his black jeans had hidden the oozing blood.

The gash was long and jagged, but superficial. He cleaned the wound and, since there were no bandages in the medicine cabinet, ended up wrapping a clean towel around his thigh. Then he washed the blood from his jeans.

In his room, he laid the jeans out near a window, hoping they'd dry by morning.

He stretched out on the bed, but knew sleep wouldn't come easily. As a soldier he'd learned to fall asleep in two minutes or less, but that was easier to do when you only had to worry about yourself and when your team consisted of capable soldiers.

Knowing that there were three lives in the other room depending on him was enough to have him staring wide-eyed at the ceiling, his heart thudding heavily in his chest.

He really didn't want Olivia to go into premature labor. The best way to do that was to stay three steps ahead of the Blake-Moore Group.

Duncan O'Hare would help, as would any of the Callahans. Mike, Marc, Mitch, Matthew and Miles Callahan were all brothers, and their sister Maddy was married to Noah, who was also a cop. One of them should be able to help. Hawk, too, if he wasn't on vacation. Ryker decided he'd call Duncan and Mike Callahan once they'd moved to a new location.

Feeling better about his plan, he tried to relax, yet thoughts whirled through his head. It was strange that Olivia had no idea why the Blake-Moore mercenaries had come after her. But he found himself believing her when she claimed to be in the dark.

He'd helped Hawk and the Feds arrest Todd Hayes, the former secretary of defense, for selling illegal guns to the enemy in Afghanistan. Hayes had hired the Blake-Moore Group, specifically Colin Yonkers and Tim Habush, to find and kill Hawk because he'd seen too much and because they'd both been involved in the gun selling.

With Hayes being held in a federal prison, it didn't make sense that the Blake-Moore Group was still intact, much less that they'd come after Olivia.

Somehow, he managed to sleep, because the next thing he knew, bright sunlight was streaming in through the window. His wound was still raw and prone to bleeding, but he tossed the towel on the floor and pulled on his still damp jeans. When there was time and everyone was safe, he'd find a place to get bandages.

He stared dubiously at the cold burgers he'd purchased sitting on a shelf in the otherwise empty fridge. Without a microwave, they would taste awful. He decided to head to the closest restaurant that served breakfast instead.

Aaron would be hungry, and so would Olivia.

There was a coffeepot and just enough grounds left

in a small can to make a half of a carafe, so he made coffee, then went outside to his SUV to get his laptop. No reason he couldn't start working while he waited for Olivia and Aaron to get up.

Sipping his coffee, Ryker focused on the computer screen. His phone indicated less than a fifty percent charge on the battery, but he had a charger in the SUV, so he didn't hesitate to use it as a hot spot for his computer.

The Blake-Moore Group's website hadn't been updated or changed in any way since the last time he'd checked. He did another search on both Kevin Blake and Harper Moore, but knew that both men were experts at staying off-grid.

He tried to think of another way to figure out who Blake or Moore had sent to pick up Olivia. The way the man had grabbed and dragged her backward on the street, while the other one had grabbed Aaron, led him to believe they hadn't been sent to outright kill either of them.

Not until they had whatever it was they wanted.

But what?

A physical item? He rolled the idea over in his mind. With Olivia on the run it didn't make sense that she'd have anything of value on her person. No, it must be a memory. Something she knew that must be important.

But Olivia said she didn't know anything. Didn't understand why Blake-Moore had come after her. How would they figure out what it was the mercenaries wanted?

The whole thing made his head hurt.

Ryker tried another angle, checking on some of the companies who'd provided reviews about the great work the Blake-Moore Group had done for them. As he scanned the reviews, he read about a hostage rescue the Blake-Moore Group had performed roughly four years ago.

It was old news, but he couldn't help but wonder if this was one of the first missions Olivia's husband had done. He remembered how she'd mentioned the Fourth of July celebration and how there had once been a lot of camaraderie. It made sense if they were celebrating their success.

They'd been a legitimate group once; the hostage rescue proved that. But something had changed over time. Maybe it had been taking on Todd Hayes as a client. Maybe they'd started with lower-level government workers and had eventually proved themselves worthy.

Yet he knew Colin Yonkers had played a role in selling guns to the enemy. It was possible that Tim hadn't realized how far Colin had gotten into trouble until it was too late.

He straightened in his seat. What if Tim had confided in Olivia? Could be that he shared something he shouldn't have.

"I hav'ta go potty." Aaron's young voice coming from the living room drew him from his dark thoughts.

"This way, sweetie." Olivia took her son's hand and led him to the bathroom.

Ryker quickly turned off the computer and tucked it into Olivia's large bag. He put his phone in his pocket, making a note to charge it once they were in the SUV. He finished his coffee, then quickly washed the cup and replaced it in the cupboard.

As soon as Olivia and Aaron were finished in the bathroom, it would be time to hit the road. They weren't that far from Nashville, but he'd also considered heading north to where he knew Duncan O'Hare and the Callahan family were located.

The Blake-Moore Group wouldn't expect them to double back the way they'd come.

He wasn't sure Olivia would like that idea, but having others available to help watch over her and Aaron was more important than staying hidden in the forest.

Olivia and Aaron emerged from the bathroom fifteen minutes later. She crossed over to take her bag, surprised to find the laptop in there.

"Sorry, but I thought it would be easier for me to carry it from now on," he explained.

"I just need a change of clothes for Aaron. He wants to wear big-boy undies." She set the laptop aside and rummaged around for what she needed, then replaced the computer.

"We need to leave," he reminded her. "We can stop for breakfast on the way."

"This will only take a minute." She took Aaron over to the sofa and managed to get the squirmy boy into clean clothes.

"Ready?" He took the discarded pajamas from her and stuffed them into the bag, before looping the strap over his shoulder.

"You know that's basically a glorified diaper bag, right?" She held out a hand. "I'll carry it."

"I don't mind." The surprise in her eyes made him wonder if her husband hadn't liked carrying the black-and-white zebra-striped bag. He didn't understand what the big deal was. Besides, adding the laptop made the bag heavy. Better for him to shoulder the burden. "Let's go."

He followed her and Aaron outside. The sun was nice, but would grow impossibly warm as the day went on.

Olivia buckled Aaron in his car seat, while he set the bag on the floor of the passenger-side seat. Within minutes they were on the road.

"Why are we going back the way we came?" Olivia asked.

"There was a family restaurant I thought would be a good place to have breakfast." He knew he'd have to discuss his plan to head north in more detail soon.

"I was thinking the fast-food restaurant we used last night would be better. I remember seeing a play area for Aaron." She glanced at him. "Their breakfast sandwiches are decent."

"Sure, why not?" He was more than willing to make her happy. After several miles, he turned into the parking lot. He parked off to the opposite side of the building from where the play area was located.

The restaurant was situated near the base of a mountain with a hiking trail that led down to a tree-laden ravine. Ryker looped the diaper bag over his shoulder, then swept his gaze over the area, scanning for anything out of the ordinary.

There was nothing suspicious, so they went inside and ordered their breakfast. They chose a table in the back, near the indoor play area. Aaron drank his chocolate milk in ten seconds flat, then wanted to go down the slide.

"Go ahead," Olivia said. "You can eat your breakfast bagel in the car."

Ryker had only taken a few bites of his breakfast sandwich when he caught a glimpse of a black SUV with tinted windows driving past the restaurant. It slowed dramatically, causing the driver behind it to lay on the horn.

A warning chill snaked over him. He instantly stood and stuffed his meal back into the wrapper and tucked it in the bag. "Get Aaron. We need to go."

"Go where?" Olivia turned to follow his gaze, then went pale. She stashed her sandwich with his, then rose to her feet looking for her son. "Aaron!"

"Wheee!" The little boy was laughing with glee as he came down the slide.

Ryker shouldered the oversize bag, then crossed over to get Aaron. Thankfully, the boy didn't cry, but wiggled around impatiently. "No. I wanna go down the slide."

Ryker ignored him. "This way." He headed toward the back door of the restaurant.

Outside, he could see the path going down to the ravine. He debated for a moment, then realized that if the Blake-Moore mercenaries had run his license plate, the vehicle wasn't safe.

"We're heading down the path," he whispered.

To her credit, Olivia didn't complain, but led the way down the winding trail. He worried she might fall, so he didn't rush her despite his instincts screaming that they needed to hurry.

Two car doors slammed loudly. From this angle, he couldn't see his vehicle, but imagined that the two men would check his SUV first, before going inside the restaurant. Precious seconds that they needed in order to stay ahead of them.

He and Olivia continued down the path dropping out of sight from the restaurant, but it wouldn't be long before the mercenaries realized they were on foot and likely on the hiking trail.

Escaping two armed men without a set of wheels would be impossible. He was armed, but they would have double the firepower.

Dread tightened his chest, making it difficult to breathe. Once again, he'd waited too long to call for backup and had put their lives in jeopardy.

FOUR

Her heart thundered so loudly she was surprised Ryker didn't hear it. Maneuvering down the dirt path wasn't easy because she couldn't see her feet over her stomach. The only reason she was able to move quickly was because Ryker was carrying both her bag and Aaron.

"Where are we going?" Aaron asked.

"Shh. Be quiet. We're playing a game of hide-and-seek." Ryker's attempt to keep her son silent was genius.

To be honest, she hadn't seen anything suspicious when Ryker had rushed them out of the fast-food restaurant. But once they'd gotten outside, she'd heard two car doors slamming shut. Two men? Like the two who'd come after her and Aaron in Harrisburg? She swallowed hard, horrified at the idea of more men coming after them, yet she was extremely thankful she wasn't alone.

She firmly believed God had sent Ryker to keep her and Aaron safe.

How in the world had the Blake-Moore Group found them again? They weren't that far from Harrisburg, yet she couldn't begin to understand how they'd tracked her and Ryker to the fast-food place.

Except, Ryker hadn't killed the man who'd grabbed

her on the street; he'd only knocked him out. Could the assailant have regained consciousness long enough to watch them escape in Ryker's SUV? Had he somehow used the license plate to track them down? She knew from firsthand experience that the Blake-Moore Group had connections within law enforcement.

Her right foot slipped on a rock, sending her reeling off-balance. Her weight shifted and she teetered for a long second, her arms flailing, knowing she was going to fall. Ryker's hand shot out, grabbing hers in the nick of time, holding her steady.

"You all right?" he whispered.

"Yes." Her voice cracked as she realized how close she'd come to falling the rest of the way down the trail. Ryker's hand was strong, but not painfully so and she gripped it like the lifeline it was. "Thanks."

"We have to keep going." His low voice held an unmistakable urgency. She nodded and continued down the path, doing her best to keep from slipping on another rock.

"I thought we were playing hide-and-seek?" Aaron's tone was plaintive.

"We are," Ryker assured him. "Shh."

Thankfully, Aaron stuck his thumb in his mouth.

Their progress seemed incredibly slow and she knew that it was her fault. But even though she felt Ryker's tall, lean frame behind her, she never once heard him sigh impatiently, the way she knew Tim would have.

Enough. She couldn't keep comparing Ryker to Tim in her mind. Her husband was gone, had frankly disappeared emotionally long before he'd died.

She needed to stay strong and focused on surviving, for Aaron's sake and for the baby.

When she stumbled across a fork in the trail, she paused and glanced over her shoulder at Ryker. "Which way?"

"Right."

Right? That path went uphill, while the other one led down. Her instincts were to keep going down, but she didn't question Ryker's decision.

If she thought heading down was difficult because she couldn't see her feet, climbing up was even worse. Sure, she could see the trail ahead of her as they went, but it didn't take long for her to begin panting heavily with exertion.

At this rate, the bad guys would find them within seconds by following the sound of her breathing louder than a wounded buffalo.

Her thigh muscles were on fire and it was all she could do to keep from groaning out loud as she forced herself to keep climbing. Praying helped for a while, but then even that was too much work. When she stopped, even for a moment, she felt Ryker's hand on her lower back, keeping her steady without pressuring her to go faster.

She kept climbing, for him. For Aaron. For the baby. *I can do this.*

The words became a chant in her mind, until she couldn't think of anything other than taking the next step, then the next. *I can do this.* Sweat slid down the sides of her face, dampening her hair and her clothes.

Still, she climbed.

The only good thing about heading up was that they were getting closer to the woods. Tall trees full of leaves rustled overhead, providing desperately needed shade from the hot morning sun.

When she thought she couldn't take another step, she felt Ryker's hand on her shoulder. "See the rock over there? We'll stop there for now."

She wanted to sink instantly to the ground but managed to find the strength to take the necessary steps toward the large boulder protruding from the mountain.

"Sit here, beneath the edge of the rock." Ryker's whisper along with the fact that he wanted her to hide beneath the boulder indicated they weren't safe yet.

Gratefully, she sat down and scooted as far under the outcropping as possible. Then she lifted her hands for Aaron.

"I don't wanna play hide-and-seek anymore," he complained. "I'm hungry."

Ryker set her bag beside her. "I need you to stay here. I'll be back soon."

Despite her bone-weary exhaustion, she lunged for his hand. "Don't leave us."

He knelt so he was eye level with her, his thumb lightly caressing the back of her hand. "I won't be long. I need to get up higher, to see the trail."

She knew he meant he needed to see the men who were desperate to find them.

To find *her*.

Clutching Aaron close, she tried to keep from falling apart. "Okay," she whispered. "We'll be fine."

Ryker nodded and released her, rising to his feet. He moved silently away, leaving her and Aaron alone beneath the rock, surrounded by woods.

Closing her eyes, she noiselessly prayed the way Willa had taught her.

Dear Lord, please give Ryker the strength he needs

to keep us all safe. Watch over us and guide us on Your chosen path. Amen.

Her eyes pricked with tears when she thought about Willa. The woman had willingly opened her heart and her home to a pregnant stranger, and Liv knew she'd be forever thankful for the way Willa had brought her into the church and shown her the way to God.

Why had the kind woman died? Was that really part of God's plan? She sniffled and tried to brush away her tears. This wasn't the time to wallow in pity. Willa would want her to be strong for Aaron and her unborn child.

"I'm hungry," Aaron said again, making her realize she'd forgotten.

"I have your breakfast bagel." She rummaged in the bag, finding the slightly squished sandwich. After opening it for Aaron, she gave it to him. The egg and cheese were more than a little melted, but he ate with gusto.

Knowing she needed to keep up her own strength, she unwrapped her sandwich and forced herself to take a bite. She wasn't hungry, but could feel the baby kicking and knew they both needed fuel if she were to keep going.

The idea of climbing the mountain again made her swallow a moan. She wasn't sure her legs would last for much longer. Even at rest, her thigh muscles were quivering. Not only was she carrying the extra weight of her pregnancy, but she'd never been one of those women who worked out in the gym. She'd always preferred long walks to running or lifting weights.

But now she realized just how out of shape she really was. And that her lack of physical endurance could easily get them all killed.

Silently promising to join a gym once the baby was born, she finished her sandwich. Aaron finished his, too, and then began to squirm in her lap.

"I wanna walk." He leaned forward, in an attempt to crawl off her lap.

"Shh." She squelched a surge of panic that Aaron might throw a temper tantrum that would lead the bad guys straight to them. "We're still playing hide-and-seek. We're hiding beneath the rock so that no one will find us."

For a moment, he seemed agreeable to continue the game. Aaron crawled off her lap and went farther beneath the rock. She didn't stop him, hoping that allowing him some ability to move around would help keep him quiet.

A pair of black-denim-clad legs abruptly dropped down on the ground in front of her. She almost screamed, until she recognized Ryker.

She put a hand over her racing heart, swallowing the urge to snap at him. He'd been so quiet, she hadn't heard him approach. "You scared me," she accused in a harsh whisper.

"Sorry." His hazel eyes looked at her for a long moment, and she put a hand to her disheveled hair, wishing she didn't look like a sweaty whale. "I want you to take my phone."

Confused, she looked from the cell phone in his hand back to him. "Why?"

He hesitated. "I called a couple of friends for help. I'm hoping they'll call back soon. The phone is on vibrate, so it won't ring."

"Friends?" Warily, she took the phone, the device warm from his touch. "Are you sure we can trust them?"

"With my life."

And mine? The words hovered on her lips, but she managed to hold them back. Ryker had protected her and Aaron over and over again. There was no reason to doubt his loyalty now. "Okay."

He nodded. "They're in Milwaukee, so it will take them at least eight to nine hours to get here by car."

Eight to nine hours? The spark of hope in her chest withered and died. "That's a long time."

"I know." The corner of his mouth quirked in a smile. "I'm planning to meet them halfway."

"How?"

"Trust me, okay?" She wanted to ask more, but Ryker rose to his feet. "I'll be back as soon as possible."

With that, he was gone, melting into the brush as silently as he'd arrived. It occurred to her that he must have been an incredible soldier.

She picked up the phone and stared at the screen, willing it to flash with an incoming call.

Friends of Ryker helping them would certainly level the playing field, yet she couldn't help feeling a bit guilty.

Ryker and now his friends were putting their lives on the line for her and Aaron. It was noble of them to protect her like this.

And for the moment, all she could do in return was pray.

After placing a call to both Duncan O'Hare and Mike Callahan and giving the phone to Olivia, Ryker returned to his hiding spot at the top of the hill. He watched the two men dressed in black, carrying small handguns, as they made their way down the trail. It hadn't taken them long to figure out where he and Olivia had gone.

When they'd paused at the fork, he'd held his breath, as they exchanged a short, terse discussion.

As he'd hoped, they'd split up. The taller of the two headed down the path, the shorter guy nimbly climbing up the way he and Olivia had.

That meant he only had one to deal with for now, although he suspected it wouldn't be long before the taller guy realized he'd been duped and joined the shorter man who was now hot on their trail.

With all the patience and skill embedded in him from his time in Afghanistan, Ryker watched the shorter of the two mercenaries cautiously approach. He could tell, even from this distance, the guy was nervous.

Ryker knew the guy he'd knocked out must have managed to see them getting into his SUV and leaving town to have found them so quickly. This time, he needed to make sure he did something more to ensure them a getaway.

There were moments when he lost sight of the approaching mercenary, but waited without moving for him to reappear in his line of vision.

As the guy approached the landing point Ryker had identified as the target spot, he readied himself. Three. Two. One. Without a sound, Ryker launched himself off the hill, landing on top of the mercenary with a loud thud.

They rolled together, precariously close to the edge, with Ryker managing to come out on top. He pressed against the guy's carotid arteries until he passed out, then quickly used the plastic zip ties he always carried in his pockets to bind the man's wrists and ankles.

Once he had the mercenary trussed up like a Thanksgiving turkey, he dragged him off the trail, deep into the brush. The whole takedown had gone off without either man saying a word.

For a moment, Ryker peered into the man's face, trying to remember if he'd seen him before, in those days before Christmas when he'd helped Hawk and his family escape from similar mercenaries sent by the Blake-Moore Group.

But the guy was a stranger.

For a moment he sat back on his heels, trying to understand how the Blake-Moore Group had managed to recruit more soldiers. The entire operation should have been broken up by the capture and imprisonment of Todd Hayes from the Department of Defense.

Ryker went through the guy's pockets searching for an ID but found nothing other than a password protected phone, which he tossed into the ravine. More proof, at least in his mind, that the two men were sent from the Blake-Moore Group. When he had the guy well hidden, Ryker took his weapon, tucked it into the waistband at the small of his back, then stood.

One down, one more to go.

He made his way back up to the hilltop. He wanted to go back to the large boulder where Olivia and Aaron waited, to check on them and reassure them, but he needed to keep his eye on the trail below.

There was no telling how long he'd have to wait before the second mercenary showed up. He was a patient man by nature, but couldn't help being concerned over Olivia and Aaron.

As if on cue, he heard Aaron telling his mother he was tired of playing hide-and-seek and wanted to go home. She reassured him that they'd be leaving soon, but Aaron wasn't buying it. Their voices weren't too loud; he was listening intently, which was why he'd heard them, yet he couldn't deny the sound could carry all the way down to where the second guy was lurking on the trail.

Once he might have prayed for strength, but that was before he'd lost his girlfriend and her daughter. Before his entire world had turned upside down. Right now, all he did was try to ignore their voices.

Just a little longer, he hoped.

Finally, after what seemed like forever, he heard the sound of heavy footsteps on the trail. Thankfully, he no longer heard Olivia and Aaron. The taller guy wasn't as stealthy as the first was, maybe because he was growing tired of chasing shadows through the woods.

A fact that would work in Ryker's favor.

"Steve? Where are you?" The mercenary's voice was full of annoyance and the fact that he'd called out to his buddy made Ryker smile.

Steve, huh? These guys wouldn't have lasted long in Afghanistan. It seemed the caliber of the soldiers the Blake-Moore Group recruited had gone downhill.

As before, he waited with infinite patience for the mercenary to get into position. As the guy approached, he slowed his pace, as if sensing danger. Ryker gave him points for realizing something wasn't right.

Just a few feet more…

Now! For the second time that day, Ryker launched himself from his hiding spot. Unfortunately, at the last second, the mercenary turned and lifted his hands in a defensive move as Ryker landed on him. They rolled over and over, Ryker's head hitting a rock and sending shards of pain lancing through him.

Darkness threatened, but he refused to give up. He tightened his grip and fought with every ounce of strength he possessed, finally gaining the upper hand.

The mercenary grunted and let out a harsh expletive. Ryker pressed harder on the guy's neck, willing him to surrender to unconsciousness.

A minute later, the mercenary went slack. Still, he didn't release the pressure, fearing a trap.

Finally, he eased up and hung his head for a moment. The base of his skull throbbed, but he ignored it. Once again, he reached for the plastic zip ties, and bound the second guy's wrists and ankles.

"Ryker? Are you okay?"

Olivia's voice had him spinning around so fast, the landscape dipped and shimmered. He blinked, bringing her into focus. "Fine." His tone was sharper than he'd intended, but the thought of her watching him struggle to subdue the mercenary bothered him. "Go back to the rock. I'll be there shortly."

Her gaze clung to his for a moment, before she eased backward, out of sight. He wanted to close his eyes, make the pain in his head and his thigh go away, but he needed to finish this.

After dragging the second perp to where he'd stashed the first one, he debated whether or not to wait for them to regain consciousness. He wanted to interrogate the two men, to find out who they worked for and what they wanted from Olivia. At the same time, though, he desperately needed to get her and Aaron far away from there.

Logically, he knew that sticking around to question

the men would be useless. Even if he managed to get them to talk, he doubted the men would tell him anything truthful.

He took a moment to zip-tie the two men together, and to a tree, so they couldn't get too far once they awoke. He tossed the second guy's phone into the ravine as well, then tore their T-shirts into strips to use as gags, to keep them silent. He figured the two guys would be found eventually, by other hikers or tourists, but hoped to gain enough of a head start that it wouldn't matter.

Killing them would give him and Olivia more time to escape, but he couldn't do it. No way could he outright kill a man, even a gun-wielding jerk who'd come after him, not to mention a pregnant woman and a child.

He'd seen too much death while he was in Afghanistan, and here at home.

When he'd learned of his girlfriend's and her daughter's deaths, he'd promised himself he'd only take a life in self-defense. The way he had at the nanny's house. It had been necessary to shoot the man who had Aaron, in order to save the boy's life.

Still, he hesitated. Their escape from the Shawnee National Forest wouldn't be fast, especially since Olivia couldn't exactly run back down the mountain, then back up again, the way they'd come. The last thing he needed was to send her into premature labor.

Finally, he turned away. He could only hope that Duncan and Mike would be on their way soon.

At this point, Ryker would take all the help he could get.

FIVE

In Liv's opinion, the trek back down the mountain, then up again was more difficult than before. Maybe because the rush of adrenaline had faded, leaving a shaky exhaustion in its wake.

Her leg muscles ached, but she knew that Ryker likely felt worse. Watching him wrestle with the mercenary on the ground had been a harsh reminder of the magnitude of danger.

She was blessed to have Ryker as their protector.

Biting back another moan, she pushed onward. The danger had been mitigated for the moment, but she knew that this was only a temporary reprieve.

The Blake-Moore Group wouldn't stop until they got whatever they wanted.

She just wished she knew exactly what that was.

As she crested the hill, the fast-food restaurant was a welcome sight. She wanted nothing more than to go inside to cool off, but Ryker steered her around to the front of the building.

"We'll get something for you and Aaron soon." His deep, rumbly voice was close to her ear. "Right now we need to get out of here."

She nodded, understanding he was right. The more distance they put between them and the two men from the Blake-Moore Group, the better.

But he surprised her by pulling open the back door of his SUV and gesturing to the car seat. "Pull that out of there, would you?"

Confused, she glanced up at him. "Why? Don't we need it?"

"Yes, but we're taking their SUV instead of this one."

"Oh." Understanding dawned. Since he was still holding Aaron and her diaper bag, she did as he'd asked, pulling the car seat out of the back and carrying it over to the black SUV at the end of the row.

After buckling in the seat, she stepped back so Ryker could strap Aaron inside. Then he leaned over and dropped the zebra bag on the floor of the front passenger seat.

Sliding into the mercenary's vehicle gave her the creeps, but she shook off the sensation. Who was she to argue with Ryker's plan? All she wanted was for her and Aaron to be safe.

She rubbed a hand over her belly.

"Are you okay?" Ryker's voice held a note of concern.

"Fine." She managed a weak smile. "Just tired. That's the most exercise I've had in a very long time."

"I'm sorry." A deep frown furrowed Ryker's forehead. "It was the best option we had to get away."

"I know." And his plan had worked. She rested her head back against the seat and momentarily closed her eyes.

"I'll stop soon for water, okay?"

She opened her eyes and looked over at him. Ryker

was still frowning as if he'd done something wrong. "Thank you."

His jaw tightened. "For nearly getting you and Aaron hurt or worse?"

"For saving our lives. Again." She didn't like the self-recrimination in his tone, so she reached out and lightly touched his forearm. His skin was warm, and she ignored the shimmer of awareness. "We wouldn't be alive without you. I'm not sure why you came after me and Aaron, but I believe God sent you to save us."

He looked surprised. "I run my own security consulting business, so safety is always my top priority."

"I see." She was glad that he was so good at his job. She stared out the windshield. It took a moment for her to realize they were heading north, back toward Wisconsin, where this mess had started.

She swallowed a protest and dropped her hand into her lap. Ryker had mentioned contacting two friends to help them, so she wasn't going to complain.

Even if her original plan was to never set foot in the state of Wisconsin ever again.

"I'm just glad I found you." His voice was low and gravelly, and she wondered if he wasn't a believer. Which was a shame, because he was one of the most honorable men she'd ever met.

"Me, too." She remembered how suspicious she'd been about his motives for helping her. Foolish now, when he'd done nothing but save them over and over again. "Although I'd still like to know why you decided to track me down in the first place."

He hesitated before answering. "I told you, I was at your house and noticed that you and Aaron had left in a hurry. I was concerned about your safety, especially since I knew your husband and brother were…"

Dead. He hadn't said the word, but she knew what he'd meant.

Dropping the issue seemed to be the prudent thing to do.

"Oh!" She rummaged in her zebra bag. "I almost forgot. I'm sure it's cold, but here's your breakfast sandwich."

"Thanks." He ate while he drove, downing the food in less than five bites. She was sure he was still hungry, but didn't think he'd appreciate the animal crackers she carried for Aaron.

They'd need to stop for food and fuel, sooner than later. She'd returned his phone, upset that neither of his friends had returned his call, and now wondered about that. "Would you like me to try contacting your friends again?"

Ryker pulled his phone out of his pocket and tossed it into her lap. "Why not? They're both cops, so it could be that they're at work and can't talk. We may not hear from them until their respective shifts are over."

They were both cops? She shivered, despite the June sun beating in through the windows. She turned the phone in her fingers. "I…don't trust cops."

He raised a brow. "They're my friends. They would never do anything to hurt you, the baby or Aaron. Mike is married to Duncan's sister Shayla, and they have a child of their own, a boy named Brodie who is just a little older than Aaron. I've helped them out before, and I know they're more than willing to return the favor."

She swallowed a lump of fear and tried to be rational. "I…didn't know you had friends in law enforcement."

"I would trust both of them with my life. Yours and Aaron's, too." Ryker's tone was soft. "They're good guys. And they've worked outside the lines on more than one occasion."

Worked outside the lines? Meaning, not following the rules to the strictest level of the law? Knowing that should have made her feel better, but didn't.

"Okay." She tried to inject confidence in her tone. "I hope you're right."

"I promise—it will be okay."

She made the calls, but was forced to leave messages for both men. "Still no answer."

"They'll call as soon as they're able." He paused, then added, "I know I've asked you this before, but there has to be a good reason why these guys are coming after you."

"I've been racking my brain trying to understand that myself. I mean, sure, I overheard a few things, here and there, but nothing serious enough to make them come after me."

"Like what?" There was a note of urgency in his tone.

She watched as he pulled into a drive-through fast-food restaurant and ordered several bottles of water. "Get yourself something more to eat," she encouraged.

"I'm fine." He handed her a cold bottle of water and she gratefully took a long drink. The nagging headache that she sometimes experienced when dehydrated eased off a notch.

"I heard Colin and Tim saying something about selling weapons to the enemy." It wasn't easy to discuss how her husband and brother had betrayed their country. "At the time I wasn't sure what that meant, but I soon figured out something was off when I was locked in the motel room with Jeff."

"There was no way for you to know the details," Ryker assured her. "What else?"

She thought back. The snippets of conversation were often out of context and hadn't made any sense. "Something about a stash of money, but that was likely referring to the gun sales."

"Probably." Ryker kept a keen eye on the rearview mirror in a way that convinced her they weren't safe yet. "Anything else?"

"Not really." She sighed and rubbed her stomach again. It was something she did unconsciously, to soothe both herself and the baby. "I did get the sense they were trying to keep secrets from their boss."

There was a moment of silence as Ryker digested that bit of information.

When his phone rang, it startled them both. He gestured for her to answer it.

The name on the screen was Duncan O'Hare. "Hello?"

"Is this Olivia Habush?"

"Yes. I'm here with Ryker. Let me put you on speaker." She held the phone in the palm of her hand and used the speaker function for Ryker's sake.

"I hear you're in trouble." Duncan's voice was matter-of-fact.

"I need help. We're just leaving the Shawnee National Forest, heading north through Illinois toward

Wisconsin. I was hoping you and Mike could hit the road and meet us halfway."

"I'm happy to meet up with you. I just have to find someone to cover my next couple of shifts."

"Great." Ryker sounded relieved. "I'm avoiding Interstate 57, using highway 51 instead. I was hoping you guys could meet us either in Springfield or Bloomington, depending on when you can get moving."

"I'll see what I can do, and get in touch with Mike, too." There was a pause before Duncan added, "I assume you need the usual?"

"Yes, please." Ryker smiled, and Liv realized it was probably the first time she'd seen him smile since they'd met. Had it really been only yesterday? He was even better looking when he smiled. "Appreciate it."

"Okay. Give me some time to coordinate with Mike. I'll let you know when we're on our way."

"Thanks, Duncan. Appreciate your help."

"Hey, it's the least I can do. You guys left me out of the fun when Hawk needed help, so it's my turn."

Ryker's smile widened. "Later."

Duncan disconnected the line, so she pushed the End Call button. "Left him out of the fun when Hawk needed help? I hardly view dealing with the Blake-Moore Group as *fun*."

Ryker shrugged. "That's just his way of keeping things light. Cops, like soldiers, put their lives on the line every single day. If they didn't make jokes, they wouldn't be able to do their jobs."

He had a point. "I guess."

"Duncan served with me and Hawk over in Afghanistan." Ryker glanced at her, his gaze serious. "He knew your brother and husband."

The news was sobering. She stared down at her hands resting on her belly. The indentation around the fourth finger of her left hand wasn't noticeable anymore, likely because she was retaining a bit of water weight. Still, she couldn't help rubbing the spot where her wedding ring had once rested.

She and Tim had exchanged vows to love and cherish one another, but she eventually realized their marriage was a farce.

Ignoring the signs of their marriage unraveling had been stupid. Learning about God and faith these past two months had made her error in judgment glaringly obvious.

It was a mistake she wouldn't make again. Marriage wasn't something to take lightly, and she knew that from this point on, she was better off alone.

The way Olivia was rubbing the fourth finger of her left hand bothered him. Was she grappling with the fact that he'd been a part of the team who'd killed her brother and husband? He couldn't blame her, yet if she'd known how her brother had pointed a gun at four-year-old Lizzie, she'd be horrified.

Not his place to tell her.

He decided to focus on the fact that Duncan and hopefully Mike were on the way, with new disposable phones, a new SUV and enough cash that they could stay off-grid for a long time. He didn't want anything that might leave a trail back to him.

It had been a gamble to take the Blake-Moore SUV. Most of the new models had built-in GPS devices, and once the two gunmen he'd tied up managed to get free, they'd be intent on tracking the vehicle. But they'd need to hot-wire his SUV or get another first. Time that would work in their favor.

He'd have to ditch their vehicle soon. He'd brought several thousand in cash with him, but his reserves would take a hit when he purchased a replacement car.

But it was worth it, to keep the three lives in his care safe from harm.

His headache had faded to a dull throb. He'd taken some over-the-counter medication when they'd stopped at the gas station. Then he'd cleaned up the blood from the back of his head the best he could, without mentioning the wound to Olivia. She didn't need anything more to worry about.

He was worrying enough for both of them.

"I meant to ask earlier, do you know Tim's cousin, too?"

Cousin? He turned to look at her. This was the first he'd heard of a cousin. "Maybe. What's the name?"

"Seth Willis. He served overseas with Tim and Colin, too." She frowned. "Although, now that I think about it, I don't know that they were in the same unit."

He searched his memory but came up empty. "I can't say the name rings a bell. Did Seth also join the Blake-Moore Group?"

She bit her lip, her brow wrinkling as she considered his question. "I think so. I think he might have been at the first cookout that the guys had when they initially joined the group."

"Good to know." It was a great clue to follow up on. Was it possible the cousin was out to vindicate the deaths of Tim and Colin?

No, that wasn't logical, either. Olivia and Aaron were innocent bystanders in all of this. There would be no reason on earth for Willis to come after her with armed men.

It had to be one of the two founders of the organization, either Kevin Blake or Harper Moore, or both, who had sent the mercenaries after Olivia.

Nothing else made sense.

"Um, Ryker?"

He glanced at Olivia. "What?"

"I need to go to the bathroom." Her cheeks were pink as if she was embarrassed to mention it. "And it would be good for Aaron to go, too."

"Oh sure. Of course." He mentally berated himself for not thinking of that sooner. He hadn't been around when his girlfriend was pregnant; he'd met her a year or so after she'd given birth to her daughter. But it made sense that frequent trips to the bathroom were symptoms expectant mothers dealt with.

"I think there's a gas station up ahead." She avoided his gaze, still rubbing her belly.

"Works for me." He eyed the gas gauge, deciding they were fine for now.

He wasn't inclined to leave a full tank of gas for when the mercenaries eventually found the SUV. In fact, he'd prefer to leave the tank dry as a bone.

The stop at the gas station took longer than he liked. It seemed like Olivia and Aaron were in the bathroom for a long time, then they went through the small convenience store, picking out snacks.

When Olivia reached inside her oversize bag, he stopped her with a hand on her arm. "I've got it."

"It's fine. I have money."

He ignored her protest and paid for the items in cash. When he noticed she'd included a couple of toys for Aaron, he realized that was yet another thing he should have thought about while he'd been watching over them.

To be fair, the little boy had been great while they'd hidden on the mountain. He'd expected a lot of crying or complaining. But Aaron had been remarkably well behaved.

When everyone was settled in the SUV, he hit the road again, keeping an eye on his rearview mirror. So far, there had been no sign of the mercenaries, but he knew it was only a matter of time.

Fifteen minutes later, he noticed a sign advertising a used-car lot. When they approached, he pulled off the highway and headed toward it.

"What are you doing?" Olivia's voice reflected her concern.

"We need a new set of wheels." He offered a smile. "Don't worry—this won't take long."

"But…" She rubbed her hands over her stomach, a gesture he'd noticed she used when she was upset. "I thought we'd use this car until we met up with Mike and Duncan."

"These SUVs have GPS devices built into them. The sooner we ditch it, the better."

"You mean, they could use the GPS device to find us?" Her voice squeaked in protest.

"Yes, but I have a plan." He pulled into the lot and threw the gearshift into Park. "Let's go."

Her blue eyes darkened with apprehension, but she unbuckled her seat belt and slid out of the car. She grabbed the diaper bag, leaving him to get Aaron out of his car seat.

"I'll take that." He didn't want her carrying anything heavy. He glanced around at the options available to them. "Look for something under five thousand dollars. It only has to get us to Springfield or Bloomington, so nothing fancy."

She nodded, and began peering at the stickers on the vehicles closest to them. It didn't take long for a salesman, likely the owner, to come out to meet them.

"What can I help you folks with today?"

"We're looking for a car." Ryker knew the guy was just trying to be cordial, since there was no other reason for them to stop in a used-car lot. "Something with a reliable engine, yet not too expensive."

"How about this one?" Olivia stood beside a dark blue sedan with several spots of rust.

"I have a van over here." The salesman gestured to a large Dodge Caravan. If he thought it was odd that they'd arrived in a new SUV, he didn't let on. "Perfect for a growing family."

"Maybe give us a few minutes alone." He smiled to take the sting from his tone.

"Sure, sure." The guy pulled out a business card. "Name's Bill Sommers. Let me know when you're ready."

With Bill out of the way, he made his way down the row of cars. They were more expensive than he'd planned, the dark blue one coming in at exactly five thousand.

Then he found a tan sedan with a decent price. "What do you think?" He looked at Olivia.

"Looks good. I say we take it."

Before he could call out to Bill, the salesman came rushing over. "Find something you like?"

"We'll take this one. Will you give me a deal to pay in cash?"

"Cash?" Bill's eyes practically popped out of his head. "Sure. How about five hundred off the price?"

"Sold." Ryker managed to keep smiling, but felt edgy. He wanted to pay the man and get out of there, pronto.

They followed Bill inside. Ten minutes later, they had the keys in hand.

"I'll just get the car seat." Olivia hurried over to the black SUV.

"Uh, you're not leaving that here, are you?" For the first time since their arrival, Bill looked concerned.

"Don't worry, a couple of friends will be by to pick it up, although I'd appreciate it if you would shred my personal information while I watch. I'm careful that way."

"I guess." The guy shrugged and did as Ryker asked.

Ryker smiled in satisfaction and shook Bill's hand. "Thanks again."

As they drove out of the parking lot in the tan sedan, he thought he caught a glimpse of a familiar black SUV several miles behind them. The flat terrain made it easy to watch their six. He tightened his grip on the wheel and did his best not to panic.

There were lots of black SUVs on the road, he told himself. It was a popular color. They were safe, for now.

He sped up, putting more distance between them. Maybe it was time to try the interstate, where the speed limit was higher.

As he approached an entrance ramp, he noticed the black SUV wasn't on the road anymore.

Because the mercenaries had turned into the used-car lot?

If so, it wouldn't take long for the two men to get back on the trail. Despite his warning, he figured Bill would blab all about the vehicle they'd just purchased for cash.

Ryker knew they needed to get to Duncan and Mike as soon as humanly possible.

Before the mercenaries caught up to them.

SIX

Something was wrong. The way Ryker kept staring up at the rearview mirror was concerning.

"What is it? Have they found us?" She twisted in her seat, no easy feat with her belly, to glance behind them. There were plenty of cars on the interstate, but nothing that seemed out of the ordinary.

Not that she was an expert.

"We'll be fine." Ryker's calm voice didn't quite match the dark shadow in his hazel eyes. "We'll have help from Duncan and Mike soon."

"I know." She told herself that Ryker had already gotten her and Aaron safely out of harm's way several times already. No reason to think he couldn't do it again, if needed. Besides, they were in a different car now, a tactic that should help them escape the men from the Blake-Moore Group. Although she still didn't understand why they were after her.

Smoothing her hand over her belly, she tried to remain calm. Stress wasn't good for her or the baby.

She was glad to know she had six weeks left before her due date. Surely all this running would be over before then.

Wouldn't it?

"Whee, I'm flying." Aaron held the toy plane in his chubby fist and waved it around in the air, making dips and turns. "Mommy, I wanna be a pilot someday."

"I'm sure you will."

"He's a great kid." Ryker's voice was low. "I'm amazed he's holding up so well."

"Me, too." She glanced back at her son, who was content to play by himself for a while. The cheap toys she'd purchased at the gas station were a welcome diversion. "He hasn't asked for his father in months." The statement popped out before she could stop it.

"He hasn't?" Ryker threw her a sidelong glance.

She slowly shook her head and stared blindly out the windshield for a bit. "Tim wasn't around much, even before…" Her voice trailed off.

Before he was killed.

"I'm sorry." She wasn't sure if Ryker's apology was for her loss, or for the role he'd played in her husband's death.

She shook off the dark thoughts. "It's okay. I'm just glad Aaron isn't missing him too badly."

Ryker nodded but didn't say anything else. She wondered about his past personal relationships. He didn't wear a wedding ring and never indicated he was married, but for all she knew, he had a woman waiting for him back home—wherever that was.

Not that Ryker's personal life was any of her business.

Except hadn't he said something about tracking her for the past few weeks? Did that mean his girlfriend didn't mind him being gone for long periods of time?

If the situation was reversed, she'd mind.

She cast another glance at him, subtly studying his profile. His dark hair was short, his cheekbones prominent. There was a dark stubble shadowing his cheeks, which normally wasn't her thing, but now made him look even more attractive in a rugged sort of way. His strong muscles beneath his black T-shirt were not bad on the eyes, either.

Enough. She peeled her gaze away to stare out the windshield. They were running for their lives from armed men. Why was she noticing Ryker's looks? Must be that her hormones were all out of whack.

Yep, that was it. Hormones.

She didn't want a man in her life. Honestly, all she wanted was to be safe. To raise her son. To bring her baby into the world.

And a place to call home.

Tears pricked her eyes, and she quickly brushed them away. There wasn't time for a pity party. Hadn't she learned from church services that God was always with her? Always watching over her? She often felt His presence when she prayed.

Between God and Ryker, she and Aaron and the baby were safe.

And that was all that mattered.

Exhaustion swept over her. She closed her eyes and rested her head against the window.

The baby moved and kicked, making her smile. She placed her hand over the motion, wishing she dared share the moment with Ryker.

"Active today?" Ryker's dry comment made her realize his keen gaze missed nothing.

"Apparently only when I want to rest." She wryly shook her head. "Happens all the time."

Ryker's gaze landed briefly on her belly, then shifted quickly back to the road. Before she could say anything more, his phone rang.

She picked it up from the center console, then pressed the Talk and Speaker buttons. "Hello?"

"Olivia?"

"Yes." She glanced at Ryker. "Duncan, is that you?"

"Yeah, I assume Ryker is there listening in?"

"I'm here," Ryker said.

"Well, I've got good news and bad." Despite the former, Duncan's tone held regret. "The good news is that I have Mike following me in his own SUV, so we can give you guys one to use. The bad news is that we're running late. We weren't planning on a semitruck colliding into a pickup. As if the stupid toll roads and Chicago traffic didn't slow us down enough."

"Yeah, I hear you on the tolls. We're about two hours out of Bloomington. We'll still plan to meet there. When we arrive, I'll let you know which motel we're at."

"Sounds like a plan. Later." Duncan disconnected from the call.

She dropped Ryker's phone back in the pocket of the console. "I hate to tell you, but I'll need another bathroom break in the not-too-distant future."

If he thought she was annoying, he didn't let on. "Can you make it another ten miles to the rest stop?"

"Sure." She winced when the baby kicked her bladder. This pregnancy felt very different from her first and she couldn't help wondering if the difference was just the fact she was completely on her own, or if this baby might be a girl.

Honestly, the gender didn't matter to her, as long as the baby was healthy.

No premature labor allowed.

Ryker pulled off at the rest stop. Hopefully this would be the last time they'd need to take a break before reaching their destination. She unbuckled her seat belt and levered herself out of the car, her thigh muscles groaning in protest after the morning climb.

Ryker pulled Aaron out of his car seat, then swung her zebra bag over his shoulder. Oddly, she found the way he carried the diaper bag endearing.

"Let Aaron walk," she suggested. "He needs to burn off some energy."

Ryker put the boy down and he immediately started to run toward the building. Liv hurried after her son.

The bathroom break lasted longer than it should have, but considering how good Aaron had been, she couldn't make herself cut his playtime short. To his credit Ryker didn't say a word, although she could sense his impatience to hit the road.

Unlike her husband, whose temper had been razor sharp and quickly triggered the last few weeks of their marriage.

"Thanks," she said, when they were finally back on the interstate. "I know that waiting around made you crazy."

He shrugged. "Not really. The extra time was helpful in making sure no one followed us. So far, so good."

Her smile dimmed. "I'm glad."

Ryker's intuition, the way he stayed alert at all times, was instinctive for him. He didn't even have to think about what to do. And he never complained.

She couldn't imagine living like that, constantly watching your back.

This was clearly his world. One she didn't particularly care for.

Once the danger was over, she knew Ryker would move on to something else. And that was a good thing.

She wanted nothing more than to find another accounting job and settle down in a quiet place to take care of her new baby and her son. And while she'd miss the calming, supportive side of Ryker's nature, she knew their worlds would never mesh.

It was foolish to wish for something more between them.

Ryker's gut was twisted in knots, although he did his best to hide the tension. The last thing he needed was for Olivia to pick up on his concern.

He desperately wanted to meet up with Duncan and Mike. The two men flanking his six would make him feel much better. While Aaron had run around chasing butterflies, he'd secretly watched the highway, trying to decide which of the black SUVs that went past might be the mercenaries.

The vehicles whizzed past without slowing, so he felt certain they were safe.

But ditching the tan sedan was still a top priority.

The vehicle ran well enough, eating the miles to Bloomington, with flat, boring countryside whizzing past them. He preferred woods or mountains that were nice to look at while providing cover, but the lack of cover went both ways.

And hopefully they'd be back in Wisconsin in the next day or so.

He passed the first few Bloomington exits, searching for something a bit more remote. Maybe the north side of town, where they'd be just a little closer to their ultimate destination.

Olivia shifted in her seat, and he knew she was uncomfortable sitting for so long.

"Almost there," he assured her.

"There, where?" The smile that curved her lips made his breath catch in his throat. She was stunning when she smiled, and he told himself he was a jerk for even thinking of her as an attractive woman.

Not only was she pregnant but he'd helped kill her brother and the father of her children. The fact that she didn't seem to blame him was humbling. Still, he knew more of the grim details than she did. "Keep your eyes peeled for something farther off the interstate. Something that won't be easy to target."

"Not easy to target." She paled and he inwardly smacked himself for using such a blunt term. "Okay, then."

"Use my phone to find something small and outside the city proper."

"I found a motel that advertises two-bedroom suites for a decent price," she said to him a few minutes later. "Take the second exit."

He did and found the place. It wasn't a highly rated motel, but it would work. After pulling up near the lobby, he took his phone and called Duncan to let him know where they were.

"Got it. We're finally past the accident scene, so we should make good time from here."

"Great." He couldn't hide the relief. Soon he'd have more than enough backup. "See you soon."

He booked a suite on the first floor for easy access. He paid in cash, but was forced to use a credit card for incidental expenses. He convinced the manager not to run the card until they checked out by giving him another fifty bucks.

The suite was a bit musty, but overall clean. He carried the car seat and Olivia's bag in and set them near the doorway. Aaron was thrilled to be out of his car seat, running around the room with his new toys. Olivia stretched out on top of the bed with a low groan.

"Where are my ankles?" She looked down toward her elevated feet with a forlorn expression. "I had them a month ago, but now they've disappeared."

He wasn't sure how to respond, so he changed the subject. "Are you hungry? I can grab us something to eat while we wait for the guys to arrive."

"I'm always hungry, but it feels like we should wait for the guys."

"They won't mind. There's a fast-food restaurant across the street. I'll pick up something to go."

She didn't look thrilled, but pushed herself upright. "Okay."

He didn't want to leave her alone, but he could see how tired she was. "You look exhausted. Why don't you rest for a bit? Just tell me what you'd like, and I'll head over with Aaron."

She hesitated, uncertainty shadowing her gaze. Finally, she nodded. "Thanks. I'll have a grilled-chicken sandwich if they have it. Otherwise a cheeseburger."

"Grilled chicken." He nodded and held out his hand toward Aaron. "Ready to take a walk?"

For the first time, the child hung back, as if he wasn't sure about leaving with a stranger. Ryker was glad the boy was wary, but didn't like the idea of scaring him.

"Go on, Aaron," Liv encouraged. "I'll be here when you get back."

"All right. But can I get a toy?"

"Sure." He felt certain there would be a toy in the kid's meal.

Aaron crossed over and put his small hand in Ryker's. The trust in Aaron's gaze was nearly his undoing. He couldn't stand the idea of the little boy and his pregnant mother being in danger.

They needed to track down the men in charge of the Blake-Moore Group, and soon.

Outside, the warm early June sun was still high in the sky. He swept his gaze around the motel parking lot before heading out toward the restaurant.

He didn't think they'd been followed, but couldn't shake the impending sense of doom. Maybe once Duncan and Mike arrived, he'd be able to relax a bit.

The line was long at the height of the dinner hour. While he and Aaron waited, the kid changed his mind several times before settling on chicken strips.

When he had their meals and more bottles of water securely tucked into the to-go bags, he took Aaron's hand again and walked him back over to the motel. Still nothing appeared out of place, but he hoped Duncan and Mike would get there soon.

He entered the suite and tiptoed across the main living area to the bedroom where Olivia had been resting. She was asleep. The peaceful expression on her face was like a sucker punch to the gut.

She deserved to look that restful every day. Not chased by jerks with guns.

"Mommy?"

"Shh." He put a finger to his lips while closing the

door. He steered the boy toward the television. "Let's unpack your meal, then find something for you to watch, okay?"

"Okay." Aaron knelt in front of the coffee table, waiting for him to place the chicken strips, French fries and carton of chocolate milk in front of him. The toy was a plastic lion, but Aaron pounced on it. "Mustafa!"

"Sure, kid." He had no clue who that was, but was grateful Aaron was happy. He found a children's channel on the television and gestured to the table. "Eat your food, okay?"

"Okay." Aaron chomped on a French fry.

Ryker sat on a chair near the door, instinctively taking the defensive position, and quickly ate his meal.

His phone vibrated, and he picked up Duncan's call. "Are you close?"

"Ten minutes. Do you need something to eat?"

"We're good. Just grabbed something from across the street. But pick up something for yourselves. Once you get here, we'll need to find a place to ditch the sedan. It's not safe to have it nearby."

"Okay, make that fifteen minutes, then, so we can swing by and get food."

"Not a problem." Ryker smiled as he disconnected from the call. It felt good to have backup so close.

"Ryker?" Olivia's sleepy voice came from the doorway. He swung around to face her, relieved that the color had returned to her cheeks. "I didn't hear you return."

"You needed the rest." He stood and gestured to a chair near Aaron. "Have a seat. I'll get your food."

"Thank you." She'd finished her meal by the time Duncan and Mike arrived.

"Thanks for coming, guys. Olivia, this is Duncan O'Hare and Mike Callahan." He gestured to the two men. "Duncan is a cop and former soldier who served with me in Afghanistan, but Mike is just a cop." He cocked a brow toward Mike, letting him know he was teasing.

"Just a cop." Mike let out a snort. "Gee, thanks. It's nice to meet you, Olivia."

"Yes, it is," Duncan chimed in. "Ryker, are you ready to roll out to ditch the car?"

"Sure." He gestured toward Mike. "Would you mind staying here with Olivia and Aaron?"

"Are you sure you trust me? After all, I'm just a private investigator turned cop."

"Yeah, I trust you." One of the things Ryker had missed after leaving the army was this brotherly ribbing. Having no siblings of his own, he'd enjoyed the camaraderie of the men who'd fought beside him. "We won't be long."

"I think I can handle it," Mike said dryly.

Ryker nodded at Olivia before leaving the motel. He drove the tan sedan to a strip mall he'd remembered seeing on the way in. Leaving the car behind gave him a measure of satisfaction.

One less way for the Blake-Moore Group to track them down.

Back at the motel, he drew the two men aside to fill them in on everything that had taken place in the past twenty-four hours.

"Blake-Moore strikes again." Mike scowled. "Hawk I could understand. After all, he'd witnessed a crime. But coming after a pregnant woman and her son? What kind of threat are they?"

"I don't know." Ryker glanced between the two men. "I'd like to move again tonight, but Olivia is exhausted. I'm afraid to push her too far. If she goes into premature labor…"

Duncan and Mike exchanged a glance. "I think we're safe here," Duncan said. "We're armed. We can take care of anything that comes up."

"Yeah. That's good." Ryker relaxed for what felt like the first time in hours. His head still throbbed, as did the wound on his thigh, but he didn't care. "I need to hit the shower and get a couple hours of sleep, but I can take the second watch."

"Go." Duncan waved a hand. "I've got first watch and Mike can take the second watch. You're no good to us if you're not one hundred percent."

Ryker nodded, knowing they were right.

A hot shower did wonders to ease his pain. The wound on his thigh didn't look too terrible. If it got worse, he'd pick up gauze and antibacterial ointment.

He fell into a deep sleep, secure in the knowledge that Mike and Duncan were watching over things.

But then a loud thudding noise brought him upright. He blinked, trying to get his bearings.

Another thud, then a muffled shout. He shot off the bed and grabbed his weapon.

Blake-Moore had found them!

SEVEN

A thud woke Olivia from a sound sleep. Had someone fallen? She pried open her eyes and peered at the cheap alarm clock on the nightstand.

Two in the morning. She glanced down at Aaron who was curled next to her. The noise hadn't woken him.

Another thud and a muffled shout sent fear spiking through her body. What in the world was going on?

She slid out of bed, steadying herself with a hand on the wall. Her bladder urged her toward the bathroom, but before she could take a step, she heard a sharp report.

A gunshot?

No! Please, Lord, help us! She bent over and scooped Aaron into her arms, although she wasn't sure where to go or what to do. Where was Ryker? Duncan? Mike?

She had no weapon of any sort. Not that she'd know what to do with one anyway. There was a bathroom within the suite, so she went inside, locked the door and glanced around, her thoughts whirling.

The Blake-Moore Group must have found her. Again. She wanted to cry, to rant and scream in frustration, but forced herself to swallow the cries burning the back of her throat.

Think. *Think!* Her gaze landed on the toilet. The motel hadn't been updated in years, and the toilet tank was similar to the one she had at home, with a heavy ceramic cover on it.

"Mommy?" Aaron raised his head, rubbing at his eyes.

"Shh. We have to be quiet." Olivia set him down in the bathtub, the safest place she could think of. "Stay here, okay?"

"I don't wanna." His lower lip trembled and she was very much afraid that he'd begin wailing at any moment.

She lifted her heart in prayer. *God, please protect us!*

"Mommy?" Her son lifted his arms toward her, his gaze begging.

"Shh. Please, Aaron. I need you to be quiet. We don't want the bad guys to find us." She hated scaring him but was more worried about what would happen if he cried loud enough to draw attention. She quickly lifted the heavy porcelain cover off the tank and held it over her head, positioning herself behind the door.

If anyone came inside, she'd whack him over the head, hopefully with enough force to knock him unconscious.

Time passed in slow motion. The noises coming from the main suite area concerned her. What if something happened to Mike and Duncan?

To Ryker?

Her heart squeezed painfully in her chest and her arm muscles quivered beneath the weight of the toilet tank lid. She blinked back tears, trying to convince herself that Ryker would survive.

That they would *all* survive.

"Olivia? Are you in there?" Ryker's familiar voice made her knees go weak.

Thank You, God!

"Yes, we're in the bathroom." She lowered the lid of the toilet tank and moved out from behind the door. After setting the tank cover back in place, she opened the door, grateful beyond belief to see Ryker standing there. "What happened? Is everyone all right?"

"Yeah, but we need to hit the road." His face was drawn into tight lines, his gaze grim. "Now."

"They found us?" Silly question, since she knew they must have. "How?"

Ryker slowly shook his head. "They must have followed us. I didn't see them, but they must have had a line on our vehicle. Get your things together."

"Okay." She didn't need to be told twice. She quickly used the bathroom, then carried Aaron back into the bedroom. Her zebra bag was in the main living space, and she only had the one set of clothes, so there wasn't anything to grab other than Aaron's plastic lion and toy plane.

When she stepped into the suite, she stopped abruptly, her gaze landing on the two men dressed in black lying on the floor. One of them was bleeding badly; the other didn't show any signs of blood.

"Are they dead?" She couldn't help asking.

"Just one of them." Ryker's voice was low and harsh, as if it pained him to know that one of the men had died.

Mike and Duncan were tying the wrists of the guy who wasn't bleeding. The man let out a low moan and she knew then that he'd only been knocked out.

Not dead. Like the other.

Nausea swirled and she did her best to stave it off. Ryker had the zebra bag over his shoulder, watching as Mike and Duncan hauled the guy up and into a chair.

Ryker leaned close. "Who sent you?"

The man stirred, but didn't say a word. His eyes remained closed, and she couldn't tell if he was only pretending or if he was semiconscious.

Ryker gave him a hard shake. "Wake up! Who sent you?"

Still nothing. The man's eyes remained shut, his head lolling to the side. She felt sick, realizing he likely had a head injury of some sort.

Which wasn't good, but was better than being dead.

Mike and Duncan stood back, watching, their expressions grim. She shifted Aaron in her arms. "Come on, Ryker. Let's just go."

He ignored her. "What does Blake-Moore want with Olivia?" he asked the intruder.

"Nuther." The word was mumbled in a way that made it difficult for her to understand. The man's eyes were still closed, but he frowned as if confused about what was happening.

"Nothing? Don't tell me nothing. Why are you here?" Ryker shook him again. "What do you want with her?"

"Nub…ber…" His voice trailed off again, his jaw hanging slack.

If it was an act, it was a good one. Her stomach swirled again and she had to swallow hard to stop from throwing up.

"Ryker, we need to get out of here." Duncan stepped forward. "They could have called for additional support from the mercenary group. Or the noise may have drawn attention from the local police. We can't stick around."

"Fine." Ryker left the man on the chair and stood, raking a hand over his hair. "Let's go."

Liv headed toward the door, but Ryker stopped her with a hand on her arm. His voice was kind now. "Let me carry Aaron."

"All right." She handed her son over. By this time, Aaron was used to being in Ryker's arms and didn't protest.

Instead, her little boy snuggled against Ryker's chest, sucking on his thumb again, as if instinctively knowing he was safer there with Ryker than anywhere else.

Duncan led the way outside. Ryker remained behind Duncan, with Mike covering her back. She wasn't sure what she'd do if they came upon other men from the Blake-Moore Group. How much more could they take?

She straightened her spine and shook off the overwhelming sense of despair. They were alive, which was the most important thing right now.

She felt humbled to realize Ryker and his friends had risked their lives to keep her and Aaron safe.

Just as he'd promised they would.

"Get in." Ryker held the passenger door of a black SUV open for her. She glanced in the back, relieved to see Aaron's car seat was already buckled in.

Moments later, Ryker slid behind the wheel. He gestured for Mike and Duncan to roll out first, in an identical SUV, then followed them.

"Are you sure you're okay?" She reached out and lightly rested her hand on his forearm. His skin was warm beneath her fingertips. "I heard a lot of noise."

"I'm fine." His words were clipped and she realized he was angry. "I should have moved from the motel as soon as we ditched the sedan."

"If they had followed us from the dealership, they likely would have followed again."

He let out a heavy sigh. "Thankfully, they must not have realized I had Duncan and Mike with me. I'm sure if they'd known, they would have come with more men."

More men. She shivered despite the warm June night air. It was horrifying to think that there would be more men coming after them.

Forever, or at least until they'd gotten what they'd wanted.

Whichever came first.

"Why had he said *nothing* in response to your question?" Olivia's voice interrupted his dark thoughts. "If he was only partially conscious, you'd think he'd spill the truth."

"Blake-Moore must have used some heavy-duty training to have them answer that way." He paused, then added, "Although, I thought he said numbers."

"Numbers?" She looked at him in horror. "You know I'm an accountant, right?"

No, he hadn't known that. He glanced at her. "Did you do accounting work for Blake-Moore?"

"No." She rubbed her hand over her belly and he knew she was troubled by what had gone down at the motel. Duncan had pulled the trigger, killing the first mercenary, but it may as well have been him. "I offered, but Tim refused my help. Said the bosses wanted a big-shot accounting firm to help manage their funds."

"Interesting." Ryker watched the taillights of the SUV in front of them. "So you wouldn't know of any numbers they might be looking for?"

"No idea. Hey, I thought we were heading toward Milwaukee?"

The Peoria sign had caught her attention. "We will, but I think it's better to stop for what's left of the night."

"It's because of me, isn't it?" Her voice was a bit shaky, and he again wished she hadn't had to witness so much violence. "I'll be fine if we need to drive longer."

He flashed a reassuring smile. "It's no problem. I need to discuss our strategy with Mike and Duncan anyway."

"If you're sure?"

"Positive." Ryker kept his eye on the taillights of Duncan's SUV. Olivia didn't say anything as they drove through the darkness. When he caught sight of a motel that offered suites, he flashed his lights.

Duncan tapped the breaks, signaling he understood, and slowed down so they could pull into the parking lot.

"Connecting suites?" Duncan asked from the driver's-side window.

"Yes." He stayed where he was, letting Duncan get the rooms this time. He thought about the dead man they'd left behind. Ryker figured the police would be on his tail thanks to the credit card information he'd had to provide in order to get the room. A wave of frustration washed over him. Having the police and the Blake-Moore Group after him would only complicate things. Good thing he had a couple of cops with him, to help corroborate his side of the story.

There was nothing he could do about it now. Olivia and Aaron needed to be safe. He could only hope that the guy Mike had knocked out would stay tied up and unconscious until the authorities arrived.

When Duncan emerged five minutes later, Ryker waited for his friends to open the rooms before sliding out from behind the wheel. He fetched the diaper bag and carefully lifted a sleeping Aaron from the car seat. Olivia went first, and he placed a hand on the lower part of her back, steering her toward the room on the left.

Inside, she turned the lamp on low.

"Where do you want him?" His voice was a low whisper.

"This way." She crossed over and pulled the covers down so that he could gently place Aaron on the bed. She stared at her son for a long moment and he wondered what was going through her mind.

Guilt stabbed him deep. Security was his specialty, he should have been more careful. He should have been able to figure out they were being followed.

He'd nearly gotten Olivia and Aaron killed.

Backing out of the bedroom, he returned to the living room of the suite. He double-checked the dead bolt on the door, then hooked the chain as an added measure. He dropped the diaper bag onto a chair. The connecting door between the suites was open, but he didn't hear Mike or Duncan.

"What kind of strategy?"

Olivia's soft voice had him spinning toward her. He'd assumed she would have crawled in beside Aaron, to get the sleep she badly needed.

He shrugged, striving for a casual tone. "Just a plan for where to go from here. Nothing to worry about." He hated knowing she was chin deep in this mess as it was. The last thing he wanted to do was cause additional stress.

She rubbed her hands on her arms as if she were chilled. "I keep thinking about the guy saying *numbers*."

He moved closer, fighting the urge to pull her into his arms. "You think you know what numbers he's talking about?"

She grimaced and shook her head. "I wish. If I had them, I'd gladly give them away."

No way was he going to allow her to do anything of the kind. If the Blake-Moore Group was willing to kill for the numbers, then Ryker knew they had to do with something illegal.

Money laundering? Or money socked away from their scheme of selling guns to the enemy?

"I'm scared." Olivia's soft admission was like a punch to his gut. "Oh!" She put a hand on her belly. "Sure, now the baby wakes up."

His fingers itched to feel the baby's movements, but he kept his hands at his sides. He wondered if his longing had shown on his face, because she unexpectedly grabbed his hand and put it on her belly.

"Can you feel it?"

"Yes." Feeling the baby move filled him with awe. The intimacy of the moment was humbling, and he was honored she'd shared this with him. "Amazing."

"It is, isn't it?" She smiled. "Thank you, Ryker. For everything you're doing for me. For us."

His throat swelled with emotion. Her gratitude was misplaced, but he also knew that if he hadn't tracked her down when he did, the outcome would have been much worse.

"You're welcome." He forced the words through his tight throat. "Get some sleep. I'm going to talk to Mike and Duncan to figure out how we can drop off the Blake-Moore Group's radar."

She nodded, but didn't move away. She continued

covering his hand on her belly with hers, as if she didn't want to let go.

Unable to help himself, he reached up and tucked a strand of dark hair behind her ear with his other hand. "I'm going to do everything possible to keep you and Aaron safe." The baby kicked again, making him smile. "Him, too."

"Her." Olivia's lips curved in a smile. "This pregnancy is very different, so I'm thinking the baby is a girl."

Since he knew nothing about it, he didn't argue. "Her, then. I'm going to keep all three of you safe."

"I know you will." Her trust leveled him. "I know God sent you to help us, Ryker, guiding us on His chosen path."

He stilled, her simple faith washing over him. Was she right about God? Was He really watching over them, guiding them to safety? The Callahans believed that, as did Hawk.

Were they right?

"Ryker." She let go of his hand, shifting closer. He told himself to back off, to give her room, but his boots didn't move. She leaned forward, resting her head in the crook of his shoulder. "I'm blessed to have you here with us."

Blessed? If either one of them was blessed, it was him. He couldn't think of a response, so he simply lowered his head and pressed a chaste kiss on her temple.

She lifted her head to gaze up at him. He wished he could see her eyes more clearly, but the lack of light made it difficult to observe beyond the shadows.

"Is something wrong?" He didn't know what she was thinking, or why she continued looking up at him.

"Nothing." A smile curved her lips and she surprised him by reaching up to wrap her hand around his neck. Then she gently pulled him down as she went up on her tiptoes.

It never occurred to him to resist. She kissed him. Sweetly at first, but then with a longing that he couldn't ignore or deny.

He wrapped his arms around her, pulling her close and deepening the kiss, the way he'd wanted to since they'd first met. She tasted like sunshine and wildflowers after the rain. He wanted nothing more than to keep holding her, but the baby kicked between them, and he couldn't help but laugh.

"Well, I'm not sure my kiss has ever spurred that reaction," she said with a wry smile.

"It's beautiful and so are you." He was about to kiss her again when he heard a small voice call out, "Mommy?"

Aaron's plaintive cry made Olivia sigh. "I'm sorry but I need to go to him."

"I know." He reluctantly loosened his grip. "Get some sleep. We'll talk in the morning."

She nodded, turned and rushed to Aaron's bedside. He listened as she reassured the little boy. Peering through the open doorway, he saw her cuddling the child close. His chest ached as he watched them.

It was a full minute before he could make himself move away from the doorway, her taste lingering on his lips.

She'd kissed him, but now that the cloud of attraction had faded, he knew he shouldn't read too much into their embrace. She'd been scared, had hidden in the bathroom with a toilet tank cover as a weapon. The stress of being on the run for her life, was probably getting to her. Coming to him for comfort didn't mean anything.

He couldn't let it mean anything.

Getting emotionally involved wasn't smart. He needed his wits about him to figure out how to stop the Blake-Moore Group, while keeping her and Aaron safe.

Another lapse in judgment on his part could prove deadly.

EIGHT

Had she lost her mind? Why on earth had she kissed Ryker? He'd been trying to comfort her, the way any friend might after running from bad guys with guns, but she'd turned a sweet embrace into something romantic.

Long after Aaron had fallen asleep, she'd replayed those moments over and over in her mind.

It's beautiful and so are you.

Just remembering the words made her shiver with awareness. An attraction she hadn't felt in a very long time.

It was impossible not to compare Ryker and Tim. Her husband had lost interest in her while she'd been pregnant with Aaron. At the time, she'd blamed his new job with Blake-Moore for the long hours Tim had spent away from home. Blamed it for his short temper and the subtle changes she'd noticed in his demeanor.

But deep down, she'd feared her husband was becoming a stranger. No matter how much she tried to find the man she'd married, he'd remained elusive. She'd attempted to rejuvenate their relationship, hoping that reconnecting with him on an intimate level would bring life back to his eyes, but it hadn't worked. She believed Blake-Moore was to blame.

Those instincts had proven correct, based on the way the Blake-Moore Group had sent armed men after her.

Only after Tim's death had she really understood that her marriage would not have survived a second pregnancy. That their relationship was damaged beyond repair.

She hadn't even had the chance to tell Tim about the baby. Frankly, she'd been afraid of his reaction. Then it had been too late.

Not that it mattered now. The relief of knowing she wouldn't have to deal with Tim made her feel guilty. He'd been her husband, a man she'd once loved. But he'd eventually turned into someone else.

A man she didn't recognize.

Which brought her back to Ryker. Sweet, caring, strong, compassionate Ryker.

It was crazy. She was getting in way over her head. Telling herself this was nothing more than some strange hero worship didn't help.

As much as she appreciated Duncan's and Mike's help, her senses were only tuned in to Ryker. A man she had no business kissing. Or wanting.

The minute she and Aaron were out of danger, Ryker would move on to his next project. Whatever that might be.

She didn't know much of anything about his personal life, other than he worked as a security specialist. But what about the women in his life? Or his family? She had no idea.

Exhaustion finally shut down her brain long enough to sleep.

The following morning, she woke up feeling well rested. But the serene feeling of hope quickly evaporated when she realized Aaron wasn't beside her.

"Aaron?" She rolled off the bed, her heart hammering in her chest. She yanked the bedroom door open and saw Ryker had Aaron on his lap, feeding him something they must have gotten from a nearby restaurant.

"He's fine. We tried not to wake you, right, champ?" Ryker grinned down at the boy.

"Right." The words were muffled by the food in her son's mouth.

"Thank you." Her panic faded and she drew a hand through her tousled hair, suddenly feeling self-conscious about her appearance. She'd been wearing the same maternity clothes for the past two days. Ugh.

The kiss they'd shared hovered in the air between them.

"We have something for you, too," Ryker added, avoiding her direct gaze. "When you're ready, let us know."

"Okay." She desperately needed the bathroom and a shower, in that order. Ducking back into the bedroom, she closed the door and made use of the facilities. It was nice to have a few minutes to herself. Normally Aaron talked to her through the shower curtain as she showered.

Another reason to like Ryker.

Enough. This idiotic preoccupation with the man had to stop. She'd obviously made him uncomfortable with her kiss. Not that she could blame him. Her hormones were raging out of control—it was the only explanation for why she was acting so strangely.

Wrinkling her nose, she dressed in the same clothes

she'd been wearing the night Ryker had rescued her from the man on the street. Maybe once they were safe, she'd be able to stop and pick up a few things.

She returned to the living room of the suite. The scent of bacon and eggs made her stomach rumble. Aaron had finished eating, and was sitting in front of the television.

"Aaron, do you need to go to the bathroom?" She approached, sniffing the air around him to see if he had soiled his pants. He normally wore Pull-Ups at night, but was potty trained during the day.

Although after everything that had happened, she wouldn't be surprised if he regressed.

"No. Mr. Ryker already helped me." Aaron didn't look away from the cartoon.

She lifted a brow and turned toward Ryker who shrugged. "Wasn't hard to find what I needed in your bag."

He'd changed Aaron? Wow. "Thank you." She crossed over and took a seat beside him. Opening the to-go container, she found scrambled eggs, bacon and hash browns. She was thankful for the food. "Looks great."

"Dig in." A smile tugged at the corner of Ryker's mouth.

She took several bites of her meal before realizing Mike and Duncan weren't around, although the connecting door between the rooms hung ajar. "Where are the guys?"

"They'll be here soon." Ryker's smile faded. "We're trying to drum up additional reinforcements, but so far there's no one else to spare."

Additional reinforcements? Another wave of guilt washed over her.

She'd just finished her breakfast when Mike walked in. "Sorry, no go. Noah is busy with Maddy and their new son. Matt doesn't want to leave Lacy as she's due any day now. Marc is out of town until tomorrow, and Miles is knee-deep in a murder case."

The names were a blur, and Ryker must have noticed her confusion.

"Mike has five siblings," he explained. "And they're all involved in some sort of law enforcement. Marc is with the FBI, Miles is a homicide detective, Matt is a K-9 cop, Noah is a cop and married to their sister, Maddy, who is an ADA." Ryker frowned. "What about Mitch?"

Mike shrugged. "He's an arson investigator, but he and Dana are vacationing in Door County. It's possible Mitch may be able to help when they return."

"Wow, six Callahans." She glanced at Duncan who'd come in behind Mike. "And you're Mike's brother-in-law."

"Yep. Mike married my sister Shayla." He clapped Mike on the shoulder. "And from what I hear, they're about to make me an uncle again."

The tips of Mike's ears turned red, but he nodded and smiled broadly, clearly happy with the news. "Not until November, though."

"Congrats." Ryker gave Mike a nod. "I'm happy for you."

"Thanks."

It was oddly reassuring to Olivia to have so many family men helping them. They no doubt understood what it was like to travel with a pregnant woman and a small child.

Mike's expression turned serious. "Actually, I think

we should all hit the road as soon as we can. Shayla told me Brodie has been throwing up nonstop all night. She hasn't been feeling very good herself, either."

"Poor kid." Duncan frowned. "Fine with me if we leave, the sooner we get back in Wisconsin the better. We have a good two and a half hours of driving before we reach the Wisconsin border, and another seventy minutes to get to Madison."

"I plan to detour to Milwaukee rather than going all the way to Madison." Mike sent Ryker an apologetic look. "I'll ask Miles to pick me up in Beloit, so I won't take you out of your way. But I really need to check on Shayla and Brodie, to make sure they're okay."

"Understood." If Ryker was upset about losing Mike and having only Duncan as backup, he didn't show it.

"I can be ready in five minutes." She stood and quickly cleaned up the mess from their breakfast. "Just let me stop in the bathroom one last time."

When she returned a few minutes later, she found Ryker and Duncan deep in conversation.

"We need to confront the cousin." Ryker's voice held a note of urgency. "He lives outside Madison, so it's on the way."

"Yeah, maybe. Although I still think we should check out the Habush house first. Could be that the numbers they're looking for may be hidden in there."

"Doubtful. They would have searched the place already," Ryker argued.

Duncan caught sight of her and stood. "Hey, Olivia. Ready?"

"Yes." She glanced at Ryker who looked sheepish at being overheard. "Are you really going to talk to Tim's cousin Seth Willis?"

Ryker exchanged a wary look with Duncan before nodding. "Yeah, that's the plan. But we have several hours of driving to do before we're even close, so let's not worry about that now."

She frowned, not liking the way he was keeping her out of the loop. "What else do you have planned?"

Ryker sighed. "Nothing. Seth is the only lead we have, other than the word *number*—if that's even what the mercenary mumbled while he was out of it." She saw the hint of frustration in his gaze. "If you're ready, let's go."

She packed Aaron's few things in the diaper bag. Ryker took the bag from her and slung it over his shoulder, then held out his hands for Aaron.

Her son went to him easily, and she was struck again by how much Ryker had become an important part of their world in such a short amount of time.

Her heart squeezed as she silently admitted how much she'd miss him once this was over.

Ryker kept his gaze on the road, his thoughts whirling. He didn't like knowing he'd only have Duncan's help for the next leg of their journey. Still, he didn't begrudge the Callahans the need to support their spouses and children. He would do exactly the same thing if the situation was reversed.

But he'd hoped to surround Olivia and Aaron with armed men who could look after her while he worked the case.

"You really think he said the word *number*?"

Olivia's voice pulled him from his thoughts. "Yeah, I do. Mike and Duncan agreed, especially once they learned you were an accountant."

"But I didn't do any accounting work for Blake-Moore."

"I know." It would have made things easier for them if she had. The way things stood now, she didn't have access or any reason to be connected to Blake-Moore's accounts.

Except through her dead husband and brother.

And what about the numbers, anyway? Why had numbers sent men searching for Olivia? Was it possible she had information she wasn't aware of? He glanced at her. "You don't happen to have a key to a safe-deposit box or anything in that diaper bag of yours, do you?"

She frowned. "No, of course not."

He'd been in the bag several times and hadn't seen anything out of the ordinary. Yet he hadn't done a full inventory of the contents, either. Something to consider once they reached their next destination.

His gaze flicked to the rearview mirror. This time, he was in the lead with Mike and Duncan covering his six. He was grateful to have them behind him, and knew they'd keep an eye out for anyone following them. He kept his speed about five miles per hour over the speed limit, keeping up with the rest of the traffic heading north.

This way he could set the pace, or rather, Olivia could, as she was the one who needed frequent rest stops.

As they rolled into Rockford, she gestured toward a gas station. "Would you mind pulling in?"

"No problem." He tapped the brake, letting Mike and Duncan know that they were stopping. The SUV behind them slowed, then followed them into the gas station.

Mike pulled up to a gas pump and jumped out of the car. "May as well fill up."

"Okay." He pulled in behind him, then slid out from behind the wheel. "I'll go inside with Olivia and Aaron first."

"I'll fill it up for you." Duncan waved him off.

"Thanks." He lifted Aaron out of his car seat, then followed Olivia inside. She had the diaper bag, and he wondered if he should look through it now or wait until later.

Olivia took Aaron's hand and led him into the restroom.

Okay, later then. He stayed near the door, but positioned himself so that he could also keep an eye on the gas pumps through the window. Duncan and Mike didn't speak, their gazes alert on the cars coming and going around them.

They were good friends and he was fortunate they'd dropped everything to come help.

"We're much better now. Thanks."

Olivia's voice had him turning toward her. He'd been so preoccupied he hadn't heard her and Aaron come out. "All set?"

"I wanna toy!" Aaron hopped from one foot to the next. "Please, Mommy?"

She sighed. "No, Aaron. You can't get a toy every time we stop to use the restroom."

"I don't mind—" Ryker stopped when she narrowed her gaze at him.

"No. Not now. Maybe later," she told her son. She took Aaron's hand in hers, but he pulled away.

"I wanna toy!" By the looks of it, the kid was gearing up for a full-blown temper tantrum.

"No." Olivia looked tired and stressed, not that Ryker

blamed her. But she ignored Aaron's cries, took him by the hand and dragged him toward the door.

Feeling helpless, he trailed behind them. Aaron dug in his heels yanking Olivia off-balance. He swooped the boy into his arms and strode outside.

"Enough." His stern tone surprised Aaron, and he stopped crying.

He gently set the boy in the car seat and buckled him in. The kid was still crying, but not nearly as out of control as he had been. When he glanced over at Olivia, she offered a weary smile. "Thanks."

"You're welcome." He hated the idea of her dealing with Aaron on her own, especially in her condition.

Sweeping his gaze over the gas station, he looked for anything out of place.

Nothing. Aaron's crying hadn't drawn much attention, either. Guess that wasn't unusual when it came to kids.

Yet, he felt unsettled, the back of his neck tingling with warning. It wasn't over yet. He slid behind the wheel, eager to get back on the road. Mike and Duncan let him pull out first, then followed.

"We'll be at the Wisconsin border soon." He could tell by the toll station looming up ahead. "Beloit is only thirty miles from here."

"Good, I guess." She looked hesitant about returning to Madison as she rested her hands on her abdomen. "I'll be sorry to see Mike go."

"We'll be okay." He infused confidence in his tone. He slowed to get through the toll, then increased his speed. The roads were wide open now, without much traffic. There weren't a lot of homes or businesses along this stretch of the highway and the prickly feeling wouldn't leave him alone.

He plucked his phone from the console between them and called Mike.

"What's up?" Mike's tone was on alert.

"Let's change the meeting spot to Delavan."

There was a pause. "Okay, any particular reason why?"

"It's smaller, easier to pick up a tail." Beloit was a larger city, and he felt better about going to a smaller, contained area.

"Okay, I'll let Miles know." Mike hung up.

Olivia's gaze showed her concern. "You think they're still following us?"

"I don't know." And he didn't like the feeling of being in a fishbowl, where their two SUVs could be seen for miles. "Probably not."

She didn't relax, but grasped the hand rest on her door like a lifeline.

Several miles had passed by, when his phone rang. Olivia picked it up and put it on speaker. "What's wrong?"

"We've got company." Duncan's terse tone filled him with dread.

"How many?"

"Just one SUV that I can see. But we have to assume they have reinforcements nearby."

Farm fields stretched on either side of them, and Ryker second-guessed his decision to bypass Beloit for Delavan. But it was too late to change direction now. He pressed on the gas, increasing their speed. "Where's Miles? Can he meet us?"

"Yes, he's on his way. We'll take care of the tail. You get Olivia and Aaron to safety."

"Got it." He tightened his grip on the wheel. When he saw an abandoned field without crops, he knew it was the best option. "Hang on, we're going off-road."

"Off-road?" Her appalled echo was cut off as they bounced off the highway and headed straight through the empty field.

"Hang on." The vehicle bucked and rolled over rocks and chunks of earth. The four-wheel drive helped keep them steady, and he took the shortest route directly toward another road he could just barely see off in the distance.

He darted a quick glance at the rearview mirror. Mike and Duncan were farther back now, and he knew they would do whatever was necessary to keep the guys from Blake-Moore from coming after them.

The sound of gunfire had him clenching his teeth. He didn't normally pray, but it may be that the Callahans' and Hawk's faith was rubbing off on him, because he found himself asking for help and guidance now.

Lord, if You can hear me, please give me the strength I need to get Olivia and Aaron away from the Blake-Moore Group. Help me keep them safe!

NINE

Liv clutched the door handle in a tight grip, trying not to cry out at the way the SUV jolted and rolled over the dirt and rocks of the field. With the other hand, she held her stomach, as if willing the baby to stay put.

No premature labor. Please.

"Mommy!" Aaron's fearful cry stabbed her heart.

"Isn't this fun?" She glanced over her shoulder at her son and forced a reassuring smile. "Mr. Ryker is taking us four-wheeling."

"No! Don't wanna go four whee-ing." Aaron's lower lip trembled and he tucked his thumb into his mouth, a sure sign he was upset. "I'm scared."

"It's okay. There's no reason to be scared. Mr. Ryker is getting us to safety." A quick glance at Ryker's grim expression was not reassuring. "How about we sing nursery rhymes?"

Aaron seemed to consider her idea then plucked his thumb from his mouth. "Humpty-dumpty sat on a wall," he sang.

"Humpty-dumpty had a great fall," she chimed in.

Ryker raised a brow, but didn't interrupt their singing as they finished the nursery rhyme. She was glad to see the highway was getting closer now, and thought it was possible that he'd make it to safety.

Pop! Pop!

Liv sucked in a harsh breath and turned to look through the back window. The men from Blake-Moore were shooting at them? An SUV that looked much like the one they were using had followed them onto the field.

Why wouldn't they just leave her alone?

Because of the numbers? Numbers she didn't know anything about. She didn't understand. It didn't make any sense.

Ryker's jaw was tight as he pressed harder on the gas, the SUV swaying even more as he obviously tried to shake off whoever was following them.

And what about Duncan and Mike? Were they okay? Or had the Blake-Moore Group gotten to them? She closed her eyes and prayed for all of them.

Dear Lord, help us! Protect us! Show us the way out!

Time seemed to move in slow motion. Each jerky, rocky movement of the SUV made her feel sick to her stomach. She prayed she wouldn't throw up her breakfast.

Then abruptly, Ryker reached the end of the field, going up and over the ditch to the highway. The moment the SUV was on level ground, he hit the gas hard, going from fifteen miles per hour to fifty, then more.

"Mommy, let's sing another one."

Her son's request helped keep her from screaming in frustration. She darted a glance behind them, realizing the pursuing SUV was far back, still in the field.

"Hey, how about 'Three Blind Mice'?" Ryker's suggestion had her gaping at him in surprise.

"Three blind mice, three blind mice," Aaron sang. "See how they run. See how they run."

When Ryker joined in, tears pricked at her eyes. He was so understanding, so sweet. So kind and gentle toward her and Aaron.

She didn't know what she'd do without him.

Ryker didn't let up on the gas for several miles. When Aaron grew tired of the nursery rhymes, Ryker handed her his phone.

"See if you can reach Duncan."

Her fingers were slick from sweat, but she managed to call Duncan, placing the phone on speaker. Her throat grew tight as the phone rang several times without an answer.

Finally, she heard Duncan's voice asking, "Are you safe?"

"Yeah, for now." Ryker glanced again at the rearview mirror. "But I think both of our vehicles have been compromised."

"Ya think?" Duncan's droll tone almost made her smile. "We'll stick with the plan to meet in Delavan for now. We'll find a way to get new wheels once we get there."

There was a moment of hesitation before Ryker agreed. "Yeah, sounds good. You and Mike are okay, too?"

"Yep. We took out their tires. Should slow them down."

"Thanks. We'll be in touch." Ryker turned his attention back to the highway.

She blinked. "You mean, that was Duncan and Mike shooting? Not the Blake-Moore Group?"

He met her gaze for a brief moment. "I was hoping so."

She slumped in her seat as relief washed over her. "I thought—" She abruptly stopped, glancing back at Aaron.

"I know. I'm sorry." Ryker reached over to take her hand in his. "The good news is that we managed to get away unscathed."

"Yes." She had to force the word past her constricted throat. He was right, and she knew God was continuing to watch over them.

But those moments when she feared a bullet would find its way into the car, hitting Aaron or Ryker, had been awful.

Her stomach cramped and she gasped and held her breath, rubbing her fingertips over her belly in a soothing manner. Stress was bad for the baby.

They'd been under stress pretty much nonstop over the past three days. And she had a horrible feeling the ongoing stress wasn't about to end anytime soon.

"Olivia?" A hint of fear threaded Ryker's tone. "What's wrong?"

"Nothing. We're fine." She did her best to sound confident, even though she was anything but. "Everything is fine."

Ryker's gaze was skeptical and she knew he didn't believe her. But she refused to consider the prospect of being in premature labor.

No way. Uh-uh. Not happening.

Ryker fell silent, although ripples of concern emanated off him like heat waves. Ignoring his negative energy, she continued to concentrate on breathing deeply, in and out, while smoothing her hands over her belly.

The odd cramping sensation faded away. After a full ten minutes, she decided there was nothing to worry about.

She and the baby were fine.

The sign for Delavan indicated they were only ten minutes away. For once, she didn't need to use the restroom and hoped they could switch vehicles quickly and get out of town, before anyone from the Blake-Moore Group caught up to them.

She longed to feel safe. To not constantly glance over her shoulder to see if anyone was behind them.

Was it too much to ask to bring her baby into a secure world where danger didn't lurk behind every corner?

The depths of despair pulled at her, and she did her best to shove it aside.

Willa had told her several times that God helps those who help themselves. Now that they'd been found for the fourth time in less than three days, she needed desperately to keep believing that God was watching over them.

She couldn't give up. Not now, and maybe not ever. If she needed to change her identity and disappear for good, then fine.

That's exactly what she'd do.

It would be worth starting over under a new identity in order to have the safety and security she needed to raise her family.

Ryker was thankful that Mike and Duncan had bought him time to escape the mercenaries. Yet the fact that they kept coming was gravely concerning.

Whatever they wanted from Olivia was big. Big enough to risk losing several good—if misguided— men in order to get it back.

As they came into the town of Delavan, he slowed his speed, unwilling to draw undue attention from the locals. His goal was for the three of them to look like a happy little family.

And if his chest tightened at the thought of having a family of his own, he ignored it.

Glancing around the quaint town, he tried to think of a way to ditch their current SUVs for something untraceable. As much as they'd managed to stay one step ahead of the Blake-Moore Group, if by the skin of their teeth, he didn't like the way they kept showing up.

Especially knowing they wouldn't stop until they had what they wanted. Which meant he needed to find it first. Whatever it was.

His phone rang, and he handed it to Olivia, who put the call on speaker. "Yeah?"

"We're about ten minutes out of Delavan. Miles is bringing an unmarked SUV to a small restaurant called the Early Bird Café." Duncan's voice was calm and steady. Ryker was relieved to have a fellow soldier with him. "We'll meet there, but you'll want to park the SUV a good distance from the restaurant."

"What's the ETA for Miles?" He glanced around as he headed into the downtown area, searching for the café. It was located on the corner of Main and Birch streets.

"Hopefully ten to fifteen minutes."

"I see the café." He drove past it, looking for a good spot to leave the SUV. "We'll see you there."

"Will do." Duncan disconnected from the call.

"Where are you planning to leave the car?" Olivia's voice held a note of uncertainty.

"Not sure." He turned right on the opposite side of

Main Street. When he saw a small police station, he grinned and gestured toward it. "There."

"Won't the police be all over an abandoned SUV?" Olivia looked apprehensive.

"Under normal circumstances, yes, but with Duncan's and Mike's connections to the Milwaukee Police Department and Sheriff's Department we can get the locals to let the SUV sit for a while."

She didn't look convinced. He pulled into the parking lot, then slid out from behind the wheel. After looping the zebra-striped bag over his shoulder, he unbuckled Aaron and lifted the boy into his arms.

"I wanna walk." The kid squirmed in his arms, and he glanced at Olivia. She wearily nodded.

It went against the grain, but he bent over to set the child on his feet. Then he reached into the back and quickly unlatched the car seat. He knew Miles had a daughter and a son of his own, but wasn't sure he'd thought ahead to bring a car seat for Aaron.

He took one of Aaron's hands in his, Olivia took the other, and the three of them walked toward Main Street.

Like your average, everyday family.

He hoped.

The walk to the café seemed to take forever. He breathed a tiny sigh of relief when they entered the restaurant. After choosing a table toward the back, sitting so that he could face the doorway, they settled in to wait.

Duncan and Mike arrived first, dropping into chairs on either side of him.

"Thanks again," he said. "I appreciate you watching my back."

Duncan waved him off. "You'd do the same for us. Coffee, please," he added as the server approached.

Breakfast was only a couple of hours ago, but he thought it might be good for Olivia and Aaron to eat something. "Lunch menus, please."

"Not for me. I'm fine," Olivia protested.

"I want chocolate milk." Aaron shot a glance at his mother, who nodded.

When they all had something to drink, Duncan leaned forward. "Okay, so Miles is bringing a clean SUV, but I'm feeling like we need two sets of wheels. It worked pretty well to have us hanging behind to cover your back."

Ryker nodded. There was no denying the strategy had worked. "Maybe we can pick up something else later tonight."

"I can meet up with you later, after I check on Shayla and Brodie," Mike offered.

Ryker was touched, but knew that Mike belonged with his wife and son. "Focus on taking care of your family. We'll think of something."

The door opened and Miles Callahan walked in. Without hesitation, he made his way toward them. "What's going on? Mike wouldn't say much when he called."

Ryker quickly filled him in on the Blake-Moore Group and the way the mercenaries continued to come after them.

Miles let out a low whistle between his teeth. "You're deep in a hot mess."

"Exactly. I have to believe they've been tracking the vehicles we're using. Maybe they have connections who can get registration information through the DMV, since we've only used disposable cell phones for the past twenty-four hours. With a clean SUV, we should be able to shake the tail."

"I took the SUV from the Milwaukee PD undercover lot." Miles grinned. "It's untraceable to you, or to the police, as I changed the vehicle's status to damaged in the computer system. Should be safe enough."

"Good." For the first time in what seemed like forever, Ryker felt a sense of relief. "If you don't mind, I'd like to get going."

"Not a problem." Miles set the keys on the table. "It's parked around the corner across from the police station."

"That's where I left our car." Ryker picked up the keys. "Maybe you could put in a good word with the locals to leave it there for a while. Or have it towed somewhere out of sight."

"Will do." Miles glanced at his brother. "Guess we're taking the hot SUV back to Milwaukee, huh?"

"Hey, it may help be a diversion for Ryker and Duncan." Mike didn't seem concerned about the potential danger.

"Thanks again, Miles." Ryker rose to his feet. He helped Olivia stand, then tossed the zebra bag over his shoulder. "I owe you one."

"Nah." Miles waved him off. "You came to bail us out last year. It's only fair we return the favor."

Duncan picked up the car seat. Olivia took Aaron's hand and made a quick trip to the restroom before they headed outside. Ryker led the way, with Duncan covering their backs.

At the car there was no sign of anyone lurking around. Olivia volunteered to sit in the back near Aaron, which irked Ryker for some reason. Duncan rode shotgun, as Ryker slid behind the wheel. He kept a keen eye on the rearview mirror, but didn't relax until they were out of town and back on the highway. Avoiding the interstate, he took the less traveled highway toward Whitewater, which would eventually get them to Madison.

"Where do you want to stay for the night?" Duncan asked.

"Somewhere remote and outside the Madison area, while being close enough to drive there as needed."

"Cambridge? We passed a sign. It's a few miles ahead and they have a motel."

"Just one motel?" He glanced at Duncan, who nodded. Great, just great. Although one motel was probably okay for now. He was hopeful that the mercenaries would assume they'd head to the Milwaukee area, rather than Madison.

Unless they already knew that Seth Willis was the lead they were following up on. He swallowed hard.

"Cambridge has beautiful hiking trails," Olivia said. "I've been there before."

"Okay, sounds like Cambridge is our next destination. Once we're settled in the motel, I need to drive out to do some recon on Tim's cousin." He glanced at Duncan. "I'd like you to stay back to watch over Olivia and Aaron."

"Wait, what? You're leaving?" Olivia's tone was sharp. "I'd rather come with you when you talk to Seth."

"No." His blunt, flat tone came out harsher than he intended, but he was tired, his head ached, the wound on his thigh burned and he was running out of patience. "I just managed to get you out of danger, Olivia. I'm not letting you step back into the middle of it."

"You don't understand, Ryker. Seth knows me. I think he'll talk more if I'm there to smooth things over." The stubborn streak he'd once found attractive was wearing thin.

He could feel Duncan's gaze on him, but thankfully his former army buddy didn't say anything. If he was honest, he'd admit leaving Olivia and Aaron with Duncan didn't sit well. It wasn't that he didn't trust Duncan, but every cell in his body shunned the idea of having Olivia out of his line of sight. Out of arm's reach.

He felt attached to her in a way that wasn't healthy. He wanted her to stay glued to his side, which was ridiculous. Wouldn't it be better to know she was safe with Duncan while he grilled Seth for inside information about the Blake-Moore Group?

Yes, it would. But he still didn't like it.

"Ryker? Did you hear me? Seth is more likely to cooperate if I'm there with you."

Duncan coughed and he speared him with a narrow look. "Olivia, please. I appreciate you want to help, but I don't think involving you and Aaron is smart. These men are playing a deadly game. And you're thirty-four weeks pregnant on top of that. I'm sorry, but you'll be better off staying at the motel with Duncan."

There was a long silence and he knew Olivia was trying to find a way to change his mind.

"I can always question Seth for you," Duncan offered.

It was tempting, very tempting to let Duncan take on the interrogation. But this was his problem, not Duncan's.

Actually, it was Olivia's problem, but that made it his problem. One he refused to let go. "No, I'd rather be the one to confront him. I'll feel much better knowing you're watching over Olivia and Aaron."

"Your call." Duncan was easygoing that way.

"Does it matter what I want?" Olivia's tone held an underlying note of panic. "Can't we just skip talking to Seth? I doubt he knows anything."

He caught her gaze in the rearview mirror. "Olivia, I need you to please trust me on this."

Her gaze pleaded with him to reconsider, and it was the hardest thing in the world to ignore it.

The kiss they'd shared still haunted him. He longed to kiss her again, and again.

Yep, he was in way over his head.

And the way things were going, he didn't think a life preserver would be tossed his way anytime soon.

TEN

Swallowing her frustration wasn't easy. Liv didn't want Ryker to leave her and Aaron with Duncan, so that he could confront Seth on his own. And for what? The slim chance of getting information?

It wasn't that she didn't trust Duncan's abilities to keep them safe. Without him and Mike covering for them in the field, they wouldn't have been able to escape. She owed both men a deep debt of gratitude.

Yet what she felt toward Ryker was different. She was in tune to him in a way that she didn't feel toward Duncan and Mike. She cared about him on a personal level. The very idea of him being harmed by Seth made her sick to her stomach.

The motel in Cambridge that Ryker identified for their next stop was in rough shape, a stark contrast to the pretty scenery. The neon vacancy sign had more letters burned out than lit. The paint on the building was faded and peeling, the shingles on the roof curling beneath the heat. She frowned, hoping the ceiling of their room didn't leak.

Duncan slid out of the passenger seat, then closed the door behind him with a solid thunk.

"Are we home?" Aaron asked.

Home. Her heart squeezed in her chest. It was a sad testament that she had no place to call home. "No, sweetie, we're staying in a motel. Won't that be fun?"

Her son wasn't buying her fake enthusiasm. "I don't wanna go to a motel. I wanna go home!"

"Aaron." Ryker's firm yet gentle tone caught her son's attention. Ryker turned in his seat so he could see the boy. "We can't go home until we're safe. No more complaining, okay? I'm sure there's a TV for you to watch, if your mom says it's okay."

Aaron eyed Ryker with a hint of confusion, as if he vaguely remembered what it was like to have a father, then surprised her by giving in. "Can I take my toys with me?"

"Of course." She sent Ryker a grateful smile. "And we'll find a movie for you to watch, too."

"With cars?" Her son's fascination with cars had made him badger her incessantly to play certain movies at home. She'd enjoyed watching it with him, although that seemed like a time in their lives that was far removed from where they were now.

"We'll see." She had no idea what sorts of movies were available and didn't want to make a promise she couldn't keep.

Duncan returned, getting back in the passenger seat. "We're all set. I have two connecting rooms at the end of the row. No suites here, I'm afraid."

"Thanks." Ryker put the car in gear and swung around toward the designated rooms. He pulled in and parked. "I don't like leaving the SUV out in the open like this. I'm going to park it behind the building."

"Good idea," Duncan agreed. He jumped out of the

vehicle and quickly used the key to unlock the motel-room door.

Liv gathered Aaron's things from the SUV, tucking them in her diaper bag before she slid out. Ryker was already on the other side, extracting Aaron from his car seat.

The way he took on the fatherly tasks of caring for Aaron caused a lump to lodge in the back of her throat. It wasn't just that he didn't seem to mind, but more so that he took control of what needed to be done without being asked.

Almost as if he knew what it was like to have a child of his own.

She followed Ryker and Aaron into the motel room, wrinkling her nose at the musty smell. She didn't say anything, but Ryker flipped a switch on the air-conditioning unit as if reading her mind.

"It will air out soon." He set Aaron on the floor.

"It's fine." In those first few nights she'd been on the run she'd stayed in worse places. No use complaining.

Being safe was all that mattered.

"Excuse me." She ducked into the bathroom for what seemed like the fiftieth time. The muted sounds of the television reached her ears, and she knew Ryker was getting Aaron settled. When she emerged a few minutes later, Aaron was watching *Cars* and Ryker was hovering near the connecting door between the rooms. She noticed his laptop was open and a picture of Seth Willis was up on the screen.

"I'll be back as soon as possible." Ryker met her gaze straight on. "If anything happens, Duncan will get you safely to the authorities."

"Please don't go." She wasn't proud of how pathetically desperate she sounded. "Duncan can question Seth just as easily as you can."

"No, Olivia. I'm the one responsible for getting to the bottom of this. Duncan has done more than enough for me."

By the stubborn glint in his eye she knew Ryker wasn't budging. She bit her lip. "Okay, but please be careful. Worrying about you will only add to my stress level."

Ryker's gaze dropped to her belly, then shifted away. She felt a pang of guilt at using her pregnancy as a way to convince him not to go. "This won't take long."

Ryker turned to leave. She rushed over and grasped his arm. "I'll pray for you."

He paused, then surprised her by nodding. "Thanks. At this point, I'll take all the prayers I can get."

He would? Surprised, she dropped her hand, and he swiftly moved through the connecting door and out to the SUV. Pushing away the edge of the curtain, she watched as he slid behind the wheel and drove away.

The SUV was nothing but a black speck on the horizon when she finally let the curtain drop. A peculiar warmth spread through her at the way Ryker had agreed to accept her prayers.

She hadn't found God and faith until she'd met Willa. And the idea of sharing her faith with a man was even more foreign. Her life before, with Tim, hadn't revolved around God.

But the knowledge that Ryker actually believed in the power of prayer reassured her in a way nothing else did.

God must have a plan for him. For *them*.

She just needed to be patient until she understood what that plan entailed.

* * *

Ryker hated leaving Olivia behind, even though he knew in his heart it was the right thing to do. There was no doubt in his mind that Duncan would protect Olivia, the baby and Aaron with his life.

He prayed such a sacrifice wouldn't be necessary.

Keeping his attention focused on the road, he followed the directions to Seth's home. He'd memorized the location by looking at the map he'd pulled up on the computer in the motel, while Olivia had been in the bathroom.

Thinking of Olivia brought a new surge of guilt. She was becoming far too dependent on him, and that wasn't good.

The fact that he was just as emotionally involved with her didn't help. This brief time apart would be good for both of them.

He made sure there were no signs of the mercenaries as he drove toward Madison. The closer he got to the capital city of Wisconsin, the harder it was to figure out if anyone was on his tail.

Seth's address was in Sun Prairie, which was on the other side of the city. The traffic was crazy busy, often bumper-to-bumper, as he made his way around the city, bypassing the congested downtown area, toward the suburbs.

Finally, he found Bakerville Street and drove past without stopping, taking a quick survey of the neighborhood. It was quiet, without a lot of people around, indicating many of the homeowners might be at work.

After making a large loop around the subdivision, he parked on the street that ran behind Bakerville. On foot, he went through a yard that was overgrown with weeds, then crouched behind a bush to watch the rear of Seth's house.

There wasn't any hint of activity within the house or in the surrounding area. Had he come too early? It was the middle of the afternoon, and for all he knew, Seth was one of the mercenaries that had been sent after Olivia.

The thought was depressing. Still, he didn't move for a full five minutes. Finally, he retreated, after deciding he'd need to return after dark. If Willis wasn't home then, he'd search the place for any potential clues.

After he was back in the SUV and driving away, Ryker realized he'd jumped on the chance to leave the motel, without considering the possibility that Seth wasn't home.

Idiot. That was what happened when you let a woman mess with your concentration.

Ten minutes outside of Sun Prairie, he pulled into a parking lot and called Duncan.

"Find him?"

"Not yet. Place looks deserted." He wondered if Duncan thought he was an idiot, too. "Looks like I'll need to stick around until later tonight, to go in under the cover of darkness."

Duncan remained silent, no doubt questioning Ryker's judgment. "Well, you should come back here, then. Better to work together to come up with a plan."

Because he liked the idea of returning far too much, he rejected it. "No, traffic through the city was ridiculous. Besides, I want to keep an eye on the place. If Willis shows, I'll go in and talk to him. I just wanted you to know this will take longer than planned."

"And you want me to tell Olivia you'll be delayed indefinitely."

"Yes." He inwardly winced. "I'm sorry, Dunc. I know she won't be happy."

"We'll be fine. I'll pick them up something for dinner."

His gut clenched. "Don't leave them alone. Take them with you."

"Telling me how to do my job, Tillman?" Thankfully, there was a note of wry humor in his tone. "I think I can handle it."

"Yeah. Sure. I'll be in touch." Ryker disconnected before he could make a bigger mess of things.

It had been a long time since he'd done any stakeout work. After leaving the army, he'd done private bodyguard work for a while, then opened his own security business. Different from what the Blake-Moore Group did, Ryker's job was to enhance the safety measures for private companies.

Not take out anyone perceived to be a threat.

After doing a little more recon, Ryker decided to buy a pair of binoculars and hide out in the tree house located catty-corner from Seth's house.

An hour later, he was safely settled in the tree house, savoring the partially obstructed view of Seth's driveway and front door. The garage was out of sight, but if a car pulled into the drive, he'd see it.

Ignoring the discomfort, he watched and waited. Being here like this reminded him of his tour in Afghanistan. The temperature was unseasonably cool for June, which was better than the heat and dust he'd experienced overseas.

Activity in the neighborhood picked up around din-

nertime as residents returned home after a long day of
work. He was about to give up on Seth ever returning
home, when he finally caught a glimpse of a dark blue
car pulling into the driveway.

He sharpened the scopes on the binocs and felt a
surge of satisfaction when he recognized Seth's face
behind the wheel. The guy glanced nervously over
his shoulder, as if sensing Ryker's gaze, before the car
rolled out of sight, presumably into the garage.

Ryker watched for several minutes, hoping to catch
a glimpse of Seth through the living room window. But
the windows were all covered with blinds in a way that
indicated Seth was taking precautions to remain hidden.

Because he was in trouble with the Blake-Moore
Group? Or because it was second nature to him, the
way it was to any soldier who'd seen combat?

There was no way of knowing for sure, but he hoped
there was a way to convince Seth to cooperate once he
had him alone.

Which might prove to be a problem. Seth was bun-
kered down in the house and Ryker didn't exactly rel-
ish breaking in.

He sat back against the rough-hewn boards of the
tree house. How could he get Seth to come out of the
house? He snapped his fingers as an idea came to him.

A diversion.

Digging into the front pocket of his black jeans, he
pulled out a lighter. He'd never smoked but had learned
that they were handy devices when you needed to start
a fire in the woods.

Or, in this case, a small fire to draw Seth out of the
house.

The minutes dragged by slowly, turning into one

hour, then two. By seven o'clock, the normal brightness was dimmed by the dark clouds accumulating overhead. Thanks to the impending storm, he was able to make his move earlier than planned.

After leaving the tree house, he made his way to the garbage and recycling bins sitting curbside a few doors down. Rummaging in the recycle bin provided him with discarded newspaper.

Moving slowly and quietly, he once again went through the unkempt yard to the rear of Seth's house. Crouching behind the bush, he could see a tiny bit of light around the blinds of the kitchen window.

He looked for a vent that might lead inside. A dryer vent, maybe? There wasn't one anywhere in sight. After agonizing for several minutes, he made a quick dash to the back door.

There was a screen door covering the interior one. Twisting the handle, he found it wasn't locked, although the inside one was.

He found a large rock and used it to prop open the screen door. Then he balled the newspaper and set it on fire.

Stepping back from the door, he pressed himself against the side of the house and waited. The scent of smoke was strong, but he couldn't be sure any of it was actually getting inside.

But his patience was rewarded when the door abruptly opened. "What in the world—"

Ryker jumped over the burning paper, which was quickly becoming nothing but ashes, forcing Seth backward into the house.

Having been caught off guard, Seth tried to fight. He swung at Ryker, but Ryker slid to the side and grabbed

Seth's arm, pulling him off-balance. They tumbled to the floor, Seth continuing to struggle. But Ryker had a position of strength, not to mention sheer determination. He had to find out what the Blake-Moore Group wanted with Olivia.

Finally, he had Seth pinned to the floor. "Tell me what I need to know and you'll live to see another day."

Seth glared up at him, his mouth pulled into a grim line. He didn't say a word, which wasn't unexpected.

Each of the mercenaries he'd come up against so far had been the exact same way. Too well trained to talk, to rat out their comrades. Unless they happened to be semiconscious.

Ryker was tired of the act.

Thunder boomed overhead and within moments rain began to fall. He was glad to know the fire he'd started would be out soon.

"You won't talk? Fine, just listen. I was one of the men who helped take down Tim Habush and Colin Yonkers. You want to be next? Fine with me. But you should know that we're onto Kevin Blake and Harper Moore. They're not going to win this thing, do you understand? We will not stop until we take them down."

Still nothing. With an abrupt move, Seth tried to twist out of Ryker's grip, but he'd been expecting it, and managed to stay on top, tightening the pressure.

"There's an innocent pregnant woman and child in the middle of this mess. Do you really want to be responsible for their deaths? A pregnant woman and her baby? A three-year-old boy?"

Something flared in Seth's eyes and Ryker felt certain the news of Olivia's pregnancy had caught the guy off guard.

Good. He needed something, anything to convince the man to talk.

"Why are mercenaries from Blake-Moore coming after Olivia Habush?"

No response.

"What possible threat could a pregnant woman be to their organization?"

Still nothing, but again the flicker in Seth's eyes betrayed the fact that Tim's cousin hadn't known about the baby.

Maybe there was at least one line the mercenary wouldn't cross.

"I have all night, Willis. I'm not leaving until I get what I want."

Seth glanced away, focusing on some spot behind Ryker's ear. He hoped and prayed the slight movement meant the guy's resistance was weakening.

He really didn't want to be here all night.

"Are you worried about Blake-Moore seeking retaliation against you? I can help you get away from them. I happen to be on a first-name basis with Senator Rick Barton and he has friends in the FBI. I'm sure we can arrange protection."

Seth's eyes met his briefly, then slid away, staring blindly at the same spot behind his ear.

"It's your funeral." Ryker lowered his voice in a tone that he hoped sounded threatening. "It's one thing to die serving our country, but do you really want to die for Blake-Moore? What have they done for you?"

Another long silence, but the way Seth's mouth tightened made him think he was finally getting through.

"You're not the first to die over this." He hadn't intended to kill anyone, but Seth didn't need to know that.

"I took out the first two mercenaries who came after Olivia, then took care of two more. How many others does Blake-Moore have in their back pocket? You're disposable, Willis. They don't care about you. All they want is Olivia. When you're dead, they'll easily find a replacement." He leaned down, getting into Seth's face. "They won't miss you when you're gone."

Seth's expression remained stoic but Ryker felt certain his words were getting under Seth's skin. What he'd said about the Blake-Moore Group was true. They wouldn't care one bit if Seth died here tonight.

"Numbers."

The word was so unexpectedly familiar, he wondered if he'd imagined it. "Numbers? Blake-Moore is looking for numbers?"

"Yeah."

Ryker waited for him to elaborate. "I need more, Seth. Why is Olivia involved? Do they think she has these numbers? And what are they related to?"

"I want protection."

Ryker wondered if this was a trap. If the minute he let up on the pressure, Seth would fight to get away. "I can get Senator Barton and the FBI to provide protection. If you cooperate with me. But so far, you've given me squat."

"Bank accounts." Seth's body relaxed beneath his, but Ryker didn't let up. "Tim and Colin were skimming from the company."

That was an angle he hadn't considered. At the same time, it wasn't a complete surprise. Men who would threaten to kill innocent women and children would just as easily steal from their employer.

"They think Olivia has access to the bank accounts?" He remembered the receipts in Olivia's house.

"I don't know. I walked away after Tim and Colin died. Decided I wasn't going to put my life on the line for Blake-Moore." His tone was bitter. "I work as a hospital security guard now. The money isn't great, but I'm dating a nurse, which is better than getting shot at."

It was. "I'm going to let you up. But if you try anything, you'll never get the protection you need."

Seth nodded, his gaze weary. Ryker surged to his feet. He checked the fire he'd started, made sure any lingering flames were out, then rattled off the personal phone number for Senator Rick Barton. Seth scrambled for a piece of paper and a pen, taking notes.

Ryker now had the information he'd come for, but it wasn't very helpful. Olivia hadn't known about her husband's embezzling.

Had she?

He strode toward the doorway, determined to find out.

ELEVEN

On a whim, Ryker decided to stop at Olivia and Tim's house prior to heading back to the motel. Logically, he didn't think there would be additional clues to uncover. Certainly someone from Blake-Moore would have already checked out the place, but he figured it was worth a shot.

And it wouldn't take too long.

Remembering the stack of receipts he'd found back in December made him think there was a slim possibility that there may be something valuable buried in there. Were they all just receipts for household items? Or was there something important hidden in plain sight?

The place looked even more forlorn and neglected than before. It occurred to him that once the danger was over, Olivia and Aaron would have a home to return to. The house was hers, if she could continue making the payments.

Which made him wonder if the bank was on the brink of foreclosing on the property already. For her sake, he hoped not.

The back door was still unlocked, the way it had been six months ago. As he entered, the sour milk smell hit hard, worse than before, and intermingled with other rotten food likely from the fridge. The interior looked just as bad as last time he'd been there, but not much worse. Blake-Moore had evidently tried to cover their tracks, leaving no obvious signs behind.

He found the receipts in the kitchen, appearing untouched from his last visit. Quickly reviewing a few of them didn't reveal anything interesting, but he swept them into a pile to take back to the motel anyway. It wouldn't hurt to go through them one by one.

Scanning the interior of the house, he tried to think about where proof of the bank accounts may be. Was there a ledger stashed somewhere? Or some other place where bank-account numbers were written down? If there was, the men Blake-Moore had sent should have found them, but maybe they hadn't looked hard enough.

He could only hope they'd missed something.

He worked his way methodically through the house, feeling a bit like he was invading Olivia's privacy, especially when it came to searching the master bedroom. Yet he didn't find anything remotely related to bank-account information. Just as he was about to leave, he hesitated, then decided he should pack a bag for Olivia, knowing she'd love fresh clothes to wear.

At least the trip here wouldn't be a total waste of time.

When he'd finished packing some of Olivia's and Aaron's things, he searched Aaron's room. A child's bedroom would be a great hiding spot. He lifted the mattress off the small bed, and searched the box of Pull-Ups that had been left behind, along with the dresser drawers and closet.

Nothing.

Dejected, he returned to the kitchen, grabbed the receipts and stuffed them into an empty envelope. After placing the envelope in the overnight bag, he swung it over his shoulder and left the house the way he'd come. As he made his way back to his vehicle, he decided to ask Olivia about the mortgage payments. If she wanted a place to return to once the danger was over, he could help make the house payments until things had settled down.

Even if she didn't want to live here anymore, she could still sell the place, then use the money to start over somewhere new.

Near him?

Yeah, right. He pushed the ridiculous idea aside. No doubt, once Olivia and Aaron were safe, and her baby was born, she wouldn't want anything to do with him.

Except she *had* kissed him.

A rash decision in the heat of the moment. He'd been her sole protector and she probably hadn't been thinking clearly. Best not to remember how much he'd enjoyed her kiss.

He focused his attention on driving back to Cambridge, making sure he didn't pick up a tail.

When he arrived at the motel, he found Duncan pacing in agitation, like a caged wild animal. Duncan rushed over when he walked in, putting Ryker instantly on alert. "What happened? What's wrong?"

"Olivia's having labor pains."

"What?" Panic washed over him, and he hurried through the connecting door to her room. He found her seated upright on the bed, her back resting against the headboard. She looked calm as she smoothed her hands over her rounded stomach. "Are you okay? Do we need to go to the hospital?"

"I'm fine." Her smile was strained. "These aren't real labor pains, just Braxton-Hicks."

"Braxton who?" He wanted to do something, anything to make sure she didn't go into early labor. "We should at least have a doctor look at you."

"Relax, Ryker. I had these with Aaron, too."

Some of the tension left his shoulders, but not much. He'd never felt more helpless than he did at this moment. He didn't care what she experienced before, being on the run these past few days had been stressful.

And stress wasn't good for Olivia or the baby.

He wasn't a total stranger to God and faith, after all; he knew Hawk and Jillian were churchgoers. Still, he hadn't thought much of it for himself, until recently. He'd never known his father, and his mother had abandoned him when he was young, leaving him a ward of the state. He'd eventually found a home with a nice couple, but he had moved around frequently for several years before that happened.

It wasn't until he'd started hanging around the Callahans and now Hawk, that he'd learned about church and faith. At first he hadn't understood why it was such a big deal, but now with Olivia and Aaron depending on him, he liked the idea of God watching over them.

He was prepared to do whatever was necessary to keep Olivia safe, but he had never anticipated she might go into labor. He had no idea how to deliver a baby!

Another swell of panic rose within him, nearly choking him.

He found himself sending up a quick prayer on their behalf.

Please, Lord, keep Olivia from delivering her baby early. Keep her, Aaron and her baby safe!

Olivia really wasn't worried about the Braxton-Hicks, but the stark fear on Ryker's face gave her pause. For the first time since he'd rescued her from the men in the Blake-Moore Group, he looked as if he might throw up.

That was her role to play, not his. She closed her eyes and concentrated on slow, deep breathing. The contractions weren't regular or strong, which were both good signs. And they were very similar to the Braxton-Hicks contractions she'd experienced with Aaron.

Still, she'd prayed hard over the past thirty minutes, asking for God's grace and mercy in watching over her unborn child. Thankfully, Aaron had remained preoccupied with his television show, oblivious to what she was experiencing.

"Olivia?" Ryker's low voice sent shivers of awareness skating down her spine. She really, really needed to get a grip on her hormones.

"I'm fine, Ryker." She opened her eyes and offered a faint smile. "I think the contractions have stopped."

"Good." Ryker hesitated for a moment, before taking a seat on the edge of the bed beside her, his expression serious. "I don't want you to wait too long. You need to tell me when we need to go to the hospital, all right?"

"I will." She wasn't going to take any chances on having a premature baby. Aaron had been a week late, so she hadn't been expecting a problem with this pregnancy. "You were gone a long time. How did it go with Seth? Did you find him? Talk to him?"

"Yeah. I convinced him to talk." His brow furrowed.

"I don't want to add any more stress, Olivia, but I need to ask you about the bank accounts."

She looked at him blankly. "What bank accounts?"

"Seth mentioned bank accounts. He seems to think they're the reason Blake-Moore is coming after you." His hazel gaze searched hers. "You really don't know anything about them?"

"Tim and I have a joint bank account, or at least we did. I didn't dare use or access it since the first few days after leaving the motel."

"I don't mean to intrude on your personal business, but how much money is in there?"

She didn't understand where he was going with this line of questioning. "Maybe six or seven thousand dollars? Tim made good money, and we didn't spend above our means." In fact, she'd preferred shopping for bargains, especially once she'd learned she was pregnant.

"Do you think that money has been going toward your mortgage payments?"

"Yes. The bank takes the money automatically from our account each month." She hadn't really thought of it until now. "Although if that's the case, I think the money will run out very shortly if it hasn't already." She blew out a heavy breath. "I hate the thought of the bank foreclosing on the house."

"I don't want you to worry about it." Ryker put a re-assuring hand on her arm. "I'll take care of everything."

"You can't pay my mortgage." She was horrified at the offer. "I'm sure this will be over soon. I doubt the bank will foreclose until I miss several payments." At least, she hoped not.

"Don't stress. It will be fine."

The idea of going back to the house she'd shared

with Tim filled her with distaste. No way. She wouldn't do it. But she could sell the property. Yes, that was the answer. She'd sell and move back to the small town of Harrisburg. Except… Willa wouldn't be there. Remembering how Willa had died helping to protect Aaron made her grimace.

Far better to find somewhere else to live. Somewhere just like Harrisburg. A smaller community where neighbors knew each other and watched out for each other.

Where she could find a wonderfully welcoming church like the one Willa had taken her to in Harrisburg.

"What about these receipts?"

Ryker's voice pulled her attention back to the issue at hand. She looked down at the envelope of receipts he'd spread out on the bed. "Where did you get these?"

"Your house."

Her gaze collided with his. "You went back there?"

He nodded. "I brought a bag back with some clean clothes for you and Aaron." He cleared his throat as if embarrassed. "I hope you don't mind."

"Normally I would, but I'm so desperate to get out of these old things, I'll gladly take whatever you brought for us, as long as they fit me. Thank you." She dropped her gaze to the receipts and picked one off the top. "These are just household items I purchased. Groceries, toiletries." She picked up another, feeling despondent over the loss of the life she once had. Not that she necessarily missed the man Tim had become, but still, living from day to day in relative safety had been nice. Something she'd never again take for granted. "A discount store where I purchased items for Aaron." Her gaze met his. "Why did you bring these here?"

"I'm not sure. I just thought they might be helpful."

He held her gaze, then added, "You need to know that Seth informed me Tim and Colin were stealing money from the Blake-Moore Group."

"What?" She didn't think she could be shocked at anything Tim had done, but the news was startling. "Are you sure?"

He lifted a shoulder. "According to Seth, they'd been at it for a while. I take it you didn't know anything about it."

"No." She felt light-headed, the blood leaving her face in a rush, and was grateful she was already sitting down. "Why would they do such a thing? Tim made good money, enough that he encouraged me to quit my part-time job as an accountant."

"I don't know." His eyes were filled with empathy. "Greed often has no limit."

"Greed." She let out a harsh laugh. "I guess that sums it up right there. Tim always wanted more, felt he deserved more, but Colin…" She shook her head unable to finish. "I hate knowing how Tim dragged my brother down with him."

"Tell me about the morning you left the house."

The change in subject made her sigh. "That was months ago. What good will it do to go over it all again?"

"Please, humor me."

She blew out a frustrated breath, thinking back to that morning just before Christmas. She'd started the day full of hope, thinking that maybe once Tim learned she was pregnant, he'd change. That he'd go back to the way things used to be.

Although based on what she'd just learned, she knew that things would never have changed. Except for the worse.

"Colin and Jeff came into the kitchen as Aaron and I were eating breakfast."

"Did he have a key?" Ryker asked.

"My brother did, yes. Not Jeff." She waved an impatient hand. "Anyway, Colin told me that we were all in danger and that we had to leave immediately."

"But he didn't say what the danger was?"

"No." She gave him an exasperated look. "Are you going to keep interrupting me or are you going to let me tell the story?"

"Sorry." Ryker looked chagrined. "Tell the story."

She thought back. "I asked Colin what was going on, even as I washed Aaron's face and hands from his breakfast. Colin told me he didn't have time to explain, because we had to move in a hurry. I asked if I could pack a bag for both of us, since it sounded like we'd be gone for at least a couple of days, but Colin said there was no time."

When she paused, Ryker asked, "So then what?"

"I told Colin we needed Aaron's car seat, so he sent Jeff out to grab it. Then as I carried Aaron to the door, Colin told me to make sure I took Aaron's diaper bag."

Ryker's eyebrows levered upward. "He actually said that? To take the diaper bag?"

She nodded. "I figured he mentioned it specifically because of the car seat. Like I should take some important things, but not worry about clothes and toiletries."

She followed Ryker's gaze as he turned and looked at the zebra-striped diaper bag. "We need to empty that thing."

A wave of frustration hit her hard. "Come on, Ryker. I've been using that bag on and off for the past six months. Don't you think I would have noticed if there was some sort of notebook full of bank-account information hidden inside?"

"Probably." Ryker leaned over and grabbed the bag. "But it can't hurt to check again."

He set the bag on her lap, and she took out the Pull-Ups diapers first and set them aside. Then she pulled out a change of clothing she always carried for Aaron and set the outfit on top of the diapers.

"Hold on." Ryker reached for the clothes. She watched as he quickly went over the seams of the clothing. When he finished, he noticed her gaze and shrugged. "Hey, it doesn't hurt to check."

"You want to go through the container of wipes, too?" She pulled that out next.

"No, thanks. You made your point."

She pulled out her wallet and handed it over. "You should probably check this. I've used the cash I'd managed to smuggle away from Jeff, but none of the credit cards."

He peered into every pocket and card slot of her wallet, then handed it back. "Nothing."

It didn't take long for her to empty the rest of the bag. "I told you—there's nothing here." She sat back against the headboard, suddenly exhausted.

The Blake-Moore Group continued to come after her because of the money. Everything came down to pure greed.

Maybe if she could find a way to explain to them that she didn't have their stupid numbers, they'd leave her and Aaron alone.

Maybe.

"Let me see the bag." Ryker lifted it off her lap and began running his fingers along the seams. She wondered if the stress was getting to him, too, because he wasn't exactly behaving normally.

But then he pulled out the cardboard covered in plastic at the bottom of the diaper bag. Liv frowned as he turned it over in his hands.

"There's a slit along the side." He used the tip of his fingernail to lift the edge of the plastic up from the cardboard.

A slip of paper floated out, landing on her legs.

For a moment they both stared at it, in shocked surprise. Ryker reached it first, then met her gaze.

"The bank-account information has been in the diaper bag all along." He showed her the small printed rows of account numbers with corresponding deposits. Her breath caught when she took note of the total.

Just over five million.

She couldn't believe it. Nausea swirled and she swallowed hard. "I don't understand. Why would Colin hide this in the diaper bag?"

"I don't know, unless Tim told him to do it. After all, Colin is the one who took you to the motel. Could be that Tim hoped to finish the job with Hawk and then get out of town before accessing the money."

Her shoulders slumped in defeat. More evidence of how far gone her brother and husband had been.

And their greed had put her and Aaron right in the bull's-eye of danger.

TWELVE

Setting aside the slip of paper he'd found hiding in the bottom of the zebra bag, he slid over along the edge of the bed and placed his arm around Olivia's thin shoulders. She looked pale and wan, as if she might pass out at any moment.

"It's okay." He tried to sound reassuring even though he knew this new evidence wasn't going to make things any better for them. Finding the information was one thing. Figuring out the next step in bringing down the Blake-Moore Group was something else.

"It's not," she whispered. He felt her draw in a deep breath and rest her head against his shoulder. "Tim and Colin are dead, and for what? Money?"

Five million was a life-changing amount of cash, but frankly, he didn't get it, either. Especially because Olivia had claimed the Blake-Moore Group paid her husband a decent salary. He rubbed his hand up and down her arm. "I'm sorry they dragged you and your son into this."

She sniffled and he felt awful knowing she was crying. "He never loved me or Aaron."

He couldn't find the words to argue, because her late

husband's actions spoke for themselves. No man should ever put his wife and son in danger the way Tim Habush had. No man should sacrifice his entire family for the contents of a bank account. Five million was nothing compared to a wife and child, especially considering the guy hadn't lived long enough to spend a dime.

He couldn't understand why Tim had thrown away the precious gift of his family, but Ryker was very glad to be with Olivia now. And he was more determined than ever to keep all of them—Olivia, her baby and Aaron—safe.

Duncan poked his head through the connecting door. When he saw Olivia in Ryker's arms, his brow raised and he flashed a knowing grin, then quickly disappeared.

"I wish Tim had been more like you, Ryker."

Her statement caught him off guard, and an unexpected flash of longing hit hard. His feelings for Olivia and Aaron were getting out of control. He cared about her, about them, far too much.

He tried to remind himself about how he'd gone down the path of having a family with Cheri and Cyndi. How they'd been killed before he'd had a chance to know what having a real family of his own would be like. Growing up in the foster-care system, he'd dreamed of having a family. But since losing Cheri and Cyndi, he had no interest in trying again.

Last Christmas he'd silently promised to find Olivia and her son, in order to help keep them safe. The way he wished someone had helped Cheri and her little girl.

After finding Olivia, he'd learned to admire her strength and courage. Her sweetness when she talked about her baby. She was everything he'd once liked about Cheri, only more.

Unable to think of a coherent response, Ryker bent down to press a kiss to her temple.

Olivia shifted in his arms, tipping her head back to look up at him. For a long moment their gazes clung, her eyes searching his. His throat seemed to have stopped working, along with his brain, since he couldn't think of anything to say.

She reached up and cradled his cheek with her palm. "You are a wonderful man, Ryker. I'm so blessed God sent you to come and find me."

Her gratitude battered the wall he'd built around his heart, knocking several bricks loose. He dropped his gaze to her lush mouth. Before he could blink, she drew his head down so she could kiss him.

Their lips clung, then melded together in a heart-stopping caress. Her sweet taste made him long for more.

Not just having her in his arms, which he absolutely wanted, but having her, Aaron and the baby in his life.

The thought brought him up short. Olivia must have noticed, because she broke off the kiss.

"Sorry, I don't know what's wrong with me." She looked adorably flustered, but he didn't like the self-recrimination in her eyes.

He finally found his voice. "There is absolutely nothing wrong with you, Olivia."

She grimaced. "Except that I keep kissing a man who has been nothing but kind to me."

He threaded his fingers through her chin-length dark hair. "I've imagined kissing you several times. You've just been brave enough to take action."

"Yeah, right." She rested her hand on her belly. "I highly doubt there's a man out there who dreams of kissing a pregnant woman who resembles a baby whale."

He placed his hand over hers. "You're beautiful, Olivia. Don't sell yourself short. But you need to know that being in danger like this heightens emotions that wouldn't normally develop on their own."

She frowned. "Duncan put his life on the line for me, but I don't feel this way toward him."

He was ridiculously pleased at her assertion, but knew she was oversimplifying the situation. "But I was the one who found you first. If the situation was reversed, and it was Duncan who came after you, I think you'd be sitting here right now with him."

"No." The stubborn glint was back in her eyes, and he was a bit relieved that she seemed to have momentarily forgotten about the bank-account numbers that had sent the Blake-Moore mercenaries gunning for her. "I wouldn't."

He didn't believe her, and decided it was time to change the subject. "We can talk more about this once you and Aaron are safe. For now, I need some time to discuss our next steps with Duncan."

"I want to give the bank information over to the Blake-Moore Group. Once they have what they've wanted all along, they'll leave me and Aaron alone."

He went still. "We can't do that."

Her gaze narrowed. "Why not? The money belongs to them, doesn't it? Tim and Colin stole from the company. It's only fair they get it back."

Ryker blew out a frustrated breath. "It's blood money. Men have died because of it. And it's highly likely that the money is what they received from dealing weapons to the enemy."

"We don't know that." She pulled her hand out from beneath his and edged away. "Don't you understand? I just want this to be over. I want to live my life with Aaron and have my baby without worrying about someone coming after us."

He didn't want to scare her, but there was no way in the world it would be as easy as handing over the banking information. "They're not just going to let you walk away, Olivia. Or me, for that matter."

A hint of worry flashed in her eyes. "The money is likely more important than revenge."

"And what's to stop us from going to the police to tell them what the Blake-Moore Group has done?"

"We'll give them our word that we won't." A thread of doubt underlined her tone, as if she was finally beginning to understand the magnitude of the danger they still faced.

Ryker rose to his feet and picked up the account numbers. "Give me some time to talk this over with Duncan, okay? Maybe we can come up with a couple of options."

She hesitated, then nodded. "Fine, but think about all the options we have available to us. Sometimes easier is better."

Ryker smiled. "I will. Now do me a favor and get some rest."

"I will."

Every cell in his body wanted to draw her into his arms again, to kiss her until they both couldn't breathe, but he forced himself to take one step, then another toward the connecting door.

"Good night, Ryker."

Her soft voice gave him pause, and he glanced over his shoulder. "Good night, Olivia."

Leaving the connecting door open about an inch, he listened as she and Aaron prepared to go to sleep.

This was the wrong place and the wrong time for him to fall for another single mother. He knew that Olivia's feelings were intermingled with hero worship after the way he'd come to her rescue.

But his weren't. They were all too real, and frankly, they scared him to death.

More than the Blake-Moore Group did.

The next morning, Olivia woke early, after having one of the best night's sleep she'd had since this nightmare had started.

Because of Ryker and Duncan watching over her, she felt safer than she had in a long time.

A shower and change of clothes felt wonderful, even if it was a bit embarrassing to know Ryker had gone through her things.

After she'd changed her son, she took Aaron's hand and walked to the connecting door that was hanging ajar. She lightly rapped on the door frame. "Ryker? Duncan?"

The door opened almost immediately. Ryker's smile made her knees go weak and she hoped she wasn't blushing. "Hey, how did you sleep?"

"Great." He opened the door wide, giving her and Aaron room to come inside. She nodded toward Duncan who was seated at a small desk with an open laptop computer before him. "Did you guys get any rest?"

"Sure." Duncan's brief grin made her wonder if he

was glossing over how much they'd slept. "Take a seat. We have a plan we'd like to discuss."

"A plan?" She glanced at Ryker. His hazel stare was steady and she had the feeling that no matter what she thought about it, their plan was already a go. "I thought you were going to come up with a few options?"

"Just listen first, okay?" Ryker's tone was gentle. "And please sit down."

"Standing isn't going to make me go into labor." She inwardly winced at her cranky tone. Why was she annoyed? After all, she'd slept well and so had Aaron. She set him up with cartoons on the television, then eased down onto the edge of the bed. "Okay, tell me your plan."

The two men exchanged a glance, then Ryker pulled up a chair so that he was eye level with her.

"Remember how I mentioned the Callahans all work in law enforcement?"

"Yes. They're a large family, and all their names start with the letter *M*." She'd thought that hilarious and wondered how many times their parents had called the wrong kid by the wrong name.

"That's right. The oldest, Marc Callahan, works for the FBI."

Oh yes, she remembered that. She straightened and glanced at Duncan, before meeting Ryker's gaze. Then it hit her. "You think the FBI is interested in the guns being sold to the enemy."

"Yes, we do. And it's not just that, but Hawk became acquainted with an FBI agent while he was trying to find who was behind the attempts to kill him and his family."

"Special Agent in Charge Dennis Ludwig," Duncan

added. "We think it's a good idea to reach out to Marc Callahan and explain what's going on. Marc can be our liaison with Ludwig."

"Why not give Blake-Moore the account numbers?" She knew she sounded like a broken record, but it seemed very logical to her. Give them what they wanted in exchange for being left alone. "With five million they could likely disappear forever."

"And what would stop them from killing us all?" Again, Ryker's tone was gentle. "No witnesses to ever come forward against them."

She reached up to rub her temple. The feeling of being well rested was fading fast beneath the harsh reality Ryker and Duncan were presenting. "We aren't witnesses to anything."

"We know the bank accounts that house the money that was siphoned away by your husband and brother." Ryker hesitated, then added, "And don't forget, two of their men died by our hands, three others assaulted and tied up. Don't you see? We absolutely need to bring the authorities in on this."

She sighed and nodded, admitting defeat. "You're right. Okay, we'll bring in the authorities. But how long will it take for the FBI to arrest Harper Moore and Kevin Blake? Days? Weeks? Months? A year?"

The two men exchanged another knowing glance. "We don't know," Duncan admitted. "But hopefully not longer than a few months."

She placed a protective hand on her stomach. "We don't have a few months. This baby is due in just under six weeks. A little less, now."

"I know. Don't worry, Olivia. It's going to be okay." Ryker put a reassuring hand on her arm. "We're going to protect you, Aaron and the baby. I'm sure the FBI will help us."

She should be relieved to know that the FBI would be helping to protect her, but she wasn't. The idea of having a couple of straitlaced FBI agents dressed in suits and ties watching over her was not reassuring. While he might be a perfectly nice guy, she didn't know or have a reason to trust Dennis Ludwig or any other FBI agent.

She wanted Ryker. Yet for the first time, it occurred to her that maybe he was tired of being in the line of fire on her behalf. After all, he'd done more than his fair share of fighting off the bad guys since he'd found her in Harrisburg.

Her cheeks burned at the memory of how she'd kissed him. Twice. Why on earth had she done that? Based on the fact that he'd tried to convince her that her emotions were some form of hero worship made her realize just how one-sided they were.

The way he'd been kind enough to tell her she was beautiful, when she was as big as a house, was sweet. His way of trying to soften the blow.

He didn't want her or care about her the way she was beginning to care about him. This plan of going to the FBI for help was obviously twofold.

Get the feds involved in bringing down Harper Moore and Kevin Blake, while extricating himself from her life.

Okay, then. She straightened her shoulders. "All right."

A momentary confusion washed over Ryker's face. "All right, what? You're in agreement with us reaching out to Marc Callahan?"

"Yes. And to bringing in the FBI, that agent in charge." She searched for his name. "Dennis Ludwig."

"Great." Duncan pounced on her agreement. "I'll call Marc now. He should be back in Milwaukee by now."

Ryker looked as if he wanted to say something more, but Aaron's plaintive tone interrupted them.

"Mommy, I'm hungry."

She turned away from Ryker. "Okay, sweetie. I'll get you some animal crackers."

Ryker jumped up and crossed through the connecting doors to get her zebra bag. She stared at it for a moment, hating the idea that she'd been carrying the stupid bank-account numbers in there all this time, then told herself not to be foolish.

The bag wasn't the problem, the numbers were.

"Duncan, see if Marc can meet us for breakfast," Ryker said. "We'll meet him halfway if necessary."

Duncan raised a hand to acknowledge him, but remained focused on his call. "Marc? Hey, it's Duncan O'Hare. Do you have a minute? We have a bit of a problem…"

Duncan left the motel room, talking to Marc as he went. She wasn't sure why he needed privacy. She knew everything that had gone down, but decided it was better for Aaron not to hear any of the specifics.

Her son was satisfied with a couple of animal crackers, his gaze locked on the television.

She second-guessed her decision several times over the next twenty minutes. Marc had agreed to meet with them in about an hour, so Ryker had advised her to pack up their things.

"We won't be back."

"But won't it take time for Marc to get in touch with Dennis Ludwig?"

Ryker nodded. "We'll still find somewhere else to stay. Better to keep moving."

"All right." It didn't take long for her to gather their things, stuffing everything into the zebra bag.

Thirty minutes later they were on the road. This time Duncan was tucked in the back seat beside Aaron. He was great with her son, keeping him entertained by reciting stories that he must have memorized from children's books.

"How does he know so many of them?" she asked Ryker.

"He spends a lot of time with his nephew Brodie."

She remembered hearing about Mike Callahan and Shayla's son. "He must have a really good memory."

"Nah. I've just read the books about a hundred times each," Duncan said in a wry tone. "I could recite them in my sleep."

The family restaurant wasn't too far off the interstate. They chose a circular booth that offered room for four seats and a high chair for Aaron.

Her stomach rumbled at the enticing scent of bacon and eggs. Ryker must have heard, as he grinned. "Let's order."

"I'll be fine. We can wait for Marc," she protested.

"Marc is running a bit late," Duncan said with a glance at his phone. "He said to go ahead and order. He'll eat on the way."

Their meal arrived in what seemed like record time. She dove into her over-easy eggs, then realized she forgot to pray, so sent up a quick, silent *Thank You, Lord* before continuing to eat.

Based on the liberal smears of syrup over his face, Aaron was enjoying his French toast.

She glanced longingly at the coffee Ryker and Duncan were drinking, but told herself to forget it. She remained determined to avoid anything that may impact the baby. Sipping her water, she watched as the two men quickly devoured their meals.

Pushing her empty plate away, she sighed. "That was good, thanks. Please excuse me for a moment." She slid out of the booth intending to use the restroom.

Ryker's hand clamped on her arm. "Wait. Duncan, do you see that SUV that just pulled in? Notice the dark tinted windows? Just like the other SUV Blake-Moore used?"

"Yeah." He lifted his phone to his ear. "Marc? We've got company."

SUV? Company? Her heart squeezed in her chest. No, this couldn't be happening again. Could it?

How was it possible that the Blake-Moore Group had found them again?

THIRTEEN

"We're getting out of here." Ryker wasn't about to take any chances. He tossed cash on the table, lifted Aaron out of his high chair, grabbed the zebra bag and placed his hand in the small of Olivia's back, steering her toward the opposite end of the restaurant. Duncan followed, still talking to Marc.

"I don't understand…" Olivia began.

"Not now." He didn't mean to sound terse, but this wasn't the time for a detailed conversation. "Go through the kitchen."

"The kitchen?" Olivia's voice rose in agitation. "They won't let us in."

He ignored her, since he wasn't planning to ask permission, and pushed the swinging door open with one hand. With the other, he gently nudged her through.

"Hey!" The kitchen help gaped at them. "Customers aren't allowed back here."

"Don't worry, we're just moving through." Ryker raked his gaze over the area, searching for the back door that he knew all restaurants had for employee use. When he saw the dark green door, he urged Olivia toward it.

He half expected someone to physically attempt

to stop them, but they didn't. Instead, the staff stayed where they were, as if momentarily frozen in time, watching them. Thirty seconds later, they were outside near a large Dumpster, with an open field behind it.

The lack of coverage made him nervous.

"Where's Marc?" He glanced toward Duncan. "We need an escape strategy."

"I know." Duncan still had his phone to his ear. "He's coming up now."

"I see him." A silver SUV came around the corner, with a dark-haired man behind the wheel. Ryker had met the entire Callahan family several times, but it wasn't always easy to tell them apart. Marc was the oldest and most serious of the bunch. Although he was a different man when he was around his wife, Kari, and his two young children.

"Wait. I need a car seat for Aaron." Olivia dug in her heels in protest when he urged her toward the SUV.

"Marc has kids, too," Duncan assured her. "See? There's a car seat in the back."

That was all Olivia needed. She rushed forward, opening the back passenger door. She reached for her son, but Ryker was already setting the boy in the car seat and securing the buckle.

"Get in. We'll have to squish together," he told her.

She didn't argue, and he hugged the door frame as much as possible to give her enough room to put on her seat belt.

The moment they were all inside the vehicle, Marc took off. Ryker kept his gaze on the parking lot, as did Duncan.

The black SUV was parked next to the one they'd driven here. Two men dressed in black were disappearing inside the restaurant. He hadn't recognized them, not that he'd expected to. Apparently the Blake-Moore Group had more than enough mercenaries working for them. A never-ending stream of disposable resources, which made him feel sick at heart. Why were these men so anxious to put their lives on the line like this? Didn't they realize how much danger they were placing themselves in? He simply didn't understand it.

"How did they find you?" Marc's question drew him from his dark thoughts.

"I have no idea." He glanced at Olivia who was doing her best to soothe her son. The boy had seemed confused by their abrupt departure, but thankfully wasn't crying.

"What if they've picked up on the fact that we're using the Callahans to back us up?" Duncan turned in his seat to look at Ryker. "First Mike, then Miles and now Marc."

Ryker blew out a breath. "Could be. We all helped Hawk six months ago, including several of the Callahans. It's not a stretch for them to assume we'd use them again."

"I wasn't followed," Marc protested.

"I know you weren't. They showed up minutes before you did." Which was an interesting fact now that he thought about it. "Could they have somehow tapped into your phone?"

Marc let out a snort. "I can't see how they could trace an FBI phone."

"But you use it as your personal device, too." Duncan's tone was mild. "Could be they have your family under surveillance."

"Maybe. I'll call and have one of my colleagues sit

on my place, just in case." Clearly Marc didn't want to believe his phone had been traced, but what other explanation was there? Especially considering the mercenaries had beaten him to the restaurant. They had to have had prior knowledge that the place was a meeting point. "But there's been no sign of that. And I only called the office in Madison to help coordinate things."

"Now what?" Olivia's voice held a noticeable tremor.

Ryker reached for her hand. "We'll continue protecting you and Aaron. Just trust us, okay?"

She nodded, and didn't say anything more. But she continued clutching his hand as if it was a lifeline.

"I want to go back to Madison," Marc said. "To the FBI office there."

Olivia tensed, but he nodded his agreement. "Whatever you think is best."

"You know, I'd think they'd have sent more than two men if they knew we'd reached out to the Callahans."

Duncan's observation made him nod. "Yeah, you would think so. Although these guys tend to believe they're better than anyone else."

"Yet we keep proving them wrong," Duncan added thoughtfully. "I wonder if they're running out of men?"

"I sure hope so." That would be the best news ever, in his opinion. What good was the Blake-Moore Group if they only had a handful of men working for them?

Except they wouldn't need any more, would they? Once they had the money Tim and Colin had skimmed from them, the two owners could easily disappear for good.

"Do you think both Harper Moore and Kevin Blake know about the embezzled money? Or just one of them?" Marc asked.

It was a good question. "I don't know. Why? Do you think we can play one owner off the other?" It made sense in a way, to have the entire five million going to one person instead of being split down the middle.

"Maybe." Marc's expression was thoughtful. "Although I can't believe they weren't aware of the gun-selling scheme, which makes me believe they're both in this up to their beady little eyeballs."

"Yeah." And it still burned him to know that while he'd been fighting in Afghanistan, the enemy had used American guns against him and his teammates. "Although, if that's true, why hasn't either one of them been arrested yet?"

Marc met his gaze in the rearview mirror. "From what I hear, there isn't any proof of their culpability. Both Blake and Moore are claiming that their men were acting alone without their knowledge."

"Yeah, right," Duncan muttered.

Marc shrugged. "Once we get the proof we need, they'll both be arrested and charged in federal court. But until then, there isn't much more we can do."

"The money stashed in overseas bank accounts might be the proof we need," Ryker pointed out. "Although we'd have to find a way to trace it back to Colin and Tim. Seth's testimony may help us, there."

"I hope so," Marc agreed.

For several miles no one said anything.

Ryker glanced over at Olivia to see she was resting her head against the edge of Aaron's car seat, her eyes closed. Her fingers still clung to his, so he didn't think she was sleeping.

"Hey, are you okay?" He kept his voice low.

She opened her eyes. "Fine. Except the Braxton-Hicks contractions are back."

He felt the blood drain from his face. "How long have you had them?"

"Since we rushed through the kitchen." She closed her eyes again.

It was the stress of being on the run for their lives. She hadn't said it, but he knew that's what she'd meant. He felt terrible that she was having to go through all of this in her condition.

"Problem?" Marc asked.

He tried not to look as panicked as he felt. "Braxton-Hicks contractions."

"Again?" Duncan swiveled around to face him, alarm in his gaze. "I don't like this. We need to get her in to see a doctor."

"Couldn't agree more." When Olivia's fingers tightened around his, he looked at her. "What's wrong?"

"Nothing, but I really would like to see a doctor." Her voice was low and steady.

Terror gripped him. "You think this is it? Real labor pains?"

The corner of her mouth tipped up in a half-hearted smile. "No, but I haven't been to see an OB in just over a month, and I'm supposed to go in monthly until I'm four weeks out, then weekly. I've missed one appointment so far, and in another two weeks, it will be two missed appointments."

"That settles it." Ryker wasn't about to take any chances. "Let's find her an OB doctor."

"Where are we?" Olivia frowned as she looked through the window. "I don't recognize this place."

"We're in McFarland, less than fifteen miles outside

of Madison," Marc said. "Do you know any OB doctors in Madison?"

"I know Dr. Bowman. He delivered Aaron. I was planning to go to him for this baby, but never had the chance."

"Will he see you without an appointment?" Ryker cradled her hand between both of his. "Or should we go to the emergency room?"

She wrinkled her nose. "This isn't an emergency. Can you look up his number? Maybe he or one of his associates has an opening."

He reluctantly let her go, then used his phone to pull up the name of the obstetrician. He found the number easily enough and called it, but quickly handed the phone to Olivia as he had no clue what to say.

Olivia politely asked for the next available appointment after explaining that she hadn't been able to see her OB in Illinois as originally planned. After several moments, she said thank you and handed him his phone.

"Tomorrow morning is the earliest they can see me."

"Not today?"

She shrugged. "I'm sure I'll be fine till the morning. They told me to call if anything changes."

A wave of helplessness washed over him. He didn't like it, but what could he do? Other than drive her to the closest hospital and insist she be seen. "That's stupid advice," he mumbled.

"I'll be fine." She rested her head against Aaron's car seat and smoothed her hands over her stomach. "As long as I can relax and remain calm."

He met Marc's concerned gaze in the rearview mirror. Having two kids of his own, Marc was better versed in what a pregnant woman might need.

"We'll find another motel," Marc offered. "We'll stop for a break before I touch base again with the field office here in Madison."

"Yeah, okay." Ryker couldn't seem to tear his gaze from Olivia. Her expression was serene, as if she was deep inside herself, thinking happy thoughts.

If anything happened to her, Aaron or the baby, he'd never forgive himself.

Slow and easy. Breathe in while counting to ten. Breathe out counting to ten.

Olivia repeated the internal monologue over and over, refusing to allow any negative thoughts into her mind. The contractions were already beginning to ease off. She knew God was watching over them and that her baby would be fine.

The SUV stopped and she pried her eyes open, blinking in confusion. After a moment she recognized they were on the outskirts of the city, the state capitol building visible in the distance.

"Just sit tight. We're almost at the hotel," Ryker said.

"Good. I could use a bathroom." Every contraction had only punctuated her need to go. "A suite would be nice if they have one available."

"Not a problem."

The hotels around them seemed nicer than the previous ones they'd stayed in, not that she'd ever complain. All she wanted, needed, was to be safe.

It didn't seem so much to ask.

Think positive, she told herself, drawing in a long, deep breath. They were safe. She had three men watching over them, one of them a federal agent no less. Between God and Ryker, she couldn't be in better hands.

"How about that one?" Marc gestured to a hotel a few miles ahead.

"Fine with me," Ryker agreed.

"Anything that nice will require a driver's license and credit card on file," Duncan pointed out.

"I know."

A twinge of concern had her meeting Ryker's gaze. "Do you think that's wise?"

"Don't worry—we'll keep you safe." Ryker's smile was reassuring and she didn't doubt his sincerity. He'd done nothing but keep her and Aaron safe since the moment they'd met.

Three days ago? It seemed much longer.

She felt bad that protecting her had become such a monstrous job. Logically, she knew it wasn't her fault Colin had put the stupid account information in her diaper bag. And her brother and Tim had skimmed the money from their employer in the first place.

Five million. She still couldn't quite comprehend that much money.

A contraction tightened her belly and she drew in a slow, deep breath. No stress, remember? She repeated her mantra as Marc navigated the busy Madison traffic.

When Marc passed the hotel, a niggle of fear encroached her inner peace. "What's wrong?"

"Just taking precautions," Marc responded.

She frowned when she noticed the silent look Marc and Ryker exchanged. Being wedged as she was between Ryker and Aaron's car seat, she couldn't see behind them.

"Are we being followed?"

"Please try not to worry." Ryker rested his hand on her knee. "We're just being careful."

No, there was more to it. The tension between the men had risen sharply over the past five minutes.

Breathe in—count to ten. Breathe out—count to ten.

It wasn't working. Marc took a quick left turn, then a right. The jerky movements weren't helping her discomfort.

"Head out of town," Ryker said. "It'll be easier to pick up a tail with fewer cars on the road."

"I'm trying." Marc seemed to be concentrating on the road before him.

"I wanna get out," Aaron cried, picking up on the tension between the adults. "I hav'ta go to the bathroom."

She did too, but had been doing her best to ignore the urge. "Soon, Aaron."

Aaron kicked his feet and she suppressed a sigh. Remaining calm and peaceful under these circumstances was impossible.

The cars thinned out around them, and just as she was about to breathe a sigh of relief, Marc pressed the accelerator, picking up speed.

"What is it?"

"Black SUV with tinted windows, but could be nothing," Duncan said. "We're just trying to put distance between us and them."

Oh no, not again. Please, not again!

Marc increased their speed another notch, making her wonder if the black SUV was keeping pace. She wanted to turn in her seat to look out the window, but couldn't.

Another contraction tightened across her belly and she caught her breath at the intensity of it. It was stronger than the Braxton-Hicks she'd been experiencing until now.

Please, God, keep my baby safe!

She breathed through the contraction, trying to imagine the sound of ocean waves hitting the sandy shore. She had one of those white-noise machines and the wave sound was her favorite.

"They're closing the gap. We need to call for backup." Marc picked up his phone from the center console and handed it to Duncan. "Call 911 first, then I'll get in touch with the FBI field office."

While Duncan spoke into the phone in a low, urgent tone, she reached for Ryker's hand. "Pray with me." She looked up at him. "Please?"

"Of course." He cleared his throat. "Dear Lord, keep all of us safe in Your care."

"Guide us on Your chosen path," she added, "and show us the way to escape these men. Amen."

"Amen," Ryker echoed.

For several long moments there was nothing but silence, then suddenly Marc shouted, "Brace yourselves!"

Before she had a chance to react, something hard hit the back of their SUV, jarring them. Marc fought to keep control of the wheel, even as he picked up speed. He moved from one lane to the other, in an attempt to avoid the vehicle behind them.

Another contraction tightened her stomach and she felt a stab of fear.

What if this wasn't false labor? What if she was about to have her baby five and a half weeks early? She told herself that less than six weeks wasn't the end of the world, but that was under normal circumstances.

And these were anything but.

FOURTEEN

The crunch of metal hitting metal was jarring. The vehicle rocked a bit, but Marc kept it under control. Ryker clenched his jaw, hating how vulnerable they were. It was disturbing to know Olivia and Aaron were in danger. The police needed to get here, and soon!

"Mommy, I'm scared." Aaron began to cry.

"Shh, we're okay." Olivia's tone lacked conviction as she reassured her son.

Marc hit the accelerator, hard, doing his best to get them away from the SUV behind them.

"Is there a place we can go to get away? An off-ramp, maybe?" Ryker knew it wasn't likely. The highway up ahead only showed woods flanking the road.

They'd left the city limits far behind.

"I'm trying." Marc continued pushing the speed even faster, which was also worrisome if they were to be hit from behind again. If Marc lost control of the vehicle, they could all die.

"The police are on the way," Duncan said.

"They better be." Ryker couldn't help turning to look back at the SUV. Marc had gotten some distance away, but their attackers were doing their best to close the gap. "Step on it, Marc."

"I am." Marc sounded tense, too.

Olivia moaned softly under her breath and he felt a stab of fear. "What's wrong?"

"Nothing." She bit the word out between clenched teeth and the way she held on to her stomach was concerning.

"More Braxton-Hicks contractions?" He didn't want to believe she was truly in labor. It wasn't time for the baby to be born yet.

"I don't think so." Her voice was strained. "These might be real."

"Real?" Duncan twisted in his seat to face them. "No way."

Olivia didn't answer, clearly concentrating on what she was experiencing. The fact that she didn't continue to talk to Aaron said volumes.

"You need to get us out of danger, Marc." Ryker hated feeling helpless, and sitting next to Olivia without being the one behind the wheel was driving him nuts.

"I'm trying," Marc repeated as he shifted their car into the left lane to go around a pickup truck. The driver shot them a dirty look, which Marc ignored. The SUV followed them into the left lane, keeping pace.

Ryker swallowed hard and silently repeated the prayer he and Olivia had shared moments ago.

Dear Lord, keep all of us safe in Your care...show us the way to escape these men. Amen.

A minute later, the wail of sirens filled the air. Ryker craned his neck, trying to locate the source of the sound. Highways were under the control of the Wisconsin State Patrol and he hoped they'd arrive soon.

"There!" Duncan must have been on the lookout for them, too. He gestured to the side-view mirror. "They're about three miles back, but coming up from behind."

"The police will save us, right?" Aaron asked.

"For sure." Ryker smiled at the little boy, then peered back over his shoulder. He still couldn't see the police from this angle. But he did notice the black SUV abruptly slow down and veer into the right lane. "Hey, I think Blake-Moore is giving up the chase."

"I hope so." Marc's voice was calmer now. "Can you make out the license plate?"

Ryker narrowed his gaze, trying to see the letters and numbers. It wasn't easy since they were going so fast and the SUV was slowing down. "Frank, Oscar, Tom…" He sighed. "I can't see the rest. They're exiting the highway."

"Call dispatch. Let them know what we have on the license plate so far," Marc said.

Duncan spoke into the phone again as Marc gently slowed his speed. Within seconds, the police car came up behind them.

Marc pulled over to the shoulder and stopped the car. He peeled his fingers from the steering wheel, but kept his hands visible after pulling out his badge and lowering the driver's-side window.

"FBI Special Agent Marc Callahan," he said as the state patrol officer approached. He opened his badge so the trooper could look at it more closely.

"And I'm with the Milwaukee PD, Officer Duncan O'Hare," Duncan added. "I made the 911 call."

"I saw the dent in your rear bumper and just heard the first three letters of the license plate number come through over the radio." The state patrol officer bent forward to look into the back seat of the vehicle. "Who are you?"

"Former army Sergeant Ryker Tillman," he introduced himself, using his military background, rather than his security-consulting business. "And this is Olivia and Aaron." He purposefully left off their last names.

"Hi, Mr. Police man." Aaron's initial fright after being hit by the SUV seemed to have faded under the novelty of having the police arrive.

"Hi." The patrol officer flashed a quick smile.

"As you can see, Olivia is pregnant and having contractions," Ryker continued. "We need to get her to the closest hospital as soon as possible."

"Contractions?" The patrol officer appeared taken aback by the news. "Hey, no one mentioned a pregnant woman and a kid."

"My fault," Duncan said, although Ryker knew he'd omitted the details about Olivia and Aaron on purpose. "I was just so worried we'd crash. Thanks for getting here so quickly."

The patrolman looked at Marc who had replaced his badge in his pocket. "Are you working a case? Is that why you were targeted?"

"I am on a case, yes, and this incident may be related." Marc shrugged. "I have a call in to the FBI office in Madison. I'd like to discuss this with them first, before I give you additional details."

The patrol officer frowned. "The attempt to run you off the road happened in my jurisdiction."

"I know, and I very much appreciate your quick response." Marc's smile was strained. "I'm happy to give you more information as soon as I run it through official channels. You know how the upper brass is. They always have to be in charge. They act like those of us with boots on the ground can't make a decision, which is bull."

"True that." The patrol officer must have appreciated Marc's honesty, as he nodded and handed over a business card. "Okay, Agent Callahan. I'll expect to hear from you soon. In the meantime, we have a BOLO out on the black SUV with a partial plate of Frank, Oscar, Tom." The guy hesitated, then added, "You want a police escort to the hospital?"

"I think we're okay, but if you'd put the word out to the other patrol officers, I'd appreciate it."

"Will do." He tipped his hat.

"Thanks again." Marc rolled up his window and waited for the trooper to return to his squad car before easing their SUV back onto the interstate.

"Where to? Do we need to go to the Madison FBI office?" Ryker could tell Olivia was still experiencing contractions.

"No, the hospital." Marc met his gaze in the rearview mirror. "I want Olivia to be seen by a doctor ASAP."

"Me, too." He took Olivia's hand in his. "You'll go to the ER, won't you?"

"Yes." The way she readily went along with the plan only emphasized the seriousness of the situation. Olivia would never agree to be seen unless she was truly concerned about her condition.

About the baby's condition.

Ryker listened to her deep, rhythmic breathing, hoping, praying that this was nothing more than Braxton-Hicks brought on by stress. Being rear-ended by the

Blake-Moore SUV could have made the contractions worse, right?

Maybe now that they were safe, at least for the moment, the contractions would stop.

Olivia's hand tightened over his, killing his feeble hope. The tightness corresponded with whatever new contraction she was experiencing. Her grip remained tight around his hand until the pain eased.

Oh yeah, there was no doubt about it.

Olivia was in labor.

He closed his eyes on a wave of despair, knowing he'd almost failed in his mission to keep her, Aaron and the baby safe.

The contractions were a good ten minutes apart, but strong enough to steal her breath.

"Where's the closest hospital?" Ryker asked.

"Not any hospital," she protested. She shifted in her seat, trying to get into a more comfortable position. "I want to go to the teaching hospital where my original OB works."

She sensed Ryker's impatience. "It's too far away."

"I have time—the contractions aren't that close. Besides, if this baby is coming early I want to be in the best hospital with the best neonatal intensive care unit." She gritted her teeth as her abdomen tightened with another contraction. "Go back to Madison."

"The baby?" Aaron's innocent question drew her attention.

"Yes, sweetie. Soon you're going to have a baby brother or baby sister."

"I wanna baby brother," Aaron announced.

She didn't have the heart to tell him she suspected

the baby was a girl. She tried to smile. "You're going to be Mommy's helper with the baby, aren't you?"

"Yep." Aaron nodded.

The pain intensified and she found herself grabbing Ryker's hand again as she breathed through it. It was always easier to practice in those birthing classes than to actually do it. She remembered getting upset with Tim when she was in labor with Aaron, because he kept telling her she was breathing wrong. She'd finally yelled at him not to tell her how to breathe. Instead of apologizing, Tim had plopped into a chair and sulked.

Unlike Ryker, who tried to be supportive. He didn't say anything, his gaze stricken with guilt and fear as if he had never planned to be around long enough to see her give birth.

Yeah, big surprise.

But he let her squeeze his hand without making a sound of protest, brushing a kiss across her knuckles when the pain eased.

"You're doing great," he said encouragingly.

"I'm not sure I have much of a choice." Her attempt at humor was weak. "Baby has a mind of her own."

"Just like her mommy," Ryker agreed.

That made her smile. She was touched by his willingness to support her through this.

"We're fifteen minutes from Madison." Marc caught her gaze. "Sure you're okay?"

"Positive." Although she was worried about Aaron. "Ryker, will you watch Aaron for me?"

"Hey, why don't I give Mike and Shayla a call," Duncan offered. "If Brodie is feeling better, maybe they'll watch Aaron. Brodie is just a little older than Aaron. I'm sure they'll have fun playing together."

"Can I play with Brodie?" Aaron asked.

"If he's feeling better, sure." She glanced at Ryker. "You may need to stay close to Aaron. He trusts you."

Ryker hesitated, then nodded. "If Mike can't help, I will. But I'd like to be there for you, Olivia."

It was the sweetest thing he'd ever said to her and it made her eyes mist with tears. "Watching Aaron will help me."

"Okay." He lightly rubbed his thumb over the back of her hand. "Whatever you want."

The stark contrast between Ryker and Tim was obvious. Was Ryker always like this? Or was this an exception under dramatically stressful and dangerous circumstances? She didn't know for sure, but would be forever grateful for his steadfast support.

"Hey, Mike, it's Dunc. How's Brodie? Better? That's great." She listened as Duncan made arrangements for Mike, Shayla and Brodie to meet them in Madison and take care of Olivia's son.

"Let me know when you're close," Duncan said. "I'll give you the details when we know them."

"All set?" Ryker asked when Duncan disconnected from the call.

"Yep. Brodie must have had a twenty-four-hour bug, because he's fine now." Duncan flashed a grin at Aaron. "He's looking forward to meeting you."

Olivia began to relax. Trust Ryker, Duncan and the Callahans to come to the rescue.

She breathed through another contraction, just as they arrived in the ER. Ryker helped her out of the back seat, and it was difficult to leave Aaron behind with Marc and Duncan, even though she knew the two men would keep him safe.

"You're in labor?" The triage nurse wasted no time. "Let's get you back to a room right away."

Ryker came with her, and the nurse assumed he was the father of the baby. "Dad, have a seat here, while the doctor examines your wife."

Olivia opened her mouth to correct them, but Ryker quickly shook his head. "Don't worry, sweetheart, I'll be right next to you the entire time."

"Okay." She understood he wanted her to play along, and why not? Honestly, she needed Ryker's support now more than ever.

The doctor asked a series of questions then performed a quick exam. "No sign of the baby's head yet, so that's good. We have an OB on her way down. She'll be here in a minute. We're also getting you a bed up in Labor and Delivery."

"So, she's really going to have the baby today?" Ryker's tone rose in surprise.

"It's possible, but Dr. Regner will know more. Oh, there she is now."

Dr. Regner flashed a reassuring smile as she entered the room, then proceeded to ask her the same questions she'd just answered for the ER doctor. The only difference was that Dr. Regner's exam was more thorough. "Okay, you're about three centimeters dilated. Once we get you settled in Labor and Delivery, we'll put a monitor on the baby so we can see how he or she is doing."

"But aren't you going to do something to stop the contractions?" Olivia had assumed they'd want her bun to stay in the oven a little longer.

"You're early but I'd estimate the baby is roughly five pounds. We'll do an ultrasound to be sure."

The next hour passed in a flurry of activity. When

she arrived in the labor and delivery room, the nurse started an IV to provide fluids. Once that happened, her contractions slowed way down.

"I might not be in labor after all." She glanced at Ryker who'd remained at her side through the IV and the ultrasound. "The contractions seem to have stopped."

"That happens sometimes once you're rehydrated," the nurse said. "But if it's true labor, they'll return."

Olivia secretly hoped they wouldn't return, at least not for another couple of weeks.

When the nurse finally left them alone, Ryker leaned over and took her hand. "I want you to know Marc has an FBI agent by the name of Tony Seavers from the Madison office stationed outside your door for protection."

"Really? I'm sure that's not necessary."

"Yes, it is. And I've heard from Mike that Brodie and Aaron are getting along great. Since you were admitted, Mike and Shayla took Aaron home with them."

"That's good to know." She could rest easier, knowing her son was in good hands. "Although all of this fuss may be for nothing, since the contractions seem to have stopped."

"Wait and see what Dr. Regner says, okay?" Ryker bowed his head for a moment, before meeting her gaze. "I'm just glad we made it here safely. I was worried you might deliver this baby in the car."

"Nah, she's too stubborn for that." Olivia tried to make light of the situation, but truthfully, she'd had the same fear. "Thanks for staying with me."

"Of course." His gaze turned serious. "I'd never let you go through this all alone, Olivia."

Tears pricked her eyes again. Hormones. And maybe something more. She cared about Ryker, way too much. Her head knew he was just being nice, her knight in shining armor, rescuing her from certain danger, but her heart yearned for something more.

His love.

A contraction tightened her belly, making her suck in a harsh breath. "I guess I was wrong."

"About?"

"They're back. The contractions, I mean." She concentrated on breathing.

"Easy now," Ryker crooned. "Do you want me to get the nurse?"

"In a minute." She rode the crest of the contraction, then relaxed as the pain eased.

Ryker's phone rang. He gave her hand a quick pat, then stood. "I'll answer this and get the nurse, okay?"

"Okay." She wasn't going to argue. If the baby insisted on coming early, then she needed to be prepared.

Ryker left the room. She imagined him chatting briefly with the FBI agent outside her door before moving on.

When her door opened, she turned her head to greet the nurse. Only it wasn't the nurse standing there. It was Tim's cousin Seth Willis.

Her blood ran cold for a moment, as she registered the fact that Seth was wearing a uniform and a name tag identifying him as a hospital security guard. "What do you want?"

Seth didn't answer, but the flatness in his eyes reminded her of Tim. She reached for her call button a second too late. Seth slammed one hand over her mouth, the other pinning her wrists together in a painful grip.

Kicking the side rail with her foot, she tried to make as much noise as possible. But to no avail.

With Seth's hand over her mouth, it was impossible to breathe. The room spun. No! This couldn't be happening. Where was the FBI? Ryker? The nurse?

Please, Lord, help me! Save me and my baby!

FIFTEEN

Ryker paced the hallway as Marc updated him on the SUV that had tried to run them off the interstate. "We found it abandoned at the side of the road, wiped clean. Not a single fingerprint or piece of trace evidence."

"Figures." They really needed a break, some way to get directly to Kevin Blake and Harper Moore. They were the ones behind these attempts against Olivia and he wanted them held responsible. "Anything else?"

"We're working with local law enforcement to find Blake and Moore but so far we don't have any idea where they are. The good news is that the banking information is legit. Our team was able to track down the embezzled funds with an electronic trail back to the Blake-Moore Group. Once we get our hands on Blake and Moore, we should have what we need to arrest them."

"Good." Ryker heard a muffled thump and turned toward the door of Olivia's room. Tony Seavers, the FBI agent posted there on guard duty, abruptly turned and pushed open her door and let out a shout.

"Hey! Get away from her!"

Shoving the phone in his pocket without disconnecting from the call, Ryker ran into Olivia's room hot on

Tony's heels. When he realized Tony was pulling a man off Olivia, he ran toward them. His blood ran hot when he saw it was Seth Willis.

He grabbed on to Seth, helping to pull him away. Between them, he and Tony wrestled Willis to the floor and cuffed him.

"What are you doing, Seth? I thought you wanted to turn your life around." Ryker didn't hide the anger in his tone. "What did you hope to accomplish by hurting Olivia?"

"I didn't want to hurt her. I just wanted the bank-account information." Seth glared at him. "If she had handed it over, I would have left her alone."

Ryker couldn't believe he'd bought into the guy's story about going straight. That he'd actually given Willis the phone information for Dennis Ludwig, their FBI contact.

"Ryker!" Hearing his name from his pocket, he realized Marc Callahan was still on the phone.

"Seth Willis tried to attack Olivia," he said into the phone. "I'll call you back." Without waiting for a response, he ended the call and rushed over to Olivia, raking his gaze over her. Her cheeks were pink, her hair disheveled and her breathing seemed labored. "Are you hurt?"

"I'm not sure. Please get the nurse." Both of her hands were splayed over her belly. "I'm not having any contractions and I'm worried something is wrong."

No way was he leaving. He reached over and pushed the call button. "The nurse is on her way. Please, Olivia, I need to know if he hurt you."

She shook her head. "Scared me more than anything, because I couldn't breathe. I kept kicking the side rails, hoping to make enough noise to attract attention. I knocked him off-balance, which helped."

His jaw tightened when he saw her bare feet, imagining the bruises that would likely mar her beautiful skin within the next day or so.

"I heard you." Tony Seavers finished zip-tying Seth's ankles then came over to stand beside Ryker. "I'm so sorry. When he claimed to be Olivia's husband's cousin, I didn't think to question him. Especially since he works here in security. Why wouldn't he be legit?"

Ryker wanted to snap at the Fed, but reined in his temper. This was his fault for not checking to see if this was the hospital where Seth worked. Not to mention believing the guy's innocence in the first place. "It's okay." He shot a glare at Seth who was propped in the corner of the room. "But I want him booked for assault and battery."

"Agreed. I'll call in the local law enforcement now. They can take him into custody." Tony's gaze lingered on Olivia for a moment, obviously still feeling guilty for his role in her attack, before stepping away to use his phone.

Olivia's smile was wan. "Don't blame Tony. Seth didn't lie. He is my dead husband's cousin."

"I know." Ryker lowered his chin to his chest, trying to get a grip. Normally he abhorred violence, but at this moment he wanted to punch Seth in the jaw for daring to place his hands on Olivia. For putting both an innocent woman and her unborn child in danger. He lifted his head. "I don't blame Tony. This is my fault, Olivia. I hope you can forgive me."

"Your fault? Funny, it seems to me Seth was the one who attacked me."

It was nice of her to try letting him off the hook, but he knew the truth. He turned toward Seth. "The Feds have the banking information, so hurting Olivia wasn't necessary."

Seth looked away, unable to hold his gaze.

There was a slight knock at the door, before it opened revealing a woman in scrubs. "I'm your nurse, Olivia. What can I do for you?"

Ryker reluctantly moved away from Olivia's bedside to make room for the nurse. He crossed over to Willis. "Tell me the truth. Are you still working for Blake-Moore?"

Seth hunched his shoulders. "No. I told you, I didn't want to put my life on the line for them. You were right that they treat us as disposable assets, easily replaced."

"You came here to assault an innocent woman, all on your own? Blake-Moore didn't put you up to this?" He was hoping Willis might be able to contact one of the owners to set up a sting, but it didn't seem likely.

"Yeah, I came on my own. Five million is a lot of cash." Willis thrust out his jaw toward Olivia. "Why should she get it all?"

"I told you the Feds have the banking information." He repeated the words slowly, hoping they would sink into Seth's tiny brain. "The money is evidence of a crime, not to mention motive for hurting Olivia. No one is going to be spending that money, do you understand?"

Seth's expression turned uncertain. "So this was all for nothing?"

"Exactly. Your greed will land you in jail, you moron." Ryker turned his back on the guy, unable to stand looking at him. Instead, he listened to what the nurse was saying.

"—doctor. She'll decide the next steps."

He edged closer. "What's going on?"

"Looks like you'll have to wait awhile to become a daddy," the nurse told him. "She doesn't seem to be having any more contractions."

"But the baby is okay?"

"So far, so good. I'll talk to the doctor. She may want to keep your wife here longer or send her home. We'll see what Dr. Regner thinks."

The nurse left as the local police arrived to take Seth into custody. They wanted a statement from Olivia, who provided her story.

"Listen, I'll fill you in on the rest," Ryker said, when they pressed her for more information on the bank accounts. "She doesn't need additional stress right now. All you need to know right now is that Seth Willis attacked her."

"We need to understand the motive behind this," the officer argued.

"Here, call Marc Callahan. He's with the FBI. He can provide more details."

The officer reluctantly took Marc's cell number, then cut the zip ties around Seth's ankles and hauled him to his feet.

When Ryker was alone with Olivia, he bent down and kissed her forehead.

"I'm sorry," he repeated. "I hope the stress of all of this isn't going to hurt you or the baby."

"I was having contractions before Seth came in here." She grimaced and put a hand on her belly. "I can't deny feeling worried about how the baby is doing. Hopefully the added stress doesn't cause any harm."

Her words hit hard. She was right; the stress she'd

suffered not just today but throughout the past few days hadn't helped one bit.

Ryker almost sank to his knees in despair. If her baby suffered any untoward complications from being born too early, he'd never forgive himself.

The contractions had completely disappeared, and for some reason, that bothered her more than the idea of having the baby arrive early. Olivia was doing her best not to show her panic and fear, but it wasn't easy.

None of this was Ryker's fault, but he looked so upset and miserable, she knew he was still blaming himself.

"Will you stay with me?" She reached for his hand. "Whatever the doctor decides to do, I can't bear the thought of delivering this baby alone."

"Yes." His simple statement warmed her heart. "I won't leave you."

"Thanks." Over his shoulder, she was relieved to see Dr. Regner enter the room.

"I hear your contractions have stopped." Dr. Regner's voice was cheerful. "I've been watching your baby's heartbeat on the monitor, and everything is looking great. I'd like to continue observing you for a bit longer, just to be sure you don't unexpectedly go back into labor."

"I don't feel great." Olivia tried not to show her fear. "Are you sure the baby will be okay?"

"Your ultrasound confirms the baby's at five pounds. That's plenty far enough along to avoid serious complications. Besides, babies under stress often develop their lungs faster." Dr. Regner patted her arm. "If the baby decides to come early, you'll both be just fine. I'd like to do a quick exam, okay?"

"Sure."

Ryker stepped back to provide her some privacy, and she reluctantly let go of his hand. The exam was over in moments.

"You're still dilated at three centimeters." Dr. Regner pursed her lips thoughtfully. "No progress there, so it seems like your baby has decided to stay put for a little while longer."

"Really?" Ryker's expression brightened with hope. "So no premature baby?"

"Not yet." Dr. Regner's tone held a note of caution. "But I'd like to keep Olivia here, maybe until dinnertime. If the contractions don't start up by then, we'll consider discharging her."

Olivia should have been relieved at the news, but she had to swallow a protest. Of course she didn't want her baby to be born prematurely, but on the other hand, she was hesitant to be back outside the walls of the hospital where Blake-Moore would have yet another chance to come after her.

"What's wrong?" Ryker's voice was soft. "You look upset."

"I'm not. It's just… I feel safer here at the hospital with you and the FBI agent standing outside my door. I'm not sure I want to leave."

His brow furrowed. "I'm surprised to hear you say that, especially after the way Seth managed to get in here."

"But he was a hospital employee and I think Tony will be hypervigilant from this point forward." The poor guy was beating himself up as much as Ryker was, both of them shouldering the guilt over Seth's attack.

Seth was the bad guy here. A man callous enough to roughly hold down a pregnant woman.

Ryker stared at her for a long moment. "Do you want me to ask the doctor to keep you here overnight?"

"No, she won't do that, not if it's not medically necessary to keep me. Besides, I can't take up a bed some other woman in labor might need." Olivia forced a smile. "I'm being overly emotional about this. I'll be fine."

"You're being honest," Ryker countered. "And I can't blame you for feeling safer here than in a motel with me. I've done a poor job of protecting you."

"No! That's not what I meant at all." She tugged on his hand. "Stop putting words in my mouth. Aaron and I are alive right now because you put your life on the line for us, more than once." Her eyes misted. "I owe you a deep debt of gratitude."

"Don't." His voice was low and gravelly. He reached up to wipe away a stray tear with his thumb. "I can't stand seeing you cry."

That made her chuckle. "Guess you haven't spent much time around pregnant women, huh?"

"No, I haven't." There was a brief pause before he added, "I dated a single mom, but she and her young daughter were killed while I was in Afghanistan."

She sucked in a harsh breath. "Killed? How? Why?"

"Carjacking gone bad." His tone held a note of bitterness. "We had only been seeing each other a few months, but her death hit me hard, haunting me for a long time. Mostly because if I had been here with her, she and her daughter would be alive today."

"Oh, Ryker." She suddenly understood him a little better. Losing his girlfriend and her child must have been the impetus for him to come searching for her and Aaron. He'd assigned himself as her personal guardian angel. "You don't know that for certain."

"Yes, I do."

She sadly shook her head. "Ryker, you could have been anywhere other than Afghanistan. Try to place your trust in God's plan for us. I'm sorry your girlfriend and her daughter died, but you must know they're in a better place now. You need to have faith."

"It doesn't seem fair that Cheri and Cyndi had to die so young. Why would God do something like that?" His expression betrayed his frustration and angst.

"I know it's not always easy to understand God's plan. All we can do is pray for strength and guidance. We need to place our worries in His hands."

"Maybe." His tone held a note of doubt.

She squeezed his hand. "I am."

Ryker's gaze turned curious. "Is that what you've been doing while you've been here in the hospital?"

She was surprised by his question. "Of course. I've been praying nonstop since the moment Willa brought me into her church, welcoming me and Aaron with open arms. Praying brings me a sense of peace, as if God is assuring me that He's watching over us."

"I've never in my life prayed with anyone, until you." Ryker's soft admission tugged at her heart. "I hope God continues to grant me the ability to keep you and your baby safe."

"He will." She didn't doubt it for a moment. "And I'm happy to hear you saying that. It means a lot to me that you're discovering the power of prayer."

Her heart swelled with hope and love. Liv cared about Ryker so much, but reminded herself not to overreact. Having just learned about Ryker's past, she understood that she and Aaron were nothing more than a poor substitute for Cheri and Cyndi, the woman and little girl he'd once loved.

Still, she was blessed to have Ryker with her now. To have him staying at her side through the birth of her baby. Although, it was looking more and more like she wouldn't be having this baby today.

A knock at her door brought her out of her reverie. "Come in."

Ryker turned, putting himself between the doorway and her bed, but his protection wasn't needed. Her nurse popped into the room.

"Time for me to take your vitals." As the nurse busied herself with the blood-pressure cuff, she glanced down at Olivia. "I hear Dr. Regner is planning to discharge you in a few hours."

"Yes. Apparently my baby is being stubborn and wants to stay inside a bit longer." She rubbed her hand over her belly, avoiding the monitor strapped there picking up the baby's heartbeat.

"Well, that happens sometimes." The nurse listened to her blood pressure, took her pulse then stuck an electric thermometer under her tongue. "Dr. Regner is preparing the discharge paperwork now, so if all goes well, you'll be out of here in time for dinner." The nurse winked. "Maybe you can get your husband to take you out someplace fancy."

Since her admission, the staff had assumed she and Ryker were husband and wife, and neither one of them had said or done anything to correct them. It seemed a bit dishonest, but Olivia didn't want Ryker to leave, so she played along, forcing a smile. When the nurse removed the thermometer probe, she said, "Maybe I will."

"Absolutely. I'll take you anywhere you'd like to go," Ryker agreed, lifting her hand to kiss her knuckles. A shiver rippled up her arm and she hoped he didn't notice her innate response to his touch.

"Aw, you two are so sweet together." The nurse beamed, before turning and then leaving the room. "Call if you need anything," she added over her shoulder.

The minute the door closed, she glanced up at Ryker. "I can't help feeling guilty about not telling them the truth."

"I know, but what's the harm? Whether we're married or not, I'm here to support you. And there's no way in the world I'm leaving you alone."

"I guess." She knew he was right, but secretly wondered if every reference to them as a couple made him feel a bit panicky.

After all, this wasn't exactly what he'd bargained for when he'd come to find her. Yet he hadn't turned away.

Just the opposite.

He'd held her, kissed her and cared for her.

The fact that she wanted more, wanted it all, was her problem. Not his.

She needed to remember that once Kevin Blake and Harper Moore were in custody, she and Ryker would go their separate ways.

SIXTEEN

Ryker didn't mind others assuming he was Olivia's husband and the father of her baby. In fact, he rather liked it. Sure, he knew this was just a temporary situation for them. Once Olivia was safe, she wouldn't need him anymore.

But for now, he intended to be there for her. To support her through this. No woman should have to go through childbirth alone.

Maybe once the danger was over, she'd continue to allow him to stop by and visit, to help her with Aaron. Having a new baby and a three-year-old would be stressful. Even if she was able to sell the house and use the money to live on for a while, she'd need emotional support.

It was humbling to realize she felt safer here in the hospital, despite the way Seth had gotten to her. Maybe part of her feeling safe had to do with having access to immediate medical care. He made a mental note to ask Dr. Regner if she wouldn't consider keeping Olivia at least overnight. If the answer was no, then fine. He'd work out some sort of plan with Marc Callahan and the Feds. Now that the FBI was involved, they should be able to keep a cocoon of security around Olivia and Aaron.

"Ryker? Do you think I could talk to Aaron?" Her tone was wistful. "I haven't been away from him for this length of time since we escaped from the motel room last Christmas."

With a nod, he pulled out his phone. "Sure, here's Mike's number."

She gratefully took the phone and asked Mike to use the app that allowed Aaron to see her face. "Hey, Aaron, how are you doing?"

"Hi, Mommy." Aaron waved and leaned toward the screen as if to see her better. "Where are you?"

"I'm at the hospital, but your little brother or sister isn't going to be born today after all. Guess you'll have to wait a bit longer to meet him or her."

"I wanna baby brother." Aaron's steadfast belief in his ability to impact the gender of her baby made Ryker smile. If Olivia was right about having a girl, he hoped the little boy wouldn't be too disappointed.

"I know you do, but God is the one who decides if I'm having a boy or a girl, remember?" Olivia smiled at her son. "And you're going to be an awesome big brother no matter what."

Aaron nodded. "Yep. Brodie and I are playing dinosaurs." He picked up a plastic T. rex, showing her.

"I'm glad you're having fun. Be good for Brodie's mommy and daddy, okay?"

"I am good." Aaron's eyes widened with innocence. "You can ask them."

"I will ask them," Olivia agreed firmly.

"When are you coming to get me?" Aaron's voice was plaintive.

"Soon, baby. When the doctor says I can go home, we'll come pick you up."

"Or Mr. and Mrs. Callahan will come meet us," Ryker added. "We'll let you know, okay?"

"Okay." For a moment Aaron looked as if he might cry, but then Shayla's voice could be heard in the background. "Who wants to help make chocolate-chip cookies?"

"Me!" Aaron and Brodie both shouted at the same time. "Bye, Mommy." The little boy ran out of view of the screen, replaced by Mike.

"He's fine, Olivia." Mike's gaze was reassuring. "We're keeping a close eye on him."

"I know you are. Thank you so much." Olivia looked as if she might cry again. "We'll let you know when the doctor discharges me."

Mike hesitated, then nodded. "Sure thing. Although it might be better for Aaron to stay with us for a while longer."

Ryker secretly agreed but Olivia looked distressed. "Oh, I don't know about that," she was quick to say. "He hasn't been away from me overnight before."

"How about we talk about it later?" Ryker gave Mike a slight nod. "First we need to find a safe house of some sort. Hopefully the FBI has something we can use."

"Absolutely. Just give us a call. Later." Mike disconnected from the call.

Olivia reluctantly passed Ryker his phone. "I'm glad Aaron seems to be doing okay."

"I'm sure he's having fun playing with Brodie." He took her hand again. "How are you feeling? Any contractions?"

"Not since just before Seth came in." She looked from their joined hands to meet his gaze. "You really think the FBI will provide a safe house for me?"

"Yes. You're a key witness, Olivia. Your testimony

of finding the bank-account information, and the fact that men employed by Blake-Moore came after you in order to get it, will assist in putting Blake and Moore behind bars."

"I guess." She didn't look convinced. "But we haven't really proven that the men who came after us worked for Blake-Moore. I'm worried they'll get off on some sort of technicality."

"They won't." He was going to do everything in his power to make sure that didn't happen. "Try not to worry about that, okay? Just stay focused on your baby."

"I will." There was a steely determination in her tone.

His phone rang, and he recognized Marc Callahan's number. "It's Marc." He released her hand and turned from her bedside. "Hey, what's going on?"

"We just started questioning the mercenary you captured at the motel. He gave us his name, James Corrian, but other than that, he's not talking. Apparently he's not willing to give up his bosses. A lawyer just showed up, likely paid for by the Blake-Moore Group."

He blew out a frustrated breath. "Corrian has to know that he'll do a significant amount of jail time. Did you offer to cut him a deal if he talked?"

"Yes, but he wasn't interested. His trust in Blake-Moore is misplaced. Could be he'll need to spend time behind bars before he realizes it's better to provide evidence against them and save himself."

"Unfortunately, we don't have that kind of time." Ryker didn't like where this was going. "We need those guys behind bars now, not in three months."

"We'll keep trying," Marc assured him. "Ludwig is flying in from DC to help provide resources to find

Blake and Moore. Don't forget, we have Willis, too. Maybe we'll get more from him."

"I hope so." But Ryker wasn't really convinced of that. Seth Willis had come here to get the bank information for his own selfish reasons. It wasn't as if Blake-Moore had sent him. The fact that he'd worked full-time as a hospital security guard was evidence that Willis had left the Blake-Moore Group. "When will you question Seth?"

"Heading that way now."

Ryker glanced at Olivia who was clearly listening to his side of the conversation. As much as he wanted to shield her from what was going on, she deserved to know. "Good, keep me posted. Also, it looks like Olivia may be discharged from the hospital in a couple of hours. We're going to need a safe place to go. Have anything in mind?"

"Good question. I'll see what we can come up with. Even if we just end up going to a motel, we'll have an FBI agent assigned to her protection detail."

Just one? Ryker would have felt better with at least three additional men. Granted, he'd have Duncan's help, too, so maybe they'd be okay. "I'll let you know when she's discharged."

Ryker disconnected and tucked the phone back into his pocket.

"We're never going to get anyone to turn on Blake-Moore." Olivia looked forlorn.

"We will. Just remember at the end of the day, everyone has their own survival instinct. Someone will turn on them." He crossed over, pulled up a chair and sat down beside her. "You're the one who told me to have faith in God's plan, remember?"

A smile tugged at the corner of her mouth. "Yes, I remember. I guess sometimes it's easier to give advice than to take it."

"Exactly." She was so beautiful, he longed to kiss her. To hold her close, reassure her that everything was going to be all right. Anyone trying to hurt her would have to go through him.

He didn't mind putting his life on the line to protect her.

The nurse returned for another set of vital signs. A few minutes later, the doctor came in. Ryker went to the far corner of the room to give Olivia privacy.

"Still at three centimeters," Dr. Regner announced. "I'm going to go ahead and discharge you. There's no point in waiting. You're not in active labor."

Ryker squelched a flash of panic. "I thought you wanted to observe her until dinnertime?" It was only three in the afternoon. He'd been hoping to stick around until five or six.

"Relax, Dad. Mom and baby are doing great. You'll meet your new son or daughter soon enough." Dr. Regner glanced at her watch. "I have to check on another patient, but I would like to see Olivia back in the clinic next week."

"Understood." Ryker hoped the danger would be over by then. "We can do that."

Olivia raised a brow, no doubt wondering why he'd included himself, but didn't argue. "Thanks, Dr. Regner. I appreciate everything you've done for me."

"Of course. Now don't hesitate to call if the contractions return. I have a feeling this baby isn't going to stay put until your actual due date."

"And you're sure it's okay for her to be discharged?"

Ryker couldn't help attempting one more time to convince the doctor to change her mind.

"I'm sure. The nurse will be in shortly with your discharge paperwork." Dr. Regner turned toward the door. "Don't forget, one week."

"I won't forget." Olivia's smile didn't quite reach her eyes and he knew she didn't want to go.

He didn't, either.

When they were alone, Olivia said, "I guess this is it."

"It's going to be okay." He kept his tone confident as he pulled out his phone to call Marc. They needed a safe house ASAP. Then he filled Tony Seavers in on the plan.

He wasn't going to allow any of Kevin Blake and Harper Moore's men to touch her again.

Olivia knew she needed to stay calm and strong for the baby's sake. All along, she'd understood stress wasn't good for her, and this latest bout of labor only reinforced her belief.

Ryker was on the phone again, talking to Marc Callahan about securing a place for them to go. She stopped listening, deciding to talk to her baby instead.

"We're going to be fine, little lady," she crooned. "I want you to stay inside where you can grow big and strong for just a little longer, okay?"

The baby kicked, making her smile. She looked forward to the day she would hold her daughter in her arms and tried not to think about how it was unlikely she'd have more children in the future.

Her gaze strayed to Ryker, wondering what he'd do once the danger was over. Would he find another single mother to rescue? How many were out there, needing his skills? She had no idea, but felt certain if there was someone in danger, Ryker would be all over it.

He'd never hesitate to save others because he hadn't been there to rescue his girlfriend and her daughter. It was disconcerting to realize she was a stand-in for the woman he'd really loved.

"Yeah, we'll take it. Thanks, Marc." Ryker turned toward her. "Good news. One of the FBI agents in Madison is arranging for a hotel suite. It's not far, roughly ten minutes from here."

"I'm glad." She couldn't deny feeling relieved. "Does that mean Aaron can join us?"

Ryker hesitated. "Maybe. Let's get you settled there first, then we can discuss our options with Mike."

She nodded. The nurse entered the room with her usual cheery smile. "I'm going to discontinue the monitor on your belly and take your IV out, okay?"

Liv wanted to protest about the monitor. She'd enjoyed seeing the reassuring beat of her baby's heart on the screen.

The IV came out first, then the monitor. Free of cables and IV tubing, she swung her feet around to sit up at the side of the bed.

"Do you need help getting dressed?" The nurse glanced at her, then Ryker.

Ryker made a coughing-choking sound. "I need to talk to Tony for a moment. Why don't you help Olivia get dressed?"

The nurse looked surprised when Ryker slipped out the door, but didn't seem to mind helping Olivia off the bed and into her own clothes. Oddly enough, Olivia felt stronger now than she had before she'd been put in the hospital bed. Clearly, she needed to stay hydrated, even if that meant frequent trips to the bathroom.

"Sit down. I'll be back with a wheelchair." The nurse

left and Olivia quickly used the restroom while Ryker was outside. He came back with the nurse.

"Duncan is going to pick us up in the corner of the parking structure not far from the doorway," he informed her as she took a seat in the wheelchair. "We'll need to give him about five minutes to get here."

"Five minutes?" The nurse frowned and looked at her watch. "I'll take you down to the lobby. You can wait for your ride there."

"No need. I can take care of pushing Olivia in the wheelchair." Ryker didn't seem to like the idea of going to the lobby. "Just give her the discharge paperwork."

"If you're sure." The nurse hesitated, then shrugged. "Okay, that should be fine. Here are your discharge instructions, Olivia. Dr. Regner wants to see you in her clinic next week, so we made an appointment for you on Wednesday at one o'clock in the afternoon."

"Wednesday at one is fine." At least, she hoped this nightmare would be over by then. She took the proffered paperwork with a smile. "And I know I'm to call if the contractions start up again."

"Exactly."

"Thanks again." Liv meant it. She was grateful for the labor-and-delivery team's expertise and knew she wanted to return to this hospital when it was time to have her baby.

"You're welcome." The nurse hurried out of the room, obviously in a rush to check on her other patients. Olivia didn't blame her.

She glanced at Ryker. "Is Agent Seavers going with us?"

"I think so. If not, he'll hand us over to Agent Barnes. He's the one who arranged the hotel."

She smiled. "I'm glad Blake-Moore has no idea I'm here."

A frown creased his brow. "I hope not, but we're taking added precautions just in case."

The minutes dragged by slowly as they waited for Duncan's call. When it finally came, the shrill ringtone startled her.

She took a deep breath, reminding herself to stay calm. No Stress was her new mantra.

"Got it. See you soon." Ryker put his phone away and came to stand behind her wheelchair. "Ready?"

"Yes." Ignoring the pang she felt in leaving the safety of the hospital room, Liv kept her gaze focused straight ahead. As they passed Tony in the hall, he nodded and fell in step behind them.

Ryker pushed her into the elevator, hitting the button labeled Lobby.

"I thought we were avoiding the lobby?"

"Originally, but there's a connection from the lobby level to the parking garage. That's where Duncan is meeting us."

Her entry into the hospital through the emergency department was nothing but a blur so she didn't question his knowledge.

They made it through the lobby and into the parking garage within the promised five minutes. When Agent Seavers's phone rang, he looked at his screen and grimaced. "My boss, likely mad at the way I let Seth get to Olivia. Give me a minute, okay?" Seavers brought the phone to his ear, turning away to speak in private.

"I think I see Duncan." She gestured to the black SUV. "Stop, Ryker. I'll walk from here."

Ryker set the brakes on the wheelchair, putting his hand beneath her elbow to help her to her feet.

She'd only made it a few steps when a blur of movement caught the corner of her eye. She turned her gaze in time to see a man she recognized as one of the bosses Tim had introduced her to at the Fourth of July party. He stepped out from behind a concrete pillar, holding a gun trained on them.

"Don't move." His tone was terse.

She froze, her hands splayed protectively over her belly.

"What do you want, Moore? Or is it Blake?" Ryker's question was mild, as if he wasn't the least bit worried about the armed man standing there.

"Moore. And you know what I want." He waved the gun. "Give me the account numbers now!"

"B-but, I don't have them." Olivia couldn't seem to drag her gaze from the muzzle of his gun. If he pulled the trigger, she and her baby would die. Thankfully, Aaron was safe, but she didn't want her son to become an orphan.

"I have them," Ryker said. "But I want Olivia safe first."

"No deal." Moore lifted the gun a bit higher.

Ryker began to recite the numbers by memory, then stopped abruptly, narrowing his gaze on Harper Moore. "If you want the entire account number, you'll let me send Olivia off with my friend. You don't need her when you have me."

"No!" She didn't want to leave Ryker behind. She couldn't bear the thought of losing him.

She loved him. More than she thought possible.

And she knew, deep in her bones, that once Harper Moore had what he wanted, he'd kill Ryker.

SEVENTEEN

More than anything, Ryker wanted to protect Olivia. To keep her safe from harm. Yet here they were, being held at gunpoint by a cold-blooded killer. Ryker swallowed a lump of guilt, knowing he should have anticipated Blake-Moore would find them at the hospital.

So much for Seth Willis's claim of not being involved with the mercenary group. Obviously, Willis must have been acting on orders from Harper Moore himself. Did that mean Kevin Blake knew about the money, too? Or had the partner of the firm been left in the dark? There was no way to know for certain.

"You can't possibly remember all the bank-account numbers," Moore said with a sneer. "You're rattling off garbage. Send Olivia to me, and I'll let you and your friend live."

No way was he doing that. Moore would kill her and the baby without a second thought. He actually did know all the numbers. He'd memorized them just in case, but wasn't sure how to convince Moore. He decided to try a different path. If he stalled long enough, maybe Duncan could get a shot at him. At the moment, he and Olivia were in Duncan's way, and Ryker knew

Duncan wouldn't risk hitting Olivia. Or maybe Tony Seavers from the FBI would arrive to help. That phone call from his boss was rotten timing.

At this point, he'd welcome anyone, even someone from the hospital security team.

"Tell me, Harper, when did you learn Tim and Colin were skimming money from you and Kevin? I'm sure that made you furious."

The question caught Moore off guard, but he didn't hesitate to answer. "Seth told me what he knew. I offered to give him a finder's fee if he brought me the bank-account information, but he got himself arrested instead." The barrel of Moore's gun never wavered. "Enough talking. We need to move. I want Olivia with me now!"

Ryker met Olivia's frightened gaze and knew he needed to do something to get her out of this mess. He swept his gaze over the area in an attempt to formulate a plan. The gun he normally kept on him at all times was in the glove box, because the hospital had a no weapon rule. There had to be something he could do.

But there was absolutely nothing to use as a weapon. The wheelchair and garbage can were both too far away to be of any use.

He prayed for strength and wisdom, hoping God had a plan for them.

"Oh!" Olivia let out a loud groan, doubling over in pain. "Help me! The labor pains are back."

What? Now? Ryker felt the blood draining from his face. Her labor must have restarted because of the stress.

"Hurry!" Moore's tone was sharp. "I want the information before she drops that kid."

"Don't be stupid." Ryker lifted his hands up in a

gesture of surrender. "You don't need her when you can have me."

Olivia slowly blinked her eyes at him, and it took only a second for him to realize she was pretending. He decided to play along. "Olivia? How bad are they?"

"Bad." Her voice was low and guttural. "If I don't get inside, I'll have this baby right here in the parking garage!"

"Take me." Ryker drilled Harper Moore with his gaze. "She'll be useless to you while she's in labor. And I promise I have the bank-account numbers memorized. Don't you see? She's a liability to you. She needs a doctor!"

"Fine. I'll take you. Stuff her into the SUV." Moore gestured with the gun. "One false move and I'll shoot."

Ryker doubted the guy would shoot in a public place, even if they were in a rather isolated corner of the parking garage. But Ryker was more than willing to comply with his demand. Olivia was still bent over, pretending to be in pain, so he moved close. "Lean on me. I'll get you into the SUV, okay? Duncan will get you out of here."

"But what about the doctor?" Olivia sounded fearful and he hoped he hadn't misunderstood her exaggerated blink. That she really wasn't in labor.

"You'll be fine." He knew that his gun was in the glove box of the SUV. All he needed was the opportunity to grab it.

As it turned out, Duncan already had the glove box open. As if reading his mind, Olivia lurched forward toward the passenger seat, staying low to give Ryker access to the gun.

Ryker knew Duncan was armed, but seated as he

was behind the wheel, his buddy couldn't shoot without possibly hitting him or Olivia, considering Harper Moore was located behind them. Ryker knew he'd have to be the one to take the shot.

He pushed Olivia down toward the floor and reached for the weapon.

Several things happened at once. A loud, authoritative voice shouted, "Hey, what's going on?" At the same time, Ryker spun around to shoot at Moore. Moore must have been momentarily distracted by the man approaching the scene, because he didn't even get a shot off.

Blood spurted from Moore's chest. He sagged against the concrete pillar, then slowly slid to the ground, a look of stunned surprise on his features.

Duncan hit the horn, the blare echoing loudly off the concrete surrounding them. The approaching security guard and other people arrived on the scene from various directions, including Tony Seavers from the FBI, looking guilty for not staying with them.

Ryker rushed over to check on Harper Moore, who was pale and bleeding, but still alive. "Where is Kevin Blake?"

Moore struggled to speak. "Dea…"

Dead? "Come on, tell me where Kevin Blake is." Ryker pressed his hand against the wound, hoping to stem the bleeding. "We need an ambulance now!"

"I'll call," the security guard offered.

"You're not going to die, Harper, but you will spend the rest of your life in jail." Ryker leaned his weight on the wound, peering down into Harper's eyes, willing the guy to respond. "Do you really want Kevin Blake to get away with all the cash?"

"He's dead..." Harper Moore's eyes drifted closed and his jaw went slack.

No! Feeling frantic, Ryker continued holding pressure on the gunshot wound. "Harper! Wake up!" He raised his head, looking at the various bystanders who were blatantly gawking. "I need a doctor here now! Hurry!"

"They're on the way." The security guard came over to kneel beside him. "What can I do?"

Ryker shook his head. "I don't want him to die. The FBI has been searching for this guy and his partner. He can't die!"

"Okay, I get it." The security guard rested a hand on Ryker's shoulder. "Are you a cop?"

"Not exactly." Ryker wondered if he'd be arrested for shooting the guy, despite the fact that he'd only done it to save Olivia's life. "I need you to secure the video for this parking garage. The Feds will want to review it."

The security guard's eyes widened as he nodded. "I can do that."

"Good." Where in the world was that medical team?

"Speaking of which, Marc Callahan is on his way." Tony Seavers gestured at the area around the SUV. "He'll work with the locals to clear the scene."

"Olivia?" Ryker craned his neck in an attempt to make eye contact with her. "Are you all right? You're not really in labor, are you?"

"I'm fine." She stood leaning against the SUV, with Duncan beside her. "Don't worry about me."

He nodded, but couldn't relax. Hearing the pounding of footsteps on the ground, he was grateful to see several men and women wearing scrubs rushing toward him. He didn't move, not until the medical team was close enough to take over.

"Gunshot wound to the chest." He moved out of the way. The team surrounded Harper Moore, the tall red-headed female obviously in charge.

"Get his chest wound packed with dressings. Get his vitals."

Ryker stared at his blood-stained hands with a sense of dismay. He didn't regret doing what was necessary to save Olivia's life, but wished he hadn't hit Moore in the chest. If the guy didn't make it, they'd be no closer to finding Kevin Blake.

"So much blood," Olivia whispered.

He grimaced, knowing she was right.

"Why don't you wash up?" She gently tugged on his elbow. "You're covered in blood and the restrooms aren't far."

He didn't want to leave her alone, but he didn't want to get her covered in blood, either. He followed her back inside the hospital to the restrooms just off the main lobby. After scrubbing the blood from his hands, he returned to find her waiting for him. Ryker longed to pull her into his arms, but noticed Marc Callahan striding toward them.

"You okay?" Marc's keen gaze raked over him. "No injuries?"

"I'm fine. Olivia's the one who needs to see a doctor."

"No, I'm okay." Olivia turned toward Marc. "Moore wanted the bank-account information."

"He claims Seth Willis told him about the embezzlement scheme," Ryker added. "He didn't say one way or the other if Kevin Blake was involved. When I asked where Kevin was, he said *dead*."

"I'll need to corroborate his claim that Blake is dead, although it doesn't make sense Moore would lie about that. Why would he want Blake to get all the cash?" Marc blew out a heavy sigh. "We're going to need your statement and Olivia's before you can leave."

"Duncan's, too." Ryker knew the drill. "I asked the security guard to secure the video. Figured you and the local authorities will want to review it."

"We will." Marc held out his hand. Ryker solemnly shook it. "Nice work. Glad you were able to stop him."

"Thanks." Ryker noticed the medical team was bringing Harper Moore's gurney inside, in a flurry of activity. The beeping heart monitor was somewhat reassuring, but the grim expressions on the faces of the team members told him that Moore was only hanging on by a thread. He couldn't seem to tear his gaze away as they wheeled past him.

"It's not your fault." Olivia's soft voice drew him from his dark thoughts. "He made the decision to come after me with a gun in an effort to get his hands on the money."

"I know." He pulled her close and buried his face against her silky hair. "I'm so glad you're okay."

"We both are." The baby kicked, making him smile. "Actually, all three of us are. You saved us again, Ryker. I'm sorry you've had to face so much violence to do it." Her body shuddered as if the memory was horrifying to her.

And he couldn't blame her.

Emotion clogged his throat, and for a moment he couldn't speak. Violence. She'd witnessed him doing violent acts from the moment they'd met. All along he knew that once Olivia returned to her normal everyday life, there would be no place for him.

Now he realized that the opposite would be just as

bad. Having him around would only make her remember the horrible things she'd witnessed. All the blood she'd seen spilled.

Now that Harper Moore was out of the picture, and Kevin Blake was likely dead, there was nothing more for him to do.

It was time to let Olivia and Aaron go. To give them the normal life they deserved.

She relished being held in Ryker's warm embrace, but it was over all too soon. He eased away, looking at Marc. "Let's get these statements out of the way as soon as possible. Olivia wants to see Aaron and deserves to get some rest."

"Olivia can speak for herself, thanks." She wasn't sure why Ryker's tone irked her. It seemed as if he was pulling away from her. "I'm *fine*."

Marc's lips twitched. "Okay, I'll talk to Olivia over here. Tony Seavers will take your statement."

Ryker gave a curt nod and moved away, without giving her a second glance. She frowned, wondering what was going on with him. She knew Ryker was likely feeling a bit of guilt over his role in taking down Harper Moore, but it wasn't as if there had been an alternative.

Marc Callahan led her to a seat in the corner of the lobby cordoned off from the rest of the public. Plenty of gawkers still hung around, but the hospital security guards were doing their best to send them on their way.

"Start at the beginning," Marc suggested.

As she told the story, Marc interrupted her several times, asking additional questions. The process took far longer than she would have expected, but finally he nodded, his expression full of satisfaction.

"Okay, thanks, Olivia. Would you like me to contact Mike so you can talk to Aaron?"

"Yes, please." When he handed her his phone, she lifted it to her ear. "Aaron? Is that you, sweetheart?"

"Mommy! When are you coming to get me?"

"Soon, baby. Very soon. Are you being a good boy for Mr. and Mrs. Callahan?"

"Yes. Mommy, Brodie's daddy wants to talk to you."

"Okay, but just know I'll see you soon, Aaron." There was a brief silence before she heard Mike's voice. "Hey, heard Ryker got Harper Moore."

"Yes. But there's still Kevin Blake."

"I heard Blake is probably dead," Mike said reassuringly. "If he and Moore both knew about the money, they'd have worked together to get to you."

"Gee, thanks. That's so not reassuring."

"Sorry, but it's the truth. Do you want me to bring Aaron to you? Just tell me when and where."

"Anxious to get rid of him, huh?" Her wry smile faded. "Actually, I'm not sure where I'm supposed to go. There was a hotel room, but I'm not sure if that's still on. Let me find Ryker and we'll call you back, okay?"

"Sure, no problem. And really, there's no rush. Aaron and Brodie are playing together just fine."

"Thanks, Mike. You and Shayla are lifesavers." She handed the phone back to Marc. "Your family has been wonderful to us."

Marc waved off her gratitude. "We owe Ryker and Duncan for the way they helped us in the past. No need to worry about it. Would you like to return home?"

"Home?" She thought about the house she'd once shared with Tim. The one she hadn't seen in six months, and thought she'd never see again. The idea of returning there wasn't very appealing, but what choice did she have? Staying in motels for the indefinite future wasn't exactly an option. "Sure, I guess."

Marc frowned at her lackluster tone. "We can go to the hotel instead. It's already been arranged."

"No, it's fine. I'm being silly." She forced a smile. "Although, I would like Ryker to come with me. At least for a day or two."

Marc lifted a brow. "I'll get him. He's likely finished with his statement by now."

"Thank you." The thought of having Ryker stay with her filled her with relief. Everyone involved in the case seemed convinced Kevin Blake was dead, but how could they know for sure? Granted, Mike had a point about the fact they would have been working together if they'd both known about the money.

Marc returned with Duncan, a sheepish expression on his face. "Um, looks like Ryker already left, but Duncan agreed to take you home."

Left? Why would Ryker have taken off without telling her?

Without so much as saying goodbye?

Her heart seemed to stop in her chest. Obviously, Ryker felt his job of protecting her was over. He hadn't really cared about her and Aaron, not the way he'd loved his girlfriend and her daughter.

"Olivia? Are you ready?"

She drew in a deep breath, trying not to let her despair show on her face. "Um, sure. But will you please call Mike to let him know? He offered to bring Aaron."

"Of course." Duncan took a few steps away, speaking quietly into the phone for a few minutes before turning back to her. "He'll meet us at your place."

She nodded and wearily pushed herself to her feet. She followed Duncan back out to the parking structure where he'd left their SUV. She was surprised it wasn't being held as evidence, but remembered Ryker saying something about the security video. Maybe that was all they needed.

She was happy to leave the hospital and to know she'd be seeing Aaron again soon.

But the hollow feeling in her chest wouldn't go away.

Ryker's leaving had put a gaping hole in her heart and she knew that her life would never be the same without him.

EIGHTEEN

Walking away from a woman had never been so difficult. Ryker's heart felt as if it were being ripped out of his chest. He already missed her.

But their time together was over.

She needed to move on, and he knew having him around would only be a horrible reminder of the danger she and Aaron had been in. The violence she'd witnessed. Seeing all that blood had made her shiver.

She'd get over him, even if he wouldn't get over her.

His role in life was to save others, the way he'd always wished someone had stepped up to help his girlfriend and her daughter. Now that his mission was accomplished, it was time to move on.

Olivia would be fine with Duncan and Tony, but by the time he'd called a rideshare for a pickup, he was already doubting his decision to leave.

Shouldn't he at least say goodbye? Let her know that if anything changed for her in the future, she could reach out to him? What if the violence didn't bother her the way he'd thought it did?

The rideshare driver pulled up in a fancy black

BMW. He was staring through the passenger window at Ryker impatiently. "Well? Are you coming?"

"No." He turned and headed back through the parking structure to the hospital entrance. He frowned when he noticed Duncan's SUV was gone.

His heart squeezed and he quickened his pace. When he burst into the lobby, he raked his gaze over the area, looking for a familiar face.

"Marc!" He rushed toward the FBI agent. "Where's Olivia?"

"She left with Duncan and Tony." Marc frowned. "Tony said you left."

"I'm back." He couldn't believe he'd missed them. "Where are they headed? To another hotel?"

"No, she's going home." At Ryker's blank look, Marc added, "You know, her house. Where she once lived. Mike is bringing Aaron out to Madison to drop him off there."

The home she'd shared with Tim? Every cell in his body rejected that idea. "Why would you let her go there? Did you confirm Kevin Blake is dead the way Harper Moore claimed?"

"She can't very well stay in a hotel indefinitely. But to answer your question, we're still working on validating Blake is dead. But even if by some freak chance he's not, the mercenary group is done. If Harper Moore survives, he'll spend the rest of his life in jail."

It made sense, but Ryker still didn't like it. He turned and walked back outside, pulling up the rideshare app on his phone.

The same driver pulled up, eyeing him warily. This time, Ryker slid into the back seat of the Beamer, reciting Olivia's address.

He sat back against the leather seat, trying to think of what he'd say to her when he saw her again. He wanted to support her, without being a constant reminder of the danger she'd been in.

There was no doubt he wanted to be there when her baby was born. But again, he wasn't so sure she wanted him. She'd leaned on him at the hospital, but that was when she was anticipating a premature birth.

Her due date was less than six weeks away. Would they still be talking to each other? Or would they have already drifted apart?

He had no idea. But at the very least he could provide his contact information, before walking away.

He'd leave it up to her to make the next move.

Olivia felt ridiculously nervous when Duncan pulled up in front of her small house. Oddly, it looked different.

Or maybe she was the one who'd changed. In her head she knew the house was just a structure, but she couldn't help but shiver as she stepped out of the SUV.

"Wait here with Tony." Duncan glanced at the house. "I want to do a quick search of the place before you go inside. Just to be sure no rogue mercenaries are hanging around."

She nodded, secretly glad to postpone the inevitable for a while longer. The more she thought about it, she knew she'd end up going to a motel once Aaron arrived. Even if Blake was dead, she didn't feel comfortable here.

This house represented a chapter of her life that was over and done. Time to move on with the next phase. The sooner she could put the place on the market and unload it, the better.

Tony Seavers came up beside her and pressed something hard into her side. "You're going to walk away with me, understand?"

Huh? She belatedly realized he held the muzzle of a gun against her. "You? You're involved?"

"Let's go." Tony pressed the gun against her, leaving her little choice but to take a step away from Duncan's SUV.

"Did Harper Moore or Kevin Blake put you up to this?" She wanted to keep him talking, hoping Duncan would return before they could get very far. She wasn't sure where Tony was taking her, not that it mattered much. In her condition, she couldn't make a run for it.

"Blake isn't dead, although we faked his demise to throw Moore off track. Kevin is meeting us soon." Tony walked her farther from the house, looking up and down the street. Everything made so much more sense now. The way he'd let Seth in to see her, the way he'd hung back, leaving them to go into the parking garage alone to meet up with Harper Moore.

Now this.

"It was you and Blake against Seth and Harper Moore, wasn't it?" The fact that each owner had tried to outdo the other was so obvious now, she couldn't believe they hadn't considered the possibility sooner.

"Think you're smart, huh? But I have you now."

She swallowed hard, wishing Ryker was there with her. But he wasn't.

And if Tony Seavers and Kevin Blake had their way, she'd never see Ryker, or Aaron, again.

Tears pooled in her eyes and she tried to blink them away. She had to be smart. There had to be something she could do to get away.

She glanced at the nearby houses, trying to remember the names of her neighbors. But she didn't see anyone, much less someone she actually recognized.

A black BMW pulled up beside them. Her heart momentarily stopped in her chest as she frantically searched for a way to escape.

The driver's-side window opened only an inch. "Get in."

"Will do." Tony must have been expecting a car sent by Kevin Blake to pick them up. He held her in place as the driver rolled the window back up and edged the vehicle ahead a couple of feet.

The door behind the driver was opened by someone inside. Tony pushed her in and she stumbled, catching herself by grabbing on to the edge of the door.

A quick glance inside revealed Ryker's familiar face. Her heart soared. He'd come for her! With a quick movement, he tugged her toward him.

"Go!" Ryker shouted to the driver.

The BMW lurched forward, the rear door swinging shut behind her.

"Hey!" Tony shouted after them.

"He has a gun!" She reached for Ryker. "Keep your head down."

"Gun?" the driver shouted. "You didn't say anything about a gun!" The wheel jerked beneath his hands. "What if he shoots at me?"

"Just keep going," Ryker barked. Then he turned toward her. "Are you okay? Did he hurt you?"

"F-fine." She stared at him. "How did you know?"

"I didn't at first, but as soon as I saw the two of you together, I figured it out. And convinced the Uber driver to play along." Ryker pulled out his phone. "I have to call Duncan."

"Tony is waiting for Kevin Blake to arrive. He's not dead after all."

Ryker let out a low whistle. "I'm glad I beat him."

"Me, too." She wanted to ask him why he'd left her in the first place, but he was quickly filling in Duncan on the latest turn of events.

Next he called Marc and brought him up to speed. "Tony Seavers is working with Blake. I need you to send a team to Olivia's house ASAP."

She couldn't hear what Marc said in response. Ryker slid his phone into his pocket, then leaned forward to tap the driver on the shoulder. "Take a left here, then another left."

"Hey, I'm not going back there," he protested. "That's crazy."

"Take two left turns, then drop us off." Ryker had no sooner said the words when the sharp report of gunfire could be heard behind them.

"Duncan!" She covered her mouth with her hand, feeling sick, praying that Tony, or Kevin Blake, hadn't shot him.

"Hurry," Ryker urged the driver.

"Where's your gun?"

"Tony took it back at the hospital, said he needed it for evidence." Ryker's expression was grim. "It's protocol after a shooting, so I didn't think much about it."

"We can't go back there without any way to protect ourselves." Her voice rose with panic. "Tell the driver to take us away."

"I can't leave Duncan alone." Ryker met her gaze. "I still have a knife."

A knife? Against a gun?

The driver did as Ryker suggested, bringing the car to a screeching halt. Ryker threw a wad of cash at the guy, then helped her out and took her hand.

"This way." He gently tugged on her hand, cutting through several backyards in an effort to return to help Duncan. As they approached a line of trees, a man suddenly came barreling out toward them, a gun in his hand.

Kevin Blake! The moment she recognized him, Ryker let go of her hand and rushed toward him. Blake lifted his weapon, but didn't get a shot off before Ryker tackled him to the ground.

"Help! Someone help!" She yelled at the top of her lungs, hoping and praying someone would come to help Ryker. She held her breath as the two men struggled for the gun.

Ryker was younger and in better shape, but he'd also been going on very little sleep. She couldn't predict the outcome, but she could help him. Quickly she surveyed the area for a potential weapon—a downed branch, a discarded garden tool. Anything.

As she sent up a silent prayer, she saw Marc Callahan tear through the tree line, just as Ryker managed to get the upper hand on Kevin Blake.

Then it was over. Marc cuffed Blake's wrists as Ryker rose to his feet, immediately searching for her.

"Ryker." Her breath caught in a sob as she ran over to hug him. He caught her close, pressing his mouth to her temple.

"Shh, it's okay. It's all over. You and Aaron are safe now."

"Duncan has Tony Seavers," Marc said with satisfaction. "Looks as if each owner found his own accomplice in an effort to outdo the other. Come on, Blake. Time for you to go for a little ride." Marc dragged him back toward her house, where his vehicle was parked at a sharp angle, no doubt abandoned in a hurry.

She leaned heavily against Ryker, trying to absorb the fact that this nightmare was truly over.

"You aren't in labor again, are you?" Ryker asked.

She shook her head, unable to bring herself to let him go. He didn't seem to mind, cradling her close and rubbing a hand down her back.

"Why did you leave me?" She lifted her head to search his gaze.

"I'm sorry. I shouldn't have left until we had evidence that Kevin Blake was actually dead." Ryker's expression was full of remorse. "I had no idea Tony Seavers was on the take, but looking back, it makes sense."

"I don't care about Kevin Blake or Tony Seavers, Harper Moore or Seth Willis." She wanted to shake some sense into him. "I care about you, Ryker. I was so hurt when you left without saying goodbye."

"I'm sorry," he repeated. "I should have let you know."

That wasn't what she wanted to hear. "Why, Ryker? Why did you leave me? Is it because I'm just another case to you? You wanted to save me and Aaron the way you couldn't save your girlfriend and her daughter? Is that all this was to you? A job?"

"No." Ryker leaned forward, resting his forehead against hers. "You and Aaron mean so much more to me than that."

"Then why?" She still didn't understand.

He sighed. "I was afraid that being with you would be a reminder of all the bad things that have happened over the past several days. I felt you shiver when you mentioned all the blood around Harper Moore. I thought you might want to move forward with a clean slate."

What she wanted was to move forward with him. But she wasn't reassured by his words. "First of all, you're wrong about what I want. What I need. And secondly, what do you want?"

"You." He said the word simply. "I want you, and Aaron and the baby." He placed his palm on her belly. "But I also know that your feelings for me are confused with gratitude."

"Don't be ridiculous." She scoffed at the idea, then realized she didn't know anything about Ryker's family or even where he lived.

Did it matter? She gazed into his eyes, remembering how she'd looked into his hazel eyes the night they met, when she'd wanted to make sure he wasn't like her late husband and brother. All she saw, then and now, was sweetness and compassion.

"Listen, I know things have been crazy since we met, but you need time to rest and relax." Ryker tucked a stray strand of hair behind her ear. "Take a break, Olivia. Spend time with your son. If you want to see me, all you have to do is to ask."

"I want to see you." The words popped out of her mouth before she could think. "I know I'm pregnant and not exactly in a position to say this, but I love you, Ryker. I fell in love with you the day you put your hand on my stomach and reveled in the movement of my baby. The way you've been so kind and caring to me and Aaron—well, I've never experienced that sort of tenderness before."

His expression was filled with doubt. "Any man would have done the same. Like Duncan. If he'd come to rescue you instead of me, you'd be with him."

She shook her head, irritated he'd mentioned that twice now. "No, Ryker, I wouldn't. I like Duncan and the Callahans I've met so far, but there's only you. I love you. And if you don't feel the same way, I understand. But don't confuse what I'm feeling with gratitude."

He looked down at her, but remained quiet. She had no idea what he was thinking, what he was feeling. Despair began to build inside her, till finally she saw a smile tug at the corner of his mouth. "Okay, I won't." He swept her close and kissed her, showing her without words how he felt.

Maybe it was too early for him to say the words. That was fine with her. She loved him enough to wait.

"Hey! You're trespassing on my property!" A cranky man shook his fist at them from the doorway of his house.

Ryker broke off the kiss and grinned at the guy. "Sorry, sir. We're leaving."

The man glared at them as Ryker took her hand and led her through the gap in the trees to the backyard of her house.

"Ryker?"

"Hmm?"

"Do you have a family?"

He hesitated, and her stomach clenched. "No, I was raised in foster care, until the army became my family. Now I have friends, who are like my family."

Her heart ached for him. "You deserve so much more."

"Oh, I don't know. I've done okay. My friends are awesome."

He was awesome. And he didn't seem to realize it. "You are an amazing man, Ryker. I love you."

He stopped and turned toward her, capturing both of her hands in his. "I love you, too, Olivia. So much it scares me. I know meeting you was part of God's plan for me and I hope you feel the same way."

"Oh, Ryker." She was touched by his reaffirmation of his faith. "I do. God sent me a wonderful man to protect me, and to care about me. I feel so blessed to have met you."

"Ditto." He cleared his throat. "I don't want to rush you, but I'd like to keep seeing you. And Aaron. I want to be there with you every day, until your baby is born, and every day afterward."

Her eyes misted. "I'd like that."

"Mommy!" Aaron's voice cut through the moment and she turned in time to see her son running toward her. Aaron clutched her around the legs, until Ryker scooped the boy into his arms. Then Ryker stepped close, putting his arm around her waist so that Aaron was cradled between them.

"I missed you." Aaron leaned over to wrap his arms around her neck.

"I missed you, too." She met Ryker's gaze over Aaron's shoulder and knew this was the first day of their new life together.

As a family.

EPILOGUE

Five weeks later

Ryker placed his arm around Olivia's shoulders as she continued to push. "Come on, sweetheart. You can do it."

"She's a stubborn one," Olivia said between gritted teeth.

"Hey, at least he almost waited until his due date." The baby's gender was an ongoing joke between them. Personally he didn't care one way or the other, but Olivia was convinced she was having a girl.

"You're doing great," Dr. Regner said encouragingly. "One more big push and your son or daughter will be born."

"That's what you said last time." Olivia sounded annoyed, but he understood that this was just part of the process.

"You can do it. Let me know when you're ready." He waited for her to signal another contraction was coming.

"Now!" Olivia let out a groan as she pushed. Ryker did his best to support her although how in the world any woman survived childbirth was beyond him. He was sweating as much if not more than Olivia.

"There she is!" The baby immediately started to wail. "A beautiful baby girl!" Dr. Regner wrapped the baby in a cloth and brought her over to Olivia.

"I was right." Olivia looked down with awe at the baby cradled against her chest. "A girl. We have a girl!"

"She's beautiful, and so are you." Ryker blinked against the threat of tears. "You did it, Olivia. Aaron has a baby sister."

"He'll be disappointed," she said with a wry laugh.

"Nah, he'll get over it." Ryker kissed her, then put his hand against the baby's head. "I love you so much, Olivia."

"I love you, too." She looked up at him. "I'd like to call her Julia, in honor of your foster mother."

His eyes burned with emotion. "I'd like that."

For a long moment he gazed down at Olivia and their daughter. "Olivia, will you please marry me?"

It wasn't the first time he'd asked her. Technically it was the third, not that he was counting. Okay, yes he was. She'd always told him she loved him, but had wanted to wait until after the baby was born to commit to marriage.

Granted, she probably hadn't meant the exact moment the baby was born, but hey, why wait?

She looked up at him and smiled. "Yes, Ryker. I'd be honored to marry you."

Her agreement filled him with joy. "I love you." He kissed her again, knowing he finally had a family of his own, one he'd treasure every single day.

For the rest of their lives.

* * * * *

Aside from her faith and her family, there's not much **Shirlee McCoy** enjoys more than a good book! When she's not hanging out with the people she loves most, she can be found plotting her next Love Inspired Suspense story or trekking through the wilderness, training with a local search-and-rescue team. Shirlee loves to hear from readers. If you have time, drop her a line at shirleermccoy@hotmail.com.

Books by Shirlee McCoy

Love Inspired Suspense

Hidden Witness
Evidence of Innocence

FBI: Special Crimes Unit

Night Stalker
Gone
Dangerous Sanctuary
Lone Witness
Falsely Accused

Mission: Rescue

Protective Instincts
Her Christmas Guardian
Exit Strategy
Deadly Christmas Secrets
Mystery Child
The Christmas Target
Mistaken Identity
Christmas on the Run

Visit the Author Profile page at LoveInspired.com for more titles.

UNDERCOVER BODYGUARD

Shirlee McCoy

Because you are my help,
I sing in the shadow of your wings.
My soul clings to you; your right hand upholds me.
—*Psalm* 63:7–8

To my friends at An Orphan's Wish who work tirelessly to shower His love on China's orphaned children. May God continue to bless your efforts.

ONE

"Come on, Old Blue, don't fail me now!" Shelby Simons turned the key in the ignition of her 1958 Cadillac and prayed that *this* time, the engine would turn over.

It didn't, of course.

That would have made her morning just a little too easy.

"Fine. Stay here. I can walk the four blocks to Maureen Lewis's place," she grumbled.

She grabbed two large bakery boxes from the backseat and closed Old Blue's door with a little too much force. She loved the car, but it was as fickle as its original owner, Grandma Beulah, had been.

The scent of chocolate wafted from the boxes as Shelby picked her way across the bakery's empty parking lot, and her stomach growled. Stupid diet. Eight days of starving herself, and she still could barely fit into the little black dress her sister had sent from Paris.

But Shelby *would* fit into it before the Spokane Business Association's black-tie dinner that she'd planned to attend with Andrew Willis.

Andrew, her ex-fiancé, who'd promised her a million dreams and given her nothing but lies.

Now, he'd be attending the function with Stephanie Parsons, and Shelby would be going alone, because there was no way she was going to stay home moping about her newly single status. Sure, she'd been planning a wedding two short months ago, but God had had other plans, and Shelby had to believe they were better than the ones she'd made for herself.

Marriage.

Family.

Forever with someone who loved her.

She sighed, hefting the bakery boxes a little higher and doing her best to ignore the fragrant aroma that drifted from them. Maureen would be pleased with the assortment of pastries Shelby was providing for the early-morning kickoff to Maureen's birthday bash. She'd invited Shelby to attend the breakfast *and* the New York shopping spree she and her closest friends were going on afterward, but unlike Maureen, Shelby wasn't a bestselling true-crime writer with plenty of money to throw around. She had bills to pay and a business to run. Being at the bakery she'd opened five years ago was the only way to do it. Though, she had to admit, flying to New York to shop sounded like a lot more fun.

She walked up South Hill, heading toward 21st Street, the quiet morning making her feel more lonely than usual. Two months, and she was over Andrew. If she were honest, she'd admit that she'd been over him two *minutes* after she'd caught him kissing Stephanie and broken their engagement. But she still craved the connection she'd had with him, still missed having someone she could call when she was walking up a dark street by herself and felt vulnerable and alone. Not that

Andrew would have appreciated an early-morning call, but she'd always thought that once they were married…

She cut the thought off before it could form.

She hadn't agreed to marry him because she'd thought she could change him. She'd agreed because she'd thought she'd loved him. More importantly, she'd thought he had loved her.

Obviously, she'd been wrong on both counts.

If she'd loved him, her heart would still be broken.

If he'd loved her, he wouldn't have fallen for Stephanie while he was engaged to Shelby.

Shelby frowned, not sure why she was thinking about Andrew. She had plenty on her plate without worrying about the past. She had three deliveries to make and a car that wouldn't start. Maybe Maureen would lend her one of the three cars she owned. *If* Shelby arrived on time. Maureen was a stickler for punctuality, and if Shelby was even a minute late making the 5:20 delivery, Maureen would not be happy.

She picked up her pace. One more block. She could do that in three minutes. Which was exactly how much time she had left. Up ahead, a dark figure bounded around the corner of Maureen's street, jogging toward Shelby with a swift pace that bordered on a run.

She stepped off the sidewalk as he neared, her heart doing a funny little dance. Dark sunglasses on a nondescript face, a jacket zipped up to his neck, a hood pulled over his hair—he looked like trouble.

Why else would he be wearing sunglasses before dawn?

Why else would he have black leather gloves on his hands?

She fished her cell phone from her apron pocket,

knowing the battery was dead and wishing she'd re-membered to charge it *before* a guy who looked like a serial killer jogged by. She pressed the phone to her ear anyway, holding an imaginary conversation and pray-ing he would just keep going.

He did, but she couldn't shake the fear that shivered along her spine as he turned his head, seemed to look right at her.

Shelby clutched the boxes a little closer, watching his progress as he approached 20th Street.

Should she knock on someone's door and ask to use a phone?

What would she say if she did?

There's a guy jogging down South Hill wearing gloves and sunglasses and looking scary didn't seem all that compelling.

He stopped abruptly, stood in the shadows of the old manor house that some development company was re-storing. Turned to face her. He was a block away, but she could feel his eyes behind those dark glasses, feel them staring straight into hers. Her heart thrummed painfully as he took a step toward her.

One step, but she had a feeling he planned to take more.

Terror froze her in place, every nightmare she'd ever had coming true as he took another step.

A car passed, its lights splashing over Shelby, draw-ing her attention away from the approaching threat for a split second. When she looked back, the man had disappeared.

She wanted to believe he'd turned down 20th Street and gone on his way, but she could still feel his gaze, hot and ugly and terrifying. She stepped back, afraid to turn her back to the unseen threat, worried that he'd be on her before she even knew he was coming.

Never turn your back on a predator.

That's what Grandma Beulah had always said, but then, Beulah had been a B movie actress and had spent more time in Beverly Hills than the great outdoors. Shelby couldn't claim to know much more than Beulah had about predators, but she knew that standing around waiting for a creepy jogger to lunge from the shadows wasn't going to do her any good.

She pivoted and took off, glancing back and seeing nothing. She was still terrified, still sure she could feel him breathing down her neck, and she half expected to be tackled from behind at any second.

She turned down Maureen's street. Five houses to go, and she could ring Maureen's doorbell, see her friend's cheerful smile. Maybe then she'd be able to convince herself that Sunglasses Guy was nothing more than an early-morning jogger.

An engine revved and headlights splashed across the cracked sidewalk, spilling onto lush yards filled with blooming daffodils and flowering shrubs. Shelby glanced over her shoulder, spotted a black Hummer rolling along the street. There was no one on the sidewalk. No hint that she'd been chased or that her fear was well-founded. She slowed to a walk, lungs burning, heart thundering as she waited for the Hummer to pass.

It pulled up beside her, going so slowly she could easily have outrun it. Big and black with tinted windows, it had plenty of room in the back to stuff a woman.

Had Sunglasses Guy come after her?

Her pulse jumped at the thought. She couldn't see

through the tinted glass, but she was sure she felt his dark gaze. She ran the last few steps to Maureen's driveway, her hair standing on end when the Hummer pulled in behind her. The driver's door opened, and Shelby didn't wait to see if Sunglasses Guy would get out. She dropped the pastries and ran for Maureen's door, her pulse jumping as someone snagged the back of her apron and pulled her to a stop.

She screamed, fists swinging, lungs filling for another scream.

"Cool it, Shelby Ann. I'm not in the mood to have my nose broken." The voice was familiar, but she swung again anyway, her knuckles brushing a firm jaw.

"I said, cool it." He grabbed her hand, held it in a grip that she couldn't loosen no matter how desperately she tried.

"Let me go!" she yelled, looking up, up and *up* into the face of her attacker.

The *familiar* face of her attacker.

She knew him!

Not Sunglasses Guy.

Hercules. The muscular, too-good-looking-to-be-for-real guy who'd been coming into Just Desserts at the crack of dawn every morning for the past four months, watching her intently as she filled his order. Two doughnuts and a large coffee. Black. To go. She'd noticed him the first day he'd walked into the bakery, and she'd been noticing him ever since. What woman wouldn't? The guy should be on the front cover of a bodybuilder magazine.

"What are *you* doing here?" She managed to sputter, and he raised an eyebrow.

"Looking for you."

"Well, you found me *and* scared me, and now I've ruined three dozen pastries." Her voice shook as she tugged away. "Maureen is *not* going to be happy."

"I'm sure they're salvageable." He lifted the boxes, opened the one on the top and frowned. "Some of them."

"*None* of them. I'm going to have to go back for more." She huffed, eyeing the smashed tops of several muffins, her pulse racing for a reason that had nothing to do with fear and everything to do with the man standing beside her. There was just something about his dark, knowing gaze that unbalanced her, and having him there, talking to her, looking straight into her eyes, studying her face…

Unbalanced was exactly how she felt.

She frowned, pulling the boxes from his hands. "You said you were looking for me. Did Dottie send you?" Dottie had been part of Shelby's life for as long as she could remember. A good friend of Beulah's, she'd shown up at the bakery a week after Beulah's funeral, and she'd been hanging around ever since.

"She said you didn't take your car out for the delivery, and she was worried about you walking here alone."

"My car wouldn't start, so I didn't have much of a choice."

"Next time, call someone to give you a ride."

"Before dawn? Who would I call?" she asked, and he shrugged.

"A friend. Family. Someone who can make sure you get where you're going and back safely."

"I've been getting where I'm going and back safely for years, Herc—" She stopped short of calling him what she'd been calling him in her head since the first day she'd seen him. "I guess you have me at a disadvantage. You know my name, but I don't know yours."

"Ryder Malone."

"Well, like I said, Ryder, I've been running my own business and getting by just fine for five years. I'm not sure what possessed Dottie to worry now, but you can go back to what you were doing before she sent you out looking for me." She took a step toward Maureen's door, but Ryder pulled her up short.

"What I was doing was waiting for my doughnuts and coffee. Dottie won't sell them to me until I get you back to the bakery in one piece, so going back to what I was doing isn't going to accomplish anything."

"Oh, for goodness' sake! What is that woman up to now?" she muttered, shoving the boxes toward him. "Here. Hold these. I'll tell Maureen that I need to run back to the bakery. If you don't mind giving me a ride, we should be able to get things cleared up pretty quickly and get you on your way."

"No problem." He took a ruined muffin from the top box and bit into it. "Still tastes great. Are you sure your customer won't—"

"I'm sure." She cut him off, anxious to give Maureen the bad news and get back to the bakery. She had too much to do to waste time, and she planned to tell Dottie that. Of all the things the woman had done in the four years she'd been working at the bakery, sending Ryder Malone out searching for Shelby took the cake.

A sad attempt at matchmaking. That's what it was, and Shelby did *not* have the patience for it.

She marched to Maureen's front door, bracing herself for the tantrum she knew was coming. As much as she liked the vivacious, spontaneous fifty-year-old,

Shelby thought Maureen was a little too much like her mother and sister. Sweet but spoiled. Kind, as long as things were going her way.

Right now, things were not going Maureen's way, and Shelby expected to hear about it.

She rang the doorbell of the beautiful Victorian, glancing at her watch as she did so. Already five minutes late, and she still had to return to the bakery to get new product. Maureen was *not* going to be happy.

As a matter of fact, Shelby was surprised she hadn't already opened the door and demanded an explanation. Now that she thought about it, Shelby was surprised there were no lights on, no sign that Maureen was getting ready for her fiftieth birthday celebration. An early breakfast, a limo ride to the airport and an early flight out to New York City.

Be there by 5:20 a.m., Shelby. Not a minute later. Our flight leaves at 8:30, and the girls will be showing up on my doorstep at 6:00 expecting a birthday breakfast to die for.

Maureen's words rang in Shelby's ears, anxiety simmering in her stomach as she peered into the narrow window beside the door. Nothing. Not even a hint of movement.

Concerned, she rang the doorbell again and heard something. A muffled sound that came from deep within the house.

And then the world exploded.

Glass sprayed from the windows to either side of the door. Heat blazed from flames that shot from somewhere. Everywhere.

Another explosion, and she was flying, spinning, hurtling through space. Away from the burning door.

Away from the shattered glass. Away from the lightening morning and deep blue sky. Flying and whirling into darkness so black and deep she knew she'd never escape it.

TWO

The force of the explosion knocked Ryder Malone from his feet. He went down hard, his thigh cramping, his pulse racing, a thousand memories trying to drag him into the past. He ignored them, jumping to his feet and running across the grass that separated him from Shelby Simons. Pretty, amusing, uncomplicated Shelby Simons. Owner of the only bakery in town that knew how to make a doughnut right.

Owner of the sweetest smile he'd seen in years.

She intrigued him. Her quiet joy, her easy humor, the comfortable way she interacted with the people who entered her bakery, all those qualities set to a backdrop of quiet beauty and stunning blue eyes.

Now, she lay facedown on the ground, bits of shingle and wood falling around her like glowing confetti. They coated her back and her thick dark hair, covered the ground around her prone figure. Flames shot from broken windows on either side of the thick wood door she'd been standing in front of. A few inches to the left or right, and she'd have been sliced to bits.

He brushed an ember from silky curls, felt the pulse point in her neck. It beat slow and steady.

Alive.

No time to check for injuries. Not with the fire raging out of control and the house groaning beneath the onslaught of flames.

He scooped her up, racing back across the yard as another explosion rocked the house. It threw him to his knees, but he kept his arms tight around Shelby's soft, limp body.

Neighbors spilled from their homes, frantic cries mixing with the roar of the blaze that consumed the beautiful Victorian, the sounds background noise to Ryder's racing thoughts. He'd seen explosions, felt them, lived through them. He hadn't expected one in Spokane. Not on a sleepy spring morning.

"Shelby?" He brushed thick hair from her cheek, and she shifted, her eyes slowly opening.

"What happened?" She gasped, coughing on the acrid fumes that poured from the burning shell of the old house.

"Some kind of explosion."

"Explosion? Maureen!" She shoved away, jumped to her feet and ran straight back toward the inferno.

He snagged the bow of her apron, pulling her to a stop, and she swung around, her eyes wide with horror. "Maureen is in there."

"There's nothing we can do for her now," he said truthfully, and she yanked from his hold, spun away, running toward the house again.

He followed, heat searing his cheeks as flames whooshed through the roof and windows, consuming wood and melting wiring, the scent suffocating.

"Shelby! She's dead. There's nothing we can do to help her," he shouted, grabbing her apron again.

"She's my friend. I have to try."

"And kill yourself in the process? I can't let you do that." He wouldn't let her do that, but she turned, tears trekking down her cheeks, leaving white trails in her soot-stained face. A large knot peeked out from beneath silky curls near her temple, the swollen flesh surrounding a deep cut that oozed blood. She didn't seem to feel the pain of it. Didn't seem to know she was hurt.

"It's her birthday, Ryder. Her fiftieth. She can't be dead."

He touched her cheek, tried to make her see the futility of the situation. "People die on their birthdays all the time."

"I know, but that doesn't mean Maureen is dead. Maybe she survived the explosion. Maybe she's upstairs, trying to find a way through the smoke and flames. I can't just stand here and watch her house burn around her."

"Shelby—"

She'd turned away again, racing around to the back of the house, dark hair glowing gold in the firelight.

He followed, his thigh aching, the memories threatening to overtake him.

Smoke.

Flames.

His comrades consumed by it.

Ryder consumed.

He shoved the images down deep, refusing them the way he had so many times in the six years since an explosive device had taken the lives of four of the ten navy SEALs who'd been sent to hunt a high-level terrorist in Afghanistan.

Fire licked along the facade of the house, blazing

across the back-porch roof, snapping and crackling as it ate its way up wood posts. Engulfed, the back door offered no hope of entry, the shattered windows only serving as a conduit for black smoke and red-gold flames to pour out.

Death had come calling, and it had taken every living thing in its path.

Shelby stopped in her tracks, her face lit by flames.

"She really is dead, isn't she?" she asked quietly, the words barely carrying over the fire's crackling hiss. Tears streamed down her cheeks, mixing with blood and soot, but her voice was steady, her gaze direct.

"Yes."

"It's her birthday." She repeated the information as if doing so would somehow change what had happened to her friend.

"I know. Come on." He took her arm, urging her to the front yard. Two explosions had already rocked the house. There might be another, and he didn't want Shelby anywhere near the building if there was.

Three fire trucks were parked at the curb, firefighters hooking a hose to the hydrant across the street. The ordered chaos of the scene strummed along Ryder's nerves, making him anxious and antsy. He'd wanted a couple of doughnuts and some coffee, and he'd gotten trouble instead. Not a good morning. That was for sure.

He hurried Shelby across the street, and a tall, thin firefighter stopped them there, his gaze jumping from Ryder to Shelby.

"You okay, folks?" he asked.

"We're fine, but my friend Maureen…" Shelby didn't finish.

"Is she inside?"

"Yes."

"Anyone else in there that you know of?"

"No. She lived alone."

"Okay. We'll do what we can to find her, but it doesn't look good."

"I know." Shelby offered a watery smile, and Ryder's heart constricted, the feeling both surprising and uncomfortable. He'd noticed Shelby and her sweet smile every time he'd gone into her bakery, but noticing wasn't the same as feeling something for her.

And he *was* feeling.

Sympathy, concern, curiosity about the woman who seemed both strong and vulnerable.

"I'm going to send an EMT over. You need to get the cut on your head looked at." The firefighter hurried away, and Shelby put a hand to her temple, fingering the lump that still oozed blood.

"It doesn't even hurt," she said, shivering as she looked at her bloodied fingers.

"Shock will do that to you. Here." Ryder shrugged out of his jacket and draped it around her shoulders, his knuckles brushing the silky flesh beneath her jaw as he adjusted the collar.

She stilled, something flashed in the depth of her eyes. Fear? Anxiety? It was there and gone too quickly for him to read.

"Thanks. I've never been so cold in my life. I guess that's another thing sho—" Her voice trailed off, her eyes widening as she caught sight of his side holster. "That's a gun."

"Right."

"You're carrying a weapon."

"Right."

"But...why?"

"I'm in the security business. I protect people and property."

"You're a bodyguard?"

"A security contractor."

"Which is the same as a bodyguard."

"If you want."

"What I want is to go back to last night and insist that Maureen spend it at my place."

"It would be nice if life had a do-over button, Shelby Ann, but it doesn't."

"I know. I just wish that I'd had a chance to save her." She swayed, her face colorless. He slid an arm around her waist, motioning to the EMT who was making his way toward them.

"Ma'am, why don't you sit down and let me have a look at your head?"

"I'm all right."

"You're bleeding, and you may have a concussion." The EMT used gloved fingers to probe Shelby's wound, and she stiffened.

"Ow!"

"Looks like you're going to need a few stitches. The doctor may want to do a CAT scan to rule out any fractures or brain bleeds. Let's get you transported to the hospital and see what's what."

"I really don't need to go to the hospital," Shelby protested.

"You really do," Ryder responded, urging her onto a stretcher that had been wheeled over by two other EMTs.

"But—"

"Just relax, ma'am, and let us do all the work." They rolled her away as she continued to protest.

Ryder figured he'd have a chat with the fire marshal and then find a place to buy some coffee, eat one of the protein bars that he kept in his glove compartment and get on with his day.

He scanned the mass of people fighting the blaze, searching for the one who might be in charge. A dog yapped from the bushes at the edge of the yard, but he ignored it, focusing on the task, determined to follow through on his plan.

"Wait! Stop!" Shelby's cry sent adrenaline pumping through him, and he turned.

She hung over the side of the stretcher as she whistled and called to something. If she leaned any farther, she'd fall on her head. The EMTs seemed helpless to stop her.

Ryder was not.

He covered the ground between them quickly, grabbing her arm and hauling her up. "Are you nuts? You're going to break your neck!"

"That's Mazy. I'm sure of it." She pointed to the edge of the yard.

"Mazy who?"

"Mazy. Maureen's dog. She's probably scared to death. Come here, Mazy. Here, girl," she called, leaning over the side of the stretcher again.

"Cut it out before you kill yourself!" He grabbed her arm again. Hauled her up again.

"But—"

"*I'll* go look for the dog. You stay put." Disgusted, he tramped across the yard, following the sound of yapping dog until he found a little white puffball cowering in the bushes. It looked more like a piece of fluff than a dog, but he picked it up anyway, ignoring its rumbling growl.

"This her?" He held the puffball out for Shelby to see, and she teared up.

"Yes. Poor thing. She must be so scared and confused."

"I'll take her to the shelter. She'll get good—"

"No! The other dogs will eat her alive."

She had a point. To a bigger dog, Mazy would probably look like a tasty morsel. "I can leave her here. Maybe Maureen had family or friends who will come and get her."

"You can't leave her here. She'll be—"

"Scared and confused?"

"Yes." She offered a half smile. "Listen, I hate to ask, but could you bring her to the hospital? I'll have someone meet us there and bring her to my place. That way, she won't run off while she's waiting for rescue."

Bring the dog to the hospital?

He frowned at the little beast, and he was pretty sure it frowned back, but Shelby was waiting, her eyes big and dark with concern, and *no* refused to make its way past his lips.

"Okay, but if she chews the upholstery in my truck, she's toast."

"Mazy has good manners. She'll behave." Shelby smiled the same sweet smile she greeted him with every time he walked into her bakery, and his pulse jumped, his blood warming.

He'd dated plenty of beautiful women during his time in the navy. After his injury and recovery, he'd been more selective, dating just a few women before he'd found Danielle. Gorgeous, driven and strong in her faith, she'd been the kind of woman he'd thought he could make a good life with, but after two years of dating, the relationship had felt hollow, Danielle's clawing, grasping need to get ahead putting a wedge between them.

He'd wanted a cozy home in the suburbs of New York City, a few kids, maybe a dog. She'd wanted a high-rise apartment in Manhattan, no kids, no pets. Nothing but work and money.

In the end, they hadn't found a way to make their goals mesh.

When he'd broken up with her, he hadn't bothered looking for another relationship. Ryder had had plenty of opportunity to find The One. But he hadn't, and he figured she wasn't out there.

But Shelby appealed to him, everything about her soft and warm and inviting. No matter how much he'd tried to ignore her, he couldn't. Four months of visiting her bakery, and he was no closer to understanding why.

She was pretty, sure, but that wasn't it.

When he looked into her eyes, it was like looking into her soul, and Ryder wanted to keep on looking.

He wasn't sure what to think about that.

Wasn't sure if he should think anything about it.

He'd come to Spokane to open another branch of his company, Personal Securities Incorporated. One year, that's what he'd planned to devote to setting things up. In eight months, he'd be going home to New York City. He didn't have time to get involved in a relationship, and he wasn't sure he would have wanted to if he did have the time.

But he couldn't seem to stay away from Shelby and her quaint bakery and easy smile.

He frowned, the dog whining and wiggling as the sirens blared and the ambulance sped away.

THREE

No way was Shelby *ever* going to let Dr. Jarrod Estes sew her up. She'd dated the man for about two minutes after she'd found Andrew and Stephanie kissing outside of Andrew's apartment building. One date with the most sought-after bachelor at Grace Christian Church, because Shelby had wanted to feel as if she wasn't the biggest loser on the planet. One date had been plenty. Jarrod had spent more time checking his text messages than talking to her, and Shelby had decided there and then that she was done with the dating scene.

Done.

Finished.

No more men.

Ever.

She'd made some lame excuse about leaving an oven on at the bakery and excused herself halfway through the entrée. Now the man she'd ditched on their first date was coming at her with a needle.

"Really, Jarrod, I don't think stitches are necessary." She eased off the exam table, her bare toes curling against cold tile, the acrid scent of smoke wafting from her hair.

Smoke from the explosions and fire that had killed Maureen.

Tears clogged her throat, but she'd already cried so much that her eyes were hot and dry.

"Shelby, I know you've had a tough morning, and I know you're anxious to get out of here and take some time to grieve, but you do need stitches." Jarrod dropped the needle back on the tray, glanced at his watch and sighed. "Tell you what, why don't I call Dottie and have her come to hold your hand?"

"Do *not* call Dottie." That was the last thing Shelby needed.

"How about one of your friends, then? Someone from church? Jasmine or Faith?" He leaned forward in his chair, a hint of impatience in his tone.

"I wouldn't want them to drive all the way here. Besides, I'm opting out of the stitches. I'm sure my head will heal just fine."

"It's going to scar," he warned.

"I can think of worse things." She scooped up her clothes and the jacket Ryder had thrown over her shoulders. Since Jarrod didn't seem keen on leaving the room, she'd find a restroom and change there. Sure, Ryder had said he'd bring Mazy to the hospital, but Shelby had seen the look in his eyes, and she figured he was about as likely to follow through as she was to let Jarrod stitch her up. She hadn't even bothered calling someone to come get the dog.

The only good man is a dead husband with a good life-insurance policy.

Another one of Beulah's truisms. One Shelby's mother and sister wholeheartedly believed. Shelby had tried to believe something different. She'd opened herself up to love, tried to create what Beulah and her mother had insisted was impossible—forever with a man who loved her for who she was.

Tried twice times, actually.

Once in college.

Once with Andrew.

Both had been disastrous.

She didn't plan to try again.

"Thanks for everything, Jarrod. See you at church Sunday." She yanked the door open, colliding with a rock-hard chest.

"What's the hurry, Shelby Ann?" Broad hands grabbed her waist as she caught her balance.

She knew the voice, the hands, the dark chocolate eyes that stared into hers.

Ryder.

Her heart jumped in acknowledgment, her body humming with an awareness she knew she shouldn't be feeling. "You came."

"I said I would," he responded, frowning slightly. "Is your friend around here somewhere? That dog and I aren't getting along, and I want her out of my car ASAP."

"Mazy gets along with everyone."

"She's not getting along with me. So, *where's your friend?*" He glanced at Jarrod, at the otherwise empty hospital room and then turned the full force of his gaze on Shelby again.

Yep. Dark chocolate eyes. Only they weren't sweet, they were hard and intense.

"I…didn't call anyone. I didn't think you'd actually come. You can just leave her…"

"Where?"

"Well..." Where *could* he leave her? "Just give me a minute to get changed and I'll get her." She tried to step past him, but he blocked her path.

"It's going to take more than a minute to get your head stitched up." He edged her backward.

"I'm not planning to have it stitched up."

"Shelby, will you please just let me get this done?" Jarrod asked, exasperated and not even trying to hide it.

"Fine." She walked back to the exam table, dropped her clothes and the coat on the chair beside it.

"Don't worry. You're going to feel this first stick, and then you won't feel a thing." Jarrod leaned toward her, the needle pointed straight at her face, and she felt every bit of blood drain from her head.

"You're not going to faint, are you?" Ryder put a hand on her shoulder.

"That would be preferable to the alternative."

"Which would be?"

"Staying conscious for the entire horrifying procedure."

Ryder laughed, the sound rusty and gruff. "It's not that bad, is it?"

"I guess that depends on which side of the needle you're on." Shelby winced as Jarrod shot her with the anesthetic.

"That's the worst of it, Shelby. Let's give it a minute to take effect. So—" Jarrod turned his attention to Ryder "—were you at Maureen's, too?"

"Yes." Ryder didn't offer more than that, and Shelby wondered if Jarrod would take the hint and stop asking questions.

He didn't.

"You work at the bakery with Shelby?"

"Why would you say that?" Ryder asked, and Jarrod frowned.

"Shelby said she was making a delivery when Maureen's house exploded."

"Shelby was making a delivery."

"And you were with her?"

"Is there a reason you want to know, Doctor?" Ryder asked as Jarrod lifted a needle and bent close to Shelby's head.

"Just curious. I was shocked to hear about the explosion and Maureen's death. I'm just trying to figure out how everything went down." Jarrod had the good grace to flush, his neck and cheeks going deep red.

"That's the job of the police and fire marshal. It may take a while for them to figure it out. The house is pretty much rubble. I'm not sure how easy it will be to piece together what happened."

"Did they find Maureen's... Maureen?" Shelby asked, and Ryder nodded.

"I'm afraid so."

"Poor Maureen." The tears Shelby had thought were completely dried up began again, slipping down her cheeks as Jarrod worked.

"If it makes you feel any better, she didn't suffer. If the initial explosion didn't kill her, the smoke overcame her so quickly, she didn't have time to be scared," Ryder offered, patting her back as Jarrod continued his slow, methodical stitching.

"Dead is dead. She should be flying to New York right now, celebrating with her friends. Not lying in a morgue," Shelby said, taking a tissue Ryder shoved toward her.

"She's celebrating in a different way." Jarrod's easy

platitude did more to irritate Shelby than it did to comfort her. She knew Maureen was a Christian, but that didn't make her death any less tragic.

"I think, if given the choice, she'd rather be on the plane."

"Right," Jarrod conceded, stepping back. "Okay, you're all set. I'm going to send a nurse in with aftercare instructions. See your personal physician tomorrow. The stitches will need to come out in ten days."

"Thanks." She stood on wobbling legs, grabbing the closest thing to her, which just happened to be Ryder's arm. She jerked back, the spark of electricity that shot through her palm an unwelcome surprise.

What was it about the man that made her heart race every time she looked in his eyes? That made heat shoot through her when she touched his arm?

It certainly wasn't his winning smile or charming personality. The guy looked like a carved statue of a Roman centurion, all hard angles and cold calculation.

"I need to get changed," she mumbled, turning away.

"I'll be right outside." He stepped into the hall and closed the door.

Alone, Shelby dressed quickly, pulling on her white polo shirt and the faded jeans that were just a little looser than they'd been when she'd broken up with Andrew. Ten pounds lost so she could fit into a fancy black dress. It all seemed futile now, the worry, the wondering if she'd look beautiful enough to make Andrew regret his lying, cheating ways, a waste of time.

She sighed as she tied her lilac apron. Just Desserts' insignia emblazoned on the front, it was the only uniform she required for people working at the bakery. It was Beulah's favorite color and a nod to the grandmother who'd provided the funds to open the shop. Today, Shelby's normally immaculate apron was soot marred and grass stained, splotches of blood mixing with the green-and-black mess, a modern painting that spoke of chaos and tragedy. She'd have to throw it away. No way would she ever get the stains out, and she couldn't imagine wearing it without crying.

Someone knocked on the door, and she pulled it open, expecting Ryder to be standing impatiently on the other side.

"Hold your horses, big guy. I'm almost..." Her voice trailed off as she looked into the face of a stocky, middle-aged man.

"Sorry. I thought you were someone else." She glanced down the hall, surprised at how disappointed she was to see it empty.

"Mr. Malone is speaking with the sheriff. I'm sure he'll be back shortly. I'm Fire Chief Timothy Saddles, Spokane County Fire Marshal. How are you feeling?"

"Okay. All things considered."

"It's been a rough morning. I'm sorry to say your friend lost her life in the fire."

"Ryder... Mr. Malone told me you'd found her remains."

"We did. They've been sent to the medical examiner and will be released to the family once he's finished."

Medical examiner? That made Maureen's death sound less like an accident and more like...

Murder?

Shelby's pulse jumped, her thoughts spinning back to those moments before she'd rung Maureen's doorbell, back to the man with the sunglasses jogging away from Maureen's street.

"Is that common procedure? I thought the medical examiner only made rulings on suspicious deaths."

"Not really, ma'am. His job is to determine cause of death when an examination by a physician can't determine it. In this case, we're assuming the explosion killed the deceased, but assumptions don't make for good investigations. Now, if you don't mind, I'd like to ask you a few questions."

"Go ahead."

"Mr. Malone said you were making a delivery to the deceased's—"

"Maureen."

"Pardon?"

"The *deceased* was Maureen. A bestselling author, a mother, a good friend. I was making a delivery to her place because it was her birthday, and she had invited a dozen friends to go on a shopping trip to New York City. They were going to meet at her house, have some breakfast and then take a limo to the airport."

"My apologies if I sounded callous, Ms. Simons. What time did you arrive at Maureen's house?"

"At 5:25. Five minutes later than she had asked me to be there."

"Did you notice anything out of the ordinary? Anything different about the house?"

"There was a guy jogging down South Hill as I was heading up it. I saw him come off her street."

"Plenty of people jog on South Hill," Chief Saddles said as he jotted something in a small notebook.

"I know, but he was wearing sunglasses and gloves. It struck me as…odd."

"Did you get a good look at his face?"

"He was Caucasian. Medium complexion. Maybe five-ten. I didn't see his hair. It was covered by a hood."

"It was a chilly morning. A hood and jacket wouldn't be out of the ordinary. Gloves, either, for that matter. We'll ask around, though. Maybe he lives in one of the houses on 21st."

Maybe.

But Shelby couldn't help shuddering as she remembered the way he'd turned, taken a step toward her.

"Do you know what caused the explosion?" she asked, trying to refocus her thoughts and get ahold of her wild imagination. He *hadn't* followed her, *hadn't* tried to harm her, hadn't done anything except jog by and look, then turn and look again.

As if he were memorizing her features.

Trying to make sure he'd recognize her if he saw her again.

"A gas leak in the heater. It looks like the heating unit cracked, gas escaped. One spark of electricity from old wiring and the whole place went up."

"A spark? Like from someone ringing the doorbell?" Shelby asked, cold with the thought. Had *she* killed her friend?

"It's possible. Either that, or Maureen turned on a light—"

"All the lights were off. The only electricity was from me ringing the doorbell twice. It's my fault, isn't it? I killed her." She dropped into a chair, her stomach sick, those stupid tears back again.

"Of course you didn't, ma'am." The chief patted her arm awkwardly, and Shelby almost felt sorry for him.

"Everything okay in here?" Ryder stepped into the

room, his height and oversize muscles dwarfing the average-size fire chief, his dark gaze on Shelby.

"You're crying again." He stated the obvious, and she frowned, irritated with him, with herself and with the fire chief, who hovered uneasily a few feet away.

"Because I just realized I killed my friend."

"Ma'am, your friend may very well have been dead before the gas was ignited. The amount of gas it took to cause such a catastrophic explosion was enough to asphyxiate her while she slept."

"That really doesn't make me feel any better, Chief." But she stood anyway, refusing to meet Ryder's eyes as she shoved his jacket into his arms. "I really need to get to work. Are we done here?"

"Yes. Just give me your contact information, and I'll call if I have any more questions."

Shelby spouted off her home address and her cell-phone number, and gave the chief the bakery's address for good measure.

"Will you call me once you have news from the medical examiner?" she asked.

"Of course. You'll probably hear from me in a day or two. If not, give me a call." He handed her a business card, and she shoved it in her apron pocket.

His findings wouldn't change the fact that Maureen was dead, but they might ease some of the guilt Shelby was suddenly feeling.

She'd felt the same way when Beulah had died alone in a hospital in Beverly Hills while Shelby sat in an airport in Seattle waiting for her connecting flight. She'd been trying to get to her grandmother after receiving a late-night call from the nursing home saying Beulah had had a heart attack, but all the trying in the world hadn't put her where she needed to be when she needed to be there.

And all the crying in the world couldn't undo what had happened at Maureen's house, because crying over spilled milk never got the mess cleaned up.

That's what Beulah would have said, and Shelby knew it was true. When Dottie had shown up on her doorstep, homeless because she'd been kicked out of Beulah's Beverly Hills rental property, Shelby had let her live in her spare room, offered her a job at the bakery, made her feel like family, because she'd known it was what Beulah would have wanted. Shelby hadn't been able to be at her grandmother's side when she'd died, but she *had* carried on the legacy of kindness and compassion that Beulah had shown to the people in her life.

She might not be able to bring Maureen back to life, but Shelby could press the fire marshal and the police to find the reason for Maureen's death. It's what Maureen would want. Complete disclosure. Absolute truth. Just like she always wrote in her true-crime books.

The fire chief left the room, his shoulders stooped, his hair mussed. He'd probably been sleeping when he'd been called out to Maureen's place. Shelby had a feeling he wouldn't be sleeping much in the next few days.

"Come on. Let's get out of here." Ryder cupped her elbow, led her through the quiet hospital corridor. Shelby didn't bother telling him she needed to wait for aftercare instructions, because she didn't want to wait. She wanted to go to the bakery, lose herself in the process of creating cakes and cookies and pastries.

"Thanks again for bringing Mazy."

"I probably should say it wasn't a problem."

"But it was?"

"She chewed a hole in my car's upholstery, so yeah, it was."

"I'll pay you for the damage."

"You weren't the one who chewed the hole," he growled, but Shelby thought there might be a glimmer of amusement in his eyes.

"No, but I did ask you to give her a ride here."

"You asked. I said yes. I'm as culpable as you."

"I can pay for half of the repair cost, then."

"No need, but for future reference, when I say I'm going to do something, I follow through. I expect other people to do the same."

"I'll keep that in mind." Not that she thought that she'd have any reason to.

Dating was out of the question. Men were off-limits.

If she wanted to remember that, she needed to stay far away from guys like Ryder.

She *would* stay far away from him. As soon as she got Mazy out of his car.

They stepped outside into the bright morning sunlight, the vivid blue sky and fluffy white clouds too beautiful for the ugliness of the day. Maureen would have been so pleased with the weather, the clear skies, everything about her fiftieth birthday. Mazy barked hysterically as Ryder led Shelby to his Hummer, and Shelby was sure she must know that her owner was dead.

Poor little dog.

"Be careful. She's a menace," Ryder warned as he opened the door.

"Hey, girl." Shelby pulled Mazy into her arms, doing her best not to cry again. Unlike her mother and sister, who always looked beautiful when they cried, Shelby looked like a mess and felt even worse when the tears flowed. Blotchy skin, bright red nose, raging headache. She was heading for all three.

"Thanks again, Ryder. I'll make sure to tell Dottie to keep you supplied with doughnuts and coffee when I'm not at the bakery." She started to walk away, but Ryder snagged her hand, his palm rough and calloused and way too wonderful.

"You're not planning on walking to the bakery," he said, his forehead creased, fine lines fanning out from his eyes. He had long, golden eyelashes and dark gold hair, and he really did look like a Roman statue come to life. Sleek, hard muscles and strong lines. Beautiful in a very masculine way.

"Yes, I am. It's only two miles from here."

"Maybe I should rephrase that. You're not *going* to walk to the bakery."

"Of course I am. I make deliveries here all the time, and when the weather is nice and the deliveries are small enough, I walk. It'll take me a half hour, tops."

"Not if you pass out from your head injury on the way there."

"I haven't passed out yet. There's no reason to think I will."

"Listen, Shelby Ann." Ryder sighed, obviously holding on to his patience with difficulty. "I was supposed to be at work a half hour ago. I have a meeting in an hour. I'd really like to be there. If I drive you to the bakery, I'll make it. If I follow you to the bakery to make sure you arrive safely, I won't. So, get in the Hummer and let's get going."

"You don't have to follow me."

"Yeah. I do. So *get in*." He lifted her off her feet, plopping her onto the passenger seat with ease.

"Hey!"

"Move your legs," he ordered, nearly closing the door on her when she didn't move fast enough.

"This is kidnapping," she sputtered as he climbed in.

"If I were going to kidnap you, I'd make sure the dog wasn't with you when I did it. One hole in the upholstery is enough." His bland reply almost made Shelby smile.

"You're a Neanderthal, you know that, Ryder?" she asked without heat as she fastened her seat belt. His hands had been on her waist, and she could still feel the imprint of his thumbs on her belly. Her soft haven't-done-a-sit-up-in-ten-years belly.

She cracked open the window, letting crisp morning air cool her flushed cheeks.

"A Neanderthal, huh?" Ryder smiled as he drove through the parking lot, and Shelby's pulse had the nerve to jump in response.

"If the shoe fits…"

"Did they wear shoes back then?"

"They might have. Of course, even if they didn't, a guy who picks a woman up and throws her in his car is still…" She lost her train of thought; a man at the corner of the hospital parking lot caught her attention.

Dark glasses that glinted in the light. Hood pulled over his hair.

Medium height.

Medium build.

As she watched, he pulled down the glasses, stared straight into her eyes, his gaze hollow and icy-blue.

"That's him," she shouted, as he turned and walked around the corner.

"Who?" Ryder braked, leaning past her and looking in the direction she pointed.

"The guy I saw this morning running from 21st Street. He's heading down Main Street."

"Stay in the car. I'll go see what he has to say."

He was out of the Hummer before Shelby could respond, moving quickly, bypassing a few pedestrians as he jogged around the corner and out of sight.

Going to find the guy with the icy-blue eyes.

Shelby shuddered, smoothing Mazy's silky head. "He'll be fine, right, girl?"

The dog whined, but it wasn't the answer Shelby wanted.

She wanted to know absolutely for sure that Ryder wasn't going to run into a trap and be brought down by the strange guy with the sunglasses.

Ten minutes passed. Then another ten.

Ryder had a meeting to get to, and Shelby had a desperate need to know he was okay.

She set Mazy on the seat.

"Stay here and don't chew anything." She tossed the command out as she opened the door and jumped out. The quick movement was a mistake. Her head spun, and she grabbed the door, steadying herself as she took deep gulps of air.

"I thought I told you to stay in the Hummer," Ryder snapped, and Shelby jumped, her heart racing double-time as she met his dark eyes.

"I was worried about you."

"You should have been worried about *you*. You're pale as paper. Sit down before you fall down." His tone was gruff, his hands gentle as he helped her back into the SUV.

"Did you find him?"

"No. That doesn't mean he wasn't there. There are plenty of places to hide around here, that's for sure, and if he took off his hood and sunglasses, I could easily have looked right at him and not known it." He glanced around the parking lot, his jacket pulled back just enough to show the edge of his shoulder holster.

A security contractor, that's what he'd called himself. He looked like one. Tough and determined and very confident.

"I know it was him, Ryder. He was waiting for me." She shuddered, and Ryder patted her knee. Heat radiated up her leg and settled deep in her belly. She ignored it. Ignored the flush that raced across her cheeks.

"Just because he's the same guy you saw this morning doesn't mean he was waiting for you. He might be indigent. It's possible he spent the night at Manito Park and then came this way for something to eat."

True. The park was just a few blocks away from Maureen's, and the Union Gospel Mission was around the corner from the hospital. It all made perfect sense, but Shelby's shivering fear wouldn't leave.

"Maybe you're right."

"I'm going to call hospital security. See if they can pull up external security-camera footage for me. I want to get a good look at this guy." He pulled out of the parking lot, the Hummer's engine purring as he drove toward the bakery.

Shelby's unsettled stomach churned and grumbled as

Ryder talked to a hospital security officer on his hands-free phone, his tone brusque.

She closed her eyes. The day had started horribly, but it didn't have to continue that way. She'd go to the bakery, work for a few hours, then take Mazy to her apartment, get her set up there. Maybe she'd forget that she'd rung the doorbell and sealed Maureen's fate.

Maybe.

But Shelby doubted it.

A lone tear slid down her cheek, and she let it fall, because her friend was dead, because Shelby might have killed her and because there was absolutely nothing she could do to change any of it.

FOUR

Shelby seemed to be sleeping as Ryder parked in front of Just Desserts. Pale and drawn, a large bandage on her temple, she looked very young and very vulnerable. That worried him. *She* worried him. Despite what he'd told her, Ryder didn't believe in coincidence, and he didn't believe that the guy she'd seen was some random homeless person. He'd been there for Shelby. Ryder's gut told him that, and he always listened to his gut.

He'd called the hospital security team and spoken to the head of security, but the thirty-second conversation had revealed little. They'd check their surveillance footage and said they'd report anything suspicious, but Ryder doubted a guy standing on the street corner would be viewed as that.

He frowned, eyeing the news vans parked in the bakery's parking lot. Obviously, news of the fire, Maureen's death and Shelby's involvement had spread.

"Are we at the bakery?" Shelby opened her eyes and blinked groggily. Dark curls slid across her forehead and cheeks. Wild and silky-looking, they begged to be touched.

"I thought you were sleeping."

"It takes me longer than five minutes to fall asleep. It didn't sound as if your conversation with hospital security went well." She scooped Mazy into her arms and got out of the Hummer. Ryder followed, falling into step beside her as she made her way across the crowded parking lot.

"They're being as helpful as they can. I'll call the sheriff later. He may be interested in viewing the footage."

"Maybe, but you're probably right. The guy was hanging around waiting for the mission to open." She smiled as she walked into the bakery, the scent of vanilla and chocolate and rich yeast dough stroking Ryder's senses almost as completely as Shelby did.

He frowned, not comfortable with the thought.

"Wow. This is…insane," Shelby whispered, clutching his arm for a moment and releasing it just as quickly.

She was right.

The bakery was jam-packed.

"I'll take care of it," he responded, shoving his way through the crowd.

A team of reporters stood near the counter, shouting questions above the quiet roar of ordering patrons and busybody visitors. Shelby's harried young employees scurried from person to person, answering questions, ringing up orders.

Ryder eased his way through the crowd, sidling up next to the loudest of three news crews.

"Leave," he said quietly, and the anchorwoman frowned.

"Excuse me?" she asked as if she weren't sure she'd heard him right.

"Ms. Simons won't be answering any questions today.

If you're interested in an interview, you'll have to call ahead of time and set up an appointment."

"But—"

"You've been asked to leave, and now you're trespassing. I suggest you take my advice and go before I call the police." He left her openmouthed and unhappy, and moved on to the next crew.

Ten minutes later, the crowd had thinned to a manageable number, air circulated through the small bakery once again, the harried young girl and her tattooed male counterpart behind the counter were working in harmony once again.

Mission accomplished.

He turned to call Shelby over, but she'd disappeared. He could hear her voice drifting from the kitchen, and he knew she was safe.

He could leave, go to his meeting and get on with his day. Only he wasn't sure he should leave before he made sure Shelby was okay.

As a matter of fact, he was certain he shouldn't.

He walked to the counter, smiled at the blonde teenager. "Is Shelby in the back?"

"Yes, I think so. I mean, she could have walked out the back door, but she never does that." She glanced over her shoulder, and Ryder took the opportunity to step around the counter.

"Sir! You can't come back here."

"I just did." He smiled again and walked into the kitchen.

"What are you doing back here? Git!" A blue-haired lady came at him with a broom, and Ryder sidestepped her swing.

Dottie. The bane of his existence. Refusing to serve

him coffee and doughnuts had been bad enough. Now she was trying to beat him with a broom. He grabbed it before she could swing again, slipping it out of her hands.

"Where's Shelby?"

"Why should I tell you?"

"Dottie! There's no need to be rude." Shelby stepped out of a walk-in pantry, a huge bag of flour clutched in her hands.

"That thing is as big as you are. You should have gotten that tattooed employee of yours to carry it." Ryder took it from her hands, and she shrugged.

"I'm stronger than he is. Dottie, why don't you go up front and help? They're swamped up there."

"Are you trying to get rid of me?"

"Yes."

"Well, then! I guess I'll go." Dottie huffed away.

"Sorry about that. Dottie has…issues." Shelby opened the sack of flour and measured several cups into a standing mixer.

"Apparently I'm one of them."

"*Everyone* is one of them."

"Yet you employ her."

"I inherited her from my grandmother. They were good friends. When Beulah passed away, I got Dottie." She smiled, finally looking into his eyes. "I thought you'd left. You have that meeting to get to, remember?"

"I wanted to make sure you were okay."

"Aside from a raging headache, I'm fine."

"You need to go home, Shelby. That was a pretty serious head injury you sustained."

"It's not the head injury that's giving me a headache. It's all the tears. I always get headaches when I cry." She poured milk into the mixer, added eggs and soft butter and sugar, her hands pretty and efficient. He'd like to take her to the gun range. Show her how to handle a semiautomatic. He had a feeling she'd be a good shot.

"Yeah? Then I'll have to be sure to never make you cry."

"Why would you? You come in for doughnuts and coffee every day. That's money in my pocket. Which makes me very happy." She offered a tight smile and turned her attention to the bowl. Obviously, he'd hit a nerve.

"Is that doughnut batter? Because I never did get my breakfast," he said.

"No. It's sweet bread. I'm going to put it in the fridge to proof, and then I'm going home. I need to get Mazy settled, and I need to settle a little, too. It's been a rough morning." She covered the bowl with a damp cloth, slid it onto a rolling rack with ten other bowls and pushed everything into a walk-in refrigerator.

"Where's the dog? I'll get her for you and walk you to your car."

"Ryder, I appreciate your help, but I don't need it anymore." She brushed flour from her apron, and he brushed it from her cheek, his fingers grazing silky flesh.

She stilled.

"Ryder…"

"You had flour on your cheek."

"Oh. Okay." She rubbed the spot he'd touched, not meeting his eyes.

"So, where's the dog?"

"Dottie tied her up out back," she responded and then pressed her lips together. "You tricked that out of me."

"No trick, Shelby Ann. You're exhausted and traumatized. Whether you want to admit it or not, you need a little help."

She sighed. "Fine. Go get Mazy. I'll meet you out front. My car is—"

"The big pink Cadillac."

"How did you know?"

"It's the only car that's here every time you are."

"Right. Okay. I'll meet you out there in a couple of minutes. I just need to give my crew some instructions." She hurried away. Ran, actually.

He walked out the back exit, freed the ungrateful Mazy and carried her to Shelby's car. He waited there, holding the struggling dog as tightly as he could without squashing her. Ten minutes passed. Fifteen. Twenty. He called work, rescheduled the meeting for later in the afternoon, tapped his fingers on the Caddie's hood.

Where was she?

Probably mixing another batch of sweet bread or keeping Dottie from attacking a patron. What she needed to be doing was resting. He shoved Mazy into the Hummer and walked into the bakery.

Shelby stood at one of the small booths, talking to an elderly couple, her blue eyes widening with surprise as she met his gaze.

"Time to go." He took her arm, tugging her away.

"But I was—"

"Going home to take a nap, remember?"

"I know, but Dottie, Zane and Rae—"

"Can handle things just fine." He led her outside, grabbing Mazy from the back of his Hummer and waiting while Shelby climbed into the Cadillac.

"Come on, Old Blue. Give me a break this time and

start, okay?" she muttered as she turned the key in the ignition.

"I hate to break the news to you, Shelby. But your car is pink, not blue." He leaned in the open door and set Mazy in Shelby's lap, caught a whiff of vanilla and berry, his muscles tightening in response.

"I know. Terrible, isn't it? Beulah left it to me in her will with specific instructions to keep it pink. If I had my way, though, she'd be blue."

"She?"

"Of course. She's not just a car. Blue is an old lady with history. She's been through a lot, but she's still nice to have around. Most of the time."

"Like Dottie?"

"Exactly. Thanks again for all your help this morning. I don't know what I would have done if you hadn't been at Maureen's place." Her eyes grew moist with tears at the mention of her friend, but she didn't let them fall. Instead, she closed the door, offered a quick wave and drove away.

He watched until the pink Cadillac disappeared from view, something in him soft for Shelby, soft for her easy smile and compassionate nature. To keep a woman like Dottie around, to drive an old pink car in memory of a woman who'd been gone for years, to run a successful bakery with a ragtag group of teens and a crotchety old woman behind the counter took a special kind of person.

Shelby was definitely that.

Ryder had been attracted to women before.

He'd even thought he might love a few of them, but none of them had touched his heart so easily, so completely as Shelby seemed to.

He rubbed the knotted muscles in his thigh before

he climbed into the Hummer. He needed to work the pain out, run until the muscles heated and loosened, but he had a meeting to attend, a client to impress. He had a company to run and his own set of problems to deal with. The last thing he needed or wanted was to be pulled into someone else's life or drama.

But with Shelby, he wasn't sure he'd have to be pulled.

With Shelby, he had a feeling he'd end up fighting his way into her life, and he had a feeling it would be worth it.

Drama and all.

He pulled away from Just Desserts, his mind humming with the million things he had to do before the day ended. Plenty to keep him occupied, but Shelby's sweet smile and berry-and-vanilla scent lingered just below the surface of his thoughts, reminding him of cool summer breezes and sparkling blue waters.

Laughter and joy and home.

All the things he'd craved most when he'd been in the arid Afghanistan countryside. Everything he'd longed for when he'd been lying in a hospital bed, listening while doctors told him he'd never walk again.

Six years ago, God had given Ryder a second chance at life, and Ryder had promised to live better and love more. He'd followed through on that, honoring his fallen comrades by building a successful security business and setting up scholarship funds for their children.

But the one thing he'd longed for most since those dark, pain-filled days had remained out of reach.

Family.

Not just his parents and siblings, but that deeper, all-consuming connection built between husband and wife and children. He'd seen its power as wives and children crowded around the beds of his surviving team members, felt it in the air as he visited the widows of those he'd served with, and he'd wanted it in a way that he never had before the explosion in Afghanistan.

Wanted it.

Sought it.

Thought he might have found it in Danielle. After they'd broken up, he'd decided that family wasn't part of God's plan for his life. Maybe he'd been right, but Ryder wasn't the kind who turned away from an opportunity, and when he looked at Shelby, that's what he saw.

An opportunity.

To look one more time for forever.

Maybe he'd find it.

Maybe he wouldn't.

Either way, he had a feeling he was in for a bumpy ride.

FIVE

"**S**tart, you stupid lump of metal. Start!" Shelby turned the key in the ignition and listened to Blue's engine sputter and die for the tenth time.

"Perfect," she muttered, leaning her forehead against the steering wheel, her head throbbing from a sleepless night and a million tears. She should have stayed in bed. She'd *planned* to stay in bed, but Dottie had called to say the doughnut fryer was acting up and that she needed Shelby to fix it.

That had been nearly an hour ago, and Shelby was still sitting in the driveway of her two-story Tudor, trying to start the Cadillac as dawn stretched gold fingers across the horizon.

She'd have to walk.

There were no two ways about it.

Walk the three miles to the bakery and hope the guy who'd haunted her dreams wasn't waiting around a corner or hiding in a dark alley.

She frowned, rubbing the bridge of her nose and praying that if she gave Old Blue one last shot, she'd start.

But nothing had been easy lately.

Not breaking up with Andrew, not facing the pitying looks of her friends and the I-told-you-so's of her family. Not running the bakery with Dottie and four high-school dropouts who'd needed a place to work.

Not answering dozens of phone calls about Maureen's death.

Not trying to sleep when Maureen's dog howled and cried for her owner.

Nothing had been easy lately.

So, *of course,* Old Blue wouldn't start.

She turned the key again and again and again, tears streaming down her face and probably smearing the makeup she'd applied to try to hide the fact that she'd spent most of the night crying.

She didn't care.

Because the stupid car would *not* start, and she was too afraid to walk, and right at that very moment her life stunk.

The Cadillac door opened, and she screamed, slapping at a hand that reached in to snatch the keys, her pulse racing with terror, the metallic taste of fear on her tongue as she tried desperately to escape through the other door.

Someone snagged her belt loop, easily pulling her back.

"You need to be more careful with your key, Shelby Ann. You break it in the ignition, and then where will you be?" Ryder's deep voice poured over her, thick and rich as melted chocolate, and Shelby collapsed onto the seat, all the strength seeping out of her.

"What are you doing here?" she asked, wiping at her cheeks as she straightened.

"Dottie was worried when you didn't show at the bakery. She wouldn't—"

"Let you buy your doughnuts and coffee until you came and checked on me?"

"Exactly. Looks like you're having car trouble again. Need some help?" He leaned in, sweat trickling down his brow, his breath coming hard and steady, his blond hair dark with moisture. Had he been running? She glanced around. No Hummer. That explained why she hadn't heard him arrive.

"Blue is being fickle lately, but I'll get her started. Go on back to the bakery. I'll meet you there."

"Actually, I was hoping to catch a ride back with you. I did a five-mile run to the bakery and a three-mile run here. My leg is protesting." He rubbed the muscle of his thigh and grimaced.

"You strained it?"

"It's an old injury. It acts up once in a while. How about you let me give Old Blue a try? Maybe we'll both make it back to the bakery before Dottie sends out a search party." He slid into the car before Shelby could protest, nudging her out of the way and sliding the key into Blue's ignition.

"She's not going to start," Shelby said as he turned the key.

So, of course, Blue started.

"There. Piece of cake. Buckle up, and let's get out of here."

"I can drive."

"I thought all the black stuff around your eyes might make it difficult to see the road."

Black stuff?

Shelby pulled her compact out of the Gucci purse her sister had given her for Christmas and looked in the mirror.

Mascara ran from both eyes. Shelby grabbed tissue from the glove compartment, dabbing at the mess.

"A gentleman wouldn't have mentioned how awful I look," she grumbled as Ryder pulled out of the driveway.

"Who said I was a gentleman?" he responded. "And who said you look awful?"

"I've got mascara running down my face. Of course I look awful."

"Actually, you look beautiful. Even with black tears running down your face."

"There's no need to flatter me to get doughnuts." She tried to keep her tone light, but she was still shaky from the surprise of seeing him, sweaty and gorgeous and too perfect for words, before she'd even had her first cup of coffee.

"Flattery implies an undeserved compliment. I'm not into that sort of thing."

"Then what sort of thing are you into?" she asked, and he shot her a look that curled her toes.

"Honesty."

"Oh. Well, that's good." She felt gauche and schoolgirlish, and she didn't like the feeling at all. She took a deep breath, steadied her thoughts and her thundering heart. He might look like Hercules, but he was a man, and she was done with men forever.

"I need to apologize for Dottie. She shouldn't have sent you out looking for me." Better. Much better.

"She should apologize for herself."

"She won't. The thing is, she means well, and the good news is, eventually, she'll get over her fixation with you—"

"Fixation?"

"She thinks I should be dating. She keeps trying to fix me up with customers. Last month, it was Mr. Hampton, the president of the seniors' birding society. He's eighty-nine."

"Ouch!"

"Exactly."

"I'm curious, Shelby Ann. What does all this have to do with you crying your eyes out?" He pulled into Just Desserts' crowded parking lot, found a spot and turned to face her, his dark eyes scanning her face as if he could read the truth there.

"Nothing. This place is busy for six o'clock in the morning. I'd better get in there and fix the doughnut machine." She opened the door, but he grabbed her hand, his touch light but so compelling she couldn't force herself to pull away.

"It's fixed. Dottie had me look at it before she sent me to find you."

"I still need to get in there."

"Is there any reason why you don't want to answer my question?"

"Is there a reason why you asked?"

"Because I'd be happy to take care of him if you need me to."

"There is no him." Not anymore.

"No?" He slid one of her curls between his fingers. "I think I might be glad about that, Shelby Ann."

"Ryder…"

"So, if you weren't crying about a man, you were crying about Maureen." He changed the subject, and she was relieved. She didn't want to think about what he'd meant, didn't want to *know* what he'd meant, because she really couldn't believe he'd meant anything.

A flirt, a player, that's what he had to be, but when she looked into his eyes, she was pretty sure he wasn't either of those things.

"Look," she said, "Maureen is dead. I feel like it's my fault, like maybe I could have saved her if I'd done something different. This stupid car never starts when I want it to, and my head is pounding, and I've got a whole day of work ahead of me. That's why I was crying. Happy?" The words spilled out, and he shook his head.

"Not if you aren't. You couldn't have saved Maureen, Shelby Ann. No matter what you did. She was dead before the explosion."

"The fire marshal hasn't confirmed that yet." Though she'd called before she'd left the house and left a message reminding him to call as soon as he heard anything.

"Because he doesn't have a friend who works for the medical examiner. I do. I called this morning. The autopsy is almost complete. They're just waiting on toxicology reports before they release their findings."

"So, the gas asphyxiated her?"

"No. She was killed by blunt-force trauma to the head."

"What?"

"Someone murdered her, Shelby, and made it look like an accident. That's one of the reasons I was here before the bakery opened this morning. I wanted to let you know that you need to be very, very careful. If the guy you saw is responsible for Maureen's death, he might not be content to leave any loose ends."

Loose ends?

As in, Shelby?

She shivered, remembering his hollow, icy stare. "Thanks, Ryder. I'll be careful. Now, I guess, I'd better get inside and help Dottie handle this rush. Do you want a couple of doughnuts to go?"

"What I want is to know that you're going to be okay," he said quietly. She looked into his eyes again and was caught in his dark gaze.

"I'm always okay, Ryder. It's just part of who I am," she responded, but her voice shook, because he seemed to see beyond her cheerful facade, seemed to see so much more than anyone else ever had.

"I don't think so. I think you're always running around making sure everyone else is okay, and I don't think you spend five seconds worrying about whether or not you are. Come on. I'll walk you into the bakery." He got out of Old Blue, and she had no choice but to follow.

Because he was right.

She did have to make sure the people she cared about were okay.

The bakery teemed with people, its walls seeming to bow from the force of so many bodies, and Shelby hurried behind the counter, taking a customer's order, answering half a dozen questions about the fire and Maureen, and then moving on to the next guest.

Over and over again.

The same routine.

Serve, answer, serve, answer, her head pounding, her body sluggish, Ryder's words echoing through her mind.

Killed by blunt-force trauma to the head.

"You okay, boss?" Zane Thunderbird asked. At nineteen, Zane had lived through more than most people double his age. Kicked out of his stepfather's home when he was sixteen, he'd been homeless for nearly two years when he'd walked into Just Desserts, tattooed and pierced and offering to wash the bakery windows in exchange for food and coffee.

Shelby had given him a job instead, and now he was in college, studying to become a nurse. She couldn't be more proud, and the last thing she wanted to do was worry him. "Just a headache, Zane. You know how I get when I'm tired."

"Then go home and rest. We can handle the bakery for another day or two while you recover."

"Are you kidding? This place is hopping. We need all hands on deck."

"All *capable* hands, and yours aren't. Not today," Dottie cut in, her blue hair vibrating with the force of her words. "You get on out of here. Go home and sleep."

"You're the one who called me to come in, Dottie."

"To fix the fryer. It's fixed. So, go."

"Ms. Simons?" A tall, thin man cut in front of the line of customers and stepped to the counter, his dark hair receding from a broad forehead.

"If you're a reporter, she doesn't have time for an interview," Dottie growled, and the man pulled a wallet from his pocket, flashing a badge and ID.

"I'm Sheriff Lionel Jones with the Spokane County Sheriff's Department. I have a few questions I'd like to ask if you have a minute."

"Sure." Shelby wiped her hands on her apron and stepped out from behind the counter, stopping short when she saw Ryder sitting in a booth near the front door. She'd been sure he was gone, but there he was, watching her with a dark, steady gaze.

"Would you like to do the interview here or down at

the station?" the sheriff asked, and Shelby forced herself to look away from Ryder and focus on the conversation.

"Here is fine. I have a small office in the back, or we can sit in a booth."

"A booth is good. I wouldn't mind a cup of coffee and a blueberry muffin, if it wouldn't be too much trouble. It's been a long night." The sheriff smiled, his gaunt, solemn face transforming into something nearly handsome and much more approachable.

"Go ahead and have a seat. I'll bring you something." Shelby grabbed a muffin and a steaming cup of coffee and set them down in front of the sheriff, studiously ignoring Ryder as she slid into the booth behind him.

"So, what did you want to ask?" She brushed imaginary crumbs from the table, restless and anxious to get the interview over with. Though the morning crowd had thinned, she was sure the lunch rush would be hectic, and she needed to make sure the staff was prepared.

"Mind if I take notes?" The sheriff pulled out an iPad from its case, and Shelby shook her head.

"Not at all."

"Good. I'm sure you've heard that Maureen Lewis's death may not be an accident."

"Yes."

"We should know for sure tomorrow, but I'd like to ask you about her friends and family. Was she close to anyone in particular? Did she have a boyfriend? A love interest? Any enemies that you know of?"

"No love interest. No boyfriend. I think she broke up with the last guy she dated over two years ago."

"What about her family? Were they close?"

"She has an ex-husband, who lives in London, and a son, who lives in Chicago. She doesn't have any contact with her ex, and I don't think she and her son are… were very close."

"How about enemies?"

"I don't know. Maureen was a good friend, but she could be tough to get along with. She was demanding and expected things to be done her way. Not everyone appreciates that."

"How about her work? Did she ever complain about it? Did she receive threats from anyone she was interviewing or writing about?"

"Not recently. At least not that she mentioned. She started a new project last month, and she seemed really caught up in it."

"Do you know what she was working on?"

"A book about the Good Samaritan murders." The case had been all over the news four years ago when a nurse named Catherine Miller was convicted of murdering eleven patients at Good Samaritan Convalescent Center.

"I'll check into it. I have a report that you saw someone leaving 21st Street yesterday morning?"

"That's right." She gave a quick description, then explained that she'd seen the same man outside the hospital.

"That was reported, too. Another reason I wanted to stop by and talk to you. You're sure it was the same guy?"

"As sure as I can be."

"We've already canvassed Maureen's street. There's no one in any of the houses that will admit to being out jogging yesterday morning. I'm going to call the state police. They have a composite-sketch artist on staff. Hopefully, we can get her down here in the next day or two. Will you be able to come to the station to work up the sketch with her?"

"Sure."

"Good. I think that's it. At the moment, it doesn't seem like you're in imminent danger, but be careful."

"I will be."

"I'll give you a call if we turn up any more information. Have a good day, Ms. Simons." The sheriff finished his coffee and took his muffin as he left.

Seconds later, Ryder slid into the booth across from Shelby.

"You're still here," she said, and he smiled.

"I still haven't had my coffee and doughnuts."

"Will you leave if I bring them to you?"

"Do you want me to?"

"Well, you *are* taking up space other customers could use."

"There aren't many customers right now."

"There will be." She got up and grabbed his doughnuts and coffee, making sure everything was packaged to go and handing them to him over the counter.

No more men.

She'd promised herself that after she'd walked out on Andrew, but she just couldn't seem to keep herself from looking deep into Ryder's eyes.

"Take the sheriff's advice, Shelby Ann. Be careful," Ryder said, his gaze sweeping over her face like a physical touch. Then he turned and walked out of the bakery, left her there staring after him.

"You going to work or going home? Because right now, you're just in the way," Dottie muttered.

"I'm working. We have two weddings next weekend, remember?" Shelby walked to the kitchen, irritated with Dottie and with her own weakness when it came to Ryder.

What she needed to do, what she had to do, was immerse herself in work, forget everything else for a while.

Fifteen hours later, she was still working as Dottie muttered about die-hard foolishness, locked the front door and left for the night.

Maybe she was right.

Maybe Shelby *would* be better off at home, but working kept her mind off all the things she couldn't change.

Maureen's death.

The cold-eyed man of her nightmares.

She hummed under her breath as she wiped down the display case one last time, rolled the last tray of dough into the walk-in refrigerator to proof over night. She'd make sweet breads from it. Sticky buns and cinnamon rolls and caramel-pecan rolls that she'd bring to church in the morning.

She walked into her tiny office, grabbing her purse from under the desk and catching sight of herself in the small mirror Dottie had hung from the back of the door. A mess. That's what she was. Hair escaping the clips she'd pulled it back with, skin pale and still slightly stained with mascara—she looked gaunt and exhausted and sickly.

And that's exactly how she felt.

A soft sound came from the front of the bakery.

Subtle, but there when there should be nothing.

No sound. No whisper of another's presence.

Shelby's heart thundered in response, her muscles tight with fear as she grabbed a knife from the kitchen and peered into the serving area.

Nothing.

No one.

Just the way it should be.

But the sound came again.

Not inside.

Outside.

And her gaze jumped to the floor-to-ceiling windows, the glass door.

The man standing there.

Medium height.

Medium build.

Something covering his face, distorting his features.

He leaned close to the door handle, seemed intent on something.

Slowly, the door she'd watched Dottie lock opened, the bell above it ringing. Shelby dived for cover, falling onto her hands and knees and crawling toward the back exit, trying desperately to find her cell phone in the overstuffed pocket of her purse.

Please, God, don't let him see me!

But she could hear his feet padding on tile floor, knew that he was coming for her.

Slow and easy, because he knew she had nowhere to run, no one to help.

Please!

But there was no help, nothing but the sound of her heart thundering in her ears and the tap of feet on tile floor.

She lunged for the back door, her shaking fingers barely managing the lock. Cool air slapped her face as she raced out into the dark alley behind the bakery.

Something snagged her shirt.

Someone yanked her back, dragged her deeper into the alley's black shadows.

"Give me your money!" he demanded, pulling the purse from her shoulder.

She didn't waste her breath telling him it was empty of cash. She just shoved into him, using a move she'd learned in the self-defense class Dottie had insisted she take.

He stumbled back, and she lifted the knife, her hand shaking as she did the unthinkable. Plunged it toward her attacker, intent on harming or killing or doing whatever was necessary to make it out alive.

He knocked her hand to the side, the blade barely grazing his arm before it clattered to the ground, curses spewing from his mouth as he dragged something from his pocket.

A gun.

"No more games, lady. We're going back in the bakery, and you're emptying the till for me. Any trouble, and I kill you."

"It's already empty," she said, the sound of traffic on the street beyond the alley a siren's song. All she had to do was run.

A hundred feet, and she'd be out on the street with cars and people and safety.

A hundred feet.

With bullets flying?

Or maybe not.

Maybe he'd go into the bakery by himself. Take what he wanted while she escaped.

Never get in a car with your attacker.

That's what the self-defense teacher had said.

Did the same apply to going in a building with him?

Should she fight to the death? Or go along and pray the guy wouldn't kill her once they got inside?

He grabbed her arm, his fingers cruel and hard as he tugged her back to the door.

She looked into his green eyes, saw intent and something else, something vaguely familiar and completely terrifying.

Coldness.

Emptiness.

The same look she'd seen in the eyes of the guy who'd been jogging near Maureen's place, who had stood in front of the hospital. Only he'd had ice-blue eyes. It couldn't be the same man.

Could it?

Panicked, she slammed her foot into his knee, kicking with enough strength to knock his leg out from under him.

He cursed, swung the gun and aimed it at her face.

No more time to think.

She dived, the explosion of gunfire nearly deafening her.

The bullet whizzed by her, its heat and energy blasting through the small alley.

Run!

She took off, zigzagging like someone in an action thriller. Only this wasn't a movie and it wasn't thrilling.

Terror fueled her, egged her on.

The mouth of the alley just a few feet away, beckoning her.

Another gunshot exploded.

Something slammed into her back, knocked the breath from her lungs. Momentum carried her out into the street. Car horns blared as she stumbled into traffic. Someone shouted. Darkness and light pulsed around her as she fell to the pavement.

Get up!
Keep running!

But life and energy seemed to pour onto the ground, spill into the street.

Blood flowing like a river, and she flowed with it as someone ran toward her, knelt beside her; a stranger with horror in her eyes, talking into a phone, screaming for help as Shelby flowed away.

SIX

"One-twenty-five. One-twenty-six. One-twenty-seven. One-twenty-eigh—" Ryder's phone rang as he neared the end of his workout, and he thought about ignoring it. Just two more push-ups and he'd be done. Finished for the night. But it was late for anyone to be calling. Late for good news anyway. Bad news, that could come at any time.

He grabbed the phone, glanced at the caller ID.

Chance Richardson.

A private investigator with Information Unlimited, Chance had worked with Ryder a few months ago. They hadn't hit it off. After working together to save a woman's life, they'd formed a truce and a friendship of sorts, but they weren't chummy enough for late night phone chats.

"Malone, here. What's up, Richardson?" he asked, grabbing a towel from the weight bench he'd set up in his living room and wiping his brow and chest.

"My mother-in-law just got a call from Dottie Jamieson. They go to church together. She mentioned your name, asked Lila if there was any way to look you up."

"Why?" he asked, worry rearing up and taking hold.

"She wanted you to know that Shelby was taken to the hospital a half hour—"

"What happened?"

"An intruder tried to rob her bakery, and he shot her in the process. She was alert enough when she arrived at the hospital to have staff call Dottie, but Dottie needs transportation to the hospital. She wanted my mother-in-law to take her, but since she mentioned you, and you're closer to the hospital and to Dottie, I thought I'd give you a call first."

"What hospital?" He didn't bother asking who'd shot Shelby, where she'd been shot, what her chances were. Those questions would come after he got to the hospital and made sure she was still alive.

"Deaconess."

"Give me Dottie's address, and tell her I'll pick her up on my way there."

Chance rattled off an address that was halfway between Ryder and the hospital. He didn't want to stop, didn't want to waste a second of time doing anything other than getting to the hospital, but he knew what Shelby would want, and that tied his hands and limited his choices.

"Tell her to be outside the house. If she isn't, I'm going on without her." He hung up before Chance could reply, tugged on a T-shirt and jogged down the four flights of stairs to the apartment complex's parking area.

It took less than two minutes to reach Dottie, but it seemed like an hour.

Seemed as if it took longer than that for her to climb into the Hummer.

She refused his help, of course.

Only her haggard expression and the tears on her cheeks kept Ryder from rushing her.

"You need steps on this thing, boy," she groused as he closed the door, but he could hear the terror behind her words, feel it pulsing through the Hummer as he jumped in, started the engine and sped toward the hospital.

"How bad is she?" he asked as Dottie urged him to drive faster.

"She called me, so she's alive and breathing. They're taking her into surgery. Stopping some internal bleeding. Taking out her spleen. My poor, poor girl." Her voice broke, and Ryder patted her bony knee, regretting it when she winced away.

"She'll be okay."

"I know that," she snapped, but her voice shook.

Ryder pulled into the hospital parking lot, forced himself to wait while Dottie eased out of the Hummer.

"You can move faster than me. You go in there, and you tell those doctors they better save my girl. If they don't..."

He didn't hear the rest of Dottie's threat.

He was across the parking lot and in the emergency room in seconds. A young nurse looked up as he approached the reception desk. "Can I help you, sir?"

"I'm looking for Shelby Simons."

"She's a patient?"

"Yes."

She typed something into the computer, slowly scanning whatever she pulled up, and he wanted to jump over the counter, look for himself.

Finally, she looked up, offered a compassionate smile. "She's still in surgery."

"Is she—"

"I'm sorry, sir. That's the only information I can give you. Go up to the third-floor surgical unit and wait there. The surgeon will be out to speak with you once Ms. Simons is in recovery."

"Well? Well?" Dottie hobbled in as Ryder jabbed a finger at the elevator button.

"She's still in surgery."

"Still in surgery? What kind of hospital is this?" Dottie shouted, and Ryder was tempted to slam a hand over her mouth.

"The kind that will kick you out if you cause a ruckus."

"I'm not causing anything. I'm asking a reasonable question. Shelby called me twenty minutes ago. Seems to me they should have patched her up by now."

Internal bleeding?

Removing a spleen?

Those things took time, but Ryder didn't say that to Dottie as they made their way to the waiting area. They both knew it, and the weight of their combined worry seemed to fill the small room.

Finally, he couldn't take it anymore.

Not the hushed expectancy of the surgical ward or the loud tapping of Dottie's fingers on the armrest of her chair.

"I'm going to find out what's taking so long."

"It's about time," Dottie grumbled as he walked into the hall. He'd track someone down. Find out something.

Wide double doors opened at the end of the hall, and a short round man appeared, his surgical scrubs loosened, a mask hanging from his neck. He met Ryder's eyes, his gaze filled with the same compassion Ryder had seen in the eyes of every doctor and nurse who'd tended him in Afghanistan.

He braced himself for bad news.

Braced himself but didn't want to hear it.

"Are you a relative of Shelby Simons?"

"A friend."

"I won't beat around the bush, then. I'm sure you're anxious to hear how she's doing."

"Yes." And if the doctor didn't start talking quickly, Ryder might be tempted to shake the information out of him.

"She made it through surgery. The bullet hit her spleen and nicked her liver, but we were able to stop the bleeding. She has a cracked rib, but that should heal well. Barring any unforeseen complications, she should make a full recovery."

"Where is she?" he asked as Dottie hurried into the hallway.

"Room 415. She can only have one visitor at a time, though, and the police are waiting to interview her."

"You go on up, boy. I can wait a few more minutes," Dottie said, something calculating and sly in her eyes.

"What are you up to, Dottie?" Ryder asked, but he was pretty sure he knew. Matchmaking. Just like Shelby had said.

"Just thinking that you'll be a lot better at tracking down the guy who shot my girl than I will be. You'll also be a lot better at meting out justice."

"That's a job for the police." But he wouldn't mind taking it out of their hands. Catching the guy, giving him just a little taste of what it felt like to be on the other side of the gun appealed to Ryder in a way that thrummed through his blood, made him desperate for the hunt.

He jogged up the stairs, trying to work off adrenaline, settle into a better frame of mind before he saw Shelby. His rage would do her no good.

Two police officers stood outside Shelby's door. They eyed him dispassionately as he approached.

"You a friend of the victim?" the shorter officer asked, and Ryder nodded.

"The deputy sheriff is in there. Once he's done—"

Ryder opened the door, walked into the room.

She looked small in the hospital bed, dwarfed by the sheets tugged up around her shoulders. An IV line snaked from her arm, and a heart monitor tracked her racing pulse. Pale. Everything. Cheeks. Lips. The only color in her face the vivid blue of her eyes.

Ryder walked past a tall, hard-faced officer, lifted Shelby's hand. "How are you feeling, Shelby Ann?"

"I'm shot up so full of drugs, I can't feel anything." Her eyes drifted closed, and Ryder met the officer's eyes.

"Ryder Malone." He offered a hand.

"Deputy Sheriff Logan Randal. Spokane County Sheriff's Department. I have a few more questions to ask Ms. Simons. If you'll wait out in the hall—"

"No."

"It wasn't a request, Mr. Malone."

"Nor is it a possibility," he responded, pulling a chair to the bedside and sitting down.

"Don't get yourself thrown in jail on my account, Ryder," Shelby mumbled.

"No one is going to jail, Ms. Simons. Except the person who did this to you, and hopefully, we'll have him in custody soon." Randal gave in without a fight. A guy who picked his battles. Ryder could appreciate that.

"I hope so, because I don't want him showing up at my bakery again." She opened her eyes, wincing as she tried to sit up.

"Hold on. You're going to rip something the doctors just fixed." Ryder pushed the button to adjust the bed, and Shelby winced again.

"You *are* in pain."

"Only when I breathe."

"I'll call the nurse."

"No, you won't. I'm already groggy from whatever they gave me during surgery, and I want to answer Randal's questions. If I don't, how are they going to catch the guy who shot me?"

"Did you get a look at your attacker, Ms. Simons?" Randal cut in smoothly, and Shelby shook her head.

"He had a mask over his face. Some kind of nylon thing that distorted his features. Very creepy." She shuddered, and Ryder lifted her hand, brushing his thumb over her knuckles, trying to warm her chilled skin.

"How about hair color? Eye color?"

"Not his hair, but I saw his eyes. They were green. That surprised me, because…" Her voice trailed off, and she shrugged, wincing at the movement.

"What?" Ryder asked, and she took a deep breath.

"This is going to sound completely paranoid, but when he walked into the bakery, I was sure he was the guy I saw yesterday morning. But that guy had silvery-blue eyes, so they couldn't be the same, could they?" Shelby's voice drifted off, her eyes closing again, and Ryder met Logan's gaze.

"Contacts?" he asked, and Logan shrugged.

"Or two different people."

"They were the same height and build. They even moved the same, but maybe I just thought that because I was terrified," Shelby said, trying again to sit up, her hospital gown falling off one shoulder, revealing creamy skin and a deep black bruise.

The rage Ryder had been tamping down boiled up and threatened to spill over. He tugged the gown back into place, his heart thundering with anger and something else.

A deep, deep need to protect Shelby.

To keep her from being hurt again.

"Do you have a security camera at your store?" Randal asked, and Shelby shook her head.

"No."

"Too bad. That might have helped. Tell you what. We have a team collecting evidence at the scene. Once we're finished, I'll come back, check in with you again. For now, how about you just rest? The sheriff already put in a call to the state police. A composite-sketch artist will meet with you as soon as you're up to it. Once we have the sketch, we can release it to the public. Hopefully, that will make it easier to find our perp."

"Okay." Shelby's eyes were already closed again, her breathing deep and even.

"Can I speak to you out in the hall for a minute, Ryder?" Randal asked.

"Sure."

Shelby grabbed his hand, her heartbeat jumping, the monitor beeping loudly. "Are you coming back?"

And he knew he had to.

Come back.

Again and again and again to Shelby's side.

Because there was something about her that called to him, and he couldn't deny it. Couldn't refuse it.

"Count on it," he responded as he eased his hand from hers and followed Randal into the hall.

SEVEN

She just needed to suck it in a little more.

Just a little.

Shelby exhaled every bit of breath from her lungs, squeezed in her stomach and *just* managed to close the button of her shirtwaist dress.

Stupid bandages.

She frowned at her reflection, unhappy with the tightness of the dress, but unwilling to wear one of her brighter-colored, looser-fitting outfits to Maureen's funeral. A funeral she was going to no matter what anyone said.

It had been one day since Shelby had left the hospital.

Four days since she'd been shot.

Time to step back into the world, regain control of her bakery and her life. Despite Dottie's protests, despite her mother's insistence that Shelby fly to California to recuperate for a month, Shelby was going to attend the funeral, and then she was going back to work.

But first she had to make it out the front door.

She slid her feet into two-inch heels, wobbled to the door, and grabbed the collar and leash from the coat hook. A neighbor had fed and walked Mazy while Shelby was in the hospital, but the poor little dog hadn't been happy about it. She'd chewed up both of Shelby's throw pillows and eaten half a roll of paper towels.

"Come on, Mazy. Today is the day. I know it's hard, but you're going to have to say goodbye to Maureen." She crouched to snap the collar around the dog's neck.

Now all she had to do was stand up and walk out the door into the bright spring day.

Too bad moving made her break out in a cold sweat.

Too bad her back burned and her rib ached.

Too bad she couldn't have downed a couple of the painkillers the doctor had prescribed, but taking them would have meant not driving, and she was going to drive, because she was *not* going to ask anyone for a ride.

Especially not anyone named Ryder.

Ryder, who'd arrived at the hospital every night at six. Who'd snuck her pizza when she'd moaned about being hungry for real food. Who'd sat by her side during the worst moments of pain.

Ryder, who made her insides shake and her brain turn to mush and who made her forget that she'd sworn off men.

No. She wouldn't call to ask for a ride even though Ryder had told her she could call for anything.

She was going to do this herself. Man up and face the fear. That's what Grandmother Beulah would have expected from the granddaughter she'd willed the Cadillac to.

Of course, Grandmother Beulah had never been shot in the back.

Shelby took a deep breath, opened the door.

Bright sunlight splashed across the lawn the neighbor's

son had mowed for her the previous day. Tulips peeked up from the dark soil of the flowerbeds she'd planted last spring. Everything was as it should be on her quiet street. No stealthy movement or unusual noise. Nothing alarming. The police had assured her that she was safe. That the man with the green eyes couldn't possibly be the guy she'd seen running from Maureen's street. He'd demanded cash, after all. Made it clear he was there to rob Shelby.

A robbery gone wrong.

Nothing at all to do with Maureen's murder.

But Shelby didn't feel safe.

She hadn't felt safe in days.

She hurried to Old Blue, her body screaming in pain as she jumped into the car, slammed the door and locked it. Mazy whined and panted in the passenger seat as she drove the ten miles to the funeral home.

Empty parking lot.

Nothing to indicate a funeral was about to take place.

Had Shelby come on the wrong date?

The way her week had been going, that wouldn't be surprising. She got out of the car anyway, leading Mazy across the parking lot and into the silent building.

An usher stood at a podium beside the door, and he smiled as Shelby approached.

"You're here for the Lewis funeral?"

"Yes."

"First door on the left, but I'm afraid you'll have to leave the dog in your car."

"She's Maureen's dog."

"You'll still have to leave her in the car."

"But—"

"Ma'am, I'm sorry, but that's our rule. Some people

are allergic to dogs, and we don't want to make this time any more stressful than it needs to be."

He had a point, and Shelby would have given in quickly if she weren't so terrified of going back outside.

"Maureen would have wanted her here."

"The deceased left no indication of that, so I'm afraid we'll have to follow policy." His smile had tightened, but he managed to keep it intact. Good for him.

Shelby's smile had failed four days ago.

It didn't seem ready to return.

Fear hummed along her nerves as she walked Mazy back to the car, her eyes scanning the street, the trees that sheltered the lush lawn, the people who strolled along the sidewalk. *He* could be there. He *might* be there. She'd never know it, either. Not until the bullet slammed into her body, carried her along its trajectory.

Killed her.

It would be quite an irony to die in the parking lot of a funeral home.

That kind of dramatic, over-the-top end was exactly what Grandmother Beulah would have preferred to having a heart attack in her sleep.

Shelby, on the other hand, was hoping for exactly the type of end her grandmother had gotten. Peaceful. Quiet. Slipping easily into the next part of her journey at the ripe old age of ninety-seven.

"Get in, Mazy." She patted the seat of the Caddy, but Mazy dug in her paws and refused to budge.

"Mazy, really. I'm not supposed to lift you, so hop in." She leaned down and nudged the dog. Pain edged in over the fear, churning in her stomach. She felt sick and dizzy, her skin clammy, her heart chugging too fast and hard.

So, maybe she wouldn't die in the parking lot.

Maybe she'd just pass out.

"Please, Mazy. Cooperate." She slid her hands under the dog's belly, lifted her, felt the burn of stitched skin stretching as she tried to get to her feet.

"You're not supposed to be lifting anything." Ryder's voice spilled into the quiet afternoon, and she looked up, nearly fell over as she tried to see his face.

"Where did you come from?"

"My apartment." He grabbed her arm, tugged her to her feet, somehow pulling Mazy from her hands and setting her on the Caddy's seat at the same time.

"That's not what I mean, and you know it," she grumbled, closing the door on Mazy's excited yaps.

"Grumpy, Shelby Ann?" He watched her through deep brown eyes, his dark suit perfectly tailored to his muscular frame, and Shelby's whole being sighed with longing. She wanted to step into his arms, tell him how scared she was, how glad that he'd shown up.

"I'm tired, and I'm in pain, and I don't feel like dealing with Mazy." She turned from his dark gaze, wobbled across the parking lot. She should have worn sneakers. They'd have made for a more dignified retreat.

"You're tired and in pain, because you're supposed to be home in bed recovering. What you're not supposed to be doing is driving. Fortunately, my apartment is close enough to walk here, so I can drive us both to the cemetery in your car." Ryder opened the door, the spicy, masculine scent of his cologne drifting around Shelby. She resisted the urge to inhale deeply, pull in his scent and make a memory of it.

"You've been talking to Dottie."

"She called because she was sure you'd show up here.

I was sure you'd use a little common sense and stay home."

"How could I? Today is Maureen's funeral. We were friends."

"She has other friends." Ryder offered a curt nod in the direction of the usher, nudged Shelby into the viewing room.

"I know," Shelby whispered, because she felt compelled to keep her voice down as people trickled in, walked by the closed casket and stared at the flower arrangements.

"Anyone here you know?" Ryder asked, and Shelby shook her head.

"Maureen and I didn't run in the same social circles."

"How'd you meet, then?" He walked her to a row of chairs and urged her to sit.

"She came into the bakery the day I opened and bought every one of my cheese Danishes. They were her favorite. She came in every week after that. Five years, and she never missed a Monday Danish run." Shelby blinked back tears as she stood and walked to the mahogany coffin. Flowers cascaded over the dark wood. Beautiful lily of the valley and gorgeous white roses.

Shelby touched a velvety bloom, her fingers caressing the silken petal. "I'm so sorry that I couldn't save you, Maureen," she whispered, and Ryder slid his arm around her waist, his touch light and gentle.

"Come on. Let's sit back down before you fall down."

"I'm not going to fall." But her legs were shaky, and she let Ryder lead her back to the chair, leaned her head down on her knees, the stitches in her back pulling, her muscles protesting.

"You really should have followed doctor's orders and

stayed home, Shelby Ann." He pressed a cool palm to the back of her neck, his rough, callused skin comforting.

The touch of a very good and very old friend.

But he wasn't even really a friend at all. He was...

Ryder, and she couldn't put a label to him.

Wasn't sure she dared try.

"You're looking at me like I've grown two heads," he said, and she realized she was staring straight into his dark eyes.

"Just wondering why you're here."

"Why wouldn't I be?"

"You didn't know Maureen."

"I know you," he said, taking the seat beside her, his long legs stretched out, his thigh muscles pressing against his dark slacks.

"Ryder—" She wanted to tell him that he needed to stop whatever he was doing. Stop the caring and the concern and the sweet words. Stop convincing her heart of something that could never be true, but the service began, music swelling from a piano near the back of the room, a few of Maureen's friends speaking fondly of her, a pastor speaking of eternity. Fifty years of life summed up in twenty minutes. The music swelled again, people spilling out to head for the cemetery. Tears dripped down Shelby's cheeks, and suddenly, she was leaning into Ryder's chest, his suit jacket muffling the sound of her quiet sobs.

Had she gone to him?

Had he come to her?

It didn't matter, because she was there, in his arms, his hand making small circles on her shoulder, his quiet murmurs filling her ear. "She would want you to celebrate what she was, Shelby. Not mourn for what she can't be."

"I know."

"Then stop crying." He brushed tears from her cheeks, his palm rough and warm against her cool skin, his dark eyes filled with sadness.

"Have you ever lost someone you cared about, Ryder?" she asked, because she wanted to know what made his eyes so dark and bleak.

"Four of my military buddies. We were SEALs together. Ten of us. Six of us survived the explosion that took their lives. I was one of the lucky ones. Come on. We need to get to the cemetery."

"Ryder, wait." She grabbed his arm, felt tension in his muscles, but his voice was gentle, his gaze soft as he answered.

"It was six years ago, Shelby Ann. I'm over the worst of it, but I do know what it feels like to lose someone you respect, admire and care deeply about. Come on." He tugged her to Old Blue and helped her into the passenger seat. She didn't bother arguing about who was going to drive. She was too tired, too sad. Because of Maureen. Because of Ryder's comrades. Because she wanted to reach out and touch Ryder's hand, tell him how sorry she was, but her throat was too clogged with tears, and she wasn't nearly brave enough to risk everything that reaching out might mean.

Hadn't she learned anything from her thrice-married-and-divorced mother? From her globe-trotting, heartbreaker sister? From her tough-as-nails grandmother? From scarred and tattered Dottie?

From her own experiences with the men that she'd

wanted desperately to believe in and who had proven just how foolish believing in anyone was?

Of course she had.

Rely on yourself, because men will only disappoint you.

That was the Simons family's motto, but she'd never really believed it. Not even when her college sweetheart had broken up with her because he wanted to date her roommate. Finally, though, she *did* believe it.

Andrew had convinced her.

She'd tried.

She'd failed.

She wouldn't try again.

Coward, her heart seemed to whisper as Ryder turned the key in the ignition and Old Blue roared to life. *Coward,* it whispered again as he met her gaze, smiled into her eyes. She ignored him, because she *was* a coward, and every minute she spent near Ryder just proved it more. She turned to stare out the window as he followed the funeral processional to the grave site.

EIGHT

Ryder surveyed the cemetery as the pastor bestowed a few last words on Maureen. He saw no sign that unexpected guests were watching the proceedings, but that didn't mean none were.

Maureen's name was synonymous with titillating true-crime tales, and there was no doubt some of the hundreds of mourners were fans anxious to see how the bestselling author's final chapter would play out rather than mourners sad to say goodbye. Fans weren't who Ryder was worried about, though.

Maureen's murderer was.

The person who'd bludgeoned her to death. Aside from the skull fracture, the medical examiner had found multiple broken bones. Forearm, ribs, cheek, jaw and nose. Ryder hadn't had the heart to tell Shelby that. Not when she was still recovering, but eventually someone would. If not Ryder, the sheriff or deputy sheriff. Both men hovered at the edge of the grave site, shifting restlessly as they eyed the mourners. Like Ryder, they expected the killer to show, and they were desperate to catch him.

More than likely, he was in the crowd, relishing the

tears that were being shed. Ryder's chest tightened at the thought, anger gnawing at him. The perp needed to be caught before he hurt someone else.

Before he hurt Shelby.

Again.

Blue eyes, green eyes, brown eyes. None of it mattered, because Ryder was absolutely sure the man Shelby had seen the morning of Maureen's death was the man who'd staged a robbery at Just Desserts and shot her in the back.

He followed her as she placed a white rose on Maureen's coffin.

"Goodbye for now, my friend," she said quietly and moved to the edge of the canopied area. Sunlight poured over her, bathing her dark hair in red and gold and highlighting the deep hollows beneath her cheekbones. Dressed in a simple dress that hugged her curves, she looked beautiful and heartbroken. She hadn't been sleeping well, hadn't been eating well. She didn't need to say it for Ryder to know the truth.

"You okay?" he asked, sliding both arms around her waist and tugging her a step closer. Her eyes widened, but she didn't protest or try to move away.

"I will be. I saw the sheriff and deputy sheriff. Are they hoping Maureen's murderer will show up?"

"Yes."

"Do you think he will?"

"I *hope* he will."

"He's not here now. At least, the guy I saw jogging that morning isn't here." She stepped away, breaking the contact between them.

"You're sure?"

"Positive. I've been looking, too." She shivered, rubbing her arms against a chill Ryder couldn't feel.

"Here." He started to pull off his jacket, but Shelby grabbed his arm.

"Don't. The last thing this crowd needs is to see a bulked-up Hercules wearing a gun and holster."

"'Bulked-up Hercules'? I'm not sure if I should be flattered or insulted by that, Shelby Ann."

"Neither." She blushed, the pink tinge in her cheeks only adding to her beauty.

"Then what should I be?"

"Impressed that I came up with such a clever description? Look, there's Maureen's son." She quickly changed the subject, gesturing to the casket and a tall, dark-haired man that stood before it, his head bowed, his eyes hidden by dark glasses. Early to midthirties. Close to six feet. Maybe a hundred and eighty pounds. He looked too old to be a fifty-year-old woman's son.

"She must have had him young."

"She was seventeen. His father was her first and only marriage. She had Hunter six months later. A big mistake, she said."

"The marriage or her son?"

"The marriage mostly. Although things were strained between Maureen and Hunter. She wasn't a very maternal person, and I think she caused some damage to their relationship when he was younger. She never told me the details, though."

"Maybe we should ask Hunter." He took a step toward the man, but Shelby grabbed his arm.

"You can't ask a man why he didn't get along with his mother while he's at her funeral," she hissed, and

Ryder almost told her she was wrong. He could ask any-one anything if it meant keeping Shelby safe.

Maureen had been killed.

Someone knew why.

Someone knew who.

Maybe Maureen's son was the key.

"Come on. I need to get home and get changed. I want to go to the bakery to check—"

"You're not going to the bakery, Shelby," he said.

"Of course I am."

"Dottie and the rest of your staff have everything under control, and you'll only be in the way."

"Is that what Dottie told you to say?"

"Only if you insisted on going back to work before you were ready."

"I *am* ready. Maybe not physically," she admitted reluctantly. "But mentally."

"You need to be both."

"You don't understand, Ryder." She started walking back to Old Blue, her movements stiff with pain.

"Then explain it to me."

"I'm afraid. When I'm awake, I think I see the guy who shot me around every corner and lurking in every shadow. When I'm asleep, he's there, too. Always at the bakery, rushing at me with a gun. Every day I don't go back and prove to myself that he's gone, the fear builds. Eventually, it will be so big that I won't be able to go back, no matter how much I want to."

"Okay."

"Okay what?" She leaned against Blue's door, her eyes shadowed and wary.

"I'll take you to the bakery. Dottie will probably cut off my doughnut supply for life, but I'll take you."

"Thanks, but I don't need you to take me. I can manage on my own. It's what I've been doing for years." She offered her first real smile of the day, her eyes crinkling at the corners, a dimple flashing in her left cheek. He ran a finger over it, watching as her pupils dilated.

"You're beautiful when you smile."

"You've been using that word a lot today," she responded, getting in Blue's passenger seat, wincing as she settled in.

"*Beautiful?* What's wrong with that?"

"I'm not beautiful, Ryder. Cute, maybe. Pretty, sometimes. Beautiful, never."

"Who told you that?" he asked as he got into driver's seat and started Blue's engine.

"I lived with three beautiful people growing up. My grandmother was an actress. My mother was Miss California. My sister is a runway model. I know beautiful, and I'm not. It doesn't bother me, so you don't have to try to convince me that I am what I'm not."

"Okay."

"You're the king of the one-word responses today, you know that?"

"And you're still grumpy."

"True." She sighed, leaning her head back against the leather seat. "I am also letting you drive again, and I'm not sure why."

"Because Old Blue runs better for me?"

"She does *not* run better for you. The weather is warming up. She always starts better in warm weather. The thing is…" Her eyes widened. "That's him!" she shouted, grabbing Ryder's arm and leaning so far toward him, she was nearly in his lap. Silky hair brushed his chin, her hand clutched his thigh, and he was pretty sure lava flowed in his belly.

"Who?"

"The guy I saw the morning Maureen died. He's right there! Near that statue!" She jabbed her finger past his nose.

Several large statues decorated grave sites. Ryder scanned marble angels and stone figures, his attention caught by movement near the edge of the cemetery. Nothing concrete. Just the feeling that something had scurried out of sight. Could have been a bird or a squirrel, but the hair on the back of his neck stood on end, his pulse jumping with adrenaline. Thick trees offered plenty of cover for anyone who might have been there, their spring-rich branches shielding the area beyond.

"Stay in the car. I'm going to get the sheriff and Randal and take a look."

"You can't—"

"Stay!"

"I'm not a dog, Ryder, and I don—"

He shut the door, left her talking to Mazy.

He ran toward the statue, gesturing for the sheriff and deputy sheriff to follow. They sprinted toward him, catching up as he reached the edge of the cemetery.

"Did you see something?" Logan asked.

"Shelby saw our perp. He was behind this statue." Ryder ducked behind the stone angel, searching the ground for signs that someone had been there.

The sheriff crouched beside him, pointed at compressed grass and a lone broken dandelion. "Looks like someone was here, but it could have been anyone."

"Shelby is convinced it was him." Ryder scanned the copse of trees, moving around thick trunks and out into an open field, Logan right behind him. Thick woods were to the left, vivid green grass to the right and ahead, sloping down to a narrow road that wove its way through the cemetery grounds. Several cars sat near the edge of the road and a few mourners dotted the area. None caught his attention. No one moved quickly. Nothing indicated that someone had run down the slope and jumped in a car.

"The sheriff is heading back to check on Shelby. How about we split up, Malone? You want to check out the cemetery or the woods?"

"I'll try the woods." It seemed like the most likely path for a perp who wanted to disappear quickly, and Ryder wanted first shot at the guy. He'd work by the book, but that didn't mean he couldn't ask a few questions and demand a few answers.

The woods were as thick as he'd imagined, tree trunk pressed close to tree trunk, the heavy scent of pine and decaying leaves filling his nose as he moved. Adrenaline pumped through him, his heart beating quickly in response.

Something moved in the shadows to his left, and he froze, his hand dropping to the gun concealed beneath his suit jacket. Another movement. Subtle. Stealthy. Coming toward him rather than moving away.

Ryder stepped behind a thick pine. Waiting.

A branch broke.

Fabric brushed against tree branches.

Close.

He tensed, holding back, practicing the patience he'd learned as a SEAL. Breath stilling, pulse slowing, everything in him ready and waiting.

Shuffled footfall. Leaves displaced. A hint of movement that let him know the time was right.

He lunged, his thigh screaming as he threw himself at the dark shadow, his arms tightening around wiggling, struggling humanity.

Hints of summer and sunshine floated on the air.

Vanilla and chocolate and...

Shelby.

"I told you to stay in the car," he nearly shouted, all his hard-won, hard-earned patience failing as he looked into her terrified eyes, imagined her lying in the trees, her body limp and lifeless.

"I was worried about you."

"Worried about *me?* I was a SEAL for ten years! I faced enemy fire more times than I can count. You should have been worried about yourself. What if I'd pulled my weapon? What if I'd shot you?" He eased his hold, smoothing his fingers over the red marks he'd left on her wrist.

"You're too careful to let something like that happen."

True, but that wasn't the point.

"What if someone else had been waiting in these trees? What if you'd run into the perp out here?"

"I didn't."

"But you could have."

"I know," she finally conceded. "I guess I just wasn't thinking straight. I kept seeing Maureen's house in flames and imagining you lying dead in the woods. I didn't think I could live with the guilt if something happened to you."

"Everything okay over here?" The sheriff tromped through the woods, and Shelby looked relieved to see him coming.

"We're fine."

"Glad to hear it. I was worried when I got to your car and didn't see you there. A woman in your position shouldn't be wandering around alone."

"A woman in my position?"

"You may have seen a murderer, Ms. Simons. And if so, he saw you. Seeing as how that's the case, you can't be too careful. Of course, you're fortunate in your choice of friends. I'm sure Malone can hook you up with a security system at your house and your business."

"Good idea, Sheriff. Why don't we go get started on that now, Shelby?"

"I don't need—"

"You'd be foolish not to take him up on his offer, young lady. Personal Securities Incorporated is one of the best security contractors in the country. Did you know that?"

"No." Shelby met Ryder's eyes, and he shrugged. It was true. His company *was* among the top five in the nation, but he didn't expect that to impress Shelby. She'd never needed high-level security, probably hadn't ever even thought about it.

"Well, it is. So, like I said, take him up on his offer. We're running patrols by your place, but a good security system will help our efforts. By the way, that sketch artist I told you about will be in this Friday. I'll send a patrol car to get you at ten in the morning. Does that work for you?" The sheriff continued talking while he led them back to grave site.

"That's fine." Shelby's response was sober, and Ryder wondered if she'd finally realized just how much of her freedom she was going to have to give up in order to stay safe.

"Great. I'm anxious to get the composite. If we're lucky, we may be able to match it with someone already in the system."

"I don't believe in luck, Sheriff," she responded, dropping into Blue's passenger seat, her face colorless.

"Well, whatever you believe in, you'd better pray it's good to you, because the guy who murdered Maureen knew what he was doing. He killed her and destroyed every bit of forensic evidence he might have left. You're the last loose end. I doubt he's going to let you keep hanging."

"I'll have a security system put in, Sheriff, and I'll be careful. Now, if you don't mind, I'm exhausted, and I really need to leave."

"Of course." The sheriff closed Blue's door and speared Ryder with a hard look.

"When is the security system going in?"

"Today."

"Good, because I've got a bad feeling about things."

"You and me both," Ryder responded, watching as Sheriff Jones made his way back to Maureen's grave site.

Empty-handed, but Ryder didn't think it was because the perp hadn't been hanging around. He had been, watching from his hiding place behind the statue.

Had he purposely showed himself to Shelby, or had he made a mistake?

Ryder hoped it was the latter. One mistake meant there would be others, and mistakes would make it easier to track the guy down.

He got into Blue, driving away from the cemetery, outlining the rest of the day in his mind.

Shelby's home security system first. Then the one at

the bakery. Maybe neither would be needed, but caution kept people alive.

In Ryder's business, it was better to overreact than to underreact. Better to plan for a war rather than a skirmish.

Because anything could be around the next corner.

A friend.

An enemy.

A booby trap.

He'd learned that the hard way, and his thigh screamed a reminder as he stepped on the gas and merged onto the highway.

NINE

Double-paned windows.

Floodlights over the front and back yards.

Motion-detecting security system tied directly to Ryder's company headquarters.

New locks on all the doors.

Shelby was willing to do all those things, but there was no way in the world—*ever*—that she was going to be escorted from place to place by Ryder. Her poor heart couldn't take it.

She had to put the brakes on, come to a dead halt before she fell over the precipice.

Her hand shook as she set a kettle on her 1940s stove. A hot cup of tea, a couple of painkillers and a few hours at the bakery, that's what she needed.

It was *all* she needed.

She was going to march outside and tell Ryder that just as soon as she finished her tea. He'd gone out there after he'd finished talking to the eight-member team he'd called in to replace her windows, set up her security system and put new locks on the doors.

One day's work.

That's what Ryder had said after he'd walked her

through the house, shown her every vulnerability, every weakened defense.

Next thing she knew, she'd been converged on by a vanload of buff men and women all eager to do exactly what Ryder told them.

She poured hot water into her teacup and dunked in a bag of ginger tea. She sipped the tea, her back aching with a ferocity that left her breathless.

She wanted to crawl into bed, pull the covers over her head and try to forget the past week, but she hadn't been kidding when she'd told Ryder she had to go to the bakery. Fear was an insidious beast, and it would consume her if she let it.

Stick your head in the sand and someone might just come along and step on it.

That's what Grandmother Beulah had always said, and Shelby had every intention of keeping that from happening.

She placed the tea on the counter and walked up to her room, trying to ignore the sound of hammers and power tools and voices. She was going to change into something that didn't cut off her breathing or dig into her stitches, and then she was going to demand that Ryder take her to the bakery.

It took a little longer than usual to change. Everything hurt. Her ribs. Her back. Her head.

Moving.

She pulled on soft, faded jeans that seemed just a little looser than they'd been the last time she'd worn them, and gently maneuvered a white T-shirt over her head. She had a clean apron at work, so she left the one she'd hung from the bedpost there.

She didn't bother with refreshing her makeup. She'd be in the kitchen anyway, tucked away from the world and all its complications. Just Shelby and the stuff she really understood, like yeast and dough and flour and sugar. Those things were so much less complicated than people.

She pulled her hair back in a headband, eyeing her pale skin and the circles beneath her eyes. A week of guilt and fear had taken its toll, but she was ready to put it all behind her.

Maureen was gone.

No way to go back and undo that.

Shelby had to move on.

Just like she'd done so many times before.

She'd perfected the technique.

Get up. Get going. Keep going.

Until one day, the thing that hurt so much didn't hurt quite as much anymore.

She blinked back hot tears, the sound of some sort of power tool ringing in her ears and vibrating through the floorboards.

Time to go.

Let Ryder's team do whatever security thing he'd demanded. She'd come home to a different house and, hopefully, bring a better mood.

"I'm leaving, girl. You be good," Shelby called to Mazy, who cowered beneath the bed, the noise and people too much for her.

Shelby wouldn't have minded cowering with her, but Simons women were tough. They faced their troubles head-on. They did not turn tail and run at the first hint of danger.

Not that any of them had ever been in danger of more than a hangnail.

She grabbed her purse from the kitchen table and walked to the back door, staring out into the bright afternoon. She needed to find Ryder and tell him she was ready to go, but he'd told her he'd be working outside, and she was afraid to leave the safety of the house.

She took a deep breath, stepped out onto the oversize deck. The yard looked as it always did, steeply sloped and dotted with tall trees. When she'd purchased the house, she'd imagined children sledding down the hill in the winter, rolling down it in the spring. Imagined spending hours on the deck, cooking and laughing and making memories.

Now all she could picture was *him*.

Standing behind the trees.

Waiting with gun drawn and aimed at her heart.

"Going somewhere?" The question came out of nowhere, and she screamed, turning so quickly, she nearly toppled down the deck stairs. She grabbed the railing to steady herself, and looked up into Ryder's deep brown eyes.

"I was looking for you."

"Here I am. What do you need?" He took her hand, gently pulled her back into the kitchen.

You.

The answer danced on the tip of her tongue, but she swallowed it down.

She did *not* need him.

She needed to go to the bakery to prove that she could, and then she needed to bake.

"I need to get back to work."

"I was hoping you'd change your mind about that."

"I didn't."

"Then I'll take you. I need to check on the team that's working there anyway."

"You already have a team at the bakery?"

"Yes."

"Dottie's probably having a fit."

"I told them to lock her in the walk-in if she gave them any trouble."

"You didn't!"

"You're right, but I thought about it." He led her through the house and outside. The new windows were already in, the lights were up. Aside from a guy sitting on the porch, staring at a computer screen and frowning, the house looked normal.

"We online yet?" Ryder asked as they walked past, and the dark-haired young man shook his head.

"Five more minutes."

"Good. Lock up and bring the keys to the other location when the team is finished here."

"Will do." He bent back over the screen, and Ryder hurried Shelby into Old Blue.

"What's he working on?" she asked as Ryder opened the door.

"Do you need your apron?" he responded, closing the door before she could respond.

"What's he working on, Ryder?" she asked again as soon as he got into the car.

"Nothing you need to worry about."

"If you're saying that, then of course I need to worry about it."

"He was tapping into an information database."

"What information and what database?"

"Sometimes a little knowledge is plenty, Shelby Ann," he muttered, pulling out of the driveway.

"It's my life, and I want to have some control over it."

"You have all the control."

"Then why is a team of people setting up a security system at Just Desserts before I've approved it? And why are *you* driving Old Blue while I sit in the driver's seat? And why aren't you telling me what that guy was doing?" Her voice broke on the last word, but she refused to cry. That, at least, she could control.

She hoped.

To her surprise, Ryder didn't respond, just kept driving, his hands loose on Blue's steering wheel, his gaze focused straight ahead.

When he pulled into the parking lot of Just Desserts, Shelby grabbed the door handle, ready to run for the kitchen and her baking supplies, but she couldn't move fast, and she'd barely pushed the door open when Ryder grabbed her shoulder, pulling her back into the car.

"Don't go away mad, Shelby Ann."

"I'm not mad."

"Liar." He smiled gently, tracing her frown with a rough, warm finger.

What was it with the man and touching?

Didn't he know that every touch seared into her soul, made rational thought nearly impossible? Didn't he understand just how tempted she was to let herself slide full tilt over the edge and into free fall?

Didn't he understand just how terrifying that made him?

"What do you want from me, Ryder?" she asked, and his smile fell away.

"For now? Just to keep you safe."

"And later?"

"I guess we'll both have to decide that. Come on. You need to get back into the bakery, and I need to check on my crew's progress."

"You still haven't told me what that guy was doing."

"I know. Do you think Dottie will hand over a couple of doughnuts without complaining when I get in there?" He walked around the side of the car, his hands gentle as he slid them around her waist and helped her out, supporting her weight when she swayed.

"Your plan isn't going to work, Ryder."

"Plan?" He raised a sandy eyebrow, his eyes glittering in the late-afternoon sunlight.

"To keep me off balance and distracted."

"If I were trying to distract you, we wouldn't be standing around talking about it." His gaze dropped to her lips and heat zipped through her belly, landed right square in her heart.

It pounded and flipped and danced, carrying her closer to the precipice she wanted to avoid.

"I'm not easily distracted, Ryder."

"No?" He leaned down, his lips so close to hers, she could feel the warmth of his breath. She wanted to close her eyes, sway toward him, let whatever would happen happen, but she wasn't that big of a fool.

"No. Come on. Let's get those doughnuts."

"You're running away," he called out as she tried to hurry to the bakery door, and she didn't argue, because it was true.

She was running as fast as her beat-up, stitched-up, aching body would move.

Ryder still made it to the door before she did, holding it open as she stepped into the bakery. The store overflowed with people who greeted her as she walked inside. She knew most of them by name, but she didn't pause to chat, didn't look over her shoulder to see if Ryder followed.

She knew he was there.

Knew it by the warmth that spread along her nape, the heat that seeped through her. She sidled past Dottie, ignoring her hard look, offered Zane a quick smile and grabbed a spare apron from a hook on the wall.

Vanilla.

Chocolate.

Cinnamon.

Sugar.

The scents were familiar and comforting, washing over her as she gingerly tugged the apron over her head.

This she knew.

This she understood.

This world of pans and baking products and business. This she could handle.

She'd let Ryder do his thing. She'd do hers. Eventually, the guy who'd shot her and killed Maureen would be found and put in jail. Life would go on. Ryder would move on.

And Shelby would move right back into her routine. Only, she'd have a new security system in her house and her bakery, and a new hole in her heart.

She frowned, working flour, water, butter and sugar into a sweet dough, her muscles tightening and protesting with every movement.

She didn't care, didn't stop, because losing herself in bread dough was a whole lot less painful than losing herself in Ryder.

She had to keep that in mind.

She *would* keep it in mind.

Two strikes and she was out.

There wouldn't be a third, but every time Shelby looked into Ryder's eyes, she couldn't help wishing there could be.

TEN

Maybe work hadn't been such a good idea.

Shelby winced as she lifted the oversize round base of Terri Anderson's wedding cake.

"It's already seven o'clock, Shelby Ann. You said you were leaving at four. Go home and let me handle that cake. I'll take the bus home when I'm done," Dottie groused, but they both knew she couldn't have lifted the cake. At seventy-eight, Dottie was just beginning to slow down. What she lacked in energy, she made up for in attitude, and she'd been shoving it down Shelby's throat since the bakery closed two hours ago.

"You've been here since three this morning. You're the one who should go home, and you know that Zane said he'd come back and pick you up when you were ready. You don't have to take the bus." Shelby panted as she hefted the second layer of the cake and slid it into the walk-in fridge with the other, a sharp pain shooting through her back at the movement.

She groaned, rubbing the muscles beneath her stitches but finding no relief.

"See? You've reinjured yourself."

"I'll be fine. I just need a minute." She wiped cold sweat from her brow.

"You wouldn't need a minute if you were home in bed where you should be."

"Point taken, Dottie. Now, call Zane, grab your stuff and go home. I'll work better without you standing over me." Shelby sighed as she lifted the final tier of the cake. The crumb coat would harden overnight, and she'd cover the cake in rich buttercream the next day.

No fondant for Terri.

Just a few dozen sugar flowers that Shelby had to craft before the nuptials the following day. She'd promised Terri she'd get it done when the bride had called frantic after hearing the news about Shelby's hospitalization.

Seventeen hours before she had to deliver the cake, and the flowers weren't made, the cakes had *just* been crumb coated, and she wasn't sure she'd be able to lift the tiers when it came time to stack them, but Shelby would finish.

It was going to be a long night.

She glanced at her clipboard, flipped through to the other cake orders. Just the one for the coming weekend.

Then three more for the following weekend.

By that time, she should be feeling more herself and less like a slug.

She grabbed the tools she needed, set them on the counter and pulled a chair from her office, ignoring Dottie's glowering stare. Usually, she didn't sit while she worked, but desperate times called for desperate measures.

"You're not going to make those flowers tonight. You're going to drive me home." It wasn't a question, and Shelby chose to ignore Dottie's grumbled comment.

"Are you ignoring me, Shelby Ann? Because if you are, your poor grandmother will turn over in her grave. The disgrace of knowing that her granddaughter wasn't raised well enough—"

"Dottie, please, go call Zane."

"I don't want that tattooed kid to drive me. I want you to."

"You sound like a spoiled child, you know that?"

"I'm way too old to be called a child."

"Not if you're acting like one."

"I'm an old lady, Shelby Ann, and I want family to bring me home. Is that too much to ask?" Dottie changed tactics, and Shelby smiled at her predictability.

"You want to ride with me, then you're going to have to wait, because I can't go home until these flowers are done."

"Do them in the morning."

"The wedding is tomorrow night, which means I'm already a day behind where I should be. The flowers need to be made and then painted tonight, because they need to dry for at least—"

"I know how long they need to dry, girl. And I know that morning is plenty early enough to paint them."

"I don't like to do them the same day as the wedding, Dottie. You know that."

"I also know that you're not up to sitting here for the next five hours making flowers. You call Terri and tell her that the cake is going to have piping and icing roses. That'll be good enough."

"It's her wedding, and she's my friend. I'm not going to give her something less than what she asked for." Besides, the truth was she really didn't want to go home.

Not when she wasn't sure who would be there or what she'd find.

Bars on the windows, maybe?

Ryder making himself comfortable on her sofa?

Ryder.

At least he hadn't hung around the bakery. He'd walked her in, done his security thing with his crew, said something about a meeting with the sheriff and left.

He hadn't returned. Which should have been fine with Shelby, but somehow it wasn't.

She frowned as she rolled gum paste and started the first set of petals.

Five hours.

That's about how long it would take to make and paint the flowers.

By the time she finished, the sun would be down, darkness cloaking the street and the sidewalk and anyone who might be lying in wait. She shuddered, fear clawing at her gut, Dottie's soft snores drifting through the room.

Dottie's snores?

She glanced at her grandmother's best and oldest friend.

Head back against the wall, her bluish curls somehow deflated, her skin papery and pale, her bones brittle.

It wouldn't take much to break one.

Wouldn't take much to put a bullet through one, either.

What Shelby could easily recover from might kill a woman of Dottie's age.

Not a good thought.

Not good at all.

"Dottie! Wake up!"

"Huh? What?"

"You fell asleep." *Now you're going to get up and go home, so whoever tried to kill me won't kill you.*

"I was just resting my eyes, Shelby Ann. Now, why'd you have to go and ruin that?"

"Because, it's nearly eight, and I want to bring you home before the sun goes down."

"You said you weren't leaving until you were done."

"I changed my mind. Come on. Let's get out of here." Shelby winced as she stood to grab her purse, blood pulsing in the bruised flesh that surrounded the gunshot wound, reminding her of just how quickly the peaceful bakery could turn into a nightmare.

"You're taking me home, and then you're going home, too, right?"

"Then I'm coming back to finish the flowers."

"Then I'm not leaving."

"Of course you are, Dottie. All you're doing is sleeping anyway."

"I was not sleeping. I was resting my eyes, and if you'd wanted help, you should have asked."

"I don't want help. I want you to go home and get some sleep."

"Well, you're just going to have to keep on wanting, then, because I'm not going!"

"Stop being so stubborn!"

"Stop being so irresponsible!"

"What's irresponsible about trying to get my job done?"

"Nothing, unless it's going to get you killed!"

"You might both want to stop shouting. I could hear you outside." The deep voice cut through their argument, and Shelby whirled, her heart racing.

"Do you have to keep doing that, Ryder?" she asked, and he raised an eyebrow.

"What?"

"Scaring years off my life. At the rate I'm aging, I might not make it to my thirtieth birthday."

"No need to worry about that, girl. You're not going to make it to tomorrow if you keep acting like a fool," Dottie muttered.

"What are you doing here, Ryder?" Shelby asked, completing ignoring Dottie's words and her dark look.

"I came back to escort you home. I would have been here sooner, but I had some business I needed to take care of."

"Business that includes the laptop your employee was looking at?"

"You really are persistent, Shelby Ann. You're right. It did include that."

"What information did he find?"

"I've got a man outside ready to give you a ride home, Dottie. I'll stick around here and keep an eye on Shelby Ann, make sure she gets home safely." He completely ignored the question, taking Dottie's frail arm and leading her from the kitchen.

She went without a fuss, her shuffling footsteps worrying Shelby. Dottie might be ornery, but she was family, and Shelby loved her. If anything happened to her—

She refused to even think about it.

Ryder opened the front door, the sound of traffic and Dottie's grousing drifting back to the kitchen.

"You'd better follow through on your promise, young man. If you don't, I know people. I'd hate to sic them on you, but I will," Dottie said, and Ryder mumbled something Shelby couldn't hear.

The door closed, silence fell.

Good. That's exactly what Shelby wanted. Peace. Silence. To be alone with her tools and her gum paste and her thoughts.

She sat at the counter again, went back to shaping petal after petal, silence swirling around her, a living, breathing entity that should have comforted her.

She knew silence, after all.

Had lived alone since her mother, Laura Beth, had told her it was time to make a go of things. *You're eighteen, Shelby Ann. It's time to make your mark on the world. Try acting or modeling. You're not classically beautiful, but you've got something sweet and lovely that translates well into pictures.* That's what she'd said as she'd handed Shelby the key to a small apartment just off Rodeo Drive, her second husband hovering behind her.

Chad Mitchell had made serious money buying and selling real estate in Hollywood. He was a player. A risk taker. A womanizer. He was also handsome, charming, very, very rich and a decade younger than Laura Beth.

Shelby's older sister insisted that Laura had sent Shelby away so that she could maintain a facade of youth and keep her younger husband's interest. For years, Shelby had refused to believe it, but the older she got, the more she observed her mother's fly-by-night attitude and the easier it was to think her sister might have been right.

She sighed, not sure why she was thinking about the past.

Maybe Dottie's mention of Beulah had sparked it.

Beulah had loved unconditionally with the kind of scriptural love that Shelby was always striving for. Selfless. Sacrificing. She so wanted to live those things out in her life, but she also wanted to experience them. She wanted to know the beauty of being the recipient of that kind of love.

She'd spent years believing that God would grant her that desire, but His plans for her life had taken her in a different direction. No white picket fence. No kids playing in the yard. No husband to share life's burdens with. Just her work and her friends. It was enough. It had to be.

She was blessed, and she had no right to complain. Sure, she was going through a rough patch in her personal life, in *every part of her life,* but God would bring her through it just as He always did.

She might not have had a traditional childhood, but Beulah had insisted on church every Sunday morning when she was around, and Shelby had continued to attend when she wasn't, forging a faith that neither her mother nor her sister had understood.

Beulah had understood, though, and she'd encouraged Shelby to seek God's will for her life, cheering her on when she'd signed up for culinary school, offering her a loan when she'd decided to open a bakery, suggesting Spokane, Washington, as the perfect place to do it.

There Shelby was, in her successful bakery, a tray full of orchids beside her, her life full and somehow empty all at the same time.

She stood, trying to ease the cramp in her back. The muscles knotted, pulling so tight she couldn't breathe or move or even think. She grabbed the counter, cold sweat beading her brow, her breath coming in short, shallow gasps because deeper ones hurt too much.

"What's wrong?" Ryder stepped into the kitchen, and Shelby shook her head, because it was all she could manage.

"Try to relax." His palms smoothed down her back, his fingers light as they probed, found the seized muscles near her incision.

"Don't—"

But he'd already started kneading the spot, the pain increasing for a split second before it eased, his touch like liquid fire, melting tension.

Melting Shelby.

She shivered, tried to move away.

"Let me finish. If I don't, the muscles will seize again," he said, his gruff voice raking along her nerves, bringing them all to attention, and she knew she was so close to falling, she wasn't sure she was even still standing on the edge.

She shifted again, trying to move away from his touch. "Ryder—"

"That guy you saw on the laptop at your place? He hacked into the mainframe of the sheriff's department. The sheriff is worried that information has been leaking out, and he's hoping it's not leaking out of one of his men. He asked me to try to infiltrate the system, look up information about a case that's been open for nearly a decade, because he wanted to see how easy it would be for someone else to get in. My man was able to do it with no trouble at all," he said, his fingers and palms kneading and working.

"How is that connected to Maureen or me?" she asked, her words sluggish. She felt drugged, her muscles loose and warm. If she hadn't been standing, she might have closed her eyes and fallen asleep.

"The open case revolved around a serial arsonist who's been working in Washington. He's taken out several businesses in Seattle and Spokane, burned down a private school in Olympia. State police have connected him to at least a dozen fires statewide. His M.O. matches the one used at Maureen's place. Only, no one has ever been hurt before. The sheriff isn't sure if someone leaked information about the case or if the guy who killed Maureen is the arsonist."

"You could have told me all that earlier," she said as his hands slid to her shoulders, found the sore muscles in her neck.

"Client confidentiality, Shelby Ann. There are always going to be things I can't tell you about my work, but the sheriff asked me to share the information with you. He wants to keep you updated on the case, and he also wants to know if Maureen was working the serial-arsonist angle for a book."

"She never mentioned it."

"There's one more thing." His thumbs smoothed circles at the base of her neck, and she felt so limp, so liquidy she wasn't even sure she cared what else he had to say.

"What?"

"While I was at the sheriff's office, Hunter Lewis was brought in for questioning."

"Maureen's son?"

"He was in town the morning she died. Flew in the night before. Supposedly to surprise her on her birthday."

"That doesn't mean he's a murderer. Besides, the guy I saw didn't look like Maureen's son."

"The sheriff thinks it's possible he hired someone to murder Maureen."

"What? No way. They weren't close, but Maureen loved her son." Shock poured ice water into Shelby's veins, and she turned, found herself face to chest with Ryder.

She looked up into his dark chocolate eyes, got caught in the heat of his gaze. Her heart jumped, her pulse leaped, her palms itched to touch his razor-stubble-covered jaw.

She clenched her fist, stepped back, bumping into the counter.

"Careful," he said, his hands cupping her waist and staying there. "Maureen was worth a lot of money, Shelby, and money can bring out the worst in people. Even family. Sometimes, especially family. I'm planning to go to his hotel and have a talk with Hunter. I thought you'd like to come along."

She did not want to spend another minute with Ryder and his magical hands.

"I have to finish these flowers. They still need to be painted."

"I can think of better uses of your time." His gaze dropped to her lips, and something unfurled in Shelby's belly, begged her to lean just a little closer, stretch up on her toes, do something much, much more interesting than painting flowers.

"Ryder—"

"What are you afraid of, Shelby Ann? Me?" he asked, his finger trailing up her arm, resting in the hollow of her throat, measuring her fear in the frantic racing of her pulse.

Only it wasn't just fear that had her pulse racing.

It was Ryder and everything he represented.

All the things she'd prayed for so long for and had finally, *finally* given up on.

All the things her family had scoffed at, but that Shelby had wanted so desperately to find.

Love.

Forever.

Happiness in the arms of someone who loved her just the way she was.

She blinked back hot tears, slipping from Ryder's embrace.

"I think I would like to go see Hunter, after all," she said and then did the only thing she could think of that wouldn't lead to heartache.

She turned and ran from the kitchen.

ELEVEN

Ryder followed Shelby, slamming his hand on the door before she could open it.

"You're running away," he said, his body still humming with a need he wouldn't give in to, his hands itching to smooth the frown line from between her brows, trace the line of her jaw, cup the silky, smooth skin of her neck.

"And?"

"You don't need to. I'm not going to take something you don't want to give," he responded, forcing his voice to stay light, his breathing to remain even.

"That's the problem, Ryder. I *want* to give it." She brushed a lock of dark hair from her cheek, her hand shaking, her eyes darkly shadowed.

"Then what are you afraid of?"

"Being disappointed again. I have a track record, Ryder. Two strikes, and I'm out of the relationship game. Come on. I still have work to do tonight, and it's not getting done while we're standing here talking." She put her hand on the door handle, and he covered it with his, stopping her before she could walk outside.

"Maybe that's the problem, Shelby Ann."

"What?"

"You've been with people who make relationships into games. They're not."

"Right. Good point. Now, I really want to get out of here, because—"

"Chicken." He cut her off.

"So what if I am? We have bigger things to worry about. Like finding out if Hunter Lewis killed his mother and is trying to kill me."

"You weren't in such a hurry to do that five minutes ago."

"We've already established that I'm a chicken, Ryder. I'm also hungry, tired and just want to forget everything for a while. Make the cake for the wedding tomorrow night and pretend that things are just like they've always been, but I can't, so I'm coming to the hotel with you. Now, can we please go?" Her voice shook, and she looked as if she was on the verge of tears. He nodded, tugging her away from the door.

"Let me go first."

"So you can get shot instead of me?"

"If it comes to that, yes."

"No."

"It's my job to keep you safe, Shelby Ann."

"It's *my* job to keep me safe," she responded, standing as tall as her five-four frame would allow.

"Take it up with Dottie. She's the one who hired me and made me promise to guard you with my life."

"What?"

"Dottie hired me to be your bodyguard." For the price of two doughnuts a day for life, but Shelby didn't need to know that.

"I need to have a talk with that woman," Shelby muttered, her cheeks flushed pink. "But before I do, I'm *un-hiring* you."

"Sorry. Once I accept a client, that client is the only one who can terminate my services. Stay here. I need to make sure the area is clear."

He opened the door, motioning for Shelby to stay back as he surveyed the area. Dusk had fallen, casting long shadows across the pavement, but there was no sign of danger. Nothing to indicate they were being watched.

He signaled for Shelby to follow, shielding her with his body as she locked the door, her shoulders stiff.

"There's no need to be a sore loser."

"I'm too terrified to be a sore anything."

"There's no need to be scared. I'll protect you with my life."

"That's why I'm scared," she mumbled as he helped her into the Hummer.

"I can take care of both of us, okay? Everything is going to be fine." He skimmed a knuckle down her jaw, then forced himself to step away. She tempted him in a way he hadn't been tempted in a long time, but he couldn't afford to be distracted.

He hopped into the Hummer and started the engine, glancing her way when Shelby's stomach growled. "Hungry?"

"Seeing as how my stomach has already made the announcement, I guess it wouldn't do any good to deny it," she responded with a half smile that showcased her dimple and the pouty fullness of her lips.

"We can stop for burgers on our way to the hotel."

"A salad will be fine," she said as he pulled into a fast-food drive-through.

"You haven't eaten all day. You need more than salad." He ordered two cheeseburgers, a large French fries and a milkshake, handing Shelby the bag as he pulled away from the window.

Much as he would have liked to bring her for a real meal of decent food, they didn't have time. Hunter was expecting them, and Ryder had a feeling that he wouldn't wait around if they weren't on time.

"Go ahead and eat what you want. I'll take what's left."

"You know what, Ryder? You make it really hard not to like you." She sighed, pulling out a fry and biting into it.

"Is there a reason why you don't want to like me?"

"*A* reason? There are a million reasons, but it's already too late. I like you, and there doesn't seem to be a whole lot I can do about it." She handed him a burger half-unwrapped for easy eating. Typical Shelby, taking care of someone else before she took care of herself.

It was time for someone to take care of her, and Ryder figured that someone might as well be him.

He bit into the burger, gestured to the bag. "One fry isn't enough. Keep eating. You need the calories."

"Keep sweet-talking me, Ryder. I like it." She pulled the second burger from the bag. "Do you think Hunter will give us any information that will help us figure out who Maureen's murderer is?"

"I don't think he'll say much. The only reason he agreed to meet with me was because I was there the morning of the explosion. He wants to pick my brain as much as I want to pick his. Having you there will be a bonus for him."

"I don't think he hired someone to kill his mother.

If he did, why would he show up in Spokane the night before she was murdered?" Shelby said, passing Ryder a fry.

"Good question. One I'm sure the sheriff's department has an answer for."

"The sheriff didn't say?"

"He's not saying much about possible suspects or motives, but he did mention the Good Samaritan murders again. I'm planning to take a trip out to the state prison tomorrow to visit Catherine Miller. See what she has to say."

"Good idea. I know Maureen visited her several times last month. She was really excited about the story. *Angel of Darkness: Murders at Good Samaritan.* That's what she planned to call the book. She thought it was going to be her bestseller yet," Shelby said, tossing her half-eaten burger into the empty bag.

"Finish that up. You need the—"

"Calories? So you said, but I'm not hungry anymore." She sighed.

"Starving yourself won't bring Maureen back, and it won't solve her murder."

"I'm not starving myself. I'm just too sick to eat."

"Sick?" He pulled into Davenport Hotel parking garage, taking three spaces near the hotel lobby entrance, the Hummer angled so Shelby could exit close to the door.

"Not *sick* sick. Just…sorry that Maureen didn't get a chance to finish the book."

"That's the thing about life, Shelby Ann. We never know how long we've got, so we have to live it the best way we can every day," he said gently, brushing a stray curl from her cheek, his fingers lingering on her smooth skin.

She was definitely a temptation, but he had a job to do, a man to interview, and he couldn't let himself be distracted by Shelby.

"I'm coming around to your side. Don't get out of the Hummer until I give you the all clear." He got out before she could argue, rounding the Hummer quickly as he scanned the parking area. A few patrons walked between the cars, talking quietly, completely caught up in their worlds and their lives, completely unaware that a murderer could be nearby.

Ryder was acutely aware of the fact.

Acutely aware of every person, every corner, every dark shadow. Even before Dottie had hired him, he'd been determined to protect Shelby. Now doing so was his job, his mission, and he didn't take that lightly.

But there was something else building between them, and it couldn't be denied any more than the danger that stalked Shelby could be.

The time to explore it would come. Eventually.

For now, he had to keep doing what he'd been doing, focusing his energy on keeping Shelby safe.

State-of-the-art security system in place.

A team of operatives ready to provide 24/7 protection.

All the tools Ryder had available thrown into the mix.

He hoped it would be enough.

Prayed it would be.

He opened the Hummer door, ushering Shelby into the Davenport.

Shelby tried to keep pace with Ryder's long-legged stride, but she nearly tripped as they stepped across the threshold and into the Davenport's posh lobby. He didn't miss a step, his arm sliding around her waist, supporting her weight as he continued to walk.

She tried to move away, but he didn't release his hold, and struggling would only make a scene.

Not that they hadn't already done that.

Walking around with Ryder was like walking around wearing a giant placard that read Stare at Me.

Or maybe Stare at the Guy I'm With.

When Ryder was around, people noticed.

Not that Shelby cared much about that.

She'd spent her childhood walking in the shadow of her mother and sister. Both breathtakingly beautiful, charming and more self-absorbed than either was likely to admit.

Shelby loved them anyway.

She wouldn't love a guy *like* them, though.

She preferred men like Andrew. Good-looking in an understated way. More likely to blend in than to stand out. Unobtrusive but still confident.

Sneaky.

Two-timing.

Untrustworthy.

Being understated and unobtrusive hadn't kept Andrew from being those things. Nor had it kept him from being self-absorbed, selfish and self-serving. Shelby was happy to be rid of him. She only wished she'd kept the ostentatious diamond ring he'd given her when he'd proposed as a reminder of just how foolish she'd been. The ring hadn't been her style at all, but he'd been so proud of the large, gaudy diamond, insisting that it suited her.

Her first hint that his solicitous concern and eagerness to listen was nothing more than a well-staged act in a play he was creating.

Shelby would have preferred something less traditional.

Maybe a sapphire or ruby ring.

If Andrew had been listening to anything she'd said in the months leading up to their engagement, he would have known that. She'd accepted the ring anyway. Worn it for five months, feeling it like a lead weight on her finger.

Still, she'd worn it.

Until Andrew hadn't shown up for a friend's wedding, and Shelby had gone looking for him.

She'd wanted the dream so badly that she'd been willing to ignore the subtle signs that Andrew wasn't the man she'd thought, but she hadn't been able to ignore seeing him exchanging a long, passionate kiss with the Realtor who was listing his apartment.

She frowned as Ryder hurried her to the elevator, a gaggle of women whispering and pointing as they passed.

"Could they be any more obvious?" she said under her breath, and Ryder smiled.

"Jealous?"

"Hardly." She stepped onto the elevator, Ryder's hand firm against the small of her back. Making good choices in men wasn't high on the list of things she did well. As a matter of fact, she was pretty sure it was right there at the bottom. So, if she wanted to trust Ryder, if she wanted to lean on him, it was probably a mistake, and she most definitely should *not* give in to the urge.

Which was okay, because she was done with men.

D.O.N.E.

Done.

"You look upset. Are you sure you're up to this?" Ryder asked as the elevator doors opened onto the third floor.

"Yes. I'm just not sure Hunter is going to be happy to see us. Did you call ahead?"

"I arranged everything, and we're right on time for the meeting I set up with him. But that's not really why you're upset, is it?" He stopped walking, tugging at her apron strings to pull her back.

"Will you please stop tugging at my apron every time you want to stop me?" she asked.

"You're awfully touchy all of the sudden, Shelby Ann."

"Because I don't want to play games that I'm bound to lose."

He sobered at that, releasing his hold, but moving toward her, graceful and muscular as a jungle cat.

She shivered, but didn't back up.

Give a man an inch, and he'd take a million miles.

Another Beulah truism, but Shelby wasn't afraid of Ryder taking more than she gave. She was scared to death of handing it to him. Every inch, every mile of her foolish, fickle emotions, dreams, hopes.

"I already told you that relationships aren't games," he said quietly. Shelby nodded, because she was afraid of what she might say if she opened her mouth.

"Shelby Simons? Is that you?" The high-pitched, almost childlike voice could only belong to one person.

The one person Shelby most did *not* want to see.

She turned anyway, nearly flinching as she met Stephanie Parsons's perfectly made-up eyes and saw Andrew standing a few steps behind her.

Okay. So, *he* was the person Shelby most didn't want to see, but Stephanie was a close second.

"Hey, how are you, Stephanie? Andrew?" She smiled, but ice flowed into her heart. She might not want Andrew, might not care about him, but that didn't mean she wanted to see him at a hotel with his new girlfriend.

"How are we? We're wonderful, aren't we, dear?" Stephanie patted Andrew's arm, a huge diamond flashing on her left ring finger.

Oh, no.

No, no, no!

Andrew had *not* proposed and given her the exact ring he'd given Shelby!

Of course the scoundrel had.

"Better than wonderful. We're getting married next spring. We're here checking out the ballroom and reception area at the hotel. It's gorgeous. Just gorgeous," Stephanie continued, and Shelby wanted to gag.

"I'm sure it will be the perfect venue. If you two will excuse me, we have an appo—"

"Don't rush off just yet, Shel. We were planning to stop by your bakery earlier today to ask you a question, but didn't have the time." Andrew grabbed her hand, his palm soft and clammy and slightly disgusting.

She frowned, stepping back and bumping into the solid wall of Ryder's chest. Nothing soft or clammy or disgusting about him.

"What question?" It had better not be *Will you make the cake for our wedding?* Because if it was, Shelby couldn't be held responsible for her actions.

"We were hoping you'd make the cake for our wedding."

"You're kidding, right?"

"Why would I be? We're exes, but we're also friends, and you're the best baker in town. Stephanie and I want the best for our big day."

"We *aren't* friends, Andrew."

"Of course we are."

"No. We. Are. Not," she annunciated, but he still didn't get it.

"I know you're hurt, but try to put that aside and share this special time with us."

"I'll give you special." She attempted to lunge at them, but Ryder grabbed her apron tie again, and she boomeranged right back into his chest.

"She can't make the cake." Ryder cut in and Andrew frowned, his eyes flashing with impatience.

"And you are?"

"Ryder."

"Well, Ryder, I don't want to be rude—"

"I'm afraid I don't feel the same way. As a matter of fact, I'm more than happy to be rude. Come on. Let's go, Shelby Ann." He started walking, and Shelby hurried to follow.

"This will only take a minute. We just—"

Ryder knocked on a door, completely ignoring Andrew's sputtered protest as it opened and Maureen's son appeared.

Tall and handsome with pitch-black hair and sky-blue eyes, Hunter Lewis studied them dispassionately, light purple dress shirt wrinkled, his chin covered with stubble.

"You're Ryder, right? And you're Shelby Simons. I recognize you from some pictures Mom posted to her website. Best cheese Danishes in town, right?"

"That's right."

"Come on in. I'm sorry that our meeting will have to be quick. The sheriff asked me to take a polygraph test in an hour. My lawyer suggested I comply."

"You didn't want to?" Ryder asked as they stepped into the room.

"I have a business to run in Chicago. It's not running itself while I'm gone. Drink?" He lifted a decanter of amber liquid, setting it back down when they both declined.

"Yeah. Me, neither. Sad to say, alcohol won't fix my problems. So, you want to pick my brain about Mom, right? What do you want to know? If she was a good mother? If we got along? If I paid someone to murder her?" He directed the question at Ryder, but his gaze was on Shelby, his blue eyes seeming to be searching for something.

"I was wondering what you were doing in town the morning of her murder." Ryder didn't hold back, and Hunter shrugged.

"It was her birthday. I thought that was as good a time as any to try to mend fences with her. I guess I left it for too long."

"So, you *didn't* get along?"

"Is it possible to get along with someone who isn't around? Mom spent most of my childhood flying from city to city doing research for her books. When I was eighteen, she gave me fifty thousand dollars and told me to get an apartment and a car and find a job."

The story reminded Shelby of her own, and her heart went out to the young man Hunter must have been. Scared. On his own. No family to depend on.

"You did pretty well for yourself on that fifty thousand. You're CEO of a software company, living in a penthouse in Chicago's business district and earning a six-figure salary. Not bad for a kid who was kicked to the curb at eighteen."

"You've been doing your research, Ryder, and you're right. I did do just fine. I never took another dime from my mother, and I never planned to. Like I told the police, I don't need her money. Even if I did, I'd have rather begged on the street than ask for it. If they want a murder suspect, they're going to have to look somewhere else."

"Where else do you think they should look?" Ryder seemed completely relaxed, but Shelby could almost feel the energy humming through him.

"Back four years. The police need to reopen the Dark Angel case. If they find the real Good Samaritan murderer, they'll find the person who killed my mother."

"The murderer is in jail," Shelby said, and Hunter speared her with a hard look.

"Is she? Mom called me up a couple of days ago, almost manic with excitement. She was convinced a murderer was still on the loose, and she said she was going to prove it. I laughed. Told her there was no way she was going to be able to prove that a guilty woman was innocent. We argued, and she ended up hanging up on me. If you want to know the truth, that's why I decided to come out for her birthday. I felt guilty for upsetting her. Now, if you'll excuse me, I need to get ready for my polygraph test." He opened the door, tension oozing out of him as he waited for them to leave.

"I'm really sorry for your loss, Hunter," Shelby offered, and he nodded.

"Thanks. Mom was a huge fan of your bakery, and I'm sorry that you had to be dragged into this mess.

My mother was self-absorbed, but I know she wouldn't have wanted to cause you any trouble." He smiled, his face changing from somber and slightly angry to handsome and charming. A chameleon, but was he a killer?

Shelby didn't think so.

Then again, she hadn't thought Andrew was a lying, cheating creep, either.

She hadn't thought Andrew would kiss her best friend while wearing the tux he was supposed to marry Shelby in.

She hadn't thought either of those things, but they'd been true.

Going with her feelings wasn't a good idea.

She's proven that over and over again, but the thought of Hunter killing his mother just didn't seem to fit with what she knew about Maureen's life.

She sighed, following Ryder down the hall as the door clicked softly behind her.

TWELVE

"What do you think?" Ryder asked as he pushed the elevator button for the lobby.

"About Hunter?" Shelby asked, because she wasn't sure how to answer.

Maybe she wasn't the best judge of character, but she really didn't think Hunter had hired someone to kill Maureen. Still, saying it felt wrong. As if by giving her opinion, she might prove the opposite to be true.

Wasn't that how it always happened with her?

As soon as she decided someone was worth trusting, she was proven wrong.

"Who else? Did he plan his mother's murder and come here to try to throw the police off his scent? Or is he as innocent as he says? Come on, Shelby Ann. I know you have an opinion. Share it."

"Innocent," she said, because she couldn't seem to deny Ryder anything.

Which was another problem altogether.

"That's what I think."

"Really?" she asked as the elevator doors swung open, and Ryder pressed a hand to her back, urging her into the lobby.

She went reluctantly, bracing herself for what she knew she'd see.

There was no way Andrew had left without asking her about the cake again.

He wasn't the kind of person to give up that easily, and Shelby was sure he was lying in wait somewhere, probably smooching his fiancée.

A sight she definitely did not want to see again.

"The way I see things, Hunter would have to be a fool to have come here to throw the police off his scent. He's not a fool," Ryder continued, apparently oblivious to her tension.

Why shouldn't he be?

She shouldn't *be* tense.

Not about seeing a man she didn't love with a woman she didn't like.

"What's wrong?" he said, proving that he sensed more than she wanted him to.

"Nothing."

"Something."

"Okay. You want to know the truth? I'm sure Andrew is still lurking around here somewhere, and I'm not happy about it."

"Andrew the ex with the Barbie-doll fiancée? Why do you care if he's here?"

"Because he's going to ask me about the cake again, and he's going to keep asking."

"So, just keep saying no."

"You make it sound so easy."

"It is."

"No. It's not." She rounded on him, looking into his dark eyes and almost losing her train of thought, because maybe he was right. Maybe it really was that easy.

"Why not? He's your ex. He doesn't have any power over you."

"Of course he does. He was the last straw, Ryder. He proved what I didn't want to believe, and now he expects me to pretend he did me a favor."

"Don't." He touched her cheek, wiping away a tear she hadn't even realized had fallen.

"Pretend he owes me a favor? I don't plan to."

"No, Shelby Ann. Don't cry over someone who isn't worth it."

"I'm not. I'm crying for what he represented and what I'm never going to have. Dreams and forever and all that stuff my mother and grandmother and sister insisted I'd never find. I guess they were right."

"Maybe not," he said, his gaze lifting, his eyes focused on something just behind her.

"They're there, aren't they?" She started to turn, but Ryder wound an arm around her waist, his hand skimming across her lower spine and hooking in her apron tie.

"Don't turn around, Shelby Ann. Don't let them know you know they're watching."

"I don't care if they know, and Andrew is going to come over here whether I acknowledge him or not."

"Let him come, then." Ryder's lips brushed her ear, his rough whisper raking along her nerves, bringing every one of them to life.

"What are you doing?" she asked, her heart thundering in her ears, her body soft with longing for whatever it was he had planned.

Stupid, stupid, stupid.

But she couldn't seem to step away.

"Just a little evasive action. Nothing to be worried about." He tugged her into a cozy alcove, tracked tiny kisses along the line of her jaw, stopping at the corner of her mouth, his dark eyes staring into hers, all his amusement gone.

"Ryder—"

"Do you want me to stop?"

Did she?

"Do you?" he repeated, and she nodded her head while her foolish arms wrapped around his neck and pulled him closer.

So close.

Their lips touched, light, easy, but she felt the kiss more than she'd ever felt anything else. Felt it swirling through her, stealing away all her worries and fears and doubts.

Andrew didn't exist.

Stephanie didn't exist.

Hunter didn't exist.

The lobby, the people, the reality of where she was and who she was with and what she should *not* be doing didn't exist.

All that existed was that moment, that light touch of lips.

She sighed, pulled him even closer, let herself get lost in the moment.

"Really, Shelby. Is this the place for that kind of display?" Andrew's voice was like a splash of ice water, bringing Shelby to full awareness again.

She jumped back, her chest heaving, heart pounding, lips burning.

Ryder's kiss still swirling through her.

"She's not baking that cake for you, Andrew, so beat it," Ryder growled, his voice hard and just slightly uneven.

"I'll let Shelby tell me that."

Shelby tried to turn to face Andrew, to tell him what he claimed he needed to hear, but Ryder caught her jaw in his broad hand, his touch as gentle as a summer breeze, and kissed her again.

Kissed her as if he meant it.

Kissed her as if she'd never been kissed before.

Kissed her until she forgot all about Andrew and weddings and cakes and two strikes and being out.

She broke away, scared by the force of her emotions, scared of what she saw in his eyes. "You shouldn't have done that."

"I didn't. *We* did." He looked as shaken as she felt, and she wanted to deny that, deny the truth of his words.

But she couldn't.

Because *they* had kissed.

Right there in the lobby of the Davenport Hotel with a dozen people looking on.

With Andrew looking on.

A little evasive action had turned into something unexpectedly strong and real and undeniable.

She took a shaky breath, tried to clear her head, but it was impossible with Ryder watching so intently.

"We need to go. I've got work to do at the bakery. A wedding tomorrow night, and those flowers have to be done. I—"

"Stop," he said quietly, and she did, blinking back more of the tears that been falling since the day Maureen died.

"I can't do this, Ryder."

"You don't have to do anything."

"But I already did."

"It was just a kiss, Shelby Ann. It doesn't have to mean forever," he said gently, hooking a strand of hair behind her ear, his fingers searing her skin.

"But it could be?" she asked, the question slipping out before she could stop it.

"If you want it to."

"Don't say that."

"You asked."

"But I didn't really want to know the answer."

"Too late," he said, and she couldn't look in his eyes anymore, couldn't stand there listening to his deep voice and his easy words.

Couldn't, so she ran from him for the second time in twenty-four hours, her heart shouting *coward* as she beelined for the door.

Ryder barely managed to snag the back of Shelby's apron before she made it out the door. Slow and sluggish, his mind and body still wrapped up in the feel of her lips, the silkiness of her hair, he'd almost let her walk outside ahead of him.

Almost.

He'd meant to keep the kiss friendly and light. Meant to do nothing more than show Andrew and his insipid fiancée how little Shelby cared about their wedding, their cake, their presence.

He'd made an error of calculation.

Hadn't factored in just how deeply the kiss would affect him.

He wouldn't make another one.

"I really have to stop wearing this apron," Shelby muttered as he pulled her to a stop.

"That would be a shame, Shelby Ann, since it gives me something to grab on to when you're trying to run from me."

"I'm not running," she said, and he raised an eyebrow, waiting for the truth.

"Okay," she admitted. "So I *am* running, but I still need to stop wearing this, because I really do need to go back to the bakery, and you stopping me every five seconds isn't getting me there."

"This time I stopped you because I need to walk outside first."

"Right. While I stand here waiting for you to make the ultimate sacrifice."

"No need for dramatics. Just stay here until I signal for you to follow," he said, purposely trying to ruffle her feathers. Better to have her angry and spewing fire than embarrassed and shut down.

"I am not being drama—"

He walked outside, cool air bathing his heated skin and cooling his fevered blood.

Focus.

That's what he needed to keep Shelby safe.

Not kisses in hotel lobbies.

But he couldn't deny he'd enjoyed it.

Couldn't deny that he'd meant what he'd said.

One kiss could lead to forever if he and Shelby let it.

Sunset painted the sky in shades of gold and purple and cast long shadows across the parking lot. People strolled along the sidewalk, the busy shopping district sparkling in the dusky light. Not a good time of day to be out. Too many people. Too many shadows. Ryder scanned the area, searching for signs of trouble before gesturing for Shelby to follow him outside.

He hurried Shelby into the Hummer, closing the door quickly. She wanted to go back to the bakery to work for a few hours, and that was fine by him, but he had no intention of leaving her there alone. Even with a new alarm system and security cameras installed, she wouldn't be safe until the guy who was after her was behind bars.

He pulled out his cell phone, dialing a navy buddy who worked for the state police.

"Delaney, here. What's up?" Tyson Delaney grumbled, and Ryder imagined him pouring over a cold case, searching for new leads. As a detective with the Washington State Police, he had a reputation for solving cases others couldn't. The job kept him working late and running full tilt, which was probably how Tyson wanted it.

"You set up that appointment with Catherine Miller for me?" Ryder asked, knowing his friend had. When Tyson said he was going to do something, he followed through.

"Tomorrow morning at nine. I went and visited her myself a few minutes ago. The Spokane County deputy sheriff was walking out as I was walking in. Miller wasn't happy about so many visitors, and she refused to answer my questions."

"Hopefully, she'll be in a better frame of mind in the morning."

"Don't count on it, friend."

"I'll try not to," he glanced at Shelby, but she was staring out the window, probably trying hard to pretend she wasn't listening. "One more thing, Ty. What do you know about the serial arsonist who's been working in the area?"

"I know I was assigned the case six months ago, and I haven't found one new lead, and I know that the Spokane County Sheriff's Department just sent me information about the explosion that killed Maureen Lewis. I'm hoping I'll find a fresh lead there."

"You think the cases are connected?"

"The sheriff does, so it's worth looking into. I've got a dinner engagement in ten, so I need to go. Call me if you have any trouble getting in to see Miller."

"Will do." He hung up, pulling up next to Old Blue, the bakery dark and untouched.

"Thanks for dropping me off, Ryder," Shelby said as if he were going to let her out of the Hummer and leave her there.

"Who said anything about dropping you off?"

"Me. I need some…space."

"Because of the kiss?" he asked, and she shrugged. "Maybe."

"Tell you what, you can have all the space you need after we catch the guy who's trying to kill you. Stay here until I come for you. The less time you spend out in the open, the happier I'll be." He got out of the Hummer, not waiting for her response. In this instance, her need for space was superseded by the safety plan he'd put into place. He used the spare key to open the bakery, turning off the alarm before walking back to the Hummer. "Ready?"

"No." But she got out of the Hummer anyway, marching into the bakery and straight to the kitchen without saying another word.

"You're upset, Shelby, but this is what I have to do to keep you safe," he said as she opened edible paint and began dabbing yellow onto a flower.

"I keep telling you that *I* have to keep me safe. Not you. Not Dottie. Not anyone else." She dropped the flower onto a tray, grabbed another one.

"You're keeping yourself safe by letting experts help you."

"I don't want help. I want…silence." She painted another flower, her head bent, dark curls falling across her cheek and hiding her expression.

"Okay."

"No. It isn't okay, Ryder, because you're standing half a foot away, all big muscles and dark eyes and dependability, and I'm thinking about heroes and forevers and a dozen things I shouldn't be. Silence isn't going to change that any more than going back and undoing our kiss would." She sighed, setting the tiny paintbrush down.

"Two kisses," he corrected.

"I don't need a reminder."

"Neither do I, but like I told you before, I'm not going to take something you don't want to give. Those kisses can be nothing, Shelby Ann, or they can be a whole lot. It all depends on you." He looked deep into sky-blue eyes.

"That's the problem, Ryder. I want too much, and every time I think I've found it, it all falls apart."

"Wanting love isn't too much, Shelby. Wanting forever isn't."

"For me, it is. Before I got blown off my feet and into your arms, I was content to become the neighborhood cat lady."

"You don't have any cats."

"That's not the point. I broke up with Andrew, and I made peace with the fact that he was it. My last hurrah. I don't want to go back to wanting something I can't have."

"Shelby—"

"God puts us all on different paths, Ryder. This is mine." She gestured to the bakery. "My bakery, my friends, my family. I need to be content with that."

"You've forgotten something, Shelby Ann," he said quietly, and she met his eyes.

"What's that?"

"God puts us all on different paths, but sometimes people's paths converge, merge, become the same. When they do, He has a reason for it."

"I need to finish these flowers. How about we discuss this another time?"

"Fine. Let's talk about your work schedule instead."

"It's hanging on the wall in my office. Go ahead and take a look."

"Trying to get rid of me?"

"Yes." She placed another flower on the tray, smiling, and Ryder's gaze dropped to her lips, his thoughts skittering away so quickly he couldn't quite catch them again.

"Glad you're willing to admit it," he said, and then he turned and walked out of the kitchen, heading outside into the cool, crisp evening. He was leaving because if he stayed, he might give in to temptation and taste the sweetness of Shelby's smile, revisit those moments in the hotel lobby when all that had mattered was the yielding softness of her lips.

He leaned against the bakery's brick facade, getting ahold of himself as he rubbed the tight muscles of his thigh. Cars passed lazily, their drivers in no hurry to get wherever they were going. That seemed to be the pace of Spokane life. Slower than the big city he'd settled in after his injury. When he'd arrived in Washington State, he'd been sure he'd be bored within days, anxious to go back to New York and the frenetic pace of life there.

But he hadn't been bored.

Not even close.

He'd slipped into the slow pace of small-city living easily, let the distant white-tipped mountains and evergreen-topped hills soothe the still-raw edges of his emotions in a way New York City hadn't been able to. Still, he hadn't planned or expected to stay more than a year. He'd sublet his apartment with every intention of returning to it after twelve months.

He still planned to return, but the urgency he'd felt when he'd left New York was gone. A few more weeks, a few more months, didn't seem like such a big thing.

As a matter of fact, when he looked into Shelby's eyes, he could imagine staying for a lot longer than that.

After he'd ended things with Danielle, he'd thought he was done with the dating scene, finished searching for a woman who obviously didn't exist. A woman who wanted the same things he did, who valued the same things he did. Not fame or fortune or excitement. Faith. Family. Forever. Home and hearth and all the things he'd longed for when he'd been lying in the hospital bed wondering if he'd ever walk again.

Shelby could be those things to him.

He could be those things to her.

He knew it deeply and with a certainty that left no room for doubt, but *she* doubted, and he wouldn't push her.

Because she was Shelby, and he cared too much.

He walked around the side of the building, checking the perimeter, but not expecting to find anything. The perp would be a fool to return, and Ryder didn't think he was that.

Behind the building, an alley yawned, dark and quiet and empty. Two Dumpsters. A stray cat. Probably a rat or two. Other than that, nothing.

The scent of decay hung heavy and cloying in cool night air, and bits of crime-scene tape still clung to the building. If he looked, would Ryder see Shelby's blood staining the pavement?

The image of her as she'd been in the hospital, vulnerable and scared, filled him with anger and the dark, hot need for retribution. The law's responsibility. God's responsibility, but that didn't mean Ryder couldn't play a part. He'd go to the prison, visit Catherine Miller, dig a little deeper into the case Maureen had been researching.

Maybe the answers they needed lay there.

One way or another, he planned to find out.

And he planned to keep Shelby safe.

Keep her alive.

Maybe even keep her close for a lot longer than the time it took to figure out who wanted her dead and why.

Hopefully, keep her close for a lot longer.

Time would tell.

Time and Shelby, because Ryder wouldn't push her, wouldn't demand anything she didn't want to give. He'd bide his time, wait her out, see what the future brought.

For now, he'd just keep following the path God had placed him on and trust that it would lead him to exactly the place he was supposed to be.

THIRTEEN

She walked across the meadow, a bouquet of pink peonies in her hand, the sun kissing her cheeks and heating her skin.

There.

Just up ahead.

He waited.

Back turned, hair gleaming in the sunlight. Her heart leaped in recognition, her body humming with love.

She wanted to call out to him, but a train rumbled past, the shriek of its horn loud enough to rip the flowers from her hand and send them skittering across the meadow. She ran to catch them, her feet sinking into a pile of crumbled cake and thick white frosting.

She fell, hands clawing at empty air, a woman's scream filling her ears, filling her head, spearing through her body until she wanted to join in with the endless shriek.

She jumped to her feet, looking for the man who'd waited.

Gone.

Ashes in the wind.

But he was there. Sunglasses down low on his nose,

his cold blue eyes spearing into hers, pink peonies drip-
ping with blood held out for her to take.

"No!" Shelby screamed, coming out of her bed as
quickly as her drug-sluggish body could manage. Pain
stole her breath, but she just kept going, racing to the bedroom door, a woman's screams still echoing in her head.

Screams and screams and more screams.

No. Not a woman.

An alarm.

She pivoted back to the bed, fumbled for the bedside
light and turned it on, her brain refusing to process what
the alarm meant. Fire? Intruder?

Alarm?

Alarm!

Ryder's team. He'd assured her that they were on
the job. If the alarm went off, someone would be there
within two minutes. Hunker down and wait it out. Those
were Ryder's instructions when he'd walked her into the
house, shown her how to set the alarm and reminded
her not to set foot outside no matter what.

With the police running patrols on the quarter hour
and the alarm set up, Shelby had been confident she'd
have a good and safe night's sleep. So confident, she'd
taken two of the pain pills.

Now she was going to pay for it, because the alarm
was still ringing, help hadn't arrived and her brain was
working in slow motion, her panic muted and faraway.

Mazy cowered a few feet away, and Shelby scooped
her up, stumbling toward the door again.

She stopped.

Was someone out there waiting for her to leave her
room?

Was he?

The cold-eyed killer from her nightmare?

She backed away from the door, Mazy clutched close to her chest.

Two minutes.

That's what Ryder had said.

So where was help?

She didn't want to be shot again.

She didn't want to *die*.

So do something. Don't just stand here like a fool and wait to be attacked again!

No phone in her bedroom.

Cell phone downstairs in her purse.

Okay.

So, she'd lock the door and hunker down just like Ryder had told her to.

But two minutes had already come and gone, and the alarm still shrieked, and she was still alone. She needed another plan. A different one.

Get out of the house without being seen.

Out the window into the backyard.

It was the only way to avoid an intruder.

She locked the door, backed toward the window, expecting the old-fashioned crystal doorknob to explode and the door to open at any moment. Expecting *him* to be standing there, gun out, ready to finish what he'd started at the bakery.

Her stomach heaved at the thought, the pain medication she'd taken making her woozy and light-headed and sick.

And hot.

Really hot.

Not just hot, *roasting,* her drug-fogged brain insisting that she was about to fry like an egg on a hot rock.

She wrinkled her nose, inhaled. Coughed.

She didn't just feel as if she was cooking, she *smelled* as if she was cooking.

Smelled smoke. Saw it billowing up through the floorboards.

Fire!

The house burning around her, the alarm screaming, and Shelby cowering against a wall trying to decide if she should escape out the window.

Of course she should.

Now.

Before it was too late.

Open the window, hang from the sill, drop to the ground.

Easy as pie. Right?

Right.

"Please, God, let it be that easy," she prayed as she tucked in her cotton pajama top, cinched the drawstring of her pants and shoved Mazy down the front of her shirt.

"Don't wiggle. I don't want you to fall."

She didn't want to fall, either.

But she'd rather fall than roast.

She unlocked the window and opened it, shoved out the screen. Looked down.

Why hadn't she bought a one-story rancher like her mother had suggested?

Why, oh why, oh why had she insisted on a two-story Tudor?

Heat seared the soles of her feet, and she knew she was out of time.

Up and over the windowsill, legs dangling, Mazy wiggling, fingers clutching wood as the alarm shrieked in her ears. Nothing between her and the ground but air.

Let go.

Just let go and drop.

She knew what she had to do, but her fingers wouldn't release their hold.

Let go!

Her back seized, the pain from her injury doing what her mind could not. Her grip loosened, and she fell so fast she didn't have time to brace for impact.

Feetfirst, tumbling back onto her butt and landing so hard the breath left her lungs. Up again, bare feet on cold grass as she ran toward the neighbor's house, pain searing through her, fear spurring her on.

A dark figure lunged from the shadows, and she screamed, Mazy barking hysterically as Shelby pivoted, tried to run away.

Too late.

Arms wrapped around her waist, viselike and hard, a voice shouting words she couldn't understand.

She screamed again, spinning around, Mazy howling, the alarm still shrieking.

"Get him, Mazy! Bite him!" she shouted, but the dog just burrowed deeper into her shirt.

"You don't really want her to bite me, do you?" Ryder growled close to her ear, the voice familiar as sunrise.

"Ryder!" She clutched his shirt, her hands fisted in soft cotton. "My house is on fire!"

"The fire department is already here. They should get things under control quickly. Come on. I want you out of this yard and out of the line of fire." He ushered her around the burning house, and she let him, because she didn't know what else to do.

The entire house was in flames, smoke billowing into the predawn sky, and she wasn't sure how it had happened or what she was supposed to do about it or even if she was really awake.

Maybe the fire, the alarm, the smoke were all part of some horrible dream.

Only, she could smell the smoke, see the flames, feel blisters forming on the bottom of her feet.

"My house," she whispered as Ryder helped her into the Hummer.

"It'll be okay," he responded, his palm resting against her cheek for a second before he turned to talk to a tall, dark-haired man.

One of his employees?

Probably, but Shelby didn't want to be introduced, didn't want to do anything but lean her head against the car's seat and close her eyes.

Mazy whined, wiggling out from under Shelby's pajamas and licking her cheek.

"It'll be okay." She repeated Ryder's words, but she wasn't sure she believed them.

Houses didn't suddenly burst into flames. Not the way hers had.

Someone had started the fire, and Shelby could have died in it.

"Ms. Simons?"

She opened her eyes, looked into the face of Fire Marshal Timothy Saddles. "It's bad, isn't it?" she asked, and he nodded.

"We should have it under control shortly, but the fire

burned hot. Looks like it took out the entire lower level of the house. Do you have home owner's insurance?"

"Yes."

"You'll be able to recoup your losses, then, and you're alive. Things could be worse."

"I know."

"Did you hear anything before the fire began? See anything?"

"No. I'd only been home a couple of hours, and I was really tired. I took some pain medicine the doctor prescribed, and that's the last thing I remember until the fire alarm started shrieking."

"So, you didn't notice anything when you got home? No strange smells? No unfamiliar cars parked nearby."

"Ryder was with me. He checked everything out, and it was clear. Whoever set the fire did it while I was sleeping."

"The arsonist was fast and thorough, then. Knew what he was doing."

"What he was doing was trying to kill me. So, maybe he didn't know much, after all."

"Kill you or flush you out of the house. It's probably a good thing you went out the window rather than one of the doors. I'm going to talk to my crew. As soon as you know where you'll be staying, call me with your contact information."

"She'll be staying with me," Ryder said, stepping into sight, his blond hair mussed, his eyes flashing with anger.

"Do you have a card?" Saddles asked, and Ryder handed one to him.

"Call if you need to speak with Shelby, but she won't

be going anywhere or speaking to anyone without me or one of my team members. You can run things through the receptionist at my office, and she'll make arrangements."

"That's—"

"How it's going to be, Chief. This is the second attack on Shelby's life. We can't afford for there to be another." He closed Shelby's door, blocking out the rest of the conversation, but not the sight of the still-smoldering Tudor.

Her house. Destroyed.

Everything she'd worked so hard for in ashes, and she wanted to be okay with it. Wanted to embrace the idea that she was alive and whole and healthy, and that everything that had been lost could be replaced.

Wanted to.

But she felt hollow and empty, her stomach twisting as firefighters continued to battle the blaze.

Maybe it was for the best. None of the dreams she'd put into the house had panned out. None of the hopes she'd set her heart on while she peeled old wallpaper and removed layers of paint from woodwork had come to fruition.

The driver's door opened, and Ryder got in, reaching for her before he spoke. Or maybe she was reaching for him, pulling herself toward his broad, strong chest, burying her face in the soft cotton of his shirt.

He smoothed her hair, murmured quiet words that said nothing and everything all at once.

It's okay.

You're okay.

Everything is going to be fine.

And somehow, despite the smoke and flames and frantic fire crew, despite her fear and worry, while Shelby leaned against Ryder's chest, inhaled his familiar scent, she could almost believe it was true.

FOURTEEN

They drove an hour to go five miles.

Shelby only knew that because she knew the area, recognized River Walk Plaza and the swank apartment buildings there.

She knew she should be thankful that Ryder had whisked her away from the charred remains of her house, from the endless questions of the sheriff, from the sympathetic but nosy stares of her neighbors, but all she felt was tired.

"Is this it?" she asked, as he pulled into a parking garage.

"Yes."

"You said it was a safe house. Not a swank apartment complex downtown."

"A safe house is anywhere that you're safe."

"I know. I just pictured an old farmhouse in the middle of a barren field. Somewhere out in the open with armed gunmen standing at every window, waiting to shoot intruders."

"You've watched too many movies, Shelby Ann. Come on. Let's get inside and get you settled. We have a few hours before our appointment with Catherine. You should be able to get some sleep before then."

"I'm not going to be able to sleep," she responded as he helped her out of the Hummer.

"We'll see."

"I won't." She lifted Mazy, and Ryder scooped the dog from her arms.

"I'm not sure my apartment manager will be happy about having a dog in the building, but we'll give it a try."

"*Your* apartment manager? I thought this was a safe house."

"It's my place and a safe house."

"Maybe this isn't such a good idea, Ryder." She dragged her sore, blistered feet. She hadn't mentioned the burns, but maybe she should. Maybe that would keep her from staying in Ryder's apartment.

With him.

"You were fine with it an hour ago."

"That was before I knew you were going to be staying in the *safe house* with me."

"You're making more of this than you need to. You're not the first client I've brought here, and you won't be the last," he said calmly, taking Shelby's arm and hurrying her to the building, keeping his body between her and the parking lot as they moved.

The 1920s facade opened into a three-story foyer and a wide marble staircase, the art-deco architecture speaking of bygone eras and attention to detail. Against one wall, a bank of elevators offered a quick ride to one of four stories, but Ryder led her to the stairs, ushering her up to the second floor, down a quiet hall and into a stairwell. Another two flights of stairs, and Shelby was panting, her back aching, her feet burning and bleeding.

"This is it, right?" she asked as he opened a door and led her out into another quiet hall.

"Almost."

"Almost? Where else is there to go?"

"I rent the loft."

"Loft? You mean penthouse?"

"I mean loft. Used to be the maintenance man's place back when this was a hotel, so it's more like an attic apartment than a penthouse. This way." His hand settled on her lower back, his fingers brushing her side as he steered her around a corner and to an unmarked door. He unlocked it, gestured for her to walk up a narrow flight of stairs.

A very narrow flight.

So narrow, her shoulders brushed against the walls. Her feet rubbed raw on the cement stairs, but she kept walking because if she stopped, Ryder would bump into her, and then she might turn around, throw herself into his arms and beg to be carried the rest of the way.

Finally, she reached another door, a small, locked metal box attached to the wall to one side of it.

"Hold on." Ryder reached around, his body pressed close as he unlocked the box, punched a code into a keypad, then pushed the door open.

She stumbled into an oversize living area, anxious to be away from his heat and his scent and him.

Anxious to sit down, too, because her feet hurt, her back hurt, and if she thought about the embers of her house, she might just start crying.

"Glad you finally decided to show up," someone said, and Shelby whirled, her heart pounding as she stared into emerald-green eyes and a tan, handsome face.

"I took the long route. Just in case. Are we hooked

into the building's security system?" Ryder responded as he closed the door, locking Shelby into the loft.

"Hooked in and functioning. We have a clear view of the exterior perimeter and the lobby." The man moved with lithe grace, his slender runner's build powerful beneath a white dress shirt and black slacks. A gun holster hugged his chest and side, the black handle of a gun brushing his arm as he walked out of a small galley kitchen and into the living room.

"Glad to hear it. Shelby, this is Darius Osborne. He'll be working security detail with me tonight. Darius. Shelby Simons."

"Nice to meet you, Shelby. Sorry it has to be under these circumstances." Darius shook her hand, his grip firm and strong, his gaze direct. Comforting. That's the vibe Shelby got from him, but she also sensed a dangerous edge beneath his vivid green eyes.

"Nice to meet you, too."

"You're probably exhausted. Why don't you settle in? Get some sleep?" He took her arm, moving her down a small hall as Ryder bent over a computer set up on the kitchen counter.

"I'm not really tired." She limped into the room he indicated, stepping back as he closed shades and blocked off her view of the brick side of another building.

"Ryder has the place set up for situations like this, so you'll be comfortable for however long you need to be here. Check in the dresser and closet for clean clothes. They might not fit well, but they'll be functional." He ignored her protest, walked through an open doorway and turned on a light. "There's a bathroom through there. If you need anything, just let me or Ryder know.

We'll get it for you. No phone calls to friends, okay? No texting. No emailing. Nothing to give anyone any idea of where you are or who you're with."

"Like anyone would believe me if I told them," she said, and he frowned.

"You're in a very dangerous situation, Shelby. Someone wants you dead. If you want to stay alive, you'll do exactly what Ryder and I tell you to do. Go ahead and get some sleep." He walked out of the room, the soft click of the door sealing her in with Mazy and her thoughts.

Too many thoughts about too many things she had no control over.

As a matter of fact, it seemed she had no control over anything in her life lately. Not where she went, who she went with or what she did.

Be tough. Don't rely on anyone but yourself.

If her family had a motto, that would be it, and Shelby was trying really hard to live by it.

No more letting someone into her life. No more allowing another person to influence her decisions, determine her happiness.

No more putting her heart in someone else's hands.

Did putting her life in Ryder's hands count?

She sighed, limping across the room, the stench of smoke drifting around her, reminding her of the house she'd labored over, the dreams she'd built with every nail hammered, every wall painted.

Gone.

All of it.

She searched the closet and the drawers, found clothes in a variety of sizes, the tags still on all of them.

Darius was right.

Ryder *was* set up for this kind of thing.

Why wouldn't he be? He made a living protecting people.

She grabbed dark jeans and a T-shirt, took a quick shower in the white-tiled bathroom, washing away soot and smoke, cleaning her sore and blistered feet. Wishing she could wash away her fear, clean away her worries just as easily.

God was in control.

He'd work things out for His best.

That was the truth of the situation, so there was no reason to fret or worry or wonder how she'd ever run a business from Ryder's safe house, or how Dottie and the four teens who relied on steady work and paychecks would fare if she had to close the doors for a few days.

No, she shouldn't worry and fret, but she *was* worried and fretting and upset, and no matter how much she didn't want them to, the tears she'd been pushing away slid down her cheeks as she towel-dried her hair and lay down on the bed.

What if she did have to close the bakery for a day or a week or a month?

Would she lose the bakery?

Would the people she cared about be forced back out on the street, begging for food and places to stay?"

And what about the house?

She had a mortgage to pay on the pile of ashes that remained. Ashes of the house and of the million dreams she'd built into it.

Dreams of a normal family with normal kids and a normal husband. Not the glamour and glitz and showiness of Shelby's childhood. Just a simple day-to-day routine, all of it lived out with a backdrop of love and acceptance.

A soft knock sounded on the door, and she ignored it, hoping that whoever it was would go away.

It had to be Ryder or Darius, and she wasn't up to facing either of them.

The door opened anyway, and she closed her eyes, pretending to sleep as someone walked across the room.

"I know you're awake," Ryder said, the mattress compressing as he sat on the edge of the bed.

"I'm trying not to be," she responded, opening her eyes as he touched her foot.

"You should have told me you were burned."

"It's not bad."

"It looks bad from where I'm sitting." He walked into the bathroom, came out a minute later with a first-aid kit. "This may hurt a little."

"Then don't do it."

"Sorry, Shelby Ann. I don't want you to get an infection." He rubbed antibiotic cream into the bottom of her foot, and she nearly jumped off the bed, pain shooting up her leg.

"That did *not* hurt *a little*," she gasped, and he patted her shin.

"Sorry. The other one isn't as bad, so it shouldn't be as painful."

"I'll do it." She grabbed the ointment from his hand, sitting up cross-legged and examining her untreated foot. Two large blisters had popped and were oozing fluid, but things could have been worse.

She braced herself, smearing the ointment onto the blisters and loosely covering both feet with gauze, Ryder's gaze steady, focused and *distracting*.

"It's been a rough night. How are you holding up?" He brushed hair from her forehead, his touch just as distracting as his gaze.

"I'm okay."

"Don't tell me what you think I want to hear. Tell me the truth," he said gently, and Shelby's throat tightened.

"If I tell you the truth, I'll start crying, and then I might never stop," she responded, because she couldn't look in his eyes and keep saying that she was fine, keep trying to hide what she really felt.

"Crying because of your house?" His fingers trailed down her cheek, skimmed down her arm until they were palm to palm.

"A little, but I'm more worried about the bakery. The people who work for me depend on it being open. If I can't be there, I'm not sure how long they can keep it running. I organize everything, prepare the orders for the day."

"You'll still be able to do that. This is our base camp, but it isn't the only place I can keep you safe. I'll take you back to the bakery tomorrow. I'll go with you while you deliver the wedding cake. Then we'll come back here, and I'll take you back to work the next day. Nothing will change."

"Everything has changed, Ryder," she said, because it had. Her life. Her business. Her home.

Her heart.

He'd changed it, made it yearn for him in a way she couldn't be comfortable with. Not if she was going to keep it whole and safe.

"It's going to be okay," he murmured, his lips brushing her forehead, and she closed her eyes, afraid he'd see how deeply his tenderness affected her.

"I'm really tired. I think I should try to sleep now."
She moved away from his comforting touch and turned
on her side, listening as he walked into the hall and
closed the door.

A tear trickled down her cheek.

Then another and another until the pillow was soaked
with them, her cheeks and neck soaked with them.

Shelby didn't bother wiping them away.

There was no one to see.

No one but God.

Shelby was sure He understood.

FIFTEEN

Dawn came early in Spokane, the sun rising in a blaze of yellow-gold light. Ryder watched it as he worked kinks out of his bad leg, the computer behind him, Darius leaning over it. Three hours of staring at the monitor, and Ryder had seen nothing. Not a bird. Not a dog. Not a person.

Too bad.

He'd been hoping the arsonist would show up looking for Shelby, hoping he'd have a chance to take the guy down and bring him in to the police.

He grimaced as he rubbed a knot from his thigh and eased into a stretch that would lengthen the muscles.

"What time are you taking off?" Darius asked, and Ryder glanced at the clock, sweat beading his brow as he slowly increased the stretch.

"Ten minutes."

"I'll let Shelby know," Darius offered, and if the client had been anyone other than Shelby, Ryder would have agreed. He had another five minutes of easy stretching and exercise to do before he started the day.

But the client *was* Shelby, and he had a personal interest in making sure she was okay, an interest that went far beyond protecting her.

"I'll get her." He stood, ignoring the sharp twinge in his leg.

"I knew you would."

"Meaning?"

"You have a lot more interest in her than you ever had in Danielle," Darius answered, his gaze still focused on the computer monitor, but Ryder knew his friend noticed every twitch, every nuance. It was what had made him a good SEAL, and what made him a good security contractor.

"Shelby is…different," he said truthfully.

"She's pretty, but not as beautiful as Danie—"

"Is there some reason why we're discussing this?"

"Just curious as to what you're thinking long-term."

"All I'm thinking about is keeping Shelby safe. Everything else will work itself out," Ryder responded, and Darius grinned. The two had been friends since they'd slipped through inky darkness and made their way into enemy camps in Afghanistan together. Both had been forced into retiring after sustaining injuries during their service to their country. It had been a no-brainer for Ryder to ask Darius to join the Personal Securities team, but Darius knew him better than almost anyone, and he knew Ryder had more than a job on his mind.

Too bad.

Ryder didn't discuss his personal life on company time, and until Maureen's murderer was caught, every minute was company time.

"You can wipe the smile off your face, Darius. We

both have jobs to do, and we need to keep focused on that."

"Point taken, boss." Darius bent over the computer again, but Ryder didn't miss the amusement in his voice.

He ignored it.

Shelby's door was closed and he knocked, waiting as Mazy snorted and sniffed at the bottom of the door. He shoved his foot against the crack, and the little dog barked.

"Hold on. I'm coming," Shelby called out. Seconds later, she opened the door, her eyes shadowed and dark with fatigue.

"Did I wake you?" he asked, and she shook her head, silky brown curls sliding across her cheek and down the slim column of her neck. He knew just how it would feel if he touched it, could imagine himself giving in to temptation and brushing an errant curl away.

"I never fell asleep." She lifted Mazy, held the little dog to her chest, more vulnerable and less animated than he'd ever seen her.

"Why not?" He moved into the room, catching a whiff of berries and vanilla as she backed away.

"I don't sleep well when I'm away from home." She dropped onto the bed, patting Mazy rhythmically.

"Is that the only thing that kept you awake? Being away from home?" He dropped down beside her, and she shrugged. She'd found a fitted black T-shirt and dark jeans that gapped in the back, her creamy skin peeking out between denim and cotton, her bandaged feet peeking out from brown sandals.

"Yes. No. Maybe." She offered a brief smile and placed Mazy on the floor. "I guess you didn't just knock on the door to ask if you'd woken me. What's up?"

"We're leaving for the state prison in ten minutes. I wanted to give you a heads-up."

"You only planned to give me ten minutes to get ready to go?"

"Why not? You don't need to be fancy to go visit a felon."

"Not fancy, but presentable is nice." She limped to the dresser, frowning at her reflection in the mirror above it.

"You're always way more than presentable, Shelby Ann," he responded as Mazy nipped at his ankle. "I don't think this dog likes me."

"I wish I could say the same."

"You don't want her to like you?"

"I don't want *me* to like *you*." She paced to the window covered with a thick shade and stood with her back to Ryder.

"Because you're afraid of being disappointed again?"

"Because I have terrible taste in men, Ryder, and if I like you, there's got to be something wrong with you."

"There's plenty wrong with me. Just like there's plenty wrong with you. But that's what relationships are all about, right? Learning the good and bad about someone and accepting both."

"I don't know. I've been in too many messed-up relationships to know what a good one is."

"That doesn't mean this one has to be messed up."

"Ryder, every dream I've ever had has fallen apart, and I've gotten over it, but I don't think I could ever get over you if I started building dreams and…" Her voice trailed off, and she shrugged.

"Build all the dreams you want around me, Shelby Ann. They won't fall apart," he responded.

"How can you know that? How can I?"

"We can't if we don't try." He kneaded the tension in her shoulders, silken hair sliding over his knuckles as he leaned down, pressing a kiss to her nape.

She shivered and turned to face him, her eyes wide and wary as she met his gaze. "I think we'd better go, Ryder. If Catherine has the answers to everything that's been going on, we can't afford to miss out on an opportunity to speak with her."

She was right.

They'd better go, because they couldn't afford to miss the appointment, and because if he looked into Shelby's eyes for one more second, he might do something he wouldn't regret, but that she might.

"What time do you have to deliver the cake? The prison is an hour drive, and I want to make sure we get back in time."

"I need to be at the bakery by three. I've got to put the cake together, decorate it. I have a hundred things I need to do before I deliver it. Maybe—"

"No."

"You don't even know what I was going to say."

"You were going to ask if I could drop you off at the bakery before I went to the prison."

"I was also going to suggest that Darius come with me. That way, I'll be safe *and* productive."

"Sorry. Darius has another assignment. If he didn't, he'd be riding shotgun." He led her into the living room, grabbed a couple of protein shakes from the fridge and tossed one her way.

"Drink," he said, opening the second can and chugging the contents.

"I'd rather not."

"I'd rather not have you fainting from hunger."

She snorted but popped the lid of the can and sipped it.

"You ready to go, Darius?"

"Ready." Darius pulled a jacket over his gun holster and opened the door.

"I'll take the lead. First sign of trouble, and you take Shelby to safety."

"Will do."

"Maybe I should just stay here," Shelby said as they started down the stairs, her voice trembling slightly.

"Sorry. All my people are tied up with other assignments, and I'm not leaving you here alone." He led the way to the lobby, moving slowly, listening intently. Just because no one suspicious had showed on the monitor didn't mean they were clear. Anyone could be a threat. A friend. A neighbor. It was Ryder's job to prevent that threat from reaching Shelby.

He stepped into the lobby, scanned the area and moved to the front door.

"Stay with her, Darius. I'll get the Hummer."

He didn't wait for Darius to respond. He didn't need to. He only hired people he could count on to follow orders, people he could trust with his life, and he *could* trust Darius. Comrade in arms. Fellow SEAL. He'd give his life for a client if necessary. Ryder didn't want it to be necessary, but he knew it was true.

He surveyed the area outside the apartment, noting each person, each face, each piece of clothing. Early-morning sunlight fell across the sidewalk and gleamed on the windows of passing cars. If danger lurked nearby, Ryder didn't feel it. No hum of awareness. No hair standing on end. He got in the Hummer, driving up onto the sidewalk in front of the apartment, ignoring the shouted protests of a few disgruntled pedestrians as he opened the lobby door.

"Let's move fast." He took Shelby's arm, gesturing for Darius to fall into step beside them. Flanked on either side, Shelby seemed small, fragile and in desperate need of protection.

One bullet. That's all it would take, and she'd be lying on the pavement, her life spilling out.

He tightened his grip on her arm, adrenaline pulsing through his blood.

"Don't worry, Ryder. Everything is going to be fine," she whispered as she climbed into the Hummer, her words dancing on the cool morning air as he closed her inside.

He hoped she was right, because right at that moment they had only one lead to follow. If it didn't bring them to Shelby's attacker, they'd be at a standstill while the killer moved forward with his plans.

Catherine Miller had to be the key.

She'd been the subject of Maureen's newest project. There had to be a connection between that and Maureen's death. Ryder just had to figure out what it was.

He climbed into the Hummer, offered a quick wave in Darius's direction and pulled away.

He needed answers, and he needed them quickly, because he had a feeling the danger that was hunting Shelby was closing in. It might not have been waiting outside the apartment building, but it *was* waiting. For the right time, the right place to strike.

SIXTEEN

Catherine Miller didn't look like a cold-blooded killer.

She didn't look like the dark angel the press had portrayed her as, either.

What she looked like, Shelby thought, was a weary, wary and very tough young woman. Red hair cropped short, her face gaunt, she had a fragile build and hard blue eyes, her orange jumpsuit garish against her pale skin.

A guard led her to a chair and stood a few feet away as she settled into it.

"Thanks for seeing us today, Catherine. I'm Ryder Malone. This is Shelby Simons," Ryder began, his dark eyes completely focused on the convicted killer.

"If you're from the press, I don't do interviews," she responded, her voice softer than her eyes.

"But you allowed Maureen Lewis to interview you," Ryder said, and Catherine frowned, leaning back in the chair, blue eyes smudged with fatigue.

"I heard Maureen died. Are you family?"

"Friends," Shelby said.

"I'm sorry for your loss. Maureen was a nice lady."

"She was writing your story when she died," Ryder

said, and Catherine shrugged, her shoulders narrow and way too thin. A scar snaked around her left wrist, purplish against her pale skin.

"It would be callous for me to say I wish she'd finished it before she'd died, so I won't."

"You just did," Ryder pointed out, and Catherine offered a brief smile.

"Okay. You're right. I did. I liked Maureen, but I was also excited about what she was doing. It's been four years since anyone cared to listen to my side of things. She listened, and..."

"What?" Shelby asked, imagining Maureen sitting exactly where she was, looking at the same woman, seeing someone worth trying to save.

"She believed me. Which is more than I can say for just about everyone else I know." There was a bitter edge to her voice, and Shelby wondered if she were really as innocent as she claimed or if she were just a good actress.

"What did you tell her that convinced her?" Ryder asked, and Catherine stiffened, something dark passing behind her eyes.

"You think that whatever I said got her killed, don't you?"

"Did it?"

"I don't know. I hope not, but if it did... I warned her to be careful. I told her that he..."

"What?" Ryder leaned toward her, and she shook her head.

"Look, I'm not sure why you're here, but I suggest that you go back to wherever you came from and leave Maureen to rest in peace."

"Maureen was murdered, Catherine."

"That's exactly why you need to let her rest in peace." Catherine smoothed her spiky hair, her hand shaking slightly, the hardness in her eyes only partially hiding her fear.

"If you didn't kill the patients at Good Sama—"

"I didn't."

"Then who did?"

"Like I said, you need to let Maureen rest in peace." She stood, but Ryder held up a hand.

"Give us another minute, okay?"

"Why should I? It's not like you're here to help me. You're here to help a dead woman, and she's way past that." She sat again.

"We're here because whoever murdered Maureen has been coming after Shelby. It's imperative that we find out who he is and what his motives are. You're the key to that."

"I'm sorry, but I can't help you." Catherine's gaze shifted from Ryder to Shelby, and Shelby had the feeling she really was sorry, but that there was more she knew. More she might have said.

"Can't or won't?" Ryder asked.

"Does it matter? It amounts to the same thing." She glanced back at the guard, then leaned forward, her eyes blazing with blue fire. "Be careful, okay? You seem like nice people, and I wouldn't want you to get hurt."

"Why would we?"

"For the same reason Maureen was. She asked too many questions of the wrong person and found out something she shouldn't have. Maybe she just made him nervous. Whatever the case, she's victim number twelve, and we have no reason to think he'll stop there. Don't give him reason to strike again."

"He's already tried, Catherine. Give us his name so we can stop him before he does again."

"I've already said too much."

"You haven't said anything." Ryder's irritation seeped through his words, and Shelby put a hand on his arm, his tension radiating through her palm. He covered her hand, linking their fingers.

She didn't pull away.

Didn't want to pull away.

Catherine's gazed dropped to their hands, and she offered a smile tinged with sadness. "Like I said, it's better to let Maureen rest in peace. Let the police find her killer. It's the safest thing for everyone."

Something about the way she said *everyone* made Shelby's pulse jump. Was there someone Catherine cared about? Someone she was worried about protecting? If so, that would explain her reluctance to share the information she'd given to Maureen. "Is there someone you want to send a message to, Catherine? We'd be happy to help you if we can."

Catherine hesitated, glancing at the guard again. "My grandmother. She can't drive, and I haven't seen her since I was sentenced. She's out on our old homestead outside of Spokane, still trying to work the land. She says she's doing okay, but I worry about her. I'm all the family she has, and my friends disappeared after I was convicted. Would you mind checking up on her?"

"What's her name?" Ryder said, and relief washed away the tension in Catherine's face. She looked even younger than when she'd walked in. Twenty-six or seven. Not old enough to have worked as a registered nurse, been on trial for murder, been in jail for four years.

"Eileen Miller. Maureen went to see her once and said she was doing okay. That was our deal. I'd let Maureen write my book, and she'd take care of Eileen. It's a shame things don't always work out the way they should," Catherine said as she stood.

"What's her address?"

Catherine rattled it off, ignoring the guard, who motioned that their time was up. "When you see her, tell her I love her, okay?"

"I will," Shelby said, swallowing a lump in her throat as Catherine shuffled away with the guard.

"She's not what I expected," Ryder said, taking Shelby's arm and leading her away.

"What did you expect?"

"All the articles I read about the murders made her seem sweet and fragile. Florence Nightingale gone wrong."

"She *is* fragile."

"But she's not sweet or angelic."

"Maybe jail changed her."

"Maybe, but I don't think so. That tough edge she has came from a lifetime of hardship. Not four years of it. She seemed edgy, too. Like she wanted to say more, but was afraid. Maybe for her grandmother. Maybe for herself."

"I was thinking the same thing."

"Then I guess there's only one thing to do," he said as a guard led them back through the prison.

"What?"

"We go visit the grandmother and see what she has to say. Maybe Eileen will be more willing to talk than Catherine is, and maybe she knows what her granddaughter is hiding."

"I still need to get that wedding cake delivered," she reminded him, and he nodded.

"It's early. We should have plenty of time to stop by Eileen's place before you need to be back at the bakery."

They walked outside, bright sunlight warming the cool spring air, its heat making Shelby feel even more sluggish and tired than she already did. She had barely slept, barely eaten. Her body hurt, her head ached, and her heart....

It was going to be hurt, too.

She knew it was.

No matter what Ryder said, no matter what his intentions, eventually she'd disappoint him or he'd disappoint her. One of them would walk away and find someone else, and all the silly dreams that she kept shoving down and hiding in the deepest part of her heart would shatter.

Just like she'd told him they would.

Build as many dreams as you want around me, he'd said, and she'd been so tempted to let herself do it.

She knew better, though.

Two strikes, and she was out.

Even though she wasn't sure she wanted to be.

Ryder helped her into the Hummer, and she wondered what it would be like to be more than a client he needed to protect, more than someone he needed to keep safe. Wondered what it would be like to just let go, let herself try one more time.

"You're deep in thought, Shelby Ann," he said as he started the Hummer's engine.

"I'm just hoping that Eileen will be able to give us some helpful information, because so far, we've come up empty today."

"I wouldn't say we've come up empty. We know that

Catherine is afraid *of* someone and *for* someone. We know that she thinks the same person who murdered eleven people at Good Samaritan Convalescent Center also murdered Maureen. Assuming that she's telling the truth about her innocence—"

"I think she is."

"*If* she is, coming here has proven what was only a theory before. Maureen was killed because of the research she was doing. She was killed because she got too close to a murderer who's been hiding his crimes for years."

"I agree, but we can't prove it. Not without knowing what Maureen found. Too bad all the research was destroyed in the explosion."

"Too bad for us, but not for the person who murdered Maureen."

"I hadn't thought of that." She'd just assumed that the arsonist wanted to hide his crime and make Maureen's death look like an accident, but the explosion and fire had taken all of Maureen's research with her. Everything on her computer. Everything on her cell phone.

Her entire life gone in the ring of a doorbell.

Shelby shivered, rubbing her arms to try to chase away the chill. Maureen had been so vibrantly alive, so filled with ideas and enthusiasm. Sure, she'd been demanding, but she'd also been funny and fun, caring and compassionate. She'd believed in what she did, offered nothing but full disclosure and absolute truth in her books. Evidence and facts had been everything to her, but the people behind the stories were what drove her.

She'd deserved a happier ending than what she'd gotten, and Shelby swallowed back a lump in her throat at the thought.

"Are you thinking about Maureen?" Ryder asked, and she nodded.

"How did you know?"

"Your eyes are sad."

"You're supposed to be watching the road, not me."

"I'm watching the road *and* you. You're a distraction, Shelby Ann. One I wasn't counting on when I came to Spokane."

"Where were you before?" she asked, even though she knew she shouldn't. Asking questions about his personal life was a sure way to get to know him better, and getting to know Ryder better would probably make her like him even more than she already did. In her estimation, that would be a whole lot worse than falling for him. If she fell, she could right herself. If she liked him more and more, she couldn't turn away.

"New York City. That's where I keep the main office of my business."

"You have more than one office?"

"This is my fourth. I already had offices in New York, Florida and Texas. A friend of mine suggested I open one here, and it seemed like a good idea. Mid-Atlantic, southeast and southwest. Now, the northwest. I came here four months ago, so I could spend a year setting things up."

"And create a security monopoly?" she responded, his words leaving her hollow.

He'd been in town four months.

Was going home in eight.

Build all the dreams you want around me.

But that would be difficult to do if he wasn't around.

"Not quite."

"The sheriff said your business is one of the best in the country."

"That's a matter of opinion, and I've never been overly concerned about people's opinions."

"Then what are you concerned with?"

"Keeping you safe."

"Aside from that."

"If I didn't know better, I'd think you were curious about me." He shot a glance in her direction, his eyes filled with amusement.

"We've been spending a lot of time together. It's only natural to be curious."

"Yeah?"

"Yes," she said firmly, and he chuckled.

"So, what else do you want to know?"

"Nothing."

"Liar."

"Everything, then, but that would be dangerous, wouldn't it, Ryder? Because in a few months you'll go back to New York, and I'll be here, working in my bakery, wishing I hadn't spent so much time getting to know you."

"Just because I *planned* to stick around for a year doesn't mean I'll *only* stick around for a year," he responded.

"It doesn't mean you'll stick around longer, either."

"I guess how long I stay will depend on what I'll be leaving behind." His words hung in the air, and Shelby knew he was waiting for her to respond, waiting for her to stop being a coward and start going after what she wanted.

The problem was, what she *didn't* want kept getting in her way.

Three strikes.

And the last one would be too painful to ever recover from.

Ryder pulled onto the interstate, accelerating into sparse traffic and putting distance between them and Catherine Miller.

A woman behind bars for a crime she said she hadn't committed, stuck there because she had no power to free herself.

Sometimes, Shelby felt the same way.

Powerless to free herself from past mistakes, from self-doubt, from fear.

Powerless despite all the power she had.

Faith. Family. Friends.

She didn't live behind bars. Her prison was one of her own making, but it was no less real, and Shelby was unable to break free, no matter how much she wanted to.

Tell her I love her.

That's all Catherine had asked, but Shelby thought she wanted more. Wanted something so desperately she hadn't dared mention it.

Freedom to leave the prison, to reach out for all the things she didn't dare dream she'd ever have.

In that small way, at least, they were exactly the same.

SEVENTEEN

Ryder's cell phone rang as he pulled up in front of a faded clapboard farmhouse. He grabbed it, glancing at Shelby as he answered. She'd fallen asleep, her head resting against the window, her hair falling across her cheek. If he'd had the time, he would have driven around for a while longer, let her get the sleep she obviously needed, but he didn't.

Not just because Shelby had a wedding cake to decorate and deliver, but because danger was breathing down their necks. They couldn't afford to do anything but keep pushing hard for the answers that would lead them to the killer. Finding him was the only way to stop him, the only way to keep Shelby safe.

"Ryder Malone." He kept his voice low, hoping she'd get at least a few extra minutes of rest.

"This is Deputy Sheriff Logan Randal."

"What can I do for you, Randal?"

"Put Shelby Simons on the phone. She *is* with you, right?"

"Yes, the sheriff and I agreed she'd be safer that way."

"May I speak to her?"

"She's not available."

"Yes, I am," Shelby mumbled as she lifted her head and opened her eyes. They were red-rimmed and deeply shadowed, her skin so pale it was almost translucent.

"I thought you were asleep."

"Just resting my eyes. Is it Dottie?"

"Deputy Sheriff Randal," he said, handing her the phone. He wanted to smooth the frown line from her forehead, but she'd been on edge since they'd left the state prison, and he figured it had more to do with him than it had to do with meeting Catherine.

Afraid, that's what she was.

So afraid that she wouldn't allow herself to accept what she felt, believe it could last.

"Hello?" She pressed the phone to her ear, her eyes wide and wary as she watched him. She listened for a moment. "Monday? I think that will work."

"What will work?" Ryder asked, and Shelby slapped her palm over his mouth.

"I'm trying to hear," she whispered, her palm so smooth and silky he didn't see any reason to push it away. "Okay. I'll see you then, Deputy Randal." Her hand dropped away, and she handed Ryder the phone.

"Well?"

"They rescheduled the sketch artist because of the fire. She'll be here Monday. The sheriff is going to send a patrol car to bring me to the station once she arrives."

"I'll bring you."

"There's no need. Not if I have a police escort."

"There's every need." He got out of the Hummer and opened Shelby's door. He'd be bringing her to the sheriff's office whether she liked it or not, and no amount of arguing would change that, but she didn't seem intent on arguing.

Her gaze was focused on the old house and its overgrown yard. A storm door hung on broken hinges, the screen gutted out. Brown grass surrounded the dilapidated building, but beyond it, the land looked lush and green. The fields, at least, were being tended.

"The place looks abandoned. Do you think we're at the right house?"

"We're at the right address. Unless something happened to Catherine's grandmother, she must still be living here."

"Maybe, but she's not living very well. Look, two of the windows are broken. The roof has a hole in it. What does she do in the winter? What does she do when it rains?"

"Good question. How about we knock on the door and ask?"

"You, there! Get out of here!" a voice called from an open window on the first floor as Ryder opened the gate. The faded blue curtain rustled, but there was no sign of the speaker.

She was there, though, hidden behind the fabric.

Ryder focused his attention there and called out. "We're here to see Eileen. Is she around?"

"I said, get out of here."

"Catherine sent us to make sure her grandmother was doing all right. We're not leaving until we do that." Shelby stepped forward, and Ryder tugged her back. For all he knew, the speaker had a gun aimed at one of their heads.

He touched his weapon, the Glock warm and smooth beneath his fingers.

"Are you Catherine's friends?" The curtains pulled back, and a red-haired woman looked out, her face tan and deeply wrinkled, her cheeks hollow. She looked gaunt and jaundiced, cigarette smoke floating through the window and out into the yard.

"We met with her, hoping to get information about a case we're working on. She mentioned her grandmother, and we offered to check in and see how Eileen is doing. Is she here?"

"She's here, and she's glad you didn't say you were Catherine's friends. My granddaughter doesn't have any that visit her or me. Not anymore. Hold on a minute. I'll let you in."

A few minutes passed before the door swung open, the rusted hinges squeaking as Eileen motioned them inside. She wore faded jeans and a bright pink tank top, both her arms covered in faded tattoos, a cigarette held between her fingers. Nothing like the frail grandmother Ryder had expected, but her hand shook as she waved them toward the living room, and he understood why Catherine had worried so much about her welfare.

"Come on in. I don't have all day."

"You're Eileen?" Ryder asked, and the woman nodded, closing the door and turning the lock and bolt.

"Who else would I be? Who else would live in a dump like this? Go ahead and sit. Might as well get comfortable." She lowered herself into a worn easy chair, wincing with the movement. "So, what do you want?"

"Catherine is worried about you. She wanted us to make sure you were okay," Shelby responded, gingerly sitting on the edge of a sagging sofa.

Ryder stood, afraid to test the strength of any of the rickety furniture.

"That's not the only reason you're here, is it? It's not like you know my granddaughter, and it's not like you care about her or about me. So, what do you really want?" She stubbed the cigarette out in an overflowing ashtray, her thick-veined hand trembling violently.

Fear?

Illness?

A combination of both?

Ryder wasn't sure, and he studied her as she studied Shelby. Eyebrows drawn on. No eyelashes. Lips pale.

Cancer?

He hoped not.

For her sake and for Catherine's.

"We're here for exactly the reason I said. To make sure you're okay," Shelby responded to her question, and Eileen's scowl deepened.

"Don't lie to me, girl. I don't like it."

"Why would I lie?" Shelby stood her ground.

"Because lying is what people do. Even highbrow, fancy ladies like you."

"I'm not highbrow or—"

"Eileen, we also want to find out what you know about Maureen Lewis's death," Ryder cut in, and Eileen turned her attention to him.

"The true-crime writer, right? Got blown up in her house. Police determined that she was murdered."

"That's right."

"I heard about it on the news." Eileen pulled out another cigarette, tapped it against her knee.

"She was writing a book about the murders that your granddaughter committed."

"She was convicted, but she wasn't guilty," Eileen snapped.

"That's not what a jury of her peers thought."

"Catherine was railroaded by the system."

"Do you know how many family members of convicts think that?" Ryder didn't pull his punches, and Shelby grabbed his arm, shook her head.

He ignored her.

Whatever information Eileen had, they needed it.

"Plenty, but I'm not one of them. I know my granddaughter, and I know the things she's capable of. Murder isn't one of them."

"Someone killed those patients, Eileen," Shelby said quietly, and Eileen nodded.

"Exactly, and that's how Catherine got herself into trouble. She reported the murders. Did you know that?"

"No." Ryder knew very little about the case except what he'd read in old newspaper articles.

"It's true. There were several patients at Good Samaritan that Catherine was really close to. She met them when she was still a nurse's aide, and she continued to care for them after she became an RN. None of them had any family close by, so she'd bring them little trinkets and go to visit them when she was off duty. That's the kind of girl Catherine is."

"But?" Ryder pressed her to continue and she frowned, staring up at the ceiling as if she could find answers there.

"Flu season rolled around and four of those patients died in less than three months. Complications from the flu. That's what the families were told, but Catherine knew that none of them had been sick. She started keeping track after that. Two more patients died in the next five months. Neither of them were sick, either. Being the kind of girl she is, Catherine took the information to the local police, and they started to investigate. Next thing we knew, Catherine was being accused of murder." She lit the cigarette, took a long drag and blew a stream of smoke into the air.

"Accused based on what evidence?" Ryder asked, and Eileen shrugged.

"Three of the patients who died left my granddaughter money. One of them left her entire estate to Catherine. Really ticked off the woman's granddaughter. She requested an autopsy. The results were inconclusive, but the woman still insisted that Catherine had manipulated her grandmother into changing her will. She planted the seed of suspicion. The police watered it. They hunted for months until they found evidence to arrest Catherine. Evidence someone else planted."

"You're saying someone murdered eleven people and then framed your granddaughter?"

"That's exactly what I'm saying. Who knows whether he was trying to pin it on her from the beginning or if she offered herself up by going to the police? All I know is that it worked. She's in jail. The real murderer is free."

"Circumstantial evidence doesn't get a person convicted, Eileen," Ryder said.

"If you'd done your homework, you'd already know what got her convicted."

"I haven't had a whole lot of time for homework, so why don't you fill me in?"

"The police found a syringe with traces of potassium chloride in Catherine's purse. Her fingerprints were on it. They also found a bottle of potassium chloride in her work locker, and one under the seat in her car. It was all over the news, and she was pretty much publicly convicted before she ever went to trial," Shelby offered quietly, her eyes filled with compassion.

"What's your name, girl?" Eileen responded.

"Shelby Simons."

"Well, Shelby, here's the rest of what you need to know. Part of my granddaughter's job was to administer medications. Sometimes orally. Sometimes through injections. She touched dozens of syringes a day. Anyone could have taken a syringe she'd used, filled it with potassium and emptied it out again. Anyone could have stuck a bottle of poison in her locker or put one in her car. She never bothered to lock either. Besides, Catherine is one smart cookie. She graduated from high school two years early and had her nursing degree by the time she was twenty. No way would she be stupid enough to leave the evidence around if she *was* a murderer. Which she isn't."

"If she didn't murder her patients, who did?" Ryder asked, and Eileen shrugged.

"That's the question, isn't it? Catherine thought she knew, and she told anyone who would listen, but it didn't do her any good. The prosecutors had their scapegoat, and they knew they'd get an easy conviction. A poor girl from the wrong side of the tracks, no one but an old grandmother and a couple of troublemaking friends to help her. Catherine didn't stand a chance." Eileen took another drag of the cigarette, coughing as she blew the smoke out.

"Who did *she* think the murderer was?" Ryder's nerves hummed with excitement, blood racing through his veins in quick, hard bursts. All they needed was a name. Once they had that, they'd know what direction to go, which way to look.

"She told me not to say."

"Why?"

"Because she was worried about me. That girl's heart is too soft. She said she'd spend the rest of her life in jail if it meant keeping me safe. Like I'm going to live the rest of *her* life. Don't know where that child gets her heart from. It doesn't come from my side of the family, that's for sure."

"Did you give Maureen the person's name?"

"Of course I did. No way would I let my granddaughter rot in prison. Next thing I knew, Maureen was dead. Catherine was still in prison."

"Who did Catherine suspect?"

"A doctor. Guy named Christopher Peterson. Nice upright member of the community. A guy no one would ever suspect."

"But Catherine did?" Adrenaline shot through Ryder. Finally, a name.

"He had access to the patients who died. He was at Good Samaritan on the days of their deaths. He was arrogant enough to think he knew what was best for everyone who walked through the doors, and he wasn't as upright as he wanted everyone to believe. He had asked Catherine out a few times after she started working there. Seeing as how he was married and had three kids, it wasn't something she was interested in."

"The fact that he was a player isn't a reason to suspect him of murder," Ryder said. But it was something to go on. Which was a lot more than they'd had an hour ago.

"Didn't you hear a word I said, boy? Aside from

Catherine, he was the only one working at Good Samaritan every day that a patient died. The defense brought him up as another possible suspect, but there was nothing to link him to the potassium, and he'd been called home on emergencies before two of the patients died."

"So, he had an alibi." Shelby sounded disappointed, but an alibi didn't mean a person was innocent. It just meant he was good at covering his crimes.

"Doesn't mean he didn't do it." Eileen took another drag on her cigarette, frowning as she exhaled. "I promised Catherine I'd quit these cancer sticks, but so far I've only been able to cut back."

"Bad habits are hard to break," Ryder responded by rote, his thoughts on the information Eileen had provided. Another suspect. A man whom the community trusted, whom his patients trusted. Was it possible *he* was the real murderer?

"You're telling me. So—" she stubbed out the second cigarette "—is there anything else you need?"

"No, but before we go, Eileen, Catherine had a message she wanted us to give you," Shelby said as Eileen struggled to her feet.

"What's that?"

"She said to tell you that she loves you."

"Yeah?" Eileen blinked rapidly, her eyes moist and bright. "That girl. Her heart is too soft. That's been the problem all along."

"If you'd like, I can take you to visit her next week," Shelby offered, and Eileen's expression brightened.

"Anytime. Just give me a call. My number is listed. I can pay you for gas, but that's about it. Funds have been short since Catherine went to prison."

"I wouldn't want payment, Ms. Eileen." Shelby kept

talking as Ryder tried to hurry her out of the living room and back to the Hummer. Catherine wasn't the only one with a soft heart. Shelby had one, too. In his mind, that only made her more vulnerable.

He wanted to tell her to guard that part of herself, but Shelby's softness intrigued him as much as her silky hair and sweet smile. More than either of those things, because it stemmed from something deep in her soul.

All Ryder had to do was look in her eyes, and he saw it. All he had to do was listen to her with her employees and with Dottie, and he heard it.

She was soft, and he was soft for her, and there was nothing he could do to change either of those things.

Nothing he *would* do to change it.

"I'll call you next week," Shelby said, and Eileen nodded.

"I'll be around. Now, you two go on back to what you were doing, and watch out. It seems to me that Maureen would have been a lot better off if she'd stayed out of things that weren't her business."

"It was her business. She was writing your granddaughter's story, remember?" Ryder said as they walked to the door.

"Not Catherine's story. That scum Peterson's story. A poor choice. Better make sure you're not making any, or you might wind up the same way she did. You both seem like nice kids. I wouldn't want to see you hurt."

Shelby stiffened at her words, her muscles tightening beneath Ryder's hand. "We'll be careful."

They stepped outside, the wooden floorboards of the porch giving a little under Ryder's weight. Obviously, Eileen was falling behind on the upkeep of her property. The clapboard house was faded, its paint peeling and gray. Maybe it had been beautiful a long time ago. Now it simply looked tired, the overgrown yard edging in and threatening to overtake the house and rickety porch. He'd send some of his men over to straighten things out. A little overtime wouldn't hurt any of them.

"That was…interesting," Shelby said as she climbed into the Hummer, her borrowed jeans hugging curvy hips and long, lean legs.

He tried not to notice, but that was difficult when the breeze carried hints of berries and vanilla. Difficult when every moment of every day seemed to be filled with Shelby.

Every thought.

Every decision based on what would keep her safe.

"I'd say it was informative. I think that a meeting with Dr. Peterson will be even more so," he responded, shutting the door and shutting down his errant thoughts.

"That means we're not going to the bakery yet, doesn't it?" She brushed stray curls from her cheek, watching him as he got into the Hummer and started the engine. He shouldn't feel her gaze the way he felt the sunlight pouring in the window, but he did.

"Sorry, but we need to visit Dr. Peterson. I want to get his take on things. We should still have plenty of time for that cake you need to build."

"Stack. Not build. And I have to put flowers on it, too."

"I'll help you."

"You can help me by getting me back to the bakery by three."

"I'll give it my best shot."

"Do you really think the doctor will be willing to talk to us?"

"We won't know until we ask." He grabbed his cell phone and dialed the office, waiting impatiently while it rang.

"Personal Securities, Inc—"

"It's Ryder," he cut in, and Paisley Duncan huffed.

"You could have waited until I finished, boss," she said, and he knew she was fidgeting at the desk, wishing she were out doing something more exciting. That had been her M.O. since he'd hired the twentysomething office temp. She wanted to be a bodyguard. Not office help.

Too bad she didn't have any training.

Too bad she couldn't fire a gun.

Too bad there was no way *ever* that Ryder would assign her a case.

"I have more important things on my mind than manners, Paisley. I need you to track down a doctor named Christopher Peterson. He works at Good Samaritan in—"

"The valley. Right. I know it. My grandmother was there for a couple of years."

"Call them and see if Peterson is in today. If he is there, let me know. If he's not, ask when he'll be in next."

"You want me to set up an appointment for you to meet with him?"

"I'd prefer he not know I'm coming. I don't want him taking off to avoid a meeting."

"I can find his home address, too. We could—"

"*We're* not doing anything."

"You take all the fun out of this job, you know that, boss?"

"Call Good Samaritan. Let me know what you find

out. I should be hitting town in an hour. I need the information before then." He disconnected before Paisley could beg him to bring her to the interview. Fresh out of college with a master's degree in English, she had no business doing anything but writing the next great American novel she was working on and sitting at a desk, and that's exactly what he'd told her on too many occasions to count.

"We're not just going to show up at the convalescent center without warning and confront the doctor, are we?" Shelby sounded appalled.

"We're going to show up there, his home, the hospital. Wherever he is, because I need to talk to him, and letting him know I'm coming will only give him time to compose his thoughts."

"I have a wedding cake to prep and deliver, Ryder. I can't spend the afternoon chasing down a doctor. If he's not at Good Samaritan—"

"Then we're going to have to keep looking. Your life is more important than a wedding cake."

"Maybe not to the bride," she grumbled, and he patted her knee, his hand resting on worn denim.

She stilled, her muscles taut, and he was sure she was holding her breath, waiting for him to move away.

Or to claim more than a pat on the knee.

Velvety lips, whispered sighs, sweet smiles.

He wanted more of them all when the time was right, but it wasn't right. Not yet.

"We'll be back at the bakery in plenty of time for you to do what needs to be done." He lifted his hand, ignoring the warmth that thrummed through his veins.

"I'm already behind, so there's no way I'll have plenty of time."

"Two hands will cut the time by half."

"Or double it. You don't know your way around a wedding cake any more than I do the revolver you're carrying."

"It's a semiautomatic, Shelby Ann, and I can teach you anything you want to know about it the same way you can teach me about wedding cakes."

"But—"

His cell phone rang, and he grabbed it, knowing exactly who it was before he answered. Paisley was overly eager, but she was also smart and quick.

"Ryder, here."

"I have the information you want, boss. Peterson is stopping in at the convalescent center today. He's scheduled to be there from noon to three."

"Then we're in business. Thanks, Paisley."

"Thank me by taking me wi—"

He disconnected, cutting her off before she could ask. He'd trained people to work as security contractors, but he didn't plan to train her. She was too eager and too young, and that could get her or a client killed.

"He's there?" Shelby asked, and he nodded.

"He'll be there until three." Which worked out perfectly. They'd find him while he was working his shift and ask a few questions before he knew why they were there. Hopefully they would throw him off balance and prevent him from formulating polished, practiced replies.

Ryder would know if the doctor was lying. Gaze shifting, hands fidgeting, stance tense, subtle clues that would give him away, and Ryder would be watching for them.

Maybe the doctor wouldn't lie, though.

Maybe he'd tell the truth.

Maybe, but Ryder thought another possibility was more likely.

The doctor *would* lie, and he'd keep on lying.

Because, Ryder thought, Dr. Christopher Peterson probably had a very good reason for doing so.

EIGHTEEN

Christopher Peterson didn't look any more like a cold-blooded killer than Catherine had. The thought flitted through Shelby's mind as she followed Ryder and the doctor into a small office.

Peterson didn't look like a killer, but he didn't look happy, either. As a matter of fact, he'd been looking decidedly *un*happy since Ryder had introduced himself and Shelby and asked if they could speak to him.

"I appreciate you giving us a few minutes of your time, Dr. Peterson," Ryder said as the doctor closed the office door.

"You should, because I don't have a few minutes. As a matter of fact, I don't have any time at all."

"Then that makes us even more appreciative," Ryder responded, but there was little sincerity in his words. He looked predatory and fierce, focused and dangerous, his attention never wavering from the doctor's face.

"Right. Whatever you want to ask, ask quickly." Dr. Peterson dropped into a leather armchair, his receding hair standing up around a broad, slightly jowly face, his emerald eyes flashing with irritation.

"We were hoping you could tell us a little bit about

the murders that were committed here." Ryder didn't beat around the bush, and the doctor tensed, his eyes narrowing.

"That's old news, and you can find whatever information you need by requesting the case file from the police or visiting the library and looking at back issues of the local newspaper. Every horrible detail is there." He rubbed the bridge of his nose, age spots marring the too-smooth skin on the back of his hand.

"I'm not interested in what the police or the newspaper have to say, Doctor. I'm interested in what *you* have to say. The way I've heard it, Catherine Miller wasn't the only employee who worked every shift that a patient died on. You were working those shifts, too."

"The police knew that. The prosecutor knew it, but none of them cared, because they already had their murderer. Like I said, it's all old news."

"You were called away from the hospital during three of the shifts, right? When you returned, you found the deceased."

"It's been a long time, but that sounds about right."

"I wouldn't think any amount of time could make it difficult to remember. Eleven people died."

"Did you come here to accuse me of something, Mr. Malone?" The doctor leaned forward, his eyes narrow with anger.

"I just wanted your take on things. Catherine Miller is still insisting she's innocent. Maybe she's telling the truth. What do you think?"

"I think she's crazy. I thought it the first day we met, and I thought it every day I worked with her."

"Even the day you asked her out?" Ryder asked, and the doctor stood.

"I think this conversation is over."

"You did ask her out, right?"

"What does that have to do with the death of eleven innocent people?"

"I'm just trying to get the facts straight."

"The facts are that Catherine Miller injected potassium chloride into eleven patients over the course of her two years here. They died, and she went to prison for her crimes. Justice was served, and we've all moved on."

"Not everyone is convinced Catherine is a murderer."

"I'm convinced. People who work here are convinced. The families of her victims are convinced. What the rest of the world thinks doesn't really matter." The doctor paced to a small window that looked out over the parking area, his back ramrod straight.

"Do you know Maureen Lewis?" Ryder asked, and Dr. Peterson swung around, his eyes cold and hard.

"She's the woman that died in a house fire a few days ago, right? The true-crime writer?"

"She was investigating the Good Samaritan murders for a book she was working on. We thought maybe she'd interviewed you."

"She was here. We only had a minute to talk, though. A few days later, she was dead. A shame. It's one thing for a person to live a full life and then go peacefully, knowing they've lived long and happily, and that they won't be burdens to their families any longer. It's another thing for someone to die young." The doctor's hot, angry gaze settled on Shelby, and her skin crawled. She resisted the urge to step behind Ryder, meeting Peterson's eyes head-on.

"You think the fact that someone is elderly means he's a burden?" she asked, and Peterson frowned.

"Not at all. I'm simply saying that death is inevitable, but it's much easier to accept when the person who dies has lived a long and fulfilling life. Now, if you'll excuse me, I have some patients to see." He walked out of the room without a backward glance.

"He's not very warm and fuzzy. I wonder what his bedside manner is like," Shelby said as Ryder led her out of the office.

"I'm thinking that I'd rather not find out."

"For someone who works at a convalescent facility, he didn't seem all that compassionate toward the elderly."

"I was thinking the same thing. As a matter of fact, I can't think of any reason why a guy like that would be committed to keeping the infirm or dying alive, and I can't help wondering why he's working here."

"Because it pays the bills?"

"Or because he gets a kick out of playing God," Ryder said quietly as they walked through the corridor, his words just loud enough for Shelby to hear.

"Do you really think he's a murderer?" she whispered back, and Ryder shrugged.

"He had the means, and I'm not sure how good his alibi was. The patients aren't hooked to monitors here like they are at the hospital. Peterson could have administered the poison and left the hospital before the deaths were discovered."

"I'm sure the police thought of that."

"I'm sure they did, too, but remember what Peterson said? They knew a lot of things, but it didn't matter because they already had their suspect. One who had the murder weapon hidden in her car, her locker and her purse. It would be interesting to know if the police were as thorough in their investigation of Peterson as they were of Catherine once they found those vials. When we get to the bakery, I'm going to call the sheriff and see what he has to say."

"So, we're finally going to the bakery?" Shelby's heart jumped with anticipation, the anxiety that had been gnawing at her for the better part of the day easing slightly. It was late, but she still had time to put the cake together and deliver it.

If she hurried, and she would, because people were counting on her and she couldn't bear to let them down.

"I told you I'd bring you there when we finished here."

"You told me you'd bring me there after we finished at the prison, then after we finished at Eileen's, then—"

"I get it, Shelby Ann. You're disappointed that I didn't follow through on what I said, but I'll make it up to you."

Disappointed wasn't at all how she felt.

Scared.

Anxious.

Worried.

Those topped her list.

Compelled and intrigued rounded out the end of it.

Or maybe they were the beginning.

When Ryder was around, she didn't know up or down or sideways. She only knew that being with him felt better than being with any other man she'd ever known.

That couldn't be a good thing, but it felt as if it was.

Ryder got in the Hummer, his dark eyes skimming over her, and her heart beat hard for him, her pulse racing.

She turned away.

She didn't want to look into his eyes, not wanting to see her longings reflected in his face.

Shelby had always believed that if she worked hard, prayed hard and tried hard, she'd get the things she wanted in life. Now, she was on the cusp of her thirtieth birthday, and she had a murderer chasing after her and a too-handsome bodyguard that was bound to break her heart if she let him. She had a dog she'd inherited from a friend who should have lived way longer than fifty years and a pile of ash instead of a house.

But she also had Dottie and Zane and Rae. She had her mother and sister and her friends. She had her bakery. She had her faith.

And maybe, just maybe, she had Ryder, too.

For now.

But not forever.

As long as she remembered that, she'd be just fine.

She rubbed the itchy, achy area surrounding the stitches in her back, remembering the firm, hot touch of his hands as he'd massaged the spasms out of her muscles.

For now.

Not forever.

She really *did* need to remember that.

Which was why she needed to forget his touch, his kisses, his gentleness, and she needed to concentrate on what had to be done to get the wedding cake ready for delivery.

She grabbed the door handle as Ryder pulled up in front of Just Desserts, ready to hop out of the Hummer and run into the building, but he grabbed her shoulder, pulling her back.

"Wait until I come around."

"The door is—"

"Wait," he growled, and she decided to do what he asked rather than waste more time arguing. Finish the cake. Deliver it. Then she could retreat to the safe house, lock herself in her room there and pretend her life hadn't completely fallen apart.

Several customers stared out the bakery's front window as Ryder rounded the Hummer, his jacket swinging open to reveal his side holster and gun. He looked tough, handsome and a little terrifying, and more than one woman leaned close to the glass, ogling him as he opened the door and ushered Shelby out of the vehicle.

She couldn't blame them.

She'd be ogling, too, if she weren't so busy running beside him as he hurried her into the bakery.

Conversation ceased as they entered the building, three dozen pairs of eyes following them as they walked around the glass display case and into the service area where Dottie worked shoulder to shoulder with Rae and Zane.

"It's about time you two showed up. We've been swamped since we opened. People coming in and asking me a million questions about you and your house. Asking me if you were alive or dead. The nerve! That's what I told them, too. The nerve!" Dottie said as she handed a white box to a customer.

"Sorry. Things took longer than we expected." Shelby grabbed an apron from a hook near the register and put it on. The cake still needed work, but she couldn't leave Dottie and Rae with lines ten customers long. Besides, running into the back and hiding from the gawking patrons wouldn't change what had happened. It certainly wouldn't fix her house.

"It's been fine, Shelby. Dottie is just grumpy because she's been worrying about you. She made me drive her by your place to see how bad the damage was, and she nearly had a heart attack," Zane said as he filled a box with frosted-yellow chocolate cupcakes.

"The house can be replaced," Shelby responded, and Dottie frowned.

"But *you* can't. You could have died in that fire, just like poor Maureen. And you!" She pointed a gnarled finger at Ryder. "You're fired. I'm shipping my girl off to Europe for a month, so you're not needed anymore. Maybe by the time she gets back the police will have caught the guy who's trying to kill her." Dottie rang up another customer, shoving a half-dozen chocolate-chip cookies into a box and passing it to the wide-eyed, gap-jawed young woman who'd just paid.

"I can't go to Europe. I have a business to run and a cake to deliver to a wedding tonight." Shelby grabbed a dozen apple Danishes from the display case and packaged them for a regular customer.

"Forget the wedding and the business, doll. I promised your grandmother that I'd look out for you if she died before I did, and that's what I'm doing. I have money socked away. Enough to send you first-class to Paris. Maybe you'll meet some gorgeous French guy, and—"

"You'll have to buy two tickets, Dottie. Once you hire me, I can't be fired," Ryder responded as Shelby rang up the customer.

"Maybe if you were doing a better job, I wouldn't

have to fire you," Dottie griped, and the customer offered Shelby a sympathetic smile before walking away.

Shelby filled another order as Dottie and Ryder discussed plans for her life, and she didn't say a word. What good would it do? Both were as stubborn and hardheaded as mules. Besides, she didn't know what she could add to the conversation. She had no idea how to keep herself safe or how to end the nightmare she'd somehow found herself in.

She rang up another order and then left the service area. Silent and comforting, the kitchen offered the solace she needed. She grabbed the sugar flowers and rolled the chilled cakes out of the fridge, frosting and assembling the first two layers quickly. One large round, then another smaller round. She piped abstract swirls on the buttercream, using a pastry bag and white decorator icing that added depth and dimension to the cake.

"It's beautiful." Ryder's words cut through the silence, and Shelby screamed, whirling around, icing squirting from the end of the piping bag onto the front of her apron.

"You did it again! I told you not to keep sneaking up on me."

"Sorry about that. You okay?" He took the piping bag and wiped icing from her apron, his hand swiping her abdomen, spreading heat with every touch.

She stepped back and bumped the counter, her cheeks heating as Ryder smiled.

He knew exactly what his touch did to her.

"I'm busy. There's a lot to do before we can transport this cake." She turned back to her work, the skin on the back of her neck burning as his gaze swept over her.

"How can I help?"

"Go back up front and help in the service area." She finished the last piped swirl and lifted a flower, gently pushing the stem through buttercream and cake.

"Not a possibility. Dottie threatened me with bodily injury if I got within ten feet of her." He lifted a delicate lily of the valley and held it out to her, his long, tan fingers gentle on the gum-paste bloom.

"I can't believe a guy like you would be afraid of a woman like Dottie."

"I'm not afraid of her. I'm afraid of what it will mean for us if she decides she doesn't like me. I know how close the two of you are." He handed her another flower, and Shelby placed it on the top tier, not daring to meet Ryder's eyes.

"There is no us."

"If you say so, Shelby Ann." He took a flower from the tray, placed it next to the one she'd already affixed to the cake.

"I do." But she wasn't sure she meant it.

"Why? Because of a couple of failed attempts at love with a couple of guys who didn't deserve you? Are you really going to let them steal your possibilities?" He stepped closer, looking down into her eyes as if he could read the truth there.

"I'm not letting them steal anything. Now, if you don't mind, I really do have to work. Since you can't go up front without facing the wrath of Dottie, how about you sit in my office while I finish this? We need to leave here in less than an hour."

"Your office is a closet, and I think I'd rather watch you work."

"I'd rather you not," she muttered as she placed another flower on the cake.

You're not going to let them steal your possibilities.

His words spun through her mind as she placed another flower and another.

She didn't have time to dwell on his assessment of her life. She needed to completely cover the top tier of the cake with sugar blossoms before she transported it. That had to be her one and only focus, but the next flower she lifted broke, her grip too tight, her concentration shot.

"Better be careful, Shelby. We're not going to have time to make replacement flowers," he said.

"It wouldn't have broken if you weren't standing there staring at me."

"Watching. There's a big difference between that and staring."

"Watching. Staring. Who cares? All I know is that you're making me nervous." The words slipped out, and her cheeks heated again.

"There are lots of things you should be nervous about. I'm not one of them."

"That's a matter of opinion." She placed another flower, filling in the last of the top tier and carefully placing it in a box. One more tier, and she'd be ready to go. Out of the kitchen, out in the fresh air where she could breathe without catching a whiff of Ryder's masculine scent.

She began piping the third layer, squirted a line too thick and had to scrape it off and begin again.

"Want some help?" Ryder asked, a hint of amusement in his voice.

"It's not funny, Ryder."

"I'm not laughing." He took the piping bag from her hands and set it on the counter, smoothing his palms up her arms until they cupped her biceps.

"I have to finish," she protested, but she didn't reach for the bag, couldn't stop looking into his dark eyes.

"You have time."

"Not for this."

"There's always time for this," he murmured, leaning down so they were a breath apart. "Because there's something you don't seem to understand and that I need to explain. You are everything a man could want. Soft and sweet and strong and brave. The two failures you keep telling me about. They weren't yours, and when we finally have time for us, there isn't going to be another one."

"Ryder—" Her breath caught as he touched the corner of her mouth, traced a line from there to the hollow of her throat.

"Are you still nervous? Or is something else making your heart beat so fast?"

"Both."

"I hope that that something else is me." His lips brushed hers, light, easy. She sighed because she couldn't do anything else. Not protest. Not pull back. Not think of one reason why she shouldn't enjoy the moment.

He tugged her closer, and she went willingly, her arms sliding around his waist as he deepened the kiss, carried her away from the shop and the cake and all the worries that had been weighing her down.

"You're supposed to be her bodyguard, Malone. Not her hunk of burnin' love." Dottie's voice was like a splash of ice water in the face, and Shelby jumped back.

"Don't you have customers to help, Dottie?" Ryder asked, his tone gruff and raw.

That would have made Shelby feel better about her heaving breaths if Dottie hadn't been glowering at her.

"We cleared the crowd, and I thought I'd give Shelby a hand getting this cake out the door, but apparently she's less worried about that than I thought."

"I'm almost finished." Shelby lifted the piping bag and added a loose swirl to the side of the tier, her hand shaking so much she almost made another blob instead.

"You would have been finished if you'd kept your mind on the job." Dottie motioned for Ryder to grab the two layers Shelby had already assembled. "Let's get these out to the car while she finishes the last tier. You know this wedding is at a park, right?"

"It was on the schedule. Manito Park. The Japanese gardens, and I've already got my men doing a sweep of the area."

"Humph." Dottie seemed less than impressed by Ryder's preparedness. "Let's move, then. Time is ticking away, and the wedding reception isn't going to wait for you to arrive."

"We still have time, Dottie," Shelby said, but Dottie was too busy bustling Ryder from the room to hear her.

Shelby finished the tier quickly, her hand steadier as she piped swirls, placed flowers and boxed it up.

Done.

And she'd still be leaving on time.

Despite the kiss.

She lifted the cake box, balancing it carefully as she grabbed extra icing, and started to walk out of the kitchen.

"Wait." Ryder grabbed her arm as he walked back in, pulling her to a stop, his phone pressed to his ear.

"No. Sorry. Go ahead." He listened silently to the speaker, his gaze never leaving Shelby. "Good. I'm glad to hear that. Thanks, Sheriff." He hung up, took the box from her hand.

"Ready to go?"

"Yes. What did the sheriff say?"

"Mostly what we've already heard. The police investigated Peterson after Catharine contacted them, but the evidence against her was compelling and Peterson had an alibi for at least two of the murders. That took him off the suspect list. His name came up during the investigation into Maureen's murder, though, and he admitted to meeting with her twice."

"So, he's a suspect again?"

"He's a person of interest, but there's really no evidence that he had anything to do with Maureen's murder. He was home the entire night before the explosion. His wife is willing to testify to that."

"He wasn't the man I saw that morning. I'm sure of that, and if that guy is the one coming after me, I don't think we can accuse Peterson of murdering Maureen."

"It's not as difficult as you might think to hire someone to do your dirty work. You can buy almost anything for the right price. Even someone's death."

"But Peterson wouldn't have any reason to want me dead, Ryder. I have nothing that would lead the police to him. I'd never even met him before today."

"That doesn't mean he's not connected to the attacks. If he hired someone to murder Maureen, and if you saw that person on your way to Maureen's house, he might want to make sure you can't point the finger at him."

"So, Peterson doesn't want me dead, the assassin he hired does?"

"It's possible. We won't know for sure until we find the guy. Wait here. I'm going to put this in the Hummer, and then I'm going to escort you out." Ryder walked out the bakery door, and Shelby didn't even bother arguing with him. There were a lot of things she didn't know and a lot of things she wasn't sure about, but she knew Ryder was good at what he did, and she knew she'd be an idiot not to let him do it.

She watched as he carried the cake outside, his muscles rippling as he set the box in the back of the Hummer. He turned, his half smile making her stomach flip.

Everything about him made her stomach flip, her heart sing, her soul yearn.

If it had only been those things that drew her to him, she would have been fine. Chemistry, physical attraction, stick any name on it you wanted, and it was the same. Fleeting and shallow. Not something to build forever on.

But it *wasn't* only those things that drew her to him. She *liked* Ryder.

Liked how he argued with Dottie, but still did what she asked. Liked the way he stuck to his promises and the way he lived his faith. Liked that he seemed to like her just the way she was. No trying to change her. No telling her she needed to be different. Just wanting her to be her.

That was a powerful gift to give someone, and Shelby didn't know if she had the strength to turn it away.

"Okay. We're set." He took her arm, led her into the cool spring day, his body shielding her from the street the way it always did, offering his life to keep her safe.

Another gift, and thinking about it made her throat clog and her heart beat faster.

"Ryder," she said as she climbed into the Hummer, and he waited, his hand on the door, his eyes staring straight into hers.

"Yeah?"

"Thanks."

He nodded and closed the door.

Maybe he knew what she meant.

Maybe he didn't.

Hopefully, Shelby would have a chance to explain. Hopefully, neither of them would die before then.

She prayed they wouldn't, clutching the extra icing and box of flowers as Ryder pulled away from the bakery and headed for Manito Park.

NINETEEN

Watching Shelby work was an addiction Ryder couldn't afford to give in to. Not when her life depended on him staying focused.

He scanned the Japanese gardens as she covered a long table with a white cloth and set a fancy-looking silver cake stand on top of it. A hundred yards away, Darius watched the entrance of the gardens, his attention focused, his body taut. Knowing him, he was hoping for some action.

Ryder wanted nothing more than to get Shelby back to his place and lock her away there. She wasn't safe out in the open, and he should have refused to bring her to the park, but part of his job was to get clients where they needed to be and to keep them safe there. He'd done it dozens of times before, and this time shouldn't be any different.

Shelby made it different, though.

Protecting her was personal. Keeping her safe was personal.

He scanned the gardens again, his attention caught by a movement to his right. A man and his son passed by, probably heading home before dusk, the park's posted closing time.

He paced to a small bridge that arched over a stream, searching for signs of tampering, but his team had been thorough. The garden was pristine, the serenity of it tempting him to believe that everything would go just the way he'd planned.

Easy in.

Easy out.

No trouble.

The sun hung low in the sky, dusk falling as the park grew quiet and Shelby continued her work. Despite the peacefulness of the evening, Ryder's hackles were raised, his skin prickling as darkness spread through the garden.

A candlelit wedding was a nice idea unless someone wanted you dead. Then it became a hazard, shadows growing long and undulating in the evening breeze as a crew quietly set up rows of chairs and readied the gardens for the ceremony.

"Okay. That's it. It's as good as it's going to get." Shelby stepped away from the cake, completely oblivious to anything but her work, but Ryder felt something in the air, a breathless waiting quality that put him on edge.

Someone was watching.

He signaled Darius and Lionel Matthews, and they slid into the shadows, going on the hunt for the hunter.

"Good. Let's go." He took Shelby's hand, pulling her away from the cake, Lincoln Stanley slipping into place behind them. One of the newest team members, Lincoln moved silently, weaving through the arriving wedding guests, then disappearing as he scouted the path back to the Hummer.

"I can't leave until the bride and groom get here. The cake—"

"No one is going to touch the cake, Shelby Ann, but I'm not liking the way things are starting to feel, so we're taking off."

"But—" She tried to protest, but he dragged her from the cake and across the small bridge.

Up ahead, Darius appeared, giving an all-clear signal and then slipping into thick woods beside the path. Something wasn't right. They both knew it. Ryder just hoped his men could find the threat before it found Shelby.

Darkness fell quickly as they made their way from the Japanese gardens into the lilac gardens. Manito Park had too many gardens, in Ryder's opinion. Too many places for someone to hide.

The sweet scent of lilac hung in the air as he led Shelby past deep purple bushes, light purple ones and white ones, their shadows long in the evening light. Everything peaceful, but not everything right. Something was about to go down, and if Ryder wasn't careful, it would take Shelby down with it.

"It's quiet," she whispered, and he nodded, probing shadows, studying dark corners, waiting, knowing.

The hair on the back of his neck stood on end, and he hurried her to a ten-foot slate wall carved into the side of a steep hill. Lilac bushes pressed close to cold stone, and he shoved Shelby behind the thick branches and heavy boughs.

"Do you think—"

"Shh." He shushed her, listening to the silence. A twig cracked. Grass rustled. Then silence again, thick and expectant.

A loud blast rocked the air, a plume of smoke shooting up into the sky from the area they'd just left. The Japanese gardens or somewhere close to it. The caustic scent of explosives drifted through the lilac garden, filling Ryder's nose and throat and lungs. He expelled it and the memories of another time and another explosion.

"What was that?" Shelby cried, her eyes wide with shock, her face paper-white.

"Nothing I want you near. Stay there, and don't move until I say different."

"Where are you going?" She clutched his hand, her palm cool and dry, her grip tight and desperate.

"Nowhere." His operatives would check out the explosion. He needed to stay close, make sure he didn't let his guard down, lose his focus. The explosion was a distraction, a red herring designed to confuse.

"Then why are you leaving?"

"Because the perp knows we're together. I don't want him finding you because he sees me."

"But—"

"Stay put." He eased his hand from hers, his heart thudding hard and fast as he pulled his gun and moved away.

Dusk cast gray shadows across the garden, and he studied each one, willing the perp to walk into his line of sight.

His leg ached deep in the bone, a reminder of where he'd once been and where he didn't plan on ever being again. Helpless, hopeless, afraid. He'd fought back from it, found strength in himself and in his faith. Now, he needed to use both to keep Shelby alive.

A flash of movement to his left warned him seconds before a dark ball flew through the air.

He dived for cover, his body reacting before his brain registered the truth.

A grenade!

The world exploded, bits of earth and grass raining down, the force of the explosion knocking the breath from Ryder's lungs.

"Ryder!" Shelby screamed, jumping from her hiding place, racing toward him, her eyes shimmering blue in the evening gloom.

"Go back!" But it was too late. A soft pop. A bloom of red in a sea of lilac, and Shelby was falling. Another pop. Shouted words, but Ryder's only thought was Shelby. He ran toward her, his gun drawn and ready, his heart thundering with fear and anger.

"Shelby?" His hand shook as he touched the pulse point in her neck, felt the thready, weak throb of her heart.

Blood bubbled up from a hole in the right side of her chest, seeping into her cotton shirt and spilling onto the ground.

Too much blood.

He'd failed her, and she might die because of it.

He pressed his hand against the wound, realized blood was seeping from beneath her back, too.

Something moved to his right, and he pivoted, aiming his gun at the figure that raced toward him.

"Hold your fire!" Darius called, and Ryder turned his attention back to Shelby. Her face devoid of color, her eyes closed, she had the grayish tinge of the dying.

Please, God, don't let her die.

"I've already called an ambulance. Hopefully, it'll be here soon. She's lost a lot of blood." Darius knelt beside him, frowning at the blood that stained the ground.

"Go find the guy who did this," Ryder said, unwilling to leave Shelby and unwilling to let her attacker escape.

"Matthews is after him. I got off one good shot when he bolted from his hiding place, and I'm pretty sure I hit him. He ran into the woods on that hill." He gestured to a hill a hundred yards out, covered with trees and shrouded in darkness.

"What about Lincoln?" Ryder pressed his jacket against Shelby's wound, trying to staunch the flow of blood, trying to will the life to stay in her.

"Injured in an explosion near the reception site. Matthews was heading back to offer aid when the grenade was lobbed. We tried to get a bead on the perp, but he was behind a boulder, and I couldn't get off a shot until he ran."

"She's losing too much blood." Ryder spoke out loud, the words tasting like dust, his stomach twisting with fear. He should have been able to keep her from being hurt. Should have protected her.

Ryder pressed harder on the bubbling wound, his hand shaking.

"Shelby?" He leaned close, listening for her breath, hearing nothing.

"She's still breathing," Darius said, but the assurance did little to comfort Ryder. Breathing for now, but maybe not in a minute.

"We need that ambulance," he responded, and the sound of sirens seemed to answer, drifting from somewhere too far away.

Please, God, get it here in time.

"Come on, Shelby Ann. You're not going to die and leave Dottie to take care of the bakery, are you?"

"I was thinking about it." The words were so quiet, he wasn't sure he'd actually heard them.

"Then how about you think about something else?" He used his free hand to brush dirt from her cheek, and she opened her eyes but didn't speak.

"Shelby? What are you thinking about?" He persisted, because he was afraid if she stopped talking, she'd stop breathing.

"I'm thinking that I want to cry and that I shouldn't. I don't think I can afford to lose any more fluids." She tried to smile, and his heart responded, tightening in his chest, aching with a hot, throbbing pain.

If she died, he didn't think it would ever go away.

"It's okay to cry when you've been shot." He smoothed her hair, and she closed her eyes.

"You wouldn't cry. Not even if you were shot." Tears slipped down her cheeks, her blood still seeping through his coat, her skin growing even paler.

"Maybe not, but I'd cry if I lost you."

She opened her eyes, looked into his face. "I think I believe you."

"You should. I cried the day I found out my buddies were killed in that explosion in Afghanistan. You're not going to make me cry again, are you?"

"I'm not sure it's my choice, and I want you to know how sorry I am."

"For what?"

"I should have stayed where you asked me to. You're the best bodyguard I've ever had."

"I'm the *only* bodyguard you've ever had."

"If I'd had a million, you'd still be the best, and I should have listened to you. I'm the one who messed up. Not you. Remember that, okay?" Her hand dropped over his, the one that pressed his coat to the bullet wound, and his throat constricted.

He could not lose her.

"Where's that ambulance?" he barked, meeting Darius's concerned gaze.

"There!" Darius jumped up, racing toward the crew that ran toward them.

"Hang on. They're almost here," Ryder said, but Shelby's eyes were closed, her breathing shallow and raspy. "Shelby?"

"It's okay," she responded. "I'm not afraid to die. I just…really wanted to live a few more of my dreams first."

"You're not going to die."

"Tell Dottie that I trust her to run the bakery—"

"You are not going to die!" he nearly shouted as the EMTs crowded in, edging him out.

"Ryder!" Shelby grabbed his hand, her grip weak. "Stay with me. I don't want to be alone."

He wasn't sure if she meant go to the hospital alone or die alone, but he nodded, not trusting himself to speak.

Then he moved back and let the medics work.

TWENTY

Fading.

That's how dying felt. At least that's what Shelby figured it must feel like, and fading was exactly what she was doing. Drifting and fading and going away, but she didn't want to go. Not yet.

She groaned as she was lifted onto a gurney, the pain so intense she wanted to close her eyes and slip away, but she was afraid that if she did, she'd never find her way back.

"You're going to be okay, ma'am," a female EMT said, her nutmeg skin and dark eyes shimmering in the evening light.

Shelby wasn't sure if she was supposed to respond, but she couldn't seem to catch her breath, so she kept silent as someone jabbed her arm with a needle.

She barely felt it, barely felt anything. Just muted pain and panic that she might fall asleep and never wake up.

Please, God, I'm not ready to die.

Darkness edged in, and she fought it as the gurney bumped over grass and dirt, people talking, the sweet scent of lilac mixing with the coppery scent of blood, everything moving.

Flying.

No pain. Just darkness. Her heart pounding in her ears, in her chest. Her body vibrating with it.

Then nothing.

No fear.

No worries.

No dreams.

"You're not leaving me, are you, Shelby Ann?" a voice whispered from somewhere far away, and she wanted to ignore it, wanted to keep floating in nothingness.

"Shelby?" The tone captured her as the voice hadn't, the desperation in it tugging her back to pain and fear.

Too much effort to stay there.

To open her eyes.

To try to find the voice that called her name again.

Ryder's voice.

She wanted to reach for him, but her arms were leaden, her fingers numb.

"I'm not going to let you leave. Not before you have a chance to live those dreams." Warm words, warm breath against her ear, warm fingers twining with hers, all of it seeming to lighten her heavy lids.

She opened her eyes, stared into Ryder's concerned face, looked into his deep brown eyes.

She didn't want to leave any more than he wanted to let her go, but she had no voice to say the words, no energy to tell him she was going to stick around, so she just stared into his eyes as the ambulance sped to the hospital. Stared and stared and tried to lose herself in them instead of the darkness that wanted to sweep back over her.

"Okay, ma'am. We're here. Just relax and let us do all the work." The EMT patted her arm reassuringly, and then Shelby was moving away from Ryder. She tried to hold on to his hand, but her grip was weak, and it slipped from her grasp.

Wait! she tried to say, but no sound came out.

She was wheeled into a narrow, well-lit corridor, people shouting instructions and information that must have had something to do with her, but that she could make no sense of.

All her thoughts were foggy and thick, her thinking sluggish.

She heard words, but they were disjointed and unconnected.

Gunshot wound.

Blood loss.

Surgery.

Everything swirling and whirling in her ears, mixing with the erratic beat of her heart.

Dying.

That's what she was doing. Right there in the hospital.

"Sir, you're going to have to wait here!" a nurse barked as she ran alongside the stretcher, her fingers on Shelby's wrist.

"I'll stay with her until you reach the operating room," Ryder responded, and Shelby tried to see him past the veil of clouds that seemed to be over her eyes.

"Sir—"

"I'm staying."

More voices. More words. Men and women in uniforms. Panic in the air.

Then everything quiet and still.

"This is it, sir. You can't go any farther."

"Shelby?" Ryder leaned so close she could see him

through the clouds, count the flecks of gold in his brown eyes, see the blond stubble on his chin. Her heart beat hollowly, the light, airy feel of floating returning, but she reached out, touched his cheek.

"Don't leave me, Ryder."

"I have to," he responded, and she was sure his voice was shaking, but maybe *she* was shaking, her heart shimmering rather than beating.

"I'm so scared," she whispered, and Ryder brushed hair from her forehead, kissed her chilled skin.

"You're too brave to be scared, Shelby Ann."

"Only when you're with me. Please, don't leave me."

"You're plenty brave, even without me, but I'll be out here waiting, and I'll be here when you come out. The first person you see. I promise." He kissed her forehead again, his breath warming her cold, cold skin, and she thought there were tears in his eyes as he stepped away, but the fog had rolled in again, and she couldn't be sure.

"Everything is going to be fine, Shelby." A dark-haired man dressed in green scrubs patted her hand as she started to move again.

Flying.

Floating.

Fading.

Please, God, I don't want to leave my mother, my sister. I don't want to leave Dottie. I don't want to leave Ryder. Not before I know what we could have had together.

The prayer whispered through her mind as she floated into darkness.

TWENTY-ONE

She could die.

Ryder had seen it in Shelby's eyes and in her blue-tinged lips. She knew it, too.

Scared.

That's what she'd said, and he'd been scared, too.

Terrified that they'd roll her into the operating room and she wouldn't come out alive.

He was still terrified.

"How is she?" Darius jogged toward him, blood splattered across his white dress shirt, his face gaunt with worry.

"Not good. She's been in surgery for four hours already. Did Matthews get the perp?" Ryder ground the question out, and Darius shook his head.

"A K-9 unit was dispatched, and they're on his trail. The good news is, the one shot I got off hit him. The police found a few drops of blood on the ridge where the perp was hiding."

"The good news will be when he's in custody."

"It'll happen, Ryder."

"It should have happened before he got another

chance at Shelby," he said, anger at his failure beating hard in his chest.

"It's difficult to stop someone when you don't know who he is or where he is, and this guy is good at protecting himself. He planned things out perfectly today. An explosive device hidden ahead of time, and all he had to do was push a button to detonate it. He meant it to be a distraction, and he succeeded. We're fortunate more people weren't hurt."

"Aside from Lincoln and Shelby, were there other injuries?" Ryder asked, knowing that if there were, he'd be wearing another layer of guilt. His men had done a sweep of the area before he arrived with Shelby, covering a grid that encompassed nearly half an acre. They'd found nothing, but something had been there. That was his responsibility and failure as much as theirs.

"No. The bomb was in a copse of trees two hundred yards from the reception site. Our perp waited until we were moving away from the site, and then set it off. There wasn't a lot of force in the explosives. He obviously had only one target.

"And he found it. I should have been more careful." Ryder slammed his fist into the wall.

"You were as careful as anyone could be, and if Shelby hadn't left her cover—"

"It wasn't her fault."

"It wasn't *anyone's* fault. Accept that or you won't be able to help Shelby heal."

He was right.

Ryder knew that, and he took a deep breath. "What else have you got for me?

"Lincoln saw our perp moving through the trees right before the explosion. He gave chase, saw the guy climb into a car on the far side of the woods seconds before the explosion. A minute after the explosion, the perp tossed a grenade at you."

"I know. No need to rehash it," Ryder said wearily, and Darius frowned.

"You're not getting my point, boss. It would have taken more than a minute for the perp to run from that parking area to the ridge."

"You're saying we're dealing with two perps?" The knowledge shot through Ryder like raw adrenaline. His pulse jumped, his body hummed with it.

"Exactly."

"Ryder Malone?" A police officer strode toward him, grim-faced and timeworn, his gray hair shaggy and unkempt.

"Yes." Ryder met him halfway, and the officer offered a hand.

"I'm Detective Nick Jasper with the Spokane Police Department. I'd like to ask you a few questions about what happened this evening."

"Go ahead."

"We'll probably be more comfortable in a less public place. The hospital has provided its conference room. If you'll—"

"No."

"Excuse me?" Detective Jasper frowned.

"If you want to ask questions, ask them here. Otherwise, they'll have to wait."

"I don't think that's going to work for me, Mr. Malone."

"I don't think you have a choice." He walked back to the operating-room door, not swayed by Darius's subtle head gesture. He'd promised Shelby he'd be there when she came out, and he would be. Even if he had to stand there for the rest of the night.

"Okay. We'll do this your way." Detective Jasper stepped up beside him. "You visited Dr. Christopher Peterson this afternoon, correct?"

"That's an odd question to ask after a woman nearly died." Ryder eyed the detective, not sure where they were headed with the interview, but intrigued. He'd had a gut feeling about Peterson, and it hadn't been a good one.

"Not so odd seeing as how another woman visited him and died less than twenty-four hours later."

"Maureen Lewis?"

"That's right. You and Ms. Simons were digging into her death, right? Trying to find out who wanted to kill her and why."

"Because someone was also trying to kill Shelby." And had nearly succeeded. Might still succeed.

Please, Lord, don't let her die.

"I understand that, Malone. I know why you've been digging. I'd have done the same in your position, but you may have dug up more than any of us suspected. You've obviously made someone very, very uncomfortable."

"Right, and here's my question for you, Detective. What are you doing about it?"

"We've reopened the case files of the murders at Good Samaritan, and we're looking into Peterson's alibis again. We've also sent men out to question him regarding his whereabouts this evening. Your men reported two perps. If he doesn't have an alibi, it's possible he was one of them."

"And the other perp?"

"That's where things get interesting. The doctor has

an old army buddy who just happens to be on our short list of persons of interest in the serial-arson case."

"That's just now coming out?"

"We had no reason to try to link Peterson to the arsonist before. Once we did, we started asking around. Wallace McGregor's name was mentioned in conjunction with the doctor. Several friends and even Peterson's wife reported that the two are as close as brothers. The thing is, Wallace is a retired firefighter. Retired because he set his own house on fire for the insurance money eleven years ago. His wife was sick at the time, and he said he was desperate for the money, so the judge let him off with probation."

"It sounds like you've got your man."

"Men, and we're going to build cases so strong they'll be in jail for the rest of their lives."

"Good." But Ryder only cared about one thing at that moment. Seeing Shelby, looking into her eyes, touching her warm skin.

Please, God, let her live.

"Is there anything else you need to discuss with me, Detective?" Ryder asked.

"We're done for now. We'll have guards posted 24/7 outside Ms. Simons's hospital room if she…" His voice trailed off, and he cleared his throat. "We'll make sure she stays safe until our suspects are rounded up."

"Thanks." Ryder didn't bother pointing out that they hadn't been successful in keeping her safe so far. No one had.

The thought pounded through his head and his heart, the guilt of letting her be hurt filling him up.

The operating-room door swung open, and a dark-haired man dressed in blood-spattered scrubs stepped out. He met Ryder's eyes, and the somberness of his gaze made Ryder's heart skip a beat. "I'm Dr. Griffon. Are you related to the patient?"

"I'm a friend. How is she?"

"Holding her own. We had to repair a torn artery, and her scapula is cracked, but she should make a full recovery. We've taken her to ICU. We'll be able to monitor her condition more carefully there."

"I'd like to speak with her as soon as possible," Detective Jasper said, and the doctor frowned.

"You may have to wait several days, Officer. She's in no condition to speak with anyone."

"It's *Detective* Jasper, and I understand that she needs to heal, but—"

"You heard the doctor, Detective. She can't speak with you," Ryder cut in, his eyes still on the surgeon.

"Here's my card. Give me a call as soon as she's able to." The detective handed Dr. Griffon his card, then walked away.

"I'd like to see her. Will that be possible?" Ryder asked, but he didn't plan to take no for an answer. He'd promised Shelby he'd be there when she came out of surgery, and he would be.

"Once she's settled in. The ICU is on the second floor. I'll have a nurse—"

An alarm sounded, the siren screaming through the corridor.

"Fire alarm!" the doctor shouted over the sound. "We'd better get out of here."

"What about Shelby?"

"The ICU staff know the procedure. She'll be wheeled to safety, but only if it's necessary."

Ryder barely heard the last few words—he was already on his way to the stairwell. Detective Jasper had promised 24/7 protection, but Ryder didn't know if guards were already stationed near the ICU.

And maybe that's what the alarm was all about.

Not a real fire, a distraction. Just like the explosion had been.

Ryder's heart raced as he bounded up two flights of stairs, brushing by a half-dozen people who were running to the exit. He burst out into the second-floor corridor, ignoring a nurse who motioned for him to leave.

The sign for the ICU was at the end of the corridor, and he ran against the current of people streaming toward the stairwell.

"You going in?" Darius shouted above the screaming alarm, and Ryder nodded, glad his friend had followed him up.

"Stay out here. If you see anyone coming this way, assume that he's trouble."

The alarm cut off as Ryder opened the door to the ICU.

Several nurses stood near a computer screen, monitoring patients as they spoke quietly to one another. They looked up as Ryder approached.

"Sir, you need to stay outside until the fire department gives us the all clear."

"I'm Shelby Simons's bodyguard," he responded, and the oldest of the group frowned.

"We were told she'd have police protection. No one mentioned a bodyguard. I'll check with security after the doctor finishes with her. Go ahead and have a seat." She gestured to a row of chairs near the nurses' station, but Ryder had no intention of sitting. He'd just seen Shelby's doctor, and he'd been on his way out of the hospital.

"What doctor?"

"Her family practitioner. Dr. Peterson."

"Peterson?" Ryder's blood went cold.

"Yes. Why?"

"What room is she in?"

"I—"

"What room?"

"Room 10. He walked in right before you got here. I—"

Ryder didn't listen. He ran.

TWENTY-TWO

Drowning.

Shelby fought as she sank like lead to the bottom of the deep end of the pool. Summertime in California, and she'd been swimming since before she could walk, but she couldn't push up from the bottom, couldn't reach the crisp, clear sky that hovered above the surface of the water.

She shoved against the bottom, but felt nothing. Not the hard cement of the public pool or the tile bottom of her grandmother's.

She flailed, trying to move her arms, her legs, but they were trapped, her face suddenly pressed into the mud at the bottom of the lake.

Lake?

Her eyes flew open, but she saw nothing, knew nothing but terror and deep, throbbing pain. She tried to scream, but she had no air to do it. Something pressed against her face so hard she thought her nose would break.

She shoved at the weight with her hands. Felt fluffy softness and crisp, cool fabric.

Pillow.

She dredged up the word from the depth of her oxygen-starved brain.

She was being smothered by a pillow.

Fight!

She tried to twist away, but couldn't free herself.

I'll be here when you come out.

Ryder's words seeped through the fog of her terror.

When had he said them?

Where?

She couldn't hold on to the memories, wasn't sure if she'd really heard them—she only knew that she was about to die, and that when she did, she'd lose any chance of ever having all the things she'd once dreamed of.

Don't let your failures ruin your possibilities.

But she had.

Two strikes, and she'd been out.

But she didn't want to stay out.

She wanted to risk it all, try for number three and shoot for forever.

She bucked against the force that held her down, and suddenly, the pillow lifted.

Darkness gone.

Light and air drifting in.

Shelby gasped, pulling deep breaths of antiseptic-scented air into her lungs.

Something crashed into the side of her bed, jarring her out of the stupor she seemed to be in. Dark shadows wrestled across the floor, panted breaths carrying into the silent room.

She tried to scream, but her throat was raw and dry, and all that came out was a raspy cough. She coughed again and again, pain shooting up her back and chest and lodging in her neck.

"Calm down, Shelby Ann. You're going to pull out all the stitches the doctor spent so much time putting in." Ryder leaned over her, his eyes blazing, his cheek red and swollen.

Number three.

Forever.

The words whispered through her mind as she reached out to touch his injury, the IV in her hand tugging as she moved.

"What happened?"

"You were shot." He lifted her hand, gently kissed her knuckles.

"Not to me. To your cheek," she rasped, and he fingered the bruise.

"Dr. Peterson decided to pay you a visit. We had a disagreement about whether or not he was going to stay."

"He was trying to smother me," she said, and he nodded, glancing at the prone figure that lay a few feet from the bed.

"He won't get a chance to try again."

"Is he…?"

"Dead? No, but he may wish he was when he's thrown in jail."

"Is everything okay in here?" Two security guards raced into the room, Darius and a police officer right behind them.

"The guy on floor is Dr. Peterson, Detective Jasper. He was trying to smother Shelby when I walked into the room," Ryder responded, and the officer knelt beside Peterson, patting him down, then turning him over and placing handcuffs on his wrists.

"I guess we've proven our theory, Malone. Peterson

really was behind all of this," he said as he pulled Dr. Peterson to his feet.

"I'm not behind anything. I was checking on my patient—"

"She's not your patient, and I'm not sure how pressing a pillow to her face counts as checking on her." Ryder rested a hand on Shelby's shoulder, his touch so light and comforting that her eyes closed, the pain in her chest and back easing as her muscles relaxed.

"I want a lawyer," Peterson responded, and Shelby thought about opening her eyes and looking into the face of the man who'd tried to murder her, but she couldn't manage it.

"You'll get a lawyer, Dr. Peterson, and once you have one, you'll probably be counseled to cooperate and tell us whether it was you or your buddy Wallace who murdered Maureen Lewis." The detective's voice was gruff and filled with irritation, but it sounded far away and muted, its urgency lost as Shelby drifted further from the room and the pain, Ryder's hand all that anchored her to reality.

"Neither of us killed anyone."

"You're lying," Ryder growled.

"I'm not—"

"You might as well fess up, Doctor. Our K-9 team apprehended Wallace. He's already down at the station, singing like a canary."

"I don't know what you're talking about," the doctor insisted, and Shelby wanted to listen to the conversation, *really* listen, but she drifted instead, floating in a place halfway between reality and dreams.

"Shelby?" Ryder called her back, and she opened her eyes.

The room had emptied. No doctor. No guards. No police officer. Just Ryder.

Just the way it should be.

She smiled, because she didn't have the energy to speak, and he ran a finger along her cheekbone.

"You must have hit something when you fell. You're going to have a bruise."

"It's better than being dead." She forced the words past her raw throat.

"True." He poured water from a plastic pitcher, shoved a straw into a plastic cup and held it for her to sip. "Not too much. The doctor might not approve."

"Peterson?" she asked, her mind muddled, her thoughts confused.

"The guy who spent four hours stitching you up after I nearly let you be killed."

"You didn't. I did. I should have listened and stayed where you told me to."

"Why didn't you?" He brushed hair from her forehead, his touch tender and easy, his eyes dark and knowing.

"Because my life would be empty without you in it, and I was sure you were about to die. It made me realize something."

"Yeah? What's that?"

"Number three? It's forever. I wouldn't want to miss out on that."

"Me, neither." He smiled gently, and Shelby imagined seeing that smile in a year, in five years, in ten. She imagined seeing it when they were both old and gray and sitting in rocking chairs.

"You're smiling." Ryder traced the curve of her lips. "What are you thinking about?"

"Sunsets and sunrises and front-porch swings. With you."

"I like that idea, Shelby Ann," he responded. "I like it a lot."

"So, it's a date?" she asked, her muscles relaxing into a sleep she couldn't deny.

"Not a date, Shelby," he whispered close to her ear. "Every dream you've ever had. Every dream I've ever had. All of it finally coming true. Forever."

"I like that idea, Hercules," she said and felt his smile as he pressed a gentle kiss to her lips.

"Good. Now, stop talking and start resting."

She didn't have the energy to call him bossy, but he was.

Bossy.

Wonderful.

Heroic.

She saw the truth as she slipped deeper into dreams. Saw it so clearly she didn't know why she hadn't seen it before. Every path she'd walked, every disappointment, every heartache had led to Ryder. It was God's plan, and it was so much better than hers had been.

Her eyes drifted closed, and she didn't fight the darkness that pulled her into sleep. She knew she didn't need to. Ryder would be waiting when she woke.

Number three.

Forever.

EPILOGUE

Shelby leaned over the large sheet cake, piping a porch onto the house she'd painstakingly created. A two-story Tudor with a lush green lawn and a white picket fence. Every eave, every window, every fence post had been drawn, painted and shadowed to match her new home.

It had taken three days and a little more energy than she probably should have expended, but it looked great, and Shelby was pleased with the results.

"What do you think, Mazy? Pretty nice, huh?"

The dog barked in response, her shiny black nose pressed to the floor as she searched for crumbs.

"Exactly what I was thinking. We're just missing one thing." Shelby set the white icing bag on the kitchen counter and lifted another one. Brown this time. She piped a hanging swing on the porch.

Perfect!

"Shelby Ann Simons, I thought I told you to take a nap!" Dottie bustled into the kitchen, her voice dripping ire, her eyes filled with concern.

"My guests will be here in a few hours, and I wanted to make sure the cake was ready for the housewarming party."

"It's ready. Go to bed. And you—" she turned her attention to Mazy "—out back for a while." She scooped up the dog and plopped her on the back deck, surreptitiously slipping her an oversize dog treat in the process.

"You know the vet said Mazy needs to cut back."

"What does she know? That dog weighs less than my big toe. Now, go to bed. I'm making my famous potato salad for the party, and I don't want you trying to steal my recipe."

"How about I just go sit on the porch swing?" Shelby asked as Dottie shooed her out of the kitchen.

"I don't care what you do, girl. Just rest. You're never going to recover fully if you don't."

"I *am* fully recovered," Shelby responded, but they both knew it wasn't true. A serious staph infection after surgery had kept Shelby in the hospital for over a month. Five weeks later, she still tired easily, but she wasn't going to let that stop her from celebrating her new home. Local contractors had moved heaven and earth to build it quickly, and she'd finally moved in. She loved the new house. Free of bad memories and broken dreams, it was waiting to be filled with wonderful new ones.

She hummed a little as she walked onto the front porch and sat on the swing, closing her eyes and letting the warm summer air wrap around her.

"Have I told you lately how beautiful you are?" Ryder's voice flowed over her, and she opened her eyes, watching as he took the porch stairs two at a time.

"Every day, but I don't mind if you tell me again."

"You're beautiful. You also look tired. Dottie said you worked seven hours today."

"Dottie has a big mouth."

"I heard that," Dottie called through the screen door.

"The doctor said part-time for another week or two, remember?" Ryder settled on the swing beside her, and she scooted in close, sliding her arm around his waist and resting her head on his shoulder. He smelled of outdoors and sunshine and everything she loved most.

"I love you so much, Ryder," she said as he stroked her hair.

"I love you, too, but you're not going to distract me. You can't work seven hours yet. You need more time to recover."

"I'm ready to get back to my life. That means pushing myself sometimes."

"Push a little, but don't overdo it, okay?" His hand skimmed over her hair again, slid down her arm and back up, the caress filling her with longing. Ryder was everything she'd been searching for, every dream she'd given up on, and her heart swelled with love for him.

"For you, I'll try not to overdo it."

"Good, because fall is coming, and it's my favorite time of year."

"Mine, too," she murmured sleepily. Much as she wanted to go back to her full work schedule, she had to admit, seven hours had been too much. Her eyelids were heavy, her muscles warm and relaxed. She thought she could sit where she was forever, her head on Ryder's shoulder, his hand sliding up and down her arm.

"I'm glad we agree, because now that I've taught you how to fire a handgun, I think it's time for you to teach me how to make a cake."

"That's fair," she responded, snuggling closer and closing her eyes. "What kind of cake do you want to make? Chocolate? Red velvet? Banana?"

"Wedding."

"Wedding?" She straightened, suddenly wide-awake. "Do you know how difficult wedding cakes are to make? How much time they take? We should probably start with something simpler. A birthday cake or—"

"It's not just any wedding cake I want to make with you." He fished in his pocket, pulled out a blue velvet jeweler's box and opened it to reveal a sparkling sapphire set in a simple platinum band.

"Ryder—"

"You've owned my heart from the first time I saw you smile. Almost losing you nearly tore me in two. You've been given a second chance. *We've* been given one, and I don't want to waste a minute of it. Will you marry me?"

"I—"

"Say yes, girl. Or I'll say it for you," Dottie hollered, and Ryder smiled.

"If Dottie's response is all I can get, I'll take it, but I'd rather hear it from you. *Will* you spend the rest of your life with me, Shelby Ann?"

"Yes," she whispered, tears sliding down her cheeks as he slipped the ring on her finger.

And then she was in his arms, every breath, every heartbeat in tune with his.

She slid her hands through his hair, loving the thickness of it, loving the velvety roughness of his jaw as her fingers trailed along warm skin, drifted along granite shoulders encased in crisp, cool cotton and settled over his heart.

"Don't make me bring a broom out there," Dottie called, and Ryder broke away, his breathing uneven, his eyes burning into Shelby's.

"I wasn't kidding about a wedding cake—a fall wedding cake."

"*This* fall?" Shelby asked as he tugged her to her feet.

"Would you rather wait until next year?" He pressed kisses along the column of her throat, his lips warm and firm and wonderful, and Shelby sighed.

"No."

"Good." He smiled down into her eyes, offering her everything she'd ever wanted and so much more than she'd ever imagined she would have. Two paths had converged and merged, God guiding and leading, prodding and pushing Shelby and Ryder straight into each other's hearts.

And Shelby was so very thankful that He had.

"Come on," she said. "If we're going to make our wedding cake together, we'd better start practicing now."

She led Ryder into the kitchen, glad to see that Dottie had made herself scarce. The piping bags were still on the counter, and she handed Ryder the white icing. "Let's get started."

"We may not want to practice on your housewarming cake, Shelby Ann. I'm not sure how well I'm going to take to this," he said, and she smiled, covering his hands with hers, guiding him as they wrote two words on the seat of the swing: *Three Forever*.

"What do you think?" she asked, looking into his dark chocolate eyes, seeing his love written there. True and real and selfless, the most wonderful gift any person had ever given her.

"I think," he said, scanning her face, his gaze dropping to her white polo shirt, her faded jeans, "it's perfect."

"*Absolutely* perfect," she responded, and he pulled her into his arms, kissed her until nothing else existed.

"So, how about we start planning this fall shindig? I've got a dozen bridal magazines. Let's start looking through them." Dottie slammed a pile of magazines on the kitchen table, and Shelby jumped back.

"Dottie!"

"What?" she asked with a sly smile.

"Do you plan to always have bad timing?" Ryder grumbled.

"Not always. Just until you two get to the I-dos," she responded, and he laughed.

"What do you think, then, Shelby Ann? Should we hurry up and get there?" he asked, pulling out a chair and gesturing for her to sit.

"You know" she responded, grabbing a magazine, her heart racing with the depth of her love for him, "I think that we should."

* * * * *

LOVE INSPIRED

Stories to uplift and inspire

Fall in love with Love Inspired—
inspirational and uplifting stories of faith
and hope. Find strength and comfort in
the bonds of friendship and community.
Revel in the warmth of possibility and the
promise of new beginnings.

Sign up for the Love Inspired newsletter
at **LoveInspired.com** to be the first
to find out about upcoming titles,
special promotions and exclusive content.

CONNECT WITH US AT:

 Facebook.com/LoveInspiredBooks

 Twitter.com/LoveInspiredBks

Get 4 FREE REWARDS!

We'll send you 2 FREE Books plus 2 FREE Mystery Gifts.

FREE
Value Over
$20

Both the **Love Inspired®** and **Love Inspired® Suspense** series feature compelling novels filled with inspirational romance, faith, forgiveness, and hope.

YES! Please send me 2 FREE novels from the Love Inspired or Love Inspired Suspense series and my 2 FREE gifts (gifts are worth about $10 retail). After receiving them, if I don't wish to receive any more books, I can return the shipping statement marked "cancel." If I don't cancel, I will receive 6 brand-new Love Inspired Larger-Print books or Love Inspired Suspense Larger-Print books every month and be billed just $5.99 each in the U.S. or $6.24 each in Canada. That is a savings of at least 17% off the cover price. It's quite a bargain! Shipping and handling is just 50¢ per book in the U.S. and $1.25 per book in Canada.* I understand that accepting the 2 free books and gifts places me under no obligation to buy anything. I can always return a shipment and cancel at any time. The free books and gifts are mine to keep no matter what I decide.

Choose one: ☐ **Love Inspired**
Larger-Print
(122/322 IDN GNWC)

☐ **Love Inspired Suspense**
Larger-Print
(107/307 IDN GNWN)

Name (please print)

Address   Apt. #

City   State/Province   Zip/Postal Code

Email: Please check this box ☐ if you would like to receive newsletters and promotional emails from Harlequin Enterprises ULC and its affiliates. You can unsubscribe anytime.

Mail to the Harlequin Reader Service:
IN U.S.A.: P.O. Box 1341, Buffalo, NY 14240-8531
IN CANADA: P.O. Box 603, Fort Erie, Ontario L2A 5X3

Want to try 2 free books from another series? Call 1-800-873-8635 or visit www.ReaderService.com.

Someone was shooting at them!

Liam hit the gas and Shauna braced herself for the worst. Her body began to shake uncontrollably as the SUV sped up and jerked from side to side as Liam attempted to escape.

They were shooting at her this time. Not just attempting to run her off the road.

These people, whoever they were, wanted her *dead*.

Just like her mother.

Why? She couldn't seem to grasp why she'd suddenly become a target. It just didn't make any sense. Tears pricked her eyes, but she held them back.

After what seemed like eons but was likely only fifteen minutes, the vehicle slowed to a normal rate of speed.

"Are you okay?" Liam asked tersely.

She hesitantly lifted her head, scanning the area. "I—Yes. You?"

"Fine. Thankfully the shooter missed us. I wish I knew exactly where the gunfire came from." He sounded frustrated. "This is my fault. I knew you were in danger, but I didn't expect anyone to fire at us in broad daylight."

"At me." Her voice was soft but firm. "Not you, Liam. This is all about me."

He glanced sharply at her. "They could have easily shot me, too, Shauna. Thankfully, they missed, but that was too close. And you still don't know why these people have come after you?" He hesitated, then added, "Or why they killed your mother?"

"No." She shrugged helplessly. "I'm not lying. There is no reason I can come up with that would cause this sort of action. No one hated either of us this much."

"Revenge?" He divided his attention between her and the road. She didn't recognize the highway they were on, but then again, she didn't know much of anything about Green Lake.

Other than she'd brought danger to the quaint tourist town.

Don't miss
Hiding in Plain Sight *by Laura Scott,*
available September 2022 wherever
Love Inspired Suspense books and ebooks are sold.

LoveInspired.com

the accidental vegetarian

the accidental vegetarian

Delicious and Eclectic Food Without Meat

Simon Rimmer

CASSELL
ILLUSTRATED

This book is dedicated to Ali, Flo, and Hamish

First published in Great Britain in 2004 by Cassell Illustrated,
a division of Octopus Publishing Group Limited
2–4 Heron Quays, London E14 4JP

This edition published in 2005 by Cassell Illustrated

Text © 2004 Simon Rimmer
Design and layout © 2004 Octopus Publishing Group Ltd

A CIP catalogue record for this book is available from the British Library.

Distributed in the United States of America by
Sterling Publishing Co., Inc.,
387 Park Avenue South, New York, NY 10016-8810

ISBN 1 84403 2760
EAN 9781844032761

Photographs by Jason Lowe
Designed by Simon Daley
Edited by Barbara Dixon and Victoria Alers-Hankey

Printed in China

Contents

Introduction	**6**
Dips and morsels	**8**
Salads	**22**
Small platefuls	**38**
Big platefuls	**62**
Side dishes	**98**
Puddings	**108**
Index	**142**

Introduction

When I bought Greens in 1990 I had two cookery books, a bank loan and no idea how to cook! The plan was that I and Simon Connolly, my business partner, would swan around as the hosts with the most, drinking nice wine and chatting up women while someone else cooked and we coined it in, big-style. That was until we worked out the size of our bank loan and the cost of employing a chef—so we became the chefs.

Simon and I met while working as waiters in the Steak and Kebab restaurant in Manchester, England. It was a brilliant place to work, full of people waiting to do other things—act, write, fly to the moon—but all loving the buzz of the place. Let me tell you something about the restaurant industry, the hours seem unsociable to you, but there isn't a more sociable job in the world. You work hard, meet great people and then sit down at the end of the shift and have a few glasses with your mates.

From there I'd got the restaurant bug, so we decided to open our own place. At the time it didn't matter what sort of restaurant it was as long as it was cheap. I had always had my eye on Greens, then one morning I drove past it and saw a "For Sale" sign being put outside. It was too good to resist and after much negotiation we became the proud owners of a veggie cafe.

I should point out here that we were, and still are, carnivores, so looking through veggie cookbooks in 1990, and being confronted with brown, stodgy food that was all a little bit worthy, was not fun. So we opened with such "classics" as nut roast, vegetarian lasagne, and some dreadful generic curry—you don't have to tell me how awful it sounds.

It was chaos at the start. We had no idea how to organize our preparation and purchasing and we were working 100 hours a week for practically nothing. I hated everything we were cooking, but we were improving.

Surprisingly, we were busy; while the food left a lot to be desired, we were overtly friendly and working very hard. I'd caught the food bug; I was determined to make veggie food more exciting, to get people to eat at Greens because the food was good. I consumed cookery books, learnt techniques, researched cultures who have great vegetarian dishes—Asian, Mediterranean, African—and tried to use French and Italian techniques alongside them; I was extremely experimental and obsessed.

After two years I was getting there; the restaurant was full and the food had become unique. I sourced unusual suppliers of fruit and veg to bring exotics to the table, I looked for different pasta makers and vegetarian cheese suppliers and I made sure that the still popular generic "vegetable" term never appeared on the menu.

After thirteen years I still love Greens. It feels like home. Our customers are very protective of it, they don't like change, or the fact that they can't always get a table—we reckon we turn away 400 people a week, which is quite amazing, so if you fancy coming, book early!

I think my food is best described as magpie cuisine—I'll steal an idea from anywhere, combining an Asian curry with Jamaican rice and peas. I always try to let the availability of ingredients influence the menus: strawberry soups in summer, Italian bean and Parmesan-roasted parsnips in winter, crisp radish and watercress salads in May.

The recipes in this book are both attainable and inspiring. I don't have formal training as a chef, so I've learnt by the seat of my pants. It hasn't been easy, but it's been a fantastic journey and I'm still learning—so what are you waiting for, turn the pages and get cooking!

Dips and morsels

Feta cheese bread

There's something really satisfying about making bread—watching it rise, kneading the dough and, best of all, eating warm bread that you've made for yourself. This bread is so delicious, all you need with it is extra-virgin olive oil and some pickled chiles.

1 Dissolve the yeast and sugar in a little of the water. This takes about 5 minutes.

2 Tip the flour and salt onto a work surface and make a well in the center. Add the rest of the water and the now frothy yeast mix and mix to a dough. Knead for 7–8 minutes until it stops being sticky—the dough is ready when it will stretch out between your hands without breaking.

3 Put the dough into an oiled bowl, cover and leave to double in size—at least 2 hours.

4 Turn the dough out onto a lightly floured surface and "knock back"—to get all the puffiness out of it.

5 Knead the oil, cheese, mint, and pepper into the dough, divide into four pieces and mold each into a round loaf. Put on a buttered and floured baking sheet, cover with a damp cloth and leave to rise at room temperature for 40–60 minutes.

6 Preheat the oven to 350°F. Glaze the loaves with egg wash and bake for around 30–40 minutes. Leave to cool.

½oz (2 sachets) instant yeast

1 tsp superfine sugar

2½ cups warm water

2¼lb strong bread flour, plus extra for dusting

2 tbsp salt

4 tbsp extra-virgin olive oil, plus extra for greasing

12oz feta cheese, crumbled

handful of freshly chopped mint leaves

freshly ground black pepper

butter, for greasing

1 egg, beaten, for eggwash

Blinis with sour cream and roasted bell peppers

Makes 15

The joy of blinis is that they're dead versatile—top them with sweet, savory or a combination of the two. Have them for breakfast, lunch or supper, make them big or small. Use your imagination for the toppings.

1 First make the blinis. Sift the flours and a little salt into a bowl. Make a well in the center and add the two whole eggs and one egg white.

2 Mix together the yeast, sugar, and milk and leave for a couple of minutes. Pour this slowly into the flour mix and whisk to make a smooth batter. Stir in the butter.

3 Cover the batter and leave in a warm place for 1 hour.

4 Meanwhile, make the topping. Roast or char the peppers until the skin is blackened. Put them in a plastic bag, seal and let them go cold, when the skin will fall away. Seed the peppers and cut into wide strips.

5 Just before cooking the blinis, whisk the remaining egg white and fold into the batter.

6 Heat a little oil in a skillet. Pour enough batter into the pan to make a 4inch blini. When the batter bubbles up, flip it over and cook the other side. Keep the blini warm while you make the rest of the pancakes in the same way.

7 Spoon some sour cream onto each blini and top with some of the pepper pieces, an olive, and a twist of black pepper.

*If using dried yeast, follow the maker's instructions for quantity and use.

$1\frac{1}{2}$ cups buckwheat or
wholemeal flour
$1\frac{3}{4}$ cups all-purpose flour
2 whole eggs, plus 2 egg whites
$1\frac{3}{4}$oz fresh yeast*
2 tsp superfine sugar
3 cups warm milk
1 tbsp melted butter
vegetable oil for frying
salt

For the topping

4 red bell peppers
1 cup set sour cream
15 black Ascoloni olives
freshly ground black pepper

Spicy red bell pepper hummus with coriander seed flat bread

Feeds 6

I thought long and hard about putting hummus in the book, it's the kind of thing that you expect from a veggie cookbook—but this is different! Firstly, the hummus is lovely and garlicky, it's also lemony and it's got a great little kick at the end from the peppers. Making breads can be hit and miss at times, which is why I love making flat breads—you have a little more margin for error, plus they have a delicious taste and texture.

1 Start with the bread. Dry-fry the coriander seeds, then lightly crush them in a mortar and pestle. Don't turn them into a powder, but also don't leave them tooth-breaking size. Put them into a pan with the water and bring just to a boil.

2 Put the yogurt into a bowl and add the yeast. Pour the coriander seeds and water into the bowl and stir well.

3 Add 1½ cups of the flour, and use your hands to combine it well, then cover the bowl and leave to prove for 25 minutes. Contrary to popular belief, it doesn't have to be somewhere warm, but it helps.

4 After the proving, turn the dough out onto a lightly floured surface, add the salt, oil, and remaining flour and give this a really good mix. Put back in the bowl, cover and leave to prove again for 1 hour, when it should have just about doubled in size.

5 Turn the dough out onto a lightly floured surface and knock it back. Divide the dough into six, then roll into little balls. Roll each ball out to 4–5inch circles.

6 To cook the bread, brush each circle of dough with a little oil and cook for about 30 seconds on each side, either in a shallow skillet or on a griddle pan. Put a cooked flat bread on each plate.

7 For the hummus, put all the ingredients except the oil, olives, and fresh chile in the blender and whiz until smooth. With the motor running, add a stream of oil to loosen the mixture.Turn out into a dish, garnish with the olives and chargrilled chile and serve with the coriander seed flat bread.

15oz can chickpeas (garbanzo beans), drained and rinsed
4 garlic cloves
¼ cup tahini paste
juice of 3 lemons
3½oz sweet pickled chile peppers
olive oil to loosen
salt and freshly ground black pepper
6 olives and 1 red chile, charred or griddled, to serve

For the coriander seed flat bread

1 tsp coriander seeds
½ cup water
1–1¼ cups plain yogurt
1½ tsp dried yeast
5 cups bread flour, plus extra for dusting
1 tbsp salt
2 tbsp vegetable oil, plus extra for brushing

Fried halloumi with lemon and capers

Feeds 4

You'll not see halloumi on a cheeseboard, because raw it tastes a bit like plastic, but when dusted with spiced flour and fried it becomes a right tasty morsel. After that the zingy lemon dressing cuts through the sweetness of the cheese to perfection. Mop up the dressing with my feta cheese bread (see page 10), or a slab of crusty white if that's what you've got.

1 Combine the flour with the cayenne and season well. Dust each slice of cheese with the flour.

2 Heat some oil in a skillet until hot, then fry the halloumi for about 1 minute on each side, until golden.

3 To make the dressing, put the lemon juice, vinegar, garlic, and mustard into a bowl and whisk together. Keep whisking and slowly add the oil, a little at a time. Season to taste, then add the capers and herbs.

4 Sit two pieces of cheese on each plate (it looks good on top of some peppery watercress) and drizzle with the dressing.

3½ tbsp all-purpose flour
1 tsp cayenne pepper
8oz halloumi cheese, cut into 8 slices
vegetable oil for frying
salt and freshly ground black pepper
watercress, to serve (optional)

For the dressing

juice of 1 lemon
1 tbsp white wine vinegar
1 garlic clove, crushed
1 tsp Dijon mustard
3 tbsp extra-virgin olive oil
1½ tsp capers in vinegar
freshly chopped parsley
freshly chopped cilantro

Sticky rice and
peanut balls

Feeds—well it depends on
how many beers

*The ultimate beer snack. Be very careful, these little beasts are addictive: Thai
spices, peanuts, rice, and deep-fried—they're crying out for a beer.*

1 Blend half the rice in a food processor until it's not quite a paste. Turn out into
a bowl and combine this with the remaining rice, the curry paste, lime juice, and
salt to taste. Mix it up really well.

2 Roll the mixture into balls 1–1½inches in diameter. Now roll the balls in the
peanuts and deep-fry in hot oil until golden. Drain on paper towels and serve with
chili sauce.

2¼ cups cooked Thai jasmine rice
4 tbsp red Thai curry paste
juice of 1 lime
1 cup roasted peanuts, finely crushed
vegetable oil for deep-frying
salt
sweet chili sauce for dipping

Favetta

Feeds 4

*This is such a lovely dish whether you are a veggie or not. You can use frozen beans,
but fresh ones are so much better. Serve with coriander seed flat bread (see page 12)
or with some roasted vegetables.*

1 Blanch the beans in boiling water for 2 minutes, maximum, then plunge into really
ice-cold water. Drain the beans and peel off the hard outer skins.

2 Put the beans, thyme, garlic, and lemon juice in a blender and pulse until smooth.

3 With the motor running, pour in enough of the oil to blend until it's the consistency
of hummus.

4 Turn out into a bowl and season.

400g/14oz fresh fava beans
handful of fresh thyme
1 garlic clove
juice of 1 lemon
½ cup extra-virgin olive oil
salt and freshly ground black pepper

Tomato and mozzarella cakes

Feeds 6

Each cake is a tomato risotto filled with melting cheese. You may have eaten the little round versions of these called "arancini," or little oranges. These larger versions could make a great lunch with simply dressed arugula.

1 Melt the butter in a heavy-bottom pan. Add the rice and cook for a couple of minutes on a low heat. When the rice starts to become a little translucent around the edges, add the wine and cook for another minute.

2 Add a ladleful of warm stock (it must be warm to enable the rice to cook properly). When the stock has been absorbed, add another ladleful and continue doing this until all the stock has been added and/or the rice is tender.

3 Next, fold in the sun-dried tomatoes and the cream and season well. Leave the rice to cool.

4 Divide the rice into six and roll into balls. The rice will be nice and sticky. Make a hole in the center of each ball and press some of the cheese into it. Cover with the rice and flatten into a patty shape.

5 Roll the patties in flour, then egg, then breadcrumbs, and deep-fry at 350°F. You don't want the oil to be too hot or the outside will cook and the middle will be cold. Fry till crisp and golden, then drain on paper towels and serve with dressed arugula leaves.

½ stick butter

2 cups arborio rice, rinsed and drained

splash of white wine

3½ cups warm stock

3½oz sun-dried tomatoes, chopped

splash of cream

1½ cups cubed mozzarella cheese

all-purpose flour, for rolling

1 egg, beaten

2½–3 cups fresh breadcrumbs

vegetable oil for deep-frying

dressed arugula leaves, to serve

Thai spiced potato cakes with spicy coleslaw

Makes 8 cakes

I first went to Thailand in 1996 and I found it so inspiring—it's a food lover's delight. I'd always loved Thai food—green curries, pad-thai, sticky rice—with all their beautiful fragrances. When you're there, the smell of lime leaves, lemon grass, coconut, and charring chiles you get from the excellent street food stalls is overwhelming. So this fantastic little morsel will give you a spicy, fragrant taste of the East. If you can't get fresh lime leaves, then use dried, but the smell of fresh makes it worth a trail around the stores. You should have tingly lips from the chiles and the wasabi in the coleslaw —don't go easy on them, live on the edge.

1 First, make the potato cakes. Put the mashed and grated potatoes in a large bowl, add all the other potato cake ingredients and season.

2 Mold the mixture into eight 3inch rounds, about 1inch thick (or make sixteen mini-cakes—great for parties), and pop them into the fridge for about 1 hour.

3 Set up three plates or bowls: one with flour, one with eggwash, and one with the breadcrumbs. First roll the cakes in flour, dust off any excess, then roll them in the egg and finally in the breadcrumbs.

4 You can shallow- or deep-fry them (I find that deep-frying gives a crisper texture). If you shallow-fry, be careful not to burn them—a gentle heat is best. Either way, they're done when crisp and golden.

5 Put a spoonful of coleslaw on each plate and sit a potato cake on top. Sprinkle some chopped cilantro over and add a wedge of lime on the side—and don't forget to pour yourself a nice cold glass of Singha beer.

all-purpose flour, for rolling

2 eggs, beaten, for eggwash

2½–3 cups fresh breadcrumbs

vegetable oil for frying

1 quantity spicy coleslaw, to serve (see page 32)

freshly chopped cilantro and lime wedges, to serve

For the potato cakes

3 large mealy potatoes, say russets, peeled, cooked and mashed

1 raw potato, peeled and grated

3 tbsp mayonnaise

1 bunch of scallions, finely chopped

2 small red chiles, seeded and chopped

freshly chopped cilantro

2 garlic cloves, crushed

2 stalks of lemon grass, finely chopped

4 kaffir lime leaves, finely chopped

1inch piece of fresh ginger, finely chopped

1 tsp ground cinnamon

2 shallots, finely chopped

salt and freshly ground black pepper

Norimaki
sushi rolls

Feeds 6

Hands up if you thought "sushi" meant raw fish? Quite a lot of you I reckon. Well, I did too, but it actually means vinegared rice, so with that piece of knowledge you can make these delicious, healthy nori rolls and show off to friends and family about the true meaning of sushi. Nori is roasted and rolled seaweed and comes in sheets.

1 Put the rice in a pan with the water and bring to a boil. Cover and simmer for 5 minutes, then take off the heat, leave covered and allow to cool.

2 When the rice is cool, put it in a bowl, season and add the sugar and vinegar. Mix well.

3 Lay out the nori sheets and spread a little wasabi on each. Put a line, about 1inch wide, of rice a little way in from the bottom edge.

4 Press some cucumber and pepper into the rice. Top with more rice and roll up tightly. Chill for 30 minutes, then cut into 1½inch long pieces. Cut off and discard the uneven ends.

5 Make a dipping sauce by heating the vinegar, sugar, and chile until the sugar dissolves.

6 Serve the sushi rolls with the dipping sauce, extra wasabi paste, soy sauce, and pickled red ginger.

¾ **cup sushi rice, rinsed thoroughly and drained**

1 **cup water**

2 **tbsp sugar**

3½ **tbsp rice wine vinegar**

4 **sheets dried nori**

wasabi paste

½ **cucumber, peeled, seeded, and cut into batons**

½ **red bell pepper, seeded, and cut into batons**

salt

soy sauce and pickled red ginger, to serve

For the dipping sauce

½ **cup rice vinegar**

6 **tbsp sugar**

1 **small red chile, finely chopped**

Patatas bravas

In Spain these are made by deep-frying the potatoes, salting them and squeezing a spicy tomato "ketchup" over them. But this is the yummiest way to do it—slowly roasting the potatoes with chiles. I like to make them a day in advance so the olive oil, chiles, and tomatoes can really get to work on the potato. Whenever we have a party at home I make a bucket-load of these—they do go so well with a cold beer.

lots of olive oil
1½lb 5oz russet or Yukon Gold potatoes, peeled
2 cups canned chopped tomatoes
3 red chiles, chopped
4 garlic cloves, crushed
lots of freshly chopped parsley
salt and freshly ground black pepper

1 Preheat the oven to 425°F. Heat a load of oil in a massive roasting pan until really hot. Cut the potatoes into 1inch cubes. Chuck away any uneven bits, so you're left with neat shapes, they look nicer.

2 Throw the potatoes in the oil and give them a little shake. Season well, then pop into the oven for about 10 minutes until they begin to brown.

3 Add the tomatoes, chiles, and garlic and stir well. Cook for another 25–35 minutes until the potatoes are soft on the inside, but with a little bit of crispness outside.

4 Either add the parsley and serve, or leave them until the next day, then reheat, adding more oil, and add the parsley before eating.

5 If you're making these for a party, put a load in a secret place for yourself, you know it makes sense.

Dolmades

Whenever I'm in Greece I can't stop eating these little fellas. There's loads of different varieties—meaty, herby, veggie, and these, which have golden raisins and pine nuts. Serving them with yummy tzatziki is essential.

1 Heat the oil in a pan and fry the shallots and garlic until soft. Add the rice, golden raisins, pine nuts, and lemon juice and fry for 1 minute. Season, then add the water.

2 Cover the pan and simmer for 15 minutes, then turn off the heat and leave to cool.

3 Once the mixture is cool, add the scallions, mint, and parsley.

4 Rinse the grape leaves in water, then place them shiny side down on a board. Put about 2 tsp of the cooled stuffing on each leaf and roll into a tight parcel. Chill until ready to eat.

5 For the tzatziki, mix the cucumber with the yogurt, garlic, mint, lemon juice, and seasoning. Tip into a serving bowl and top with a dash of olive oil.

6 You can serve the dolmades either cold or warm (just heat them in a steamer). Put them on a large plate with the tzatziki in the middle and get stuck in.

1 tbsp olive oil

3 shallots, finely chopped

2 garlic cloves, crushed

$2/3$ cup short-grain rice, rinsed and drained

$1/2$ cup golden raisins

$1/2$ cup pine nuts, toasted

juice of 1 lemon

$3/4$ cup water

1 bunch of scallions, finely chopped

handful of finely chopped fresh mint leaves and parsley

20 preserved grape leaves

salt and freshly ground black pepper

For the tzatziki

1 cucumber, peeled, seeded, and coarsely grated

$3/4$ cup Greek yogurt

4 garlic cloves, crushed

handful of freshly chopped mint leaves

juice of $1/2$ lemon

extra-virgin olive oil

Salads

Santa Fé Caesar salad

A good Caesar salad is a joy to behold, but unfortunately the rise of café bars has meant that a bit of romaine lettuce, soggy croûtons, mayo, and Parmesan are masquerading as the real thing. So here is a great salad, which has the strength of a Caesar with spicy bits of the Mexican border. Hail Caesar-Gringo!

1 To make the dressing, put the mayonnaise, mustard, and garlic into a bowl and whisk in the lime juice and vinegar. Mix in the grated Parmesan and season to taste.

2 To make up the salad, cut the lettuce into 1–2inch wide slices, chuck away the bottom, and put the slices into a large bowl. Season with a little salt and pepper.

3 To make the croûtons, dry-fry the tortillas in a pan until a little charred, then break up into the lettuce bowl.

4 Chuck in the beans and chiles.

5 Add about half the dressing and toss, then add the rest (if you think it's dressed enough with half that's fine) and the avocado, shallots, and cilantro leaves.

6 Finally, top with some large Parmesan shavings (use a potato peeler to get the right effect) and serve.

1 romaine lettuce, trimmed

2 soft corn tortillas

½ cup cooked/canned pinto beans, or kidney beans, drained and rinsed

2 red chiles, seeded and chopped

1 ripe avocado, chopped

2 shallots, finely sliced

fresh cilantro

salt and freshly ground black pepper

For the dressing

¾ cup mayonnaise

2 tbsp Dijon mustard

1 garlic clove, crushed

juice of 1 lime

2 tbsp white wine vinegar

¾ cup freshly grated Parmesan cheese, plus extra Parmesan to shave for garnish

Sun-blush Niçoise

Feeds 6

This is sunshine on a plate—sun-blushed tomatoes, light baby romaine lettuce, olives, and a gorgeous creamy Italian dressing. It's a brilliant appetizer, because it doesn't fill you up too much, but really gets the juices flowing for more tastes. You'll need some foccacia to mop up the irresistible dressing.

1 Break up the lettuces and divide between six bowls or plates.

2 Toss together the potatoes, beans, and capers with a little seasoning, then divide them between the bowls.

3

4 Spoon a little of the dressing over each salad, then sit an egg half, some sun-blushed tomatoes and olives on top or arrange them around the sides of the bowl.

2 baby romaine lettuces

7oz boiled tiny new potatoes (about 12)

7oz cooked fine green beans

5–6 tbsp capers in vinegar

3 hard-cooked eggs, halved

5½oz sun-blushed tomatoes

18 large green olives

salt and freshly ground black pepper

For the Italian dressing—makes 4 cups

4 egg yolks

4 tsp superfine sugar

4 tsp Dijon mustard

2½ cups olive oil

¾ cup white wine vinegar

juice of 3 lemons

freshly chopped oregano leaves

Panzanella

I did some filming in the Tuscany region of Italy a couple of years ago and ended up doing an impromptu cookery demonstration at a wonderful cookery school near Lucca. After I'd finished, about 20 of us sat down and ate some fantastic pasta and fish, but the highlight was the panzanella, which is really just a bell pepper, tomato, and stale bread salad, but using the juice from the tomatoes and the peppery olive oil from the olive groves at the school made it one of my most memorable meals.

1 Skin the tomatoes by putting a cross on the bottom, plunging them into boiling water for about 30 seconds, then into iced water. The skins will peel off easily. Cut them into quarters, scoop out the seeds into a strainer and press to release the juice into a bowl. Put the quarters into a separate bowl.

2 Skin all the peppers by either grilling them, or roasting them until black. Put them in a plastic bag until cool—the skins will fall off. Then seed them and cut each into about eight pieces. Put in the bowl with the tomato quarters, then add the chile, capers, and olives.

3 Tear the bread into big chunks and put in a separate bowl.

4 Add the vinegar, garlic, and oil to the tomato juice, season and whisk well, then pour over the bread and leave for about 1 hour.

5 Finally, gently combine the tomatoes and peppers mixture with the bread and dressing, and garnish with basil leaves.

6 Pretend you're in Tuscany.

2¼lb plum tomatoes

2 red bell peppers

2 yellow bell peppers (you can use green, but they're a little bitter)

1 small red chile, seeded and chopped

5–6 tbsp capers, in vinegar or salt

12 large Ascoloni olives—should be black, but I don't like them so I use green

1 ciabatta loaf, preferably stale

4 tbsp red wine vinegar

5 garlic cloves, crushed

1 cup extra-virgin olive oil, preferably Tuscan

salt and freshly ground black pepper

handful of fresh basil leaves, roughly torn, to garnish

Warm stack of Greek salad with parsley pesto

Feeds 6

A delicious lunch recipe that looks good and yet is simplicity itself. While I say it's Greek, the Italians do help out a bit.

1 Skin the tomatoes by putting a cross on the bottom, plunging them into boiling water for about 30 seconds, then dropping into iced water—the skins will peel off easily. Then slice them to about ⅛inch thick.

2 Slice the zucchini to the same thickness, season and griddle on both sides until they're nicely striped.

3 To make the pesto, put the garlic and parsley in a blender and whiz together, then with the motor still running add the nuts, cheese, and oil. Taste and season.

4 To assemble, you'll need six 4inch diameter serving rings (or two rings and repeat three times). Sit the rings on a baking sheet. Plonk a layer of tomato in the bottom of each ring. (If you're using plum tomatoes, make sure the base is well covered.) Season, then spoon on a little pesto and top with a couple of basil leaves and a layer of sliced or crumbled feta. Repeat with a layer of zucchini slices. Then repeat the layering, finishing with a layer of feta.

5 Preheat the oven to 350°F. Drizzle the stacks with a little oil and cook in the oven for 10–12 minutes to warm through. You can flash them under a hot broiler to brown, if you want.

6 Unmold each stack onto a plate, and arrange the olives around. Garnish with basil, a good drizzle of oil, and a lemon wedge.

6 beefsteak tomatoes, or
12–15 decent-sized plum tomatoes
1lb zucchini
handful of fresh basil leaves, plus
extra for garnish
1lb Greek feta cheese
olive oil for griddling and drizzling
18 large Kalamata black olives
lemon wedges, to serve
salt and freshly ground black pepper

For the parsley pesto

2 garlic cloves
large handful of roughly chopped
fresh parsley
¼ cup pine nuts
½ cup freshly grated Parmesan
cheese
⅔ cup extra-virgin olive oil,
Greek of course

Coronation chickpeas and potato salad

I used to think coronation chicken was really corny—it probably still is, but I love it. Well, it set me thinking; why didn't Queen Elizabeth get anything created for veggies? So by Royal Appointment, here is something for us.

1 Cook the potatoes and, while they're still hot, cut into quarters and put in a bowl with the onions and vinaigrette. Toss them well (the potatoes will absorb the dressing) and season. Leave to cool.

2 Mix the mayo with the curry paste, then stir into the cooled potatoes with the chickpeas, golden raisins, and almonds. Garnish with cilantro leaves.

800g/1lb 12oz new potatoes, scrubbed

bunch of scallions, finely chopped

2 tbsp vinaigrette

1 cup mayonnaise

2oz smooth curry paste (maybe softened in a little hot water)

½ cup canned chickpeas (garbanzo beans), drained and rinsed

1 tbsp golden raisins

1 tbsp slivered, toasted almonds

salt and freshly ground black pepper

fresh cilantro leaves, to garnish

Asparagus, potato, and fennel salad with Italian dressing

Feeds 4

I love dishes that include a bit of leftover grub—roasties in this case—and teamed with "posh" ingredients such as asparagus. Slap a bit of tangy Italian dressing over the top and it makes a brilliant lunch salad or appetizer.

Slice the asparagus diagonally, cut up the potatoes, if necessary, and put all the salad ingredients into a large bowl. Season well and dress with about ¾ cup of the dressing. (If you like, you can serve this with warm potatoes and asparagus.)

12 cooked asparagus spears

about 20 roast potatoes

2 shallots, sliced

handful of arugula leaves

1 fennel bulb, blanched and finely sliced

1 quantity of Italian dressing (see page 25)

Pickled cucumber salad

Feeds 4

This is dead easy—a lovely sweetish pickle that gives a great lift to any Oriental dish or tired salad. The warm, fragrant Szechuan peppercorns really add to the dish, but if you can't get them use black ones.

1 Toss the cucumber batons in the salt and put in a colander for about 20 minutes to get rid of excess moisture. Meanwhile, dry-fry the peppercorns for 2–3 minutes until fragrant, then roughly grind in a mortar and pestle.

2 Heat the ground nut and chili oils in a small pan, add the garlic and chile and cook gently for 2 minutes. Add the sugar and vinegar and simmer until the sugar has dissolved and the mixture is a little syrupy. Rinse and dry the cucumber and add to the pan with the onions. Crank the heat up and count slowly to 10. Take off the heat, let it cool and serve with whatever you fancy—pie, salad, quiche, Chinese.

4 cucumbers, peeled, seeded, and cut into 2inch long batons

1 tsp salt

2 tbsp Szechuan peppercorns

2 tsp peanut oil

1 tsp chili oil

1 garlic clove, crushed

1 small red chile, seeded and finely chopped

2 tbsp sugar

2 tbsp rice wine vinegar

2 scallions, finely chopped

Sweet potato salad

Feeds 4

I do love arugula and Parmesan salad, but arugula deserves more, so I grant it the company of sweet potato and mint.

1 Brush the potato slices with the chili oil and season, then griddle for a couple of minutes on each side.

2 To make the dressing, simply whisk everything together in a small bowl.

3 Put the mint, arugula, and shallots into a serving bowl, pour over the dressing and toss gently, then sit the sweet potatoes on top.

14oz golden sweet potato, peeled and thinly sliced

chili oil

handful of fresh mint leaves

7oz fresh arugula leaves

4 shallots, finely sliced

salt and freshly ground black pepper

For the dressing

1 red chile, seeded and finely chopped

2 tbsp light soy sauce

juice of 1–2 limes

1 tsp superfine sugar

Spicy coleslaw

Feeds 2–4

Wasabi is hot green horseradish—it's seriously fiery, but very addictive.

Put the cabbage, onion, and carrots into a large bowl and season well. Add the mayo, wasabi, and lime leaves and mix it up well.

4oz red cabbage, finely sliced

½ red onion, finely sliced

2 carrots, grated

50g/2oz mayonnaise

¼ cup wasabi paste

3 lime leaves, shredded

salt and freshly ground black pepper

Fattoush

Feeds 4

I think that Middle Eastern cuisine has some of the best veggie dishes and ingredients on the planet—tabbouleh, kibbeh, borak—all great names and tastes (if you don't know what they are, that can be your homework for next time). I also love the fresh, clean tastes they do so well—this brilliant Lebanese salad is ideal for a summer's day, it's crunchy, zesty, and the dressing is divine. Sumac is a dried, crushed berry and it tastes a bit of a cross between cumin and cranberry.

1 To make the dressing, simply whisk all the ingredients together in a bowl.

2 For the salad—again, dead easy—just put all the ingredients in a large bowl and season to taste.

3 Pour the dressing over the salad and gently toss together. I love serving it in a huge bowl and letting everyone pile in.

1 pita bread, torn into small pieces

8 plum tomatoes, seeded and quartered

½ cucumber, peeled, and cut into batons

½ green bell pepper, cut into strips

8 radishes, sliced

1 shallot, sliced

a few arugula leaves

1 small baby romaine lettuce

handful of fresh mint leaves

For the dressing

1¼ cups olive oil

juice and zest of 5 lemons

1 garlic clove, crushed

4 tbsp ground sumac

salt and freshly ground black pepper

Griddled eggplant salad with nuoc cham

Feeds 6

This works brilliantly as a side dish for spicy dishes, but I think it also works as an appetizer. Beware of this Vietnamese dressing, it is HOT, so make use of the yogurt.

1 Put the eggplants into a bowl, add a little oil and the lime juice and season with plenty of salt. Toss well.

2 Next, griddle the eggplants in a hot pan until charred. Put to one side.

3 To make the nuoc cham, simply combine all the ingredients in a processor. (I tend to process the dry ingredients first to make it smooth.)

4 Next, dry-fry the cumin seeds until fragrant, then crush them in a mortar and pestle and combine with the yogurt.

5 Arrange the eggplants on plates, spoon some nuoc cham dressing over, and top with the yogurt.

4 eggplants, cut into wedges, or chunks if large
vegetable oil for griddling
juice of 1 lime
1 tbsp cumin seeds
½ cup plain yogurt
salt

For the nuoc cham

10 small red chiles
5 garlic cloves
juice of 5 lemons
5 tbsp rice wine vinegar
5 tbsp water

Watermelon salad

Feeds 6

This is a great summer dish, making use of juicy watermelon, feta cheese, and the spicy bread. I can feel the sun on my body already.

1 Combine all the ingredients for the dressing in a bowl.

2 Toss the salad ingredients in the dressing, season lightly, then sit some of the salad in a good high mound on top of a piece of coriander seed flat bread (see page 12).

7oz Greek feta cheese, cut into 1inch cubes

½ cucumber, seeded, and cut into 2inch batons

6–8 fresh basil leaves

6 wedges of watermelon, about 3oz each

For the dressing

½ cup Greek yogurt

lots of freshly chopped mint leaves

juice of 1 lime

salt and freshly ground black pepper

Arugula, fig and pecan salad with creamy blue cheese

Feeds 4

This is one of the most delicious ways of eating figs. Traditionally you'd probably expect Roquefort or Dolcelatte, but I'm a champion of trying new tastes, so see what you fancy at your favorite cheese store.

1 Whisk together the oils and vinegar and season well.

2 Put all the remaining ingredients into a large bowl, pour in the dressing, toss together and serve.

2 tbsp walnut oil

1 tbsp vegetable oil

1½ tbsp raspberry vinegar

9oz arugula leaves

½ fennel bulb, very finely sliced

6–8 ripe figs, quartered

5½oz creamy blue cheese, broken into bite-sized cubes

1 cup pecan halves

salt and freshly ground black pepper

Green papaya salad

Feeds 4

I used to eat this hot, spicy salad every day on the beaches on Koh Samui. It's one of those Thai dishes that makes your eyes water and you crave liquid. But take the pain and nibble on raw white cabbage to quell the fire, although ice-cold lager does work well.

1 Put the garlic, shallot, and salt to taste in a large mortar and pestle and grind to a paste. Put the paste in a large serving bowl.

2 Coarsely grate the papaya and add to the bowl with the chiles, tomatoes, beans, nuts, lime juice, and sugar.

3 Garnish with cilantro leaves and lime wedges and serve.

4 garlic cloves

1 shallot, sliced

1 green papaya, peeled and seeded

3 small hot red chiles, seeded and chopped

2 tomatoes, seeded and cut into strips

3 raw green beans, cut into strips

¼ cup roasted peanuts, crushed

juice of 1 lime

pinch of sugar

sea salt

fresh cilantro, to garnish

lime wedges, to serve

Lemon, fennel and oyster mushroom salad

Feeds 4

There's something quite sexy about this salad; maybe it's the lemon marinade combined with the juicy mushrooms and fennel, or maybe it's the way the sauce dribbles down your chin...

1 Trim off the fennel tops, cut the fennel in half lengthwise, or quarters if they're large. Blanch in boiling water for about 1 minute, then plunge into ice-cold water. Drain when cool.

2 Whisk together the oil, lemon juice, zest, and garlic.

3 Arrange the mushrooms and fennel in a serving dish and season well, then pour over the oil marinade. Add enough oil to just cover the ingredients. Cover and chill for at least 24 hours, then serve with warm foccacia bread to dip into the sauce.

3 fennel bulbs

lots of extra-virgin olive oil

juice and zest of 3 lemons

2 garlic cloves, sliced

7oz oyster mushrooms

salt and freshly ground black pepper

Small platefuls

Eggplant "roll-mops"

Feeds 4

I love roll-mop herrings, they remind me of my dad, as we're the only members of my family who like them. I created this eggplant version almost as a joke, but I found that everyone loved them, so now you can make them. You really need to pickle the onions for at least a week, otherwise you'll be pulling faces as you eat. If you want to make this more substantial serve with cold boiled potatoes, hard-cooked eggs, and fine green beans.

1 To pickle the onions, put all the ingredients except the onions in a pan and bring to a slow boil. Simmer for 15 minutes, then allow to cool. Pack the onions into a sterilized sealable jar and pour the spiced vinegar over them. Seal the jar and leave for at least 1 week.

2 To assemble the dish, cut the eggplants into strips about $\frac{1}{8}$ inch thick. Season the strips, then brush with the oil and cook on a griddle for a minute or so each side until nicely striped.

3 Put a little bit of pickled onion (make sure you don't have any seeds in there) at the end of a slice of eggplant, roll it up tightly and secure with a wooden toothpick. When you've rolled them all up pour a little more vinegar over and chill for about 20 minutes.

4 Make a dressing by whisking the chopped chives into the cream.

5 Sit a couple of roll-mops on a little watercress or other greenery and top with a big dollop of the chive cream.

3 large eggplants, topped and tailed
olive oil for brushing
white vinegar for drizzling
freshly chopped chives
¾ cup sour cream
salt and freshly ground black pepper
watercress, to serve (optional)

For the pickled onions

4 cups white vinegar
1 cinnamon stick
6 cloves
1 tbsp coriander seeds
1 tsp mustard seeds
2 bay leaves
2 red chiles
1 tsp black peppercorns
2 tbsp superfine sugar
1½ tbsp salt
2 onions, finely sliced

Eggplant tikka

This might seem like a bit of a hassle for lunch, but it is worth it and even though there are a lot of ingredients it's easy to prepare. The end result is fantastic, ideal for outdoor summery lunches with friends.

1 Toss the eggplants in oil and salt, then cook on a hot griddle pan on each side until striped.

2 Put all the marinade ingredients into a large bowl and stir to mix. Coat the eggplants well with the marinade, thread onto wooden skewers and put into a dish, then cover and chill for at least 2 hours.

3 To make the coleslaw, simply combine all the ingredients in a bowl.

4 Cook the eggplants under a hot broiler, basting with the butter and lemon juice and turning when golden.

5 Serve the eggplant kebabs with a few chiles, lime wedges, and the coleslaw.

4–6 eggplants, about 2lb, topped, tailed and cut into chunks
vegetable oil
3½ tbsp melted butter
juice of 1 lemon
salt
chiles and lime wedges, to serve

For the marinade

½ cup plain yogurt
juice of 1 lime
2 garlic cloves, crushed
1inch piece of fresh ginger, finely chopped
1 tbsp ground coriander
1 tsp ground cumin
1 tsp garam masala
1 tsp paprika

For the coleslaw

1 cup plain yogurt
juice of 2 limes
pinch of cayenne pepper
6oz shredded white cabbage
1 each of red, yellow and orange bell peppers
10 scallions, chopped
handful of freshly chopped cilantro leaves and stems
1 tbsp ground cumin
1 garlic clove, crushed

Eggplant "stack" with pesto

Imagine yourself in Italy—Florence with the beauty of the city, the fine ice cream and brilliant small restaurants knocking out exquisite Italian fare—then imagine a local guy has opened a sandwich bar using all these influences, that's what this is all about.

1 Preheat the oven to 400°F. To make the pesto, put the basil and a little of the oil in a food processor and blitz to make a paste. Add the garlic, pine nuts and Parmesan and blitz with enough oil to make a rich, thick sauce. Turn out into a dish, check the seasoning and keep the pesto cool.

2 Season the eggplants well and toss in oil, then cook on a hot griddle pan on both sides until striped. Do the same with the bread.

3 To assemble the dish, put four rings (about 4inches wide x 2inches deep) on a baking sheet and brush a little oil around the inside of each.

4 Press some eggplant into the bottom to form a solid base, then add a slice of tomato and a spoonful of pesto. Then it's a piece of bread, a little oil and mozzarella. Continue layering and finish with a layer of cheese. Drizzle with oil, then cook in the oven for 10–15 minutes until warmed through. Finish off under a hot broiler to brown the cheese before serving.

5 Sit each ring on a plate, run a knife around the inside edge and carefully remove the ring. Garnish with a little dressed arugula.

3–4 good-sized eggplants, topped, tailed and sliced into $\frac{1}{2}$inch rounds

vegetable oil for griddling and brushing

1 ciabatta, cut into slices about the thickness of a dollar coin

9oz beefsteak tomatoes, thinly sliced

10oz buffalo mozzarella cheese, thinly sliced

dressed arugula leaves, to garnish

For the pesto

10oz fresh basil, stalks and leaves

$\frac{1}{2}$ cup extra-virgin olive oil

2 garlic cloves

$\frac{1}{2}$ cup toasted pine nuts

1 cup freshly grated Parmesan cheese

salt and freshly ground black pepper

Goat's cheese and mango

Feeds 6

Another Greens classic and probably one of the easiest dishes ever created, it's cheese on toast for goodness sake. This has been on and off the menu for thirteen years and there's still an argument raging as to who actually created it. The dish was conceived around a table at a curry house after a good few beers. Now we all claim to be the daddy of the dish, but I think we know the truth...

1 Preheat the oven to 250°F. Dip a sharp knife into really hot water, then slice the cheese log into pieces about ⅓inch thick (this will give about six portions). Dip the knife into the water after each slice.

2 Combine the sesame seeds, chile and mint in a wide bowl.

3 Warm the honey, then brush it sparingly on one side of each piece of cheese. Press the cheese slices into the sesame mixture then shake off any excess. Put to one side.

4 Cut a circle a little bigger than a cheese slice out of each piece of bread (probably a 3inch cutter). Brush each bread slice with a little oil, then put in the oven for about 5 minutes until dry, but not colored.

5 To make the sauce, put the wine, mango, and salt into a bowl and mix well.

6 When you're ready to serve, put a piece of cheese on each slice of bread and either put under a hot broiler until the cheese softens, but not melts, or put it in a hottish oven (400°F) for a few minutes.

7 Put a swirl or small pool of sauce in the middle of each plate, top with a little arugula, then sit the cheese on toast on top.

7oz goat's cheese log, rind on

1¼ cups toasted sesame seeds

2 small red chiles, finely chopped

1 bunch of fresh mint leaves, finely chopped

5 tbsp clear honey

6 thick slices white loaf

olive oil

splash of white wine

7fl oz canned mango pulp

pinch of salt

arugula leaves, to serve

Mushroom "rarebit" on brioche toast

I love the taste and texture of field mushrooms and when you add the strong cheesy topping and serve it on toasted brioche, well, it's the food of kings and queens.

1 Preheat the oven to 350°F. Put the mushrooms in a baking dish and season. Sprinkle with garlic and cover with the oil. Cook in the oven for 10–12 minutes until softened slightly.

2 Meanwhile, toast the brioche and make the rarebit topping by combining all the ingredients in a bowl. When the mushrooms come out of the oven spoon some of the topping mix onto each of them, pressing it well in. Then place under a hot broiler until the cheese bubbles, melts and browns.

3 Serve one large mushroom on top of a piece of toasted brioche.

6 large field mushrooms, or portobellos cut in half, peeled and trimmed
2 garlic cloves, crushed
½ cup olive oil
6 slices brioche
salt and freshly ground black pepper

For the topping

2 cups grated mature Cheddar or Gruyère cheese
1 tbsp wholegrain mustard
1 garlic clove, crushed
1 egg, beaten

Proper pizza

Pizzas originated in Naples as a way of using up leftovers, such as bread dough, tomatoes, cheese, and herbs. Since then, of course, they've become a bit of a hybrid—asparagus and fontina, Sunday lunch pizza, even balti pizza. Well this is a simple, but delicious, Neapolitan pizza with tomatoes, cheese, basil, and olive oil. Once you've mastered this, then if you want to try apricot and radish tikka masala pizza, well who am I to criticize?

1 To make the base, sift the flour into a large bowl. Dissolve the yeast in a little warm water until it begins to foam, then slowly add to the flour and mix to form a dough. If it's too sticky add more flour.

2 Cover the bowl and leave to rest for 5 minutes. Turn out onto a lightly floured surface and knead the dough with the salt for about 10 minutes until smooth. Cover with a damp cloth and let it prove for about 30 minutes.

3 Preheat the oven to 475°F. Cut the dough in half, knead for a brief minute, then press it out into two circles about 1½inches diameter each (I like the edges slightly thicker, almost like a plate edge). Place the dough circles on floured baking sheets.

4 To make the topping, season the tomatoes and spread over each dough base (you probably won't need the whole can). Add some basil leaves, seasoning, and torn cheese to each one, then drizzle over some oil.

5 Put in the oven and bake for 8–10 minutes.

6 Serve with a little more oil and some black pepper.

*If using dried yeast, follow the maker's instructions for quantity and use.

For the base

4½ cups bread flour, plus extra for dusting

10g/¼oz fresh yeast*

2 tsp salt

For the topping

15oz can chopped tomatoes, well drained

fresh basil leaves

7oz buffalo mozzarella cheese, torn into pieces

extra-virgin olive oil

salt and freshly ground black pepper

Pumpkin enchilladas
with mole sauce

Feeds 6

I adore Mexican food—it can be a bit limited, but what's good is magnificent, like this dish. Mole sauce is a rich, deep, smoky sauce with both a chocolate and chile hit. I leave the seeds in the chiles, but take them out if you prefer. I like to serve this with guacamole and sour cream. Don't turn the page thinking this weird choccy sauce isn't for you—it is! Try it and be converted.

1 To make the sauce, put the chiles, coriander seeds, sesame seeds, almonds, peppercorns, and cloves in a mortar and pestle and crush. Tip into a skillet and dry-fry for a minute or so until lightly charred.

2 In a separate pan, fry the onion, garlic, and cocoa in a little oil for 2 minutes.

3 Add the tomatoes and bring to a boil, then add all the dry-fried spices, the cinnamon, sugar, and stock and cook for 25 minutes. Transfer to a blender and whiz until smooth. Turn out and fold in the chocolate.

4 Preheat the oven to 400°F. Put some oil in a roasting pan and put in the oven to heat up. Tip the squash into the roasting pan, season well and roast for 40 minutes until soft.

5 Put the squash in a bowl, add the refried beans, cilantro, and red chile and stir well to mix.

6 Divide the mixture between the tortillas, roll up and cut the ends straight. Put in a baking dish, cover, and cook in the oven for about 12 minutes, until warmed through.

7 To serve, put two tortillas on each plate and spoon over some of the sauce (it's pretty heady so not too much). Serve with some sour cream, lime wedges, and cilantro.

vegetable oil for roasting

2 butternut squash, peeled and cut into 1¼inch cubes

15oz can refried beans

freshly chopped cilantro leaves

1 red chile, chopped

12 soft flour or corn tortillas

salt and freshly ground black pepper

soured cream, lime wedges and fresh cilantro leaves, to serve

For the sauce

10 red chiles

2 tsp coriander seeds

1 tsp sesame seeds

2 tbsp slivered almonds

5 black peppercorns

2–3 cloves

1 onion, sliced

3 garlic cloves, crushed

1 tbsp cocoa powder

vegetable oil for frying

15oz can chopped tomatoes

pinch of cinnamon

sugar to taste

⅔ cup stock

3½oz best-quality dark chocolate (not unsweetened), grated

Chinese mushroom pancakes

Feeds 6 as an appetizer,
3 as a main course

Creating vegan dishes is always really difficult, so when I made this for the first time I thought I was the vegan king! It takes its inspiration from crispy duck and pancakes, but we're using oyster mushrooms instead—it really is brilliant.

1 To make the sauce, heat a little oil in a skillet and fry the shallots until soft.

2 Add the garlic and sherry, reduce a little, then add the plums and cook until they begin to break down. Add the stock and bring to a boil.

3 Simmer for 5 minutes, then pass through a strainer into a serving bowl.

4 Mix the flour and five-spice powder together with some seasoning. Toss the mushrooms in the mix, then shake off any excess.

5 Heat some oil in a large pan and deep-fry the mushrooms in batches for about 4 minutes, until crisp and brown. Drain well on paper towels.

6 Warm the pancakes either in a microwave for 20 seconds or in a steamer over simmering water for 1 minute.

7 I like to pile the mushrooms onto one big plate, put the cucumber and scallions on another and the pancakes inside the steamer. Spread a little plum sauce on a pancake, lay a strip of mushrooms down the middle, top with onion and cucumber, and roll up, tucking in the bottom edge. Guzzle down and make sure you've got extra pancakes on hand, because everyone will want more.

$7/8$ cup all-purpose flour

$7/8$ cup five-spice powder

14oz oyster mushrooms

18 Chinese pancakes, 3inch diameter (from any Asian supermarkets)

1 cucumber, seeded and cut into 2inch batons

6–8 scallions, finely sliced

vegetable oil for deep-frying

salt and freshly ground black pepper

For the plum sauce

2 shallots, chopped

1 garlic clove, crushed

splash of dry sherry

1lb plums, pitted

$1/2$ cup stock

vegetable oil

Banana dhal

You can use any type of lentil to make a dhal, but the advantage of the red ones is that they don't have to be soaked, so this makes a really quick and easy meal. Adding either fresh banana or fried plantain makes it extra special and all you need to serve with it are a couple of chapattis.

1 Fry the onion, garlic, and ginger, in the oil over a low heat for about 10 minutes until soft and golden. Add the turmeric and cook for 1 minute.

2 Add the lentils to the pan and fry for 1–2 minutes.

3 Add the warmed stock and bring to a boil, then simmer for 15 minutes.

4 Add the spices, season, and cook for a further 10 minutes.

5 A couple of minutes before serving fold in the bananas and warm through.

6 Garnish with cilantro leaves and eat with bread.

1 onion, finely sliced

2 garlic cloves, chopped

1inch piece of fresh ginger, finely chopped

2 tbsp vegetable oil

pinch of turmeric

1 generous cup red lentils, well washed and drained

3 cups warmed stock

pinch of ground cumin

pinch of ground coriander

pinch of garam masala

4 firm bananas, thinly sliced

salt and freshly ground black pepper

fresh cilantro leaves, to garnish

Gruyère-filled beefsteak tomatoes

Feeds 4

This is a really old dish from Greens, but I still love it. The intense flavor from reducing the cream, then adding yummy Gruyère cheese and tasty treats makes it what I like to call a meat-eater's veggie dish.

1 Preheat the oven to 325°F. Skin the tomatoes by putting a cross on the bottom, plunging them into boiling water for about 30 seconds, then into iced water. The skins will peel off easily. Slice off the tops and put to one side, scoop out the pulp into a bowl, being careful not to break the flesh, and put the pulp to one side. Season the cavities well.

2 Put the cream in a heavy-bottom pan, bring slowly up to a boil, then cook to reduce the volume by half.

3 Meanwhile, heat a little oil in a large pan and gently fry the zucchini, peppers, mushrooms, and garlic until soft, about 5 minutes.

4 Add ⅔ cup of the cheese to the reduced cream and stir until it melts. Remove from the heat and fold in the fried vegetables.

5 Divide the filling between the tomatoes, top with the remaining cheese, sit the lids on top and put onto a baking sheet.

6 Cook in the oven for 6–8 minutes, until the cheese melts.

7 To make the dressing, press the tomato pulp through a strainer and season the juices. Add the vinegar, then whisk in the oil.

8 Toss the arugula in the dressing and sit the tomatoes on top of the leaves.

4 beefsteak tomatoes

1¾ cups heavy cream

2 zucchini, finely diced

2 red bell peppers, seeded and finely diced

3oz white button mushrooms, finely chopped

1 garlic clove, crushed

1¾ cups freshly grated Gruyère cheese

vegetable oil for frying

salt and freshly ground black pepper

handful of fresh arugula leaves, to serve

For the dressing

tomato pulp from the tomatoes

1½ tbsp red wine vinegar

5 tbsp extra-virgin olive oil

Roasted red bell peppers
with fennel

Feeds 6

Patience is the key for this recipe, the peppers and fennel need to be soft, and the cheese needs to brown and bubble—if you rush this it'll be a big disappointment.

1 Preheat the oven to 400°F. Season the peppers well, drizzle with oil, then put in a baking pan and roast for about 10 minutes until softened.

2 Blanch the fennel pieces in boiling salted water for 2 minutes, then plunge into ice-cold water. When they're cool, pat dry.

3 Put the tomatoes and olives in a bowl with the garlic and parsley and season well.

4 Put a piece of fennel inside each pepper half, sprinkle some tomato mixture over and drizzle with oil. Top with grated cheese and put under a hot broiler until the cheese bubbles and browns.

5 To serve, put a little watercress on each plate and sit a pepper half on top. Spoon some yogurt on the side and garnish with a lemon wedge and green olives. Finish with a good twist of black pepper.

3 decent-sized red bell peppers, halved lengthwise and seeded

3 fennel bulbs, trimmed and cut into halves, or quarters if very large

3 tomatoes, skinned, seeded, and finely chopped

3–4 black olives, pitted and finely chopped

1 garlic clove, crushed

small handful of freshly chopped parsley

10oz mozzarella cheese, grated

olive oil for roasting

salt and freshly ground black pepper

watercress or mesclun, Greek yogurt, lemon wedges and green olives, to serve

Peas
and carrots

Make this and don't tell your friends and family what's in it, they'll struggle to guess. Mint, peas, carrot vinaigrette—such simple ingredients, but combined they're pretty cool, and very much removed from the frozen or tinned stuff. It makes a great appetizer.

1 Preheat the oven to 350°F. Blanch the peas in boiling salted water for 1 minute, then plunge into ice-cold water. Drain well, then purée with the mint in a food processor.

2 Combine the eggs, cream, and lemon juice in a bowl and season to taste. Pass the pea purée through a fine strainer into the egg mixture.

3 Divide the mixture between six greased ramekins. Put them in a roasting pan, pour in hot water to about half way up the ramekins, cover with foil and cook in the oven for 25–30 minutes until set. Allow to cool.

4 To make the dressing, put ¾ cup of the carrot juice into a pan, bring to the boil, reduce the heat and cook until reduced by half. Pour into a bowl, add the honey and vinegar and whisk to mix. Slowly add the oil, then stir in the rest of the carrot juice and season.

5 Turn out each pea custard onto a plate. Toss some chard in the dressing, sit this on top of the pea creation and drizzle more dressing around.

3 cups defrosted frozen peas (fresh if in season)

lots of fresh mint leaves

3 eggs

¾ cup heavy cream

squeeze of lemon juice

salt and freshly ground black pepper

red chard, to garnish

For the dressing

1 cup carrot juice (squeeze your own if you can)

1 tsp honey

1 tbsp white wine vinegar

⅔ cup extra-virgin olive oil

Leeks wrapped
in phyllo

This is a simple and delicious starter packed with flavor. Avoid using really huge leeks as they're a bit "woody" for this dish; what you need are slim, attractive leeks that will be sweet and succulent.

1 Preheat the oven to 425°F. Cut the leeks into 4inch long pieces (cut the end at an angle to make them look pretty).

2 Heat some oil in a roasting pan, then put all the leeks in, season well and add the garlic. Roast in the oven for about 5 minutes until just a little soft. Take out of the oven and cool, then peel off their outer layer.

3 When the leeks are cool, cut the phyllo to the length of the leeks and wrap a piece around each leek. Brush with butter, put in the roasting pan and pop back in the oven for another 8–10 minutes until the phyllo is crisp and golden.

4 To make the dressing, whisk the lemon juice and mustard together, then add the garlic and whisk in the oil. Fold in the chives and tomatoes and season well.

5 Sit a little watercress or other greenery on each plate, top with two leek parcels and spoon over a little dressing.

6 medium-sized leeks, trimmed, well washed and dried

1 garlic clove, sliced

6 sheets of phyllo pastry

3oz melted butter

olive oil for roasting

salt and freshly ground black pepper

a little watercress, to serve (optional)

For the dressing

---

juice of 2 lemons

3oz Dijon (Grey Poupon) mustard

1 garlic clove, crushed

2/3 cup extra-virgin olive oil

handful of freshly chopped chives

2oz sun-blushed tomatoes, finely chopped

Leek and potato rosti with "rarebit" topping

Feeds 6

Rostis are simply fried grated potato with added bits—leeks in this case—and yummy toppings. They're easy to do: simply grate the potatoes, mold into a disc and fry—but sometimes those pesky potatoes don't want to stick together and you end up with burnt potato pieces, not nice. So this is a fail-safe way to perfect rosti every time, by par-boiling the potatoes they'll stick like glue, and it means you can prepare them in advance without worrying about them.

1 Put the potatoes in a pan and just cover with water, bring to a boil and then boil for 7 minutes, no more. Drain.

2 When they're cool enough to handle, peel the potatoes and grate them into a bowl. If you use long strokes the end result is better, or you can use the grater attachment on your processor.

3 Mix the grated potatoes with the leek and garlic, then season really well.

4 Mold the mixture into six patties and chill for 1 hour.

5 Heat a good amount of oil in a pan, enough so when you put the rosti in it will lap up the side a little. Pop in the rostis (do in two batches) and fry over medium heat for about 4 minutes each side until golden, then drain on paper towels.

6 To make the topping, put the ingredients into a bowl and stir well to mix.

7 Lay out all the rostis on a baking sheet and divide the topping between them, then place under a hot broiler until the cheese bubbles and browns.

8 This is delicious served with tomato and balsamic vinegar salad, or a fried egg—honestly!

4 large potatoes, scrubbed but not peeled
1 small leek, trimmed, well washed and finely chopped
2 garlic cloves, crushed
vegetable oil for frying
lots of salt and freshly ground black pepper

For the topping
2½ cups freshly grated strong mature Cheddar cheese
1 egg, beaten
1½ tbsp wholegrain mustard

Beet tart

I love this and the combination of buttery pastry, sweet roasted beets and sharp tangy goat's cheese is delicious.

1 To make the pastry, put the butter, flour and salt in a food processor and pulse until it resembles breadcrumbs. Add the water and milk and pulse to form a dough. Turn into a bowl, cover and chill for 25 minutes.

2 Preheat the oven to 400°F. Divide the pastry into four and roll out to roughly fit deep tart pans, about 4–4½inches wide. Line the pans, letting the pastry overhang the edges a little, and bake blind for 25–30 minutes until firm and lightly golden. Remove from the oven and trim off the edges.

3 To make the chutney, fry the onions, garlic, and butter with some seasoning in a little oil over a low heat for about 20 minutes until golden but not burnt. Add the sugar and vinegar, bring to a boil, then reduce the heat right the way down and cook for about 30 minutes until "jammy".

4 To make the filling, chuck the broccoli into boiling salted water, count to 10, then spoon it out and plunge into iced water (this will stop it cooking on). Drain well.

5 Heat some oil in a skillet, then add the beets, season well and cook for a couple of minutes. Add the broccoli and pine nuts (these are yummy if you toast them a little first) and cook for a minute or two. Pour in the crushed tomatoes and toss all the ingredients quickly, then remove from the heat.

6 Divide the filling mixture between the pans and top with the crumbled goat's cheese. Either flash under a hot broiler until the cheese browns, or put back into the top of the oven for a few minutes.

7 Serve alongside the chutney. This is really fab with big fat fries with rock salt and balsamic vinegar.

For the pastry

1¾ sticks chilled butter, cut into cubes
3¼ cups all-purpose flour
pinch of salt
3½ tbsp water
3½ tbsp milk

For the filling

12 broccoli florets
4–6 cooked beets, peeled and cut into large wedges
¾ cup pine nuts
½ cup crushed tomatoes
6oz goat's cheese, crumbled
vegetable oil for frying
salt and freshly ground black pepper

For the chutney

4 large Spanish onions, sliced
1 garlic clove, crushed
½ stick butter
⅔ cup dark brown sugar
½ cup white wine vinegar
vegetable oil for frying
salt and freshly ground black pepper

Simple
tomato tart

Every time I make this I forget how easy it is and yet it looks like you've taken ages to make it. Serve with some arugula dressed with extra-virgin olive oil and balsamic vinegar.

1 Preheat the oven to 350°F. Roll out the pastry on a lightly floured surface to an 7 x 11inch rectangle and put on a greased baking sheet.

2 Cut the tomatoes into slices about ⅛inch thick. Arrange overlapping slices on the pastry, leaving a 1inch border all round. Season well, brush with butter and sprinkle with sugar.

3 Bake in the oven for 25–30 minutes, until crisp and golden and the tomatoes have caramelized.

4 Combine the oil and vinegar in a bowl and toss the arugula in it. Serve a generous slice of tart on each plate with the dressed arugula.

8oz bought puff pastry

flour for dusting

6–8 plum tomatoes, peeled

2 tbsp melted butter, plus extra for greasing

1 tbsp superfine sugar

3 tbsp extra-virgin olive oil

1 tbsp balsamic vinegar

fresh arugula leaves

salt and freshly ground black pepper

Sun-dried tomato, mozzarella and basil tart

Feeds 6

This is so simple and yet so tasty. If you ever make a cheese-filled tart, always add a little splash of cream to give a touch of richness to the filling. All you need with this is a bit of green salad dressed with simple vinaigrette.

1 Divide the pastry into six equal pieces and roll out on a lightly floured surface to fit six 4inch tart pans. Press the pastry into the pans, then chill them for about 20 minutes.

2 Preheat the oven to 400°F. Put the pans on a baking sheet and bake for 15 minutes until crisp and golden.

3 To make the filling, combine the cheese, basil, and tomatoes in a large bowl and season well.

4 When the pans are cooked, remove from the oven, divide the filling between them and add a splash of cream to each. Return to the oven and bake for about 5 minutes until the cheese melts and begins to brown.

1 quantity of shortcrust pastry (see page 92)
flour for dusting
2½ cups freshly grated mozzarella cheese
about 20 fresh basil leaves
12 sun-dried tomatoes, finely chopped
dash of heavy cream
salt and freshly ground black pepper

Spicy beet and coconut soup

Beets get a lot of bad press and everybody, except me, seems to hate pickled beet. I love it and it also has magical properties. Whenever I go to watch an important soccer match with my mates, it's tradition for me to bring the lucky cheese and beet sandwiches—they nearly always work. Anyway, this is one of the most stunning and delicious soups you'll ever make, it's both earthy and spicy at the same time and it has the best color pink. A little tip: don't blend it until you're about to serve as it will go brownish.

1 Put all the ingredients for the paste into a blender and blend until smooth (the smoother the paste the nicer the soup, so take your time).

2 Preheat the oven to 400°F. Put the scrubbed beets into an ovenproof dish, sprinkle with oil and sea salt, then wrap in foil and roast for about 35 minutes until soft. When cool enough to handle, peel and chop the beets.

3 Gently fry the shallots and cumin seeds in a little oil, then add half the paste and cook for 5 minutes to release the fragrance.

4 Add half the beets, cook for a couple of minutes, then add the stock, bring to a boil and simmer for about 7–8 minutes.

5 This is when it gets interesting—just before serving, put the soup, coconut milk, the rest of the paste and beets in a blender and blend until smooth. It will be a bright pink, like you've never seen from food before, unless you live on Mars. The soup should be hot enough, but if necesssary reheat gently for a minute or two.

6 Check the seasoning, then serve immediately topped with mint, cilantro and cucumber. It's also lovely with the coriander seed flat bread (see page 12).

1lb 2oz fresh beets, scrubbed

vegetable oil for coating and frying

2 banana shallots, finely chopped

1 tsp cumin seeds

2½ cups stock

1¾ cups coconut milk

sea salt

fresh mint, cilantro leaves and chopped, seeded cucumber, to serve

For the paste

---

2 stalks of lemon grass

2 garlic cloves

3 red chiles (seeded if you like)

1inch piece of fresh ginger, peeled

4 kaffir lime leaves

juice of 1 lime

Big platefuls

Huevos rancheros (ranch eggs)

Feeds 4

A good few years ago my dear friend Graham Peers got married in Richmond, Virginia, so a tribe of us made the trip and we all stayed at various friends of Graham's around town. Alison, my wife, and I got the best deal as we were 50 yards from a fantastic place called The Steak and Eggs Kitchen, which did the best breakfasts, and had those mini-TVs on the tables. Well, this is where I first had huevos rancheros, or fried eggs cooked with spicy salsa and flour tortillas on the side. Serve these with extra-hot chili sauce and endless cups of coffee.

1 Put all the ingredients for the salsa except the crushed tomatoes in a bowl and season. Gradually add the crushed tomatoes—you may find you don't need them all, you're looking for the veg bits to be bound by the tomato sauce, not swimming in it.

2 You need to cook this in batches. Heat a little oil in a skillet over a medium heat and warm a quarter of the salsa. Now make a hole in the middle of the pan, melt a ½ stick butter in the gap, then break 2 eggs into this space. Put a lid on the pan and leave for about 3 minutes. The dish is ready when the eggs are cooked and the whites have merged into the salsa.

3 Slide the eggs and salsa onto a large plate and top with cilantro leaves. Cook the rest of the eggs in the same way. Now dip your warm tortillas into the yolks and dare yourself to overdo the chili sauce. (Not that I'd know, but apparently this is a great hangover cure!)

vegetable oil for frying

2 sticks (1 cup) butter

8 eggs

fresh cilantro leaves

2 warm soft flour or corn tortillas, halved

hot chili sauce (Jamaican hot is pretty good)

For the salsa

1 onion, finely chopped

1 red bell pepper, seeded and finely chopped

1 small hot red chile, finely chopped

1 zucchini, finely chopped

1 garlic clove, finely chopped

1 green bell pepper, seeded and finely chopped

⅔ cup crushed tomatoes

salt and freshly ground black pepper

Savory Paris-Brest

This is traditionally a sweet dish with custard, almonds, and other yummy things inside a ring of choux pastry. I don't see any reason why you can't turn it on its head and have a savory filling—so I will.

1 Preheat the oven to 400°F. To make the pastry, put the butter and water in a pan and heat until the butter melts, then bring to a boil. Take the pan off the heat, tip in all the flour and mix well. Cool slightly, then, using a wooden spoon, beat in the eggs, one at a time (it's pretty tough on the old arms, this one). Add the salt.

2 Transfer to a pastry bag and allow to cool for a few minutes. Line a baking sheet with waxed paper, then pipe a 8inch diameter circle onto the paper, then pipe another one directly on top.

3 Put the sheet in the oven and cook for 30–40 minutes, when the choux ring should be golden and firm. The aim is to get it to dry out in the middle—I quite often put it on the bottom shelf for another 5–10 minutes to make sure. When it's cooked, take the ring out and let it cool. Increase the oven temperature to 425°F.

4 To make the filling, heat some oil on a baking sheet in the oven. Slice the zucchini and eggplant into pieces about $\frac{1}{8}$inch thick. Ideally, cook each vegetable separately—season each vegetable, place in the hot oil on the sheet, add a little garlic and roast until soft, then toss in a little thyme. Put to one side while you cook the next one. However, if you're pushed for time, roast the onions for 5 minutes, then add the peppers for 5 minutes, then the eggplant and zucchini in the same sheet.

5 When all the vegetables are roasted, reduce the oven temperature to 350°F. Slice the choux ring horizontally into two halves. Arrange the vegetables on the bottom ring and top with the sun-blushed tomatoes and goat's cheese. Cover with the top ring.

6 Pop it back into the oven for about 10 minutes until the cheese softens. Serve with a dressed mixed leaf salad.

$1\frac{1}{4}$ **sticks butter (10 tbsp)**

1 cup water

$1\frac{3}{4}$ **cups all-purpose flour**

6 eggs

pinch of salt

For the filling

2 zucchini

1 eggplant

1 red onion, sliced in quarters attached to the base

2 red bell peppers, seeded and cut into chunks

1 garlic clove

fresh thyme

12 sun-blushed tomatoes

7oz goat's cheese, crumbled

vegetable oil for roasting

salt and freshly ground black pepper

Phyllo strudel with port wine sauce   Feeds 6

OK, here we go, the recipe that changed the world, well Greens. I always say this is the dish to serve to meat-eaters because it blows their minds. I like to serve it with some fine green beans with garlic and tomato sauce (see page 106) and a few new potatoes, although a good friend of mine swears it tastes best with fries and garlic mayo. If you make only one dish out of this book, it should be this one...

1 Heat some oil in a pan, add the mushrooms, garlic, and seasoning and fry for a couple of minutes, then drain well. Then fry the leeks.

2 Mix the cheeses together in a large bowl with a good amount of seasoning until smooth. (Sometimes it helps to warm the cream cheese for a few seconds in a microwave to soften it.) Fold in the mushrooms, leeks, and tomatoes, then chill for at least 2 hours.

3 Preheat the oven to 400°F. Lay out six pieces of pastry on a lightly floured surface and brush with lots of melted butter, then cover with another layer and brush again. Add a final layer, but this time only brush the edges of the pastry.

4 Divide the chilled filling into six long sausages and place each one on the bottom edge of each pastry rectangle. Fold the bottom edge over the filling, tuck in the sides, then roll up into a tight parcel and brush with butter. Put them all on a baking sheet and cook in the oven for 25 minutes until crisp and golden.

5 Meanwhile, make the sauce. Pour the wine into a pan, bring to a boil and reduce it by half—stick a bay leaf in the wine if you want to make it a little more "herby."

6 Heat the oil in a pan and cook the onion, mushrooms, and garlic with seasoning until soft. Throw in a big slosh of port and reduce that by half. Next, pour in the reduced wine and bring back to a boil, then add the stock, bring to a boil and cook to reduce for about 15 minutes. Just before serving, whisk in the cold butter to give it a really great shine.

7 To serve, pour a little sauce on each plate and sit a strudel on top.

7oz button mushrooms, halved

1 garlic clove, crushed

7oz leeks, trimmed, well washed, drained and roughly chopped

9oz ricotta cheese

9oz full-fat cream cheese

3 tomatoes, skinned, seeded and chopped

18 pieces phyllo pastry, 9 x 6inch melted butter

olive oil for frying

salt and freshly ground black pepper

For the sauce

1 bottle red wine (a good heavy red is best)

1 bay leaf (optional)

2 tbsp olive oil

1 large onion, sliced

3oz button mushrooms, sliced

2 garlic cloves, crushed

good glug of port

½ cup stock

¼ stick (2 tbsp) cold butter, cubed

Wild mushroom pancakes

The filling for these pancakes is rich and delicious and the pecans make it a brilliant dish for the winter. Unlike in most pancake recipes, you don't need to let the batter stand.

1 First make the pancakes. Sift the flour and salt into a bowl, then make a well in the center and break the eggs into it. Whisk the eggs into the flour, then, little by little, slowly add the milk and water, whisking well to avoid lumps. Finally, whisk in the butter.

2 Heat a little oil in an 7inch skillet until really hot, then turn the heat down to medium. Spoon about 4 tbsp of batter into the pan and swirl it around to evenly coat the base. Cook the pancake for about 30 seconds, then flip it over and cook the other side. Turn the pancake out onto greaseproof paper and repeat with the rest of the batter. You should get twelve pancakes. Stack each pancake on waxed paper until you're ready to use them.

3 For the filling, mix the ricotta and Parmesan cheeses together and season well.

4 Heat a little oil in a pan and fry the fresh shiitakes and garlic for about 5 minutes, then drain on paper towels. Drain off the water from the dried mushrooms and chop them up.

5 Combine all the mushrooms, the pecans, and tarragon with the cheese mixture and check the seasoning.

6 Preheat the oven to 350°F. Put about 4 tbsp of filling across each pancake and roll up, tucking in the ends to make a neat parcel.

7 Use two pancakes per serving. Put the pancakes on a greased baking sheet or in pairs in greased individual dishes and top each pair with grated mozzarella. Cook in the oven for about 15 minutes until the cheese melts. Serve with a little ladleful of warm tomato sauce and some fine green beans with garlic and tomato sauce (see page 106).

$7/8$ cup all-purpose flour

pinch of salt

2 eggs

$3/4$ cup milk

$1/2$ cup water

$1/2$ stick (4 tbsp) butter, melted

$1\frac{3}{4}$ cups freshly grated mozzarella cheese

vegetable oil for frying

$1/2$ quantity basic tomato sauce (see page 107), to serve

For the filling

1lb ricotta cheese

$1\frac{1}{2}$ cups freshly grated Parmesan cheese

6oz fresh shiitake mushrooms

1 garlic clove, crushed

3oz dried shiitake mushrooms, soaked in boiling water for 1 hour

1 cup slightly broken pecans

2oz freshly chopped tarragon leaves

salt and freshly ground black pepper

Hazelnut and mushroom parcels

Feeds 4

This is another "meaty" dish that any carnivores will adore. Mushrooms, hazelnuts, and cheese wrapped in puff pastry—how could that not be anything but gorgeous? Great for Sunday lunch, or even Christmas, maybe with some fresh cranberries inside and a Cumberland sauce, but equally delicious for your supper tonight.

1 To make the parcels, fry the shallots and garlic in a little oil until soft, then add the cremini mushrooms and cook until soft. Add the assorted mushrooms, nuts, and port and reduce a little. Finally, add the butter, cook for 2 minutes, then remove from the heat and drain for at least 1 hour, or as long as possible.

2 Put a piece of vignotte on each piece of pastry, then top with some of the mushroom mixture. Roll up into a parcel and put on a greased baking sheet. Brush with eggwash, top with sesame seeds and chill for at least 20 minutes.

3 Preheat the oven to 400°F. Cook the parcels for 20 minutes until the pastry is golden.

4 Meanwhile, make the sauce. Heat some oil in a large pan and fry the shallots and garlic for 5 minutes until softened. Add the wine and reduce by half.

5 Chuck in the red peppers and cook for 5 minutes, then add the stock and tarragon and bring to a boil. Cook for 5 minutes, then pour into a food processor and whiz until smooth. Turn out into a dish, season and add a splash of vinegar to cut the sweet sauce.

6 Spoon a little sauce onto each plate, and top with a parcel. Garnish with watercress or other greenery.

2 shallots

1 garlic clove, crushed

7oz cremini mushrooms, cut into bite-sized chunks

29oz assorted mushrooms, cut into bite-sized chunks

1 cup shelled, roasted hazelnuts

splash of port

small piece of cold butter, plus extra for greasing

7oz vignotte cheese

4 x 6inch square pieces puff pastry rolled out to ½inch thick

1 egg, beaten, for eggwash

handful of sesame seeds

olive oil for frying

a little watercress, to garnish (optional)

For the sauce

2 shallots

1 garlic clove

splash of white wine

6 red bell peppers, roasted, skinned, seeded, and chopped

¾ cup stock

sprig of fresh tarragon

splash of white wine vinegar

Sweet potato and pineapple sandwich

Feeds 4

I love sweet potato, it has such a silky smooth texture when it's mashed and a delicious caramel flavor when it's roasted. This dish gets its inspiration from the Caribbean, where there are so many delicious sweet yet savory recipes that it's impossible to be anything other than a complete pig when you visit. You can give this an even bigger Caribbean flavor by adding a slug of rum to the pan when stir-frying the veggies.

1 Preheat the oven to 425°F. Heat the oil in a roasting pan, then add the sweet potato chunks. Season well, give them a good shake and add the chiles, thyme, and garlic. Roast for about 30 minutes until the sweet potato is soft (it's probably worth giving them the odd stir while they're roasting).

2 Brush each of the pineapple slices with oil and cook on a hot griddle pan for a couple of minutes each side until well striped. When they've all been charred, put them in an ovenproof dish with their juice and put to one side.

3 To make the sauce, cook the curry paste in a pan for a few minutes to release the flavor, then add the coconut milk and bring to the boil. Add the stock and cook for 5 minutes.

4 Heat some more oil in a skillet, add the onion and cook until it starts to brown. Add the red pepper and then the sweet potatoes. Cook for 3–4 minutes until the potato starts to break down.

5 Spoon in a little of the curry sauce to bind the mixture, then add the okra and cilantro. Stir it around for another couple of minutes.

6 Pop the pineapple slices in the oven for a few minutes to warm through. Put a slice of pineapple on each plate, then spoon a quarter of the sweet potato mixture on top (if you've got them, use small rings to make it neater). Sit another slice of pineapple on top and drizzle some of the curry sauce around the edge.

½ cup vegetable oil

1½lb golden sweet potatoes, peeled and cut into largish bite-sized chunks

2 small red chiles, chopped

handful of fresh thyme

4 garlic cloves, crushed

1 pineapple, peeled and cut into 8 slices (keep the juice)

1 red onion, sliced

1 red bell pepper, seeded and sliced

3oz blanched okra

freshly chopped cilantro leaves

salt and freshly ground black pepper

For the curry sauce

3 tbsp curry paste (mild or hot, whatever's in the cupboard)

1¾ cups coconut milk

½ cup stock

Cheese sausages with onion gravy

The joy of a good sausage is that fried, fatty quality and a strong mystery seasoning. Veggie sausages are tricky, but after years of trying I think this is a pretty good version—when you break them open they look "fatty" and they taste like a dream.

1 The sausage mix couldn't be easier—just chuck all the ingredients except the oil into a large bowl, season well, get your hands in and mix it all up. When you taste it, I reckon you need to over-season it by about 15 percent, so it's a bit more salty and peppery than you'd normally have—the mixture seems to lose some of its power as it chills and cooks. Chill the mixture for 2 hours.

2 Meanwhile, make the gravy. Heat a little oil in a pan and fry the onions, garlic, and sugar over low heat until golden. Sprinkle on the flour and cook for 3–4 minutes. Add the gravy browning and stock and bring to a boil. Season, then simmer for at least 20 minutes.

3 Mold the chilled sausage mix into sausage shapes—you should get about twelve out of it, depending how big you like your sausage... You can either shallow-fry the sausages in a little oil or deep-fry them in a lot of oil; I think the deep-fry method brings the best out of the flavor and texture. Fry them for about 5 minutes until golden, then drain well on some paper towels and serve with the gravy.

4 This fabulous grub is great with mashed potato (try it with the addition of wholegrain mustard), with a salad, or in a bun smothered in ketchup, onions, and mustard and served with fries.

*If you can find British Lancashire cheese, use instead of the Cheddar.

For the sausages

1lb 5oz Cheddar* cheese, grated or crumbled

3½ cups fresh breadcrumbs

6 scallions, chopped

2 tbsp fresh thyme, chopped

2 tbsp freshly chopped parsley

3 whole eggs, plus 3 egg yolks

2 garlic cloves, crushed

about 3 tbsp milk, to bind

salt and freshly ground black pepper

vegetable oil for frying

For the onion gravy

3 large onions, sliced

2 garlic cloves, crushed

1 tbsp brown sugar

⅔ cup all-purpose flour

⅓ cup gravy browning

3 cups stock

Penne all'arabiata

Feeds 4

This is one of the simplest pasta dishes in the world and definitely one of the most delicious. It's particularly good if you grow your own tomatoes as their sweet earthiness makes it even better.

1 Cook the pasta in boiling salted water until al dente. Meanwhile, heat the oil in a pan and gently fry the shallots, chiles and garlic until soft, then add the tomatoes and turn up the heat. Once the tomatoes begin to break up, turn down the heat and simmer for about 5 minutes to form a sauce.

2 Drain the pasta over a pan and add to the sauce with a little of the water the pasta was cooked in. Season well and stir in the parsley. Serve with big shavings of Parmesan, crusty bread, and a fruity Valpolicella red wine.

10oz dried penne

½ cup olive oil

2 shallots, finely chopped

2 small red hot chiles, seeded and chopped

1 garlic clove, crushed

8 tomatoes, finely chopped

a good handful of freshly chopped parsley

salt and freshly ground black pepper

Parmesan shavings, to serve

Macaroni cheese

Real comfort food—a bowl of creamy macaroni cheese never fails to hit the spot. In this recipe I've added both cherry and sun-blushed tomatoes to make it more of a sunshine dish. If you pack the mac-cheese into a presentation ring before it goes into the oven you can make it posh enough for an informal lunch/dinner for friends. But if you're doing it for yourself, slap it into a big bowl and wade in.

1 Preheat the oven to 400°F. To make the sauce, pour the milk into a pan, add the bay leaves and heat to scalding point. Remove from the heat and, when cooled a little, discard the bay leaves.

2 Melt the butter in a pan, stir in the flour and cook, stirring, for 3 minutes (don't let it brown). Add a little of the milk to the flour and stir to combine. Cook briefly, then gradually add the rest of the milk and stir until you have a smooth sauce. Bring to the boil, stirring all the time, reduce the heat and simmer for 3 minutes. Take off the heat and stir in the cheese, mustard, and seasoning.

3 Heat the oil in a large pan and fry the shallots until translucent, then add the pasta, all the tomatoes, and the cheese sauce. The sauce should coat, not swamp, the macaroni (you may need to add a little milk to loosen the sauce).

4 Heat through, then pour into an ovenproof dish and sprinkle with Parmesan. Bake in the oven for 6–8 minutes until the sauce begins to thicken.

5 Finish off under a hot broiler, and top with chopped parsley.

2 tbsp olive oil

4 shallots, sliced

14oz cooked macaroni

20 cherry tomatoes, halved

12 sun-blushed tomatoes

freshly grated Parmesan cheese

freshly chopped parsley

For the cheese sauce

2 cups milk

2 bay leaves

¼ stick (2 tbsp) butter

3½ tbsp all-purpose flour

1¼ cups grated mature Cheddar or Gruyère cheese

1 tsp English mustard

salt and freshly ground black pepper

Linguine with potato and pesto

More comfort food—potato and pasta is a great combination, if you don't feel like it's a carb overload. Add strong pesto and creamy mascarpone and you may never leave the house again.

1 To make the pesto, put all the ingredients except the oil into a blender and blend until smooth. Then, with the motor running, slowly add enough oil to make a thick sauce.

2 Cook the pasta in loads of boiling salted water for about 8 minutes.

3 Very finely dice the potatoes and put in water. Heat the oil in a skillet. Drain and dry the potatoes and fry, stirring continuously, until crisp and golden. Don't allow them to burn. Take them off the heat and drain on paper towels.

4 Drain the cooked pasta, then put it back in the pan. Add all the remaining ingredients and the pesto to the pasta and warm through. Check the seasoning.

5 Serve with black pepper and Parmesan shavings—this is delicious.

14oz dried linguine

2 potatoes, e.g. russet, peeled

3½ tbsp olive oil

2 garlic cloves, crushed

1 x 8oz tub mascarpone cheese

½ cup stock

salt and freshly ground black pepper

Parmesan shavings, to serve

For the pesto

1¾ cups pine nuts

large bunch of fresh basil leaves

1¼ cups freshly grated Parmesan cheese

2 garlic cloves

extra-virgin olive oil

Gnocchi with wild mushroom and rosemary ragu

Feeds 12

Once you've made this dish it will become a firm favorite in your repertoire. It's packed full of flavor, taste, and texture and the smell when you're cooking it is heaven. I reckon this'll feed about 12 of you, but I find if you reduce the quantities it doesn't work as well, so invite all those people round you haven't seen for absolutely ages.

1 To make the gnocchi, boil the potatoes for about 40 minutes until soft. Drain, and when cool enough to handle peel and mash or pass through a ricer into a bowl.

2 Make a well in the center of the mash, add the egg and mix in, then add the flour and seasoning. Mix to form a dough, then knead for a few minutes until dry to the touch.

3 Divide the potato dough into three and roll each out into ¾inch diameter ropes, then cut off at ¾inch intervals. Press one side of each gnocchi with the back of a fork to form "grooves"—this will give the sauce something to stick to.

4 Bring a large pan of water to a boil and drop the gnocchi into the water. When they rise to the top, scoop out and refresh in ice-cold water. Drain well, then pat dry, toss in oil and chill until needed. You can also freeze them at this stage.

5 To make the ragu, heat some oil in a pan and gently fry the vegetables for 5 minutes until soft. Add the tomato paste and cook for 7–8 minutes until a rich red.

6 Add the wine, stock, and rosemary, bring to a boil, then simmer for at least 40 minutes, but preferably 1 hour.

7 When ready to serve, cut the mushrooms into chunks and fry with the garlic in oil until soft, season well.

8 Warm the gnocchi in the ragu, spoon onto a plate and top with the mushrooms and Parmesan.

1½lb floury potatoes, e.g. russet, unpeeled

1 large egg

3½ cups all-purpose flour

salt and freshly ground black pepper

For the ragu

olive oil for frying and tossing

2 onions, finely chopped

2 carrots, finely chopped

2 celery stalks, finely chopped

2 garlic cloves, crushed

10oz tomato paste

3½ cups red wine

3½ cups stock

fresh rosemary to taste

For the topping

1lb Portobello mushrooms

1 garlic clove

freshly grated Parmesan cheese, to serve

Goat's cheese cannelloni with cherry tomatoes

Feeds 6

I got a bit fed up with cannelloni baked in either tomato or béchamel sauce, so I started roasting little cherry tomatoes in lots of oil, to make a semi-sauce. This is packed full of flavor and looks divine.

1 Preheat the oven to 425°F. Pour some oil into a roasting tin and put in the oven to heat up. Chuck the tomatoes into the hot pan and roast for about 10 minutes.

2 Add the thyme, balsamic vinegar, garlic, and seasoning and roast for a further 15 minutes, then remove the pan from the oven and keep warm. Reduce the oven temperature to 350°F.

3 Make the filling by combining the cheeses and spinach with lots of seasoning in a bowl.

4 Lay the pasta out and put a line of filling along the long edge of each piece, then roll up into a cannelloni shape.

5 Drizzle a little of the oil from the tomatoes on the bottom of an ovenproof dish large enough to hold all 12 cannelloni. Then pack the tubes in and pour the tomatoes over. Bake in the oven for 15 minutes until heated through.

6 Serve topped with shaved Parmesan and a crisp green salad dressed with oil and balsamic vinegar.

14oz cherry tomatoes, halved
fresh thyme
dash of balsamic vinegar
2 garlic cloves, crushed
12 sheets of fresh pasta, 4½ x 4inches square
olive oil for roasting
salt and freshly ground black pepper
Parmesan shavings, to serve

For the filling

1 x 8oz tub ricotta cheese
6oz goat's cheese
1¼ cups freshly grated Parmesan cheese
5–6 cups baby spinach leaves, well washed and drained

Lemon grass risotto
with lime leaf tapenade

Feeds 4 for lunch

As long as you add warm stock to the rice, don't stir it too much and let it know you love it, making risotto is very straightforward. This fragrant variation is delicious—the lemon grass is so uplifting.

1 Fry the shallots and garlic in a little oil until soft. Bruise the lemon grass with the back of a knife and add to the pan. Add the rice and stir gently for a couple of minutes until the edge of the rice becomes translucent. Then add the wine and cook for a minute or two.

2 Add a good ladleful of stock to the rice and cook, stirring, until it has been absorbed. Repeat with more stock until it has all been used and/or the rice is soft. Season well.

3 To make the tapenade, simply put all the ingredients except the oil in a food processor, add seasoning and blend. When it's pretty broken down, leave the motor running and slowly add the oil. Spoon out into a bowl.

4 Add a swirl of cream to the rice just before serving, then divide between four bowls and top each serving with some tapenade.

4 shallots, sliced

1 garlic clove, crushed

3 stalks of lemon grass

2½ cups arborio rice

splash of white wine

2¾ cups stock

splash of cream

vegetable oil for frying

salt and freshly ground black pepper

For the tapenade

8 fresh kaffir lime leaves, torn

⅔ cup green olives, pitted

1 tbsp capers

handful of cilantro stalks

1 garlic clove

juice and zest of 1 lime

⅓ cup olive oil

Moroccan spaghetti

Feeds 4

One of the best places I've been to is Marrakesh—the sights, sounds, smells, and people are so stimulating. The food market at Djemma el-Fna square has some of the best street food anywhere, with its wonderful aromas of cinnamon, almonds, and cumin. So this is inspired by that trip; it's simple pasta with a sauce a-la-Marrakesh.

1 Cook the spaghetti in boiling salted water until al dente.

2 Meanwhile, heat the oil in a pan and gently fry the onion and garlic until soft.

3 Add the tomatoes, cinnamon, cumin, and turmeric and cook over a medium heat for about 20 minutes until the tomatoes break down.

4 Season the sauce and then add the almonds and chickpeas.

5 Drain the pasta and divide between four plates. Fold the herbs into the sauce and mix it with the pasta.

10oz dried spaghetti

½ cup olive oil

1 onion, finely chopped

2 garlic cloves, crushed

8 tomatoes, finely chopped

1 tsp ground cinnamon

1 tsp ground cumin

pinch of turmeric

1 cup toasted, slivered almonds

½ cup cooked chickpeas (garbanzo beans), drained and rinsed if canned

bunch each of fresh parsley and cilantro leaves, finely chopped

handful of freshly chopped mint leaves

salt and freshly ground black pepper

Four-cheese and zucchini penne

Feeds 4

An easy pasta dish that shows how essential it is to use good ingredients in simple dishes. I like to cook the zucchini slowly so they almost begin to "melt." Watch out for the salt—you don't need much at all as the cheeses will provide it.

1 Cook the penne in lots of boiling salted water until al dente.

2 While it is cooking, fry the zucchini and garlic slowly in some oil until very soft. Season to taste.

3 Put all the cheeses in a separate pan with a little splash of oil and slowly warm through until they begin to melt. Add a splash of wine and the zucchini and cook very gently for 4–5 minutes.

4 Drain the pasta over a saucepan, then add the pasta to the zucchini mixture, together with a little of its cooking water.

5 Stir to mix, check the seasoning and turn out into a serving dish. Top with some Parmesan shavings and serve at once.

14oz dried penne

1lb zucchini, washed and cut into rounds

1 garlic clove, chopped

½ cup mascarpone cheese

½ cup freshly grated Parmesan cheese

1 cup crumbled Gorgonzola cheese

½ cup crumbled Dolcelatte cheese

splash of white wine

olive oil for frying

salt and freshly ground black pepper

Parmesan shavings, to serve

Eggplant tikka masala

Feeds 6

Apparently, chicken tikka masala is now the UK's favorite dish, more than roast dinner and more than fish and chips. If that's the case, then I feel it's only right and proper for there to be a vegetarian version.

1 Toss the eggplants in vegetable oil and salt. Cook on a hot griddle pan until striped on each side.

2 Combine all the marinade ingredients in a bowl, season with salt and coat the eggplant pieces well. Thread onto wooden skewers, put in a sheet, cover and chill for at least 2 hours.

3 Meanwhile, make the sauce. Put the onion, garlic, and chiles in a food processor and blend until smooth. Heat the peanut oil in a pan and fry the onion paste over a low heat for about 7 minutes until golden brown.

4 Roughly chop the cilantro leaves and put with the ginger and tomatoes in the processor (don't bother washing it out) and blend until smooth.

5 Once the onions are golden, spoon the tomato mixture into the pan and cook for a good 15 minutes, until most of the liquid has evaporated.

6 Stir in the ground coriander, cumin, paprika, fenugreek, and garam masala and add salt to taste. Cook briefly, then gently stir in the yogurt, a little at a time, to avoid curdling.

7 Add the milk, crank the heat right up and bring to a boil. Simmer for 5 minutes.

8 Cook the eggplant skewers under a hot broiler, basting with the butter and lemon juice and turning when golden. (They are delicious eaten just like this with a naan bread wrapped around them.)

9 Lay 2 skewers of eggplant tikka on a plate, spoon over some sauce and garnish with cilantro leaves. Serve with rice, naan bread, and icy cold beer.

4–6 eggplants (about 2lb total weight), cut into chunks or wedges
vegetable oil
3½ tbsp melted butter
juice of 1 lemon
salt
fresh cilantro leaves, to garnish

For the marinade

½ cup plain yoghurt
juice of 1 lime
2 garlic cloves, crushed
1inch piece of fresh ginger, finely chopped
1 tbsp ground coriander
1 tsp each of ground cumin, garam masala, paprika

For the sauce

1 onion, roughly chopped
5 garlic cloves
3–5 red chiles (seeded if you like)
3 tbsp peanut oil
1 bunch of fresh cilantro leaves
1½inch piece of fresh ginger
5 plum tomatoes
1 tbsp ground coriander, 2 tsp ground cumin, 1 tsp paprika, 2 tsp ground fenugreek, 1 tsp garam masala
⅓ cup plain yoghurt
⅔ cup milk

Rendang shallot and asparagus curry

Feeds 6

I first ate rendang in Holland—Amsterdam, where there's a large Malaysian community—it was a knockout: sweet, but not too sweet, spicy, but not too spicy. It's traditionally served with buffalo, slow-cooked to tenderize the meat, and quite dry. Well, I've teamed it with shallots and asparagus and left it a bit wetter, but to be more authentic you can reduce the sauce down.

1 Melt the butter in a pan, add the sugar and when it begins to dissolve chuck in the whole shallots. Season, turn down the heat and cook for at least 45 minutes, turning every 10 minutes or so until the shallots are golden and soft.

2 Blanch the asparagus in boiling salted water, then refresh in ice-cold water.

3 To make the paste, put all the ingredients except the oil in a food processor and blend until smooth.

4 Heat the oil in a wok and fry the paste until fragrant—be careful not to burn it.

5 Add the shredded coconut and the coconut milk, and stir well. Bring to a boil and boil to reduce the sauce by half.

6 Add the shallots, asparagus, and toasted coconut and warm through.

7 Garnish with the cilantro and serve with jasmine rice.

½ stick (4 tbsp) butter
½ cup brown sugar
20 shallots
1lb bundle asparagus, trimmed
2 cups shredded unsweetened coconut
1¾ cups canned coconut milk
⅔ cup desiccated coconut, toasted
vegetable oil for frying
salt and freshly ground black pepper
freshly chopped cilantro leaves and jasmine rice, to serve

For the paste

1 onion, roughly chopped
2 garlic cloves
1inch piece of fresh ginger
3 red chiles (seeded if you like)
1 tsp ground coriander
1 tbsp tamarind paste
1 tsp turmeric
1½ tsp curry powder
1 stalk of lemon grass
pinch of salt
2 tbsp vegetable oil for frying

Italian bean casserole

Feeds 6–8

I think there's something very sexy about this dish; we always imagine casseroles to be heavy and robust, but this one has a lightness with a simple tomato base, lots of beans and lemon. Topped with arancini it's hardcore.

1 Heat some oil in a large casserole, add the carrots, celery and leeks and fry for 3–4 minutes. Season and add the garlic and wine. Let the wine cook out and reduce by two-thirds.

2 Tip in the tomatoes and lemon zest and bring to a boil.

3 Add the stock, bring back to a boil and simmer for 20 minutes.

4 Chuck in the beans and cook for 5 minutes, then add the fresh herbs and the lemon juice. It's worth having a quick recheck of the seasoning now.

5 To make the arancini, roll the risotto into 1½inch balls, press a little cheese into the center and fold to enclose. Deep-fry in hot oil until golden. Drain on paper towels.

6 Serve a good bowlful of casserole with arancini and a little shaved Parmesan on top.

4 carrots, chopped

4 celery stalks, chopped

3 leeks, trimmed, well washed and chopped

2 garlic cloves, crushed

good glug of white wine

15oz can chopped tomatoes

juice and zest of 1 lemon

¾ cup fresh stock

½ cup each of cooked borlotti and cannellini beans, drained and rinsed if canned

fresh oregano

fresh marjoram

olive oil for frying

salt and freshly ground black pepper

Parmesan shavings, to serve

For the arancini

1 quantity cooked tomato risotto (see tomato and mozzarella cakes, page 16)

4oz mozzarella cheese

vegetable oil for deep-frying

Red Thai bean curry

Once you've mastered the art of making your own Thai curry paste you'll never buy it again. It takes a bit of marketing to get all the gear at first, but most of the big supermarkets sell Thai ingredients now, even fresh lime leaves. You won't need all the curry paste, so keep it in an airtight jar in the fridge. Incidentally, try adding a dollop of the paste to creamy mashed potato—divine.

1 To make the curry paste, dry-fry the peppercorns, cumin, and coriander seeds until fragrant, then grind them in a mortar and pestle. Put them with all the other paste ingredients except the oil into a blender and blitz until smooth—it takes a good 5–10 minutes.

2 Warm the oil in a pan and add four good spoonfuls of paste (one per person). Cook on a low heat until it becomes fragrant.

3 Crank up the heat and add the coconut milk and stock and bring to the boil. Boil for 3 minutes.

4 Add the fine green and fava beans, onions, and tomatoes and simmer for about 4 minutes.

5 Divide the luscious curry between four bowls and garnish with lime wedges and cilantro and serve with rice.

1¾ cups canned coconut milk

½ cup stock

8oz cooked fine green beans

8oz cooked fava beans

1 bunch of scallions, finely chopped

2 tomatoes, chopped

lime wedges and fresh cilantro leaves, to serve

For the curry paste

10 black peppercorns

2 tsp cumin seeds

2 tsp coriander seeds

10 red chiles (seeded if you like)

5 shallots

2 garlic cloves, crushed

piece of fresh ginger

6 stalks of lemon grass

12 kaffir lime leaves

pinch of ground cinnamon

½ tsp turmeric

splash of vegetable oil

splash of chili oil

1 tbsp palm sugar

salt

2 tbsp vegetable oil for frying

Black bean and eggplant chili

Feeds 6

You don't expect to see eggplants in a chili, but their meaty texture together with the strong taste of the black beans and the sneaky addition of chocolate make it a delicious combo.

1 Heat the oil in a pan and fry the eggplants for about 4 minutes, to color and soften. Remove and drain on paper towels.

2 Fry the onions and garlic in the same pan until soft, then add the chiles and cook for 5 minutes.

3 Add the tomatoes, coriander, cumin, cinnamon, bay leaf, and eggplants and simmer for 5 minutes.

4 Add the beans, season well and cook for 15 minutes. Stir in the chocolate and serve with grated cheese and/or sour cream.

½ cup vegetable oil

1lb eggplants, cut into 1inch cubes

2 red onions, finely chopped

4 garlic cloves, crushed

10 small red chiles, chopped (seeded if you like)

4 cups canned chopped tomatoes

1 tsp ground coriander

pinch of ground cumin

pinch of ground cinnamon

1 bay leaf

9oz cooked black beans, drained and rinsed if canned

2 tbsp grated best-quality dark chocolate (not unsweetened)

vegetable oil for frying

salt and freshly ground black pepper

grated cheese and/or sour cream, to serve

Ojja with sweet potato and okra

Feeds 6

This is one of the most bizarre success stories on recent menus. This weird little African dish managed to get voted onto the menu in the absence of anything else we could agree on, and it has been really popular. It's got a heady aroma from the smoked paprika and it gets finished with beaten egg, which makes it really creamy.

1 Preheat the oven to 400°F. Pour some oil in a baking tin and put in the oven to heat up. Put the sweet potato with lots of salt and pepper into the hot oil and roast for about 25 minutes until soft and slightly crisp.

2 Meanwhile, make the ojja. Fry the onions and garlic in oil with some seasoning. When they're soft add a splosh of wine and reduce by two-thirds, then add the paprika and cook for about 3 minutes, stirring all the time.

3 Add the tomato paste and stir for a few minutes, then chuck in the tomatoes and bring to a boil. Pour in the stock and cook for about 25 minutes over a low heat until thickened and reduced. Check the seasoning.

4 Blanch the okra and the beans in boiling water, then refresh in ice-cold water.

5 Cook the rice with the turmeric and some salt according to the packet instructions.

6 Heat some oil in a large skillet, add the potatoes and cook until they start to color up, then add the beans, okra, and ojja and bring to the boil. Beat the eggs, add to the pan and let it begin to cook, then fold it through the mixture and keep folding until it creates a lovely marbled effect through the dish.

7 Just before serving, throw in a load of chopped parsley. The texture should be thick enough so you can spoon this up high, it shouldn't be a sloppy casserole. Serve with rice.

2 golden sweet potatoes, peeled and cut into largish bite-sized pieces

3oz fresh okra

4oz fresh fava beans

2¾ cups long-grain rice, rinsed and drained

1 tsp turmeric

2 eggs

lots of freshly chopped parsley

olive oil for frying

salt and freshly ground black pepper

For the ojja

2 onions, sliced

3 garlic cloves, crushed

splash of red wine

1 heaped tbsp smoked paprika—it really needs the smoked stuff, unsmoked doesn't do it

1 tbsp tomato paste

2 cups canned chopped tomatoes

⅔ cup stock

Plantain and mango curry

I can't decide when the best time to eat this dish is—it's a neat little lunchy treat, but also great for party food, and really different because it's bright yellow, and nearly sweet enough for a dessert. Anyway try it with fresh warm naan bread—and friends.

1 Slice the plantain into pieces about ⅛inch thick. Place in a pan of boiling salted water with half the turmeric and cook for 10 minutes, then drain.

2 Fry the nigella or mustard seeds in a little oil until they pop, then add the onion, red chile, curry leaves, and some salt. Cook for 5 minutes over medium heat, stirring pretty much all the time until the onion is golden.

3 Add the ginger and green chile and cook for 1 minute.

4 Add the rest of the turmeric and mix well, then take off the heat and slowly fold in the yogurt, plantain, and mango.

5 Put back on the heat for 1 minute. Serve with rice or naan bread.

1 plantain, not too ripe, peeled

2 tsp turmeric

1 tsp nigella seeds (or black mustard seeds)

1 onion, finely sliced

1 dried red chile

about 25 curry leaves

1inch piece of fresh ginger, finely chopped

1 fresh green chile, seeded and sliced

1¾ cups plain yoghurt

1 firm mango, peeled and sliced

vegetable oil for frying

salt

Oriental pie

Sounds strange, cooks up a storm. This is really a shepherd's pie-style dish. Big strong mushroom flavors, enhanced by oriental spices and topped with a very Western, creamy mash topping. You can substitute pretty much any favorite earthy veg for the mushrooms.

1 Fry the scallions in a little oil until they wilt. Add all the mushrooms to the pan and cook for 5 minutes, then add the garlic, ginger, cinnamon, and star anise and cook for 5 minutes more.

2 Add the soy sauce and stock and bring to a boil, then simmer for about 10 minutes to reduce by half.

3 Preheat the oven to 400°F. Pour the mushroom mixture into a baking dish and add the chickpeas.

4 To make the topping, put both mashed potatoes into a pan and stir to combine. Beat in the butter and cream and season well, then warm through over low heat.

5 Spoon the mash on top of the mushroom and chickpea mixture and cook in the oven for 15 minutes. Finish off under the broiler to brown the top.

8 scallions, left whole

9oz Portobello mushrooms, halved

7oz shiitake mushrooms

1 garlic clove, crushed

1inch piece of fresh ginger, sliced into matchsticks

1 cinnamon stick

2 star anise

½ cup light soy sauce

½ cup stock

¾ cup cooked chickpeas (garbanzo beans), rinsed and drained if canned

vegetable oil for frying

For the topping

1 cup mashed potato

1 cup mashed sweet potato

1¼ sticks (10 tbsp) butter

3½ tbsp heavy cream

salt and freshly ground black pepper

Caramelized onion and mustard tart

Feeds 6

A big "meaty" dish that's great for lunch, with sweet, strong onions, the sharpness of the mustard and crisp shortcrust pastry. I serve this with a tomato salad or chutney.

1 Roll out the pastry on a lightly floured surface to fit a 8–10inch tart pan, press into the pan and chill for 20 minutes.

2 Preheat the oven to 400ºF. Bake the pastry case for 25–30 minutes until crisp and dry.

3 Meanwhile, melt the butter and oil together over a low heat, then add the onions, garlic, and seasoning. Cook the onions very slowly for 30–40 minutes until golden—don't let them burn.

4 Whisk together the whole eggs, egg yolks, mustard, and cream and stir in the cooked onions. Remove the tart case from the oven and reduce the heat to 350ºF. Spoon the filling into the tart case and bake for 20 minutes until set firm and golden.

1 quantity shortcrust pastry (see below)

flour for dusting

½ stick (4 tbsp) butter

1 tbsp vegetable oil

4 large Spanish onions, sliced

1 garlic clove, crushed

2 whole eggs, plus 2 egg yolks

2 tbsp wholegrain mustard

⅔ cup heavy cream

salt and freshly ground black pepper

Shortcrust pastry

Makes enough for 1 x 10inch pie dish

1 Put the flour, butter and salt in a food processor and pulse until "crumby". Add the milk and egg yolk and pulse until a dough forms.

2 Turn the dough out onto a lightly floured surface and knead for a few minutes, then cover and chill for at least 1 hour.

3 When you're ready to use it, roll the dough out on a floured surface and use as directed.

1¾ cups all-purpose flour, plus extra for dusting

¾ stick (6 tbsp) chilled butter, cubed

pinch of salt

3½ tbsp milk

1 egg yolk

Jerk-spiced pumpkin pie

Feeds 6

Remember eating loads of vol-au-vents filled with mushrooms at parties? You know they're corny, and that mushroom filling is vile, but you can't help yourself. Well, this is Mr vol-au-vent's cooler elder brother, he's bigger, tastier and a whole lot more handsome.

1 Preheat the oven to 375°F. Cut a 3inch circle out of the middle of six of the pastry circles. Put the whole pastry circles on a floured baking sheet and sit a cut one on top of each. Brush with eggwash and bake for about 20 minutes until golden brown and dry. Remove the pie cases from the oven.

2 For the filling, pour some oil in a roasting pan and heat to smoking, either in the oven or on the hob. Throw in the squash (not literally!) and shake around for a couple of minutes, then sprinkle on the jerk seasoning and mix well. Roast in the oven for about 25 minutes until soft with a little crispness on the outside. Remove from the pan and put to one side. Pour the oil into a skillet and fry the spinach and almonds, then season and add to the squash. Divide the fillling between the pie cases and warm through in the oven for 5 minutes.

3 For the curry sauce, heat the oil in a pan and fry the paste until fragrant, then add the coconut milk and stock, bring to a boil and simmer for 5 minutes.

4 Fry the plantain slices gently in oil until golden on each side, then put aside and keep them warm.

5 Sit a pie on each plate, spoon over just enough sauce to cover the ingredients, not to swamp them, top with a few slices of the plantain and garnish with cilantro.

12 x 6inch circles of ready-rolled puff pastry
flour for dusting
2 eggs, beaten, for eggwash
2 plantain, peeled and sliced
vegetable oil for roasting and frying
fresh cilantro leaves, to garnish

For the filling

1½lb butternut squash, peeled and cubed
3 heaped tbsp jerk seasoning
a handful of spinach leaves, well washed and drained
1 cup toasted slivered almonds
salt and freshly ground black pepper

For the curry sauce

1 tbsp vegetable oil
3 heaped tbsp mild curry paste
1¾ cups canned coconut milk
½ cup stock

Stilton, asparagus and caramelized shallot roulade with spicy chutney

Feeds 4

This roulade couldn't be more different in flavors than the following one. I've served it with a pear chutney, but I think it's a good dish for Christmas, so try adding a few fresh cranberries to the chutney.

1 First make the roulade. Melt the butter in a pan and stir in the flour to make a roux. Cook for 3 minutes, then add the milk, a little at a time, and stir until thickened. Season well, then stir in the egg yolks. Take off the heat and leave to cool. When cooled, stir in the spinach. Beat the egg whites until stiff then gently fold into the mixture.

2 Preheat the oven to 400°F. Grease and line a 15 x 10inch baking sheet and sprinkle with flour. Spoon the mixture onto the sheet and cook for about 15 minutes until firm and springy. Turn out onto a piece of waxed paper, carefully remove the lining paper and leave to cool.

3 For the filling, heat the butter in a pan and when bubbling add the shallots, season well and simmer on a very low heat for 30–40 minutes until rich and golden. Stir frequently to stop them burning. Spread the cream cheese evenly over each cooled roulade, then sprinkle on the Stilton, shallots, nuts, and asparagus.

4 Using the waxed paper to help you, roll the roulade up from one long side, then wrap in waxed paper and foil and chill overnight.

5 To make the chutney, heat a little oil in a pan and fry the shallots and garlic until soft. Add the pears and ginger and cook for 5 minutes, then add the vinegar, sugar, and chile and cook over a low heat for about 20 minutes. Season to taste, then set aside to cool.

6 When ready to serve, preheat the oven to 400°F. Cut the roulade into 8 slices and put on a baking sheet. Cook for about 10 minutes until they begin to crisp and brown. Serve the roulade with the chutney and some wilted spinach.

½ stick + 1 tbsp (5 tbsp) butter, plus extra for greasing

⅞ cup all-purpose flour, plus extra for dusting

1¾ cups warmed milk

7 eggs, separated

handful of freshly chopped spinach leaves

salt and freshly ground black pepper

For the filling

½ stick (4 tbsp) butter

15 shallots, sliced

1 cup soft cream cheese

6oz Stilton cheese, crumbled

½ cup walnut halves

about 10 asparagus spears, halved lengthways

For the chutney

olive oil for frying

2 shallots, chopped

1 garlic clove, crushed

6 unpeeled pears, cored and chopped

¼ cup chopped preserved ginger

½ cup white wine vinegar

6 tbsp superfine sugar

1 chile, finely chopped

Basil roulade with goat's cheese and sun-blushed tomatoes

Feeds 4

A particularly popular dish whenever it's on the menu at Greens. The combination of goat's cheese, sun-blushed tomatoes and basil makes everyone think of the Mediterranean. But just so you don't get too carried away, some good old beets will bring you back to earth.

Make these roulades a day in advance, so they get a chance to firm up. This is a lovely dish to serve for a special occasion.

1 First make the roulade. Melt the butter in a pan and stir in the flour to make a roux. Cook for 3 minutes, then add the milk, a little at a time, and stir until thickened. Season well, then stir in the egg yolks. Take off the heat and leave to cool.

2 Beat the egg whites until stiff, then gently and carefully fold into the cooled mixture, keeping in as much air as possible. Then gently fold in the basil.

3 Preheat the oven to 400°F. Grease and line a 15 x 10inch baking sheet. Spread the mixture onto the sheet, top with the Parmesan and cook for 15 minutes until springy and risen. Turn out onto a piece of waxed paper, carefully remove the lining paper and leave to cool.

4 To make the filling, season the ricotta cheese and spread some on the cooled roulade base, leaving a gap at each end, then sprinkle on the goat's cheese, basil, and tomatoes. Roll the roulade up from one long side, then wrap in waxed paper and foil and chill overnight.

5 When ready to serve, preheat the oven to 400°F. Slice the roulade, allowing two wedges per person, and heat in the oven for about 10 minutes, then finish off under a hot broiler to crisp slightly. Transfer to a serving plate with some watercress or other greenery.

6 Meanwhile, make the beet caviar. Heat the oil in a pan and fry the shallots, garlic, and lime leaves until soft, then add the beets and warm through. Put into a food processor and pulse until broken down but still a little chunky. Serve with the roulade.

½ stick + 1 tbsp (5 tbsp) butter, plus extra for greasing

⅞ cup all-purpose flour

1¾ cups milk, warmed

7 eggs, separated

big handful of roughly chopped fresh basil leaves

¾ cup freshly grated Parmesan cheese

salt and freshly ground black pepper

watercress, to serve (optional)

For the filling

1 x 8oz tub ricotta cheese

1 cup crumbled goat's cheese

big handful of fresh basil leaves

sprinkle of sun-blushed tomatoes

For the beet caviar

2 tbsp olive oil

2 shallots, finely chopped

1 garlic clove, crushed

4 lime leaves, shredded

6 cooked beets, peeled and chopped

Side dishes

Bubble and squeak

Feeds 4

I've heard rumors of people using cabbage, rather than sprouts, in their bubble… you, of course, would never dream of such a barbaric act. Long live the sprouts!

1 Fry the onions in half the butter until soft, but not colored. Leave to cool.

2 Combine the onions with the potatoes, sprouts, and garlic and season well (heavy on the pepper).

3 Divide the mix into four and shape into squares or rounds. Dust with a little flour and fry in the remaining butter for about 5 minutes on each side until golden.

2 onions, sliced
½ stick (4 tbsp) butter
1 cup mashed potatoes (no butter or cream)
1–1½ cups cooked sprouts
1 garlic clove, crushed
a little flour for dusting
salt and freshly ground black pepper

Pan haggerty

Feeds 4

I hope this version of the classic north-east England potato dish is accurate, otherwise Scotty and all my Geordie mates will never forgive me. It's a great side dish for a lazy Sunday supper.

1 Preheat the oven to 350°F. Heat half the butter in an ovenproof pan and fry the onion until soft, then remove from the pan.

2 Put a layer of potato in the same pan and fry for a few minutes until golden.

3 Now layer up onion, potato, onion, seasoning each layer and finishing with potato.

4 Melt the remaining butter and pour over the pan. Cook in the oven for about 40 minutes until soft.

5 Before serving, grate the cheese over the top and put under a hot broiler until the cheese bubbles.

½ stick (4 tbsp) butter
1 onion, finely sliced
7oz (about 1 fist-sized) waxy potato, peeled and finely sliced
3oz mature Cheddar cheese
salt and freshly ground black pepper

Lentils with lemon

Feeds 4

So often lentils get overcooked and taste of nothing, but this dish uses Puy lentils, which are a lovely green lentil when cooked, but a bluey/purple when raw. Adding lemon and red bell peppers makes this a yummy dish to serve on the side of just about everything savory.

1 Boil the lentils for 10 minutes in lots of boiling salted water. Drain.

2 Bring the stock to a boil and add the lentils and garlic. When it returns to the boil chuck in the lemon juice, zest, and the peppers. Adjust the seasoning and serve immediately.

1 cup Puy lentils

½ cup stock

1 garlic clove, crushed

juice and zest of 1 lemon

½ red bell pepper, seeded and finely diced

salt and freshly ground black pepper

Smoky roasties

Enough for you—and 3 others

You can't beat a good roastie, crisp on the outside, fluffy on the inside and nice and salty. Well, these chaps are so good you can eat them on their own. I'd keep these a secret from all of your friends, otherwise you'll become a roast potato factory.

1 Preheat the oven to 425°F. Pour the oil into an ovenproof dish and heat to smoking in the oven.

2 Cut the potatoes into big chunks, about 2inch-ish in an abstract way. Boil them for 4 minutes in salted water, then drain and return them to the pan. Pop them back on the heat and give them a good shake (this will break up the edges and give them that crispy/fluffy look) for a minute or so.

3 Remove the hot oil from the oven, lift the potatoes out of the pan, ignoring all the small "crumbs," and pop them into the oil. Put them straight in the oven and cook, turning them every 10–15 minutes, for 30 minutes until crisp and golden.

4 Just before serving, season them with salt, sprinkle on the paprika, give 'em another gentle shake and serve.

⅔ cup olive oil

4–6 large, floury potatoes, peeled

sea salt

good pinch of smoked paprika

Sprouts with beet

Feeds 4

Two of the most maligned and underrated veggies in the world. Sprouts aren't just for Christmas and beets aren't just to be pickled in a jar. The combination of these two is heavenly—sweet, sharp, and with garlic and chili thrown in. Don't be afraid, try them.

1 Preheat the oven to 400°F. Season the beets, wrap them in foil and roast for about 40 minutes until soft. Allow to cool, then peel them and cut into wedges.

2 If the sprouts are big, cut them in half, if not, leave them whole.

3 Heat the oil in a skillet until hot. Simply chuck in the sprouts, let them fry for a minute to begin browning, then give them a shake.

4 Now put the beets, chili flakes, and garlic into the pan. Cook for a couple of minutes, then season really well.

5 Serve as a funky veg.

2 raw beets

1½–2 cups cooked sprouts

a little olive oil for frying

pinch of chili flakes

1 garlic clove, crushed

salt and freshly ground black pepper

Glazed carrots with caraway seeds

Feeds 4

If you're bored with carrots, then tuck into these tasty, sweet little beauties.

1 Pop the carrots in a pan with a good pinch of salt and just cover them with water. Add the sugar, caraway, and butter, bring to a boil and simmer for 8–10 minutes, until just tender, but with a bite.

2 Drain the liquid into another pan and reduce by about two-thirds.

3 Add the carrots and caraway to the pan, season and serve.

1lb peeled carrots, cut into batons

1 tsp sugar

1 tsp caraway seeds

3 tbsp butter

salt and freshly ground black pepper

Stuffed pimentos with thyme and basil

Feeds 4

If you're serving something quite plain, then these sweet, slightly spicy peppers are a great accompaniment. Because they get charred and the thyme and basil are pretty strong they make the most boring dish spring to life.

1 Heat a griddle pan to smoking hot and brush it with a tiny amount of oil. Griddle the peppers on both sides until lightly charred. Meanwhile, mix together the ricotta, thyme, lemon juice, and seasoning.

2 While the peppers are still warm, roughly spread a spoonful of the mix onto each pepper. Sit the peppers side by side on a plate, sprinkle a few basil leaves on top and serve (if you want a bit more spice, drizzle a little chili oil over the peppers before serving).

a little vegetable or olive oil for griddling

6 long thin red pimento peppers, halved lengthwise and seeded

¾ cup ricotta cheese

small bunch of fresh thyme

juice of ½ lemon

a few fresh basil leaves

salt and freshly ground black pepper

Celeriac and potato dauphinoise

Feeds 6

It's a grand tradition Chez Rimmer to have dauphinoise potatoes to excess at Christmas time, so imagine everyone's surprise when that tasty, yet ugly veg the celeriac joined the celebrations. But let me tell you, he was a most welcome guest after the first large mouthful as celeriac is a brilliant addition to your creamy dauphinoise.

1 Heat the butter in a pan and gently fry the onion and garlic until soft, but not brown. Reserve a little of the cheese, then layer up the potatoes, celeriac, remaining cheese, and onion in a buttered baking dish, seasoning each layer as you go. Combine the creams and season well, then pour into the dish and leave to stand for about 20 minutes.

2 Preheat the oven to 325°F. Sprinkle the dish with the reserved cheese, then cook the dauphinoise for about 1½ hours until soft.

¼ stick (2 tbsp) butter, plus extra for greasing

1 onion, finely sliced

1 garlic clove, crushed

1½ cups grated mature Cheddar cheese

1lb floury potatoes, peeled and finely sliced

1lb celeriac (celery root), peeled and finely sliced

1¼ cups heavy cream

1¼ cups light cream

salt and freshly ground black pepper

Parmesan-roasted parsnips

Feeds 6, if you're lucky

I adore all roasted veg, but parsnips are just about my faves. Adding strong Parmesan and garlic makes them good enough to eat on their own—so if you're serving these as a veg with your roast make twice the amount because you'll eat half of them before they get to the table.

14oz parsnips, peeled and cut into 2inch batons

1 garlic clove, sliced

1½ cups freshly grated Parmesan cheese

olive oil for roasting

salt and freshly ground black pepper

freshly chopped parsley, to serve

1 Preheat the oven to 425°F. Pour some oil into a roasting pan and put in the oven to heat up. Toss the parsnips in the garlic and seasoning.

2 When the oil is smoking, add the parsnips to the pan and roast for about 25 minutes, shaking occasionally (that's the parsnips, not you).

3 Then add the cheese and roast for another 10 minutes. The cheese will begin to melt and form a yummy, stringy coating.

4 Serve the parsnips topped with a twist of black pepper and a little chopped parsley.

Fine green beans with garlic and tomato sauce

Feeds 6

Fine green beans are one of the few veg that I like cooked slowly; they become deliciously sweet and scrummy. Add a touch of cinnamon to the tomato sauce for an extra flavor.

1lb fine green beans

½ cup olive oil

4 garlic cloves, sliced

1 cup basic tomato sauce (see page 107)

salt and freshly ground black pepper

1 Preheat the oven to 325°F. Cook the green beans in boiling salted water for about 4 minutes, then refresh in ice-cold water.

2 Heat the oil in an ovenproof dish, add the garlic and as soon as it begins to "fizz" add the beans and tomato sauce. Season well and stir to mix, then cook in the oven for 25 minutes until the beans are soft and sweet.

Coconut rice in banana leaf

Feeds 6

There's a good few curries in the book, so this is a simple, yet effective way to serve rice. Good to put on the barbie as well.

1 Put the rice in a pan with the water and coconut cream. Bring to a boil and cook for about 12 minutes.

2 Take it off the heat and stir in the chiles. Divide between the banana leaves, top with some cilantro and wrap the leaves up. Secure the leaf parcels with a skewer then put in a steamer and steam for another 5 minutes.

* If you can't find block coconut cream, lift the solid cream off the surface of canned cocnut milk.

1¼ cups long-grain rice, rinsed and drained

2 cups water

8oz block coconut cream, chopped*

2 small red chiles, seeded and sliced

6 pieces banana leaf, about 12 x 8inches

fresh cilantro leaves

Basic tomato sauce

Makes enough sauce for 4 large bowls of pasta

I prefer this slightly heavier tomato sauce for my dishes as that little bit of extra depth helps with a lot of veggie food. I recommend making twice this amount if you use it on a regular basis, as you can freeze it and use at a later date.

1 Heat the oil in a large pan and gently fry the onion, celery, and garlic until soft.

2 Add the tomato paste and cook for a few minutes, then add the tomatoes, stock and wine. Season and bring to a boil.

3 Turn the heat right down, half cover the pan and simmer for about 1 hour, stirring every now and again.

4 If you want a nice smooth sauce blend in a processor and pass through a fine sieve before using, otherwise use as is.

½ cup olive oil

1 onion, chopped

1 celery stalk, finely chopped

2 garlic cloves, chopped

2 tbsp tomato paste

4 cups canned chopped tomatoes

½ cup stock

½ cup red wine

salt and freshly ground black pepper

Desserts

Popsicles

Remember when you were a kid and you made simple popsicles from cheap orange drink that was always a bit too strong, so it made you cough? Well, now is the time to rediscover your childhood and make these two yummy popsicles that kids will love, but that are also a great fun thing to have at a summer party. Serve them in a bowl of ice with the sticks pointing up.

Watermelon and lime

Makes 8 popsicles

Put the sugar, water and vanilla seeds into a pan and heat until the sugar dissolves, then cool and chill until really cold. Stir in the watermelon and lime juices, pour into eight lolly moulds and freeze. Don't forget the sticks.

½ cup + 1 tbsp superfine sugar

½ cup water

seeds of 1 vanilla bean

2½ cups watermelon juice (squeeze out some watermelon pulp)

juice of 2 limes

Strawberry and black pepper popsicle

Makes 8 popsicles

Simply blend the yogurt, fruit, and sugar together, then add a good twist of pepper. Pour into molds and freeze. Don't forget the sticks.

1¼ cups plain yogurt

4oz strawberries, hulled

4 tbsp caster sugar

freshly ground black pepper

Honeycomb ice cream

The taste of honeycomb/cinder toffee is divine, a real taste of childhood, and I even like the 3 hours it takes to pick the bits out of my teeth. Well, it's only very recently that I learned how to make it and now I can't stop, much to the delight of my dentist, Roger.

If you've tried making ice cream before and been disappointed by the results because it's too "icy," well this is a creamy winner—the secret ingredient is vodka, which has a lower freezing point and stops those ice-crystals forming. Now, where did I put that toothpick?

1 To make the honeycomb, put the sugar and syrup into a pan and warm until the sugar dissolves, then turn up the heat until it starts to form a caramel. The longer you leave it the more caramelly it becomes, but don't leave it too long as it'll burn. You want it golden.

2 Now, chuck in the bicarbonate of soda and stir well, then pour onto a greased tray and allow to cool (how easy is that?).

3 For the ice cream, whip the cream until it becomes thick, but not fully whipped. Fold in the vodka and condensed milk and whisk until firm, then break in the honeycomb and mix well. Pour into a freezer container and freeze for at least 8 hours—there's no need to churn.

For the honeycomb

6 tbsp superfine sugar

2 tbsp English golden syrup or corn syrup

2 tbsp bicarbonate of soda, sifted

For the ice cream

1 pint heavy cream

3 tbsp vodka

¾ cup sweetened condensed milk

Strawberry soup

Feeds 4–6

This is a really lovely summer dessert, full of flavour and color. The best way to describe the taste is like a good snog!—and your lips tingle afterwards.

1 Put 1¾lb of the strawberries and all the superfine sugar in a food processor and process to a purée. Pass through a strainer into a serving bowl and stir in the wine.

2 Add the nectarines, raspberries, and the pulp from the passion fruit and stir to mix.

3 Cover and chill until lovely and cold.

4 Serve each helping with a quenelle of mascarpone and fresh mint leaves.

2¼lb strawberries, hulled

6 tbsp superfine sugar

½ cup dessert wine

2 nectarines, peeled and diced

9oz raspberries, halved

4 passion fruit, halved

½ an 8oz tub mascarpone cheese

mint leaves, to garnish

Strawberry, vodka and black pepper granita

Feeds 6

This isn't really a dessert but I wanted to include it as it's a great drink to start or end a summer evening with—fruity, boozy, and refreshing, and lethal!

1 Heat the sugar and water in a pan over low heat until the sugar dissolves, then take off the heat and chill.

2 Blend the chilled syrup with the fuit, booze, and pepper.

3 Pour into a freezer container, then put in the freezer.

4 Break up the ice crystals every 40 minutes until the granita is completely frozen and has a grainy consistency.

5 Serve in chilled stem glasses with more fruit and mint.

2⅔ cups superfine sugar

2 cups water

10oz strawberries, plus extra to decorate

½ cup vodka

good twist black pepper

fresh mint leaves, to garnish

Strawberry and coconut trifle

Makes 6 individual or 1 big trifle

I love trifle, it always reminds me of big family parties when I was a kid. You just can't beat sherry-soaked cake, trapped inside jello with a big load of tinned fruit, topped with custard, cream and then decorated with hundreds and thousands and those little silver balls that break your teeth in half. Now this trifle is so gorgeous you'll want to stick pictures of it in a scrapbook and send it fan mail. Making custard with coconut milk really is spectacular, while soaking fat juicy strawberries in Cointreau is making me salivate as I write. Anyway, to the recipe.

This does take a bit of time as you've got to make the custard and then let it cool, so if you're thinking of making it for supper tonight, better eat late.

1 First make the custard. Whisk the egg yolks and sugar until they're pale and creamy, then sift in the flour and mix well. Put the coconut milk and vanilla seeds into another pan and very slowly bring it to a boil (if you want a really thick custard use just the top solid part of the coconut milk, you'll need 2 cans). When it's come to a boil, take it off the heat, pour over the egg mixture and whisk well. Pour it all back into the pan and bring back up to a boil, then simmer for 5 minutes, stirring all the time. Take it off the heat again, pour into a bowl, cover with plastic wrap and chill. When it's cold, whip the cream and fold in. Have a sneaky taste of it—how good?

2 Meanwhile, put the strawberries into a bowl, cover with confectioners' sugar and Cointreau and chill them for about 1 hour. Break the cake up into chunks and either line the bottom of a big glass bowl or divide into six glasses or little bowls. (I like it both ways, but I do love that slurping sound when you spoon a big portion out of a large bowl.) Splash some Cointreau over the cake.

3 Tip the strawberries on top of the cake, then the kiwi slices. Warm the jam with a little water to soften it, then pour it over the cake and fruit. Spoon all the chilled custard onto the cake and fruit.

4 To make the topping, whip the cream and mix with the mascarpone, then spoon over the custard. Finally, sprinkle the toasted coconut on top and serve—you'll never buy a packet dessert again.

14oz strawberries, hulled and chopped into good-sized chunks

½ cup confectioners' sugar

good glugs of Cointreau

9oz cake, pound, jelly roll, muffins—all work well

2 kiwi fruit, peeled and sliced

9oz good quality strawberry jam (say, ¾ jar Bonne Maman)

For the custard

6 egg yolks

½ cup + 1 tbsp superfine sugar

5–6 tbsp all-purpose flour

1¾ cups canned coconut milk

seeds of 1 vanilla bean

¾ cup heavy cream

For the topping

½ cup whipping cream

½ cup mascarpone cheese

½ cup desiccated coconut, toasted

Cherry tiramisu cheesecake

Feeds 12

This combines black forest gâteau with a tiramisu, both of which have become a bit corny in recent times, so the only way to rescue them is to turn them into cheesecake!

1 To make the base, put the crackers, butter, and sugar into a bowl and combine well, then press into a 9inch springform pan and chill for 20 minutes.

2 Preheat the oven to 350°F. Drain the cherries and reserve the juice. Put the juice and booze in a small pan and bring to a boil. Combine the cornstarch with a little water to make a paste, then add to the liquid. This will thicken it to a "jam." Cook over low heat for a couple of minutes, then pour over the cherries and stir to combine. Place a few cherries on the cracker base.

3 To make the topping, beat the cheeses together with the sugar and vanilla, then fold in the eggs, one at a time. Finally, stir in the chocolate and pour onto the cracker base. Bake in the oven for 45–60 minutes, until the top is firm yet yielding. Remove and cool.

4 For the sauce, simply mix the water, syrup, and butter into the chocolate.

5 To serve, spoon the rest of the cherries over the top of the cheesecake, cut a big slab, sit it on a plate with choccy sauce and cream and enjoy.

For the base

8oz crushed graham crackers

1¼ sticks + 1 tbsp (11 tbsp) unsalted butter, melted

½ cup soft brown sugar

For the filling

7–8oz can black cherries

splash of Kirsch

a little cornstarch

For the topping

1½lb ricotta cheese

8oz tub mascarpone cheese

⅔ cup superfine sugar

dash of vanilla extract

6 eggs

9oz best-quality dark chocolate (not unsweetened), melted

For the sauce

4 tbsp water

1 tbsp English golden syrup or corn syrup

1 tbsp unsalted butter

5½oz best-quality dark chocolate (not unsweetened), melted

cream, to serve

Zucotto

Remember when you couldn't move for tiramisu on restaurant menus? It always amazed me that this cracking cream- and choccy-filled dessert didn't make it into our psyche then too—maybe now is the time. Spread the word: zucotto is king.

1 Line a 2½ pint round-bottomed bowl or basin with plastic wrap. Mix the brandy, orange liqueur, and orange juice together in a separate bowl and dip the cake slices in it. Line the bowl or basin with three-quarters of the moist cake slices until all the inside is covered.

2 Fold the confectioners' sugar into the cream.

3 Grate half the chocolate and mix with all the nuts and three-quarters of the cream. Spread over the cake slices in the basin, then mold a hollow in the middle.

4 Melt the remaining chocolate and stir into the rest of the cream. Put this in the hollow and smooth.

5 Cover the cream with the remaining moist cake slices, then cover and chill for 24 hours.

6 Turn the cake out onto a plate, pour over some melted chocolate, then cut generous pieces and eat with yet more cream.

3 tbsp brandy

2 tbsp orange liqueur

5 tbsp fresh orange juice

2 shop-bought pound cakes, trimmed and cut into slices

⅞ cup confectioners' sugar

2 cups heavy cream, whipped

5½oz best-quality dark chocolate (not unsweetened), melted

½ cup slivered, toasted almonds

½ cup roasted skinned hazelnuts

melted chocolate and cream, to serve

Peanut butter and jelly cheesecake

Feeds 12 hungry horses

This is a real '"love or hate'"recipe; for me the combo is so terrific. Use Skippy supercrunch peanut butter, it has a taste and texture like no other for this recipe.

1 To make the base, put the crackers and butter into a bowl, combine well and press into a 9inch springform pan. Chill for 20 minutes.

2 Preheat the oven to 350°F. For the topping, just put the cheese, sugar, eggs, and vanilla into a blender and pulse until smooth. Don't worry if the mix seems a bit runny, the eggs will set it.

3 Spoon the mixture into a bowl and fold in the peanut butter.

4 Spread the jam over the cracker base, leaving about a 1inch gap all the way round, then spoon the peanut mixture on top.

5 Bake in the oven for about 1 hour. The cheesecake should be springy and just set in the middle. If you can turn off the oven and leave the cake in with the door just open until cool, this will help to stop it cracking, but it's not crucial as it'll get eaten straight away once it's cool.

For the base

7oz crushed graham crackers

1¼ sticks + 1 tbsp (11 tbsp) unsalted butter, melted

For the topping

2½ cups full-fat cream cheese

⅔ cup superfine sugar

6 eggs

splash of vanilla extract

⅔ cup crunchy peanut butter

⅔ cup strawberry jam

Litchi and toasted coconut cheesecake

Feeds 12

As you know, I love Asian food, but their lack of dairy makes the desserts a bit disappointing for Western palates, so this member of my cheesecake family uses lovely Asian influences in our favorite dessert. This is lovely served with mango kulfi or lime sorbet.

1 Usual base job: combine the crackers, sugar, and butter. Press into a 9inch springform pan and chill for 20 minutes.

2 Preheat the oven to 350ºF. Put the coconut under a hot broiler and shake around until it's toasted and golden. Don't even think about leaving it as I guarantee you'll burn it—I always do and so do my team.

3 Put the cheese and sugar into a food processor and pulse together, then add the eggs and pulse to combine.

4 Tip the mixture into a large bowl and fold in the litchis and 1 cup of the coconut. Spoon onto the cracker base, then sprinkle over the remaining coconut.

5 Bake in the oven for about 1 hour. You're looking for a cake that's firm yet yielding! Allow to cool before serving.

For the base

9oz crushed graham crackers

½ cup soft light brown sugar

1¼ sticks + 1 tbsp (11 tbsp) unsalted butter, melted

For the filling

2 cups desiccated coconut

2lb cream cheese

⅔ cup superfine sugar

6 eggs

15oz can of litchis, drained, or 12 fresh, peeled and pitted

More chocolate than is good for you

I recommend you make this for someone you fancy—wife, husband, girlfriend, lover, Britney Spears. As long as they love choccy, I guarantee they will be powerless to your advances as the cupid of cheesecakes takes control.

1 Crush the bourbon biscuits, add the butter and mix well, then press into a 9inch springform pan and chill for 20 minutes.

2 Preheat the oven to 350°F. To make the filling, put the chocolate in a bowl over barely simmering water (make sure the water doesn't touch the bottom of the bowl) and leave until melted.

3 Put the cream cheese and superfine sugar in a food processor and whiz until smooth, then add the eggs and pulse to mix. Add the cocoa powder and melted chocolate and pulse again.

4 Spoon the filling onto the cracker base and bake in the oven for about 1 hour until springy to the touch. Allow to cool in the pan then turn it out.

5 Ideally this should be served topped with grated chocolate, a dusting of cocoa powder and with a rich chocolate sauce. To make the sauce, melt the chocolate and cream over a bowl of simmering water, then whisk in the butter. (Serve the sauce immediately as it won't reheat.) Now wait for the magic to work.

For the base

9oz British bourbon (or Oriels) biscuits

1 stick + 1 tbsp (9 tbsp) unsalted butter, melted

For the filling

7oz best-quality dark chocolate (not unsweetened)

2lb full-fat cream cheese

$2/3$ cup superfine sugar

6 eggs

$3/4$ cup cocoa powder, plus extra for dusting

For the sauce

8oz best-quality dark chocolate (not unsweetened), plus extra for sprinkling

1 cup heavy cream

2 tbsp unsalted butter, cut into small pieces

Goat's cheese and
lemon cheesecake

Feeds 12

This is a brilliant dessert for anyone without a hugely sweet tooth, the strong goat's cheese works brilliantly with the lemon; it's the only slightly grown-up one of all the cheesecakes.

1 To make the base, put the crackers, nuts, and butter into a bowl, mix together and press into a 9inch springform pan. Chill for 20 minutes.

2 Preheat the oven to 350°F. Pop both cheeses and the sugar into a food processor and pulse till smoothish. I like a bit of texture in this one.

3 Add the eggs and lemon zest and juice and pulse to combine, then spoon onto the cracker base. Bake in the oven for about 1 hour until the cake is springy. Let it cool fully before turning out. I like to serve this with Greek yogurt, rather than cream.

For the base

7oz crushed graham crackers

½ cup crushed pecans

1 stick + 1 tbsp (9 tbsp) unsalted butter, melted

For the filling

1lb 5oz peeled goat's cheese

10oz mascarpone cheese

⅔ cup superfine sugar

6 eggs

zest and juice of 2 lemons

Pecan and white chocolate pie

Feeds 12

While I love the sophistication of a classic lemon tart and the delights of summer fruits, I think a piece of pie is second only to cheesecake in the dessert stakes. Pecan pie is a sugar junkies' delight. To make it richer I'm adding white chocolate.

1 Preheat the oven to 400°F. Roll out the pastry on a lightly floured surface and press it into a 10inch tart case. Line the pastry with foil and rice or baking beans and bake in the oven for 15 minutes. Then remove the rice and foil and cook for another 15 minutes to dry out the case.

2 Beat one of the eggs and brush the pastry case with this eggwash, then cook for a further 5 minutes to seal the case.

3 Meanwhile, make the filling. Whisk the remaining eggs well, then add the sugar, syrup, butter, and vanilla and mix well.

4 Lightly break half the nuts and fold into the mixture, together with the chocolate. Pour the mix into the cooked case and then top with the remaining nuts.

5 Reduce the oven to 350°F and bake the pie for 40 minutes until set (don't panic if the mixture looks too sloppy—it will set it fast). Leave the pie to cool.

6 Serve a large wedge with a spoonful of wicked whipped cream.

1 quantity of sweet shortcrust pastry (see page 124)

flour for dusting

7 eggs

1 packed cup soft light brown sugar

½ cup English golden syrup or corn syrup

2oz unsalted butter, melted

a dash of vanilla extract

1lb shelled pecan nuts

3½oz white chocolate, grated

whipped cream, to serve

Passion fruit tart

If you like classic French lemon tart, then you're gonna love this baby. The exotic taste of passion fruit is magnificent. In fact, the passion fruit syrup is a great sweet sauce for ice creams and poured over fruit.

1 To make the pastry, put the flour, butter, salt, and confectioners' sugar in a food processor and pulse until "crumby." Add the milk and egg yolks and pulse until it forms a dough. Turn it out onto a floured surface and knead for a few minutes, then cover and chill for at least 1 hour.

2 Turn the pastry out onto your floured surface and roll out 2inches larger than a 11inch tart case. Push the pastry into the base, leaving the excess hanging over the sides, and chill for at least 30 minutes.

3 Preheat the oven to 350°F. Line the pastry case with foil and rice or baking beans and bake in the oven for 20 minutes. Remove the rice or beans and foil, brush with the eggwash and cook for a further 10 minutes. Remove from the oven and trim off the excess pastry with a sharp knife. Leave to cool.

4 To make the filling, put the sugar and water into a pan and heat gently until the sugar dissolves. Tip in the passion fruit pulp and allow to cool.

5 Whisk the eggs and sugar together, then add the cream. Using a slotted spoon, add all the passion fruit pulp to the cream mixture with a little of the juice, probably about 1 tablespoon. Reserve the remaining juice to use as extra sauce.

6 Pour this custard into the cooked and cooled tart case. Incidentally, a little tip is to fill the tart case while it's sitting on the oven shelf, with the shelf pulled out—genius or what?

7 Reduce the oven to 325°F and bake the tart on the middle shelf for about 40 minutes. It should still be a little wobbly, but it will carry on cooking and will set. To serve, dust the tart with confectioners' sugar and a spoonful of the extra sauce.

For the pastry

1¾ cups all-purpose flour, plus extra for dusting

¾ stick (6 tbsp) cold unsalted butter, cubed

pinch of salt

⅞ cup confectioners' sugar, sifted

3½ tbsp milk

2 egg yolks

1 egg, beaten, for eggwash

confectioners' sugar, to serve

For the filling

1¾ cups superfine sugar

⅔ cup water

pulp and juice of 12 passion fruit

9 eggs

1¼ cups heavy cream

Chocolate and prune tart with Earl Grey tea custard

Feeds at least 8

If you think prunes are something to be avoided at all costs, think again, at least until you've tried this decadent tart. Soaking them in Earl Grey tea overnight brings out a really rich flavor in them, which goes particularly well with chocolate—and brandy.

1 Preheat the oven to 400°F. Roll out the pastry on a lightly floured surface and press it into a 10inch tart case. Line the pastry with foil and rice or baking beans and bake in the oven for 15 minutes. Then remove the rice and foil and cook for another 15 minutes to dry out the case.

2 Brush the pastry case with the eggwash, then cook for a further 5 minutes to seal the case.

3 To make the filling, strain the prunes and reserve the tea.

4 Put the chocolate and butter into a bowl.

5 Pour the cream into a pan and bring just up to a boil, then pour over the chocolate and butter and stir until it's all smooth and creamy.

6 Pour just enough of the chocolate mixture into the pastry case to leave a little space at the top, then press the prunes into the surface in a jolly attractive manner. Chill to set.

7 To make the custard, heat the milk to scalding point.

8 Whisk the egg yolks and sugar together in a pan, then pour the milk over them and stir to combine. Add the vanilla seeds and about 4 tbsp of the reserved Earl Grey tea and put back on a low heat. Cook, stirring, until the custard will coat the back of a spoon.

9 Cut a big fat piece of tart, sit it on a plate, pour on some custard and have a large brandy.

1 quantity sweet shortcrust pastry (see page 124)
flour for dusting
1 egg, beaten, for eggwash

For the filling

20 Agen prunes, pitted and soaked in Earl Grey tea overnight
10oz best-quality dark chocolate (not unsweetened), broken into pieces
2 tbsp unsalted butter
1¼ cups heavy cream

For the custard

1¾ cups milk
4 egg yolks
2 tbsp superfine sugar
seeds of 1 vanilla bean

Steamed suet pudding with banana and toffee

Feeds 6

This is a real, old-fashioned British pudding. It stirs memories for the "old folks" and the curiosity of their grandchildren. My version is like that long-lost friend who was a bit geeky at school, but has grown into a smooth sophisticated professional and is now everyone's best mate. Go on, you know you want to...

1 Put the flour, baking powder, suet, sugar, currants, and orange zest into a bowl and stir to mix. Add the milk and bananas and mix to a dough.

2 Roll the dough into a cylinder, about 6 x 2inches. Wrap in buttered greaseproof, leaving room for it to rise, and seal at each end. Put into a steamer and steam for 1 hour.

3 To make the custard, put the milk and vanilla seeds into a pan and bring to a boil. Pour onto the egg yolks and sugar and beat well. Return to the pan and cook over a low heat until it coats the back of a spoon.

4 For the toffee sauce, put the sugar, butter, and syrup into a pan and bring to the boil, then remove from the heat and add the cream.

5 Unwrap the steamed pudding and cut into slices. Cover with the custard and then the toffee sauce.

2½ cups all-purpose flour

2 tsp baking powder

5½oz shredded vegetable suet

6 tbsp superfine sugar

1 cup currants

zest of 1 orange

⅔ cup milk

1–2 bananas, chopped

butter for greasing

For the custard

2½ cups milk

seeds of 1 vanilla bean

6 egg yolks

6 tbsp superfine sugar

For the toffee sauce

½ cup soft dark brown sugar

¾ stick + 1 tbsp (7 tbsp) unsalted butter

⅓ cup British golden syrup or corn syrup

1½ cup heavy cream

Melting chocolate pudding

Feeds 4

I feel it my duty to issue a health warning with this magnificent dessert—OK, you have to be willing to experience rich banana cake, melting ganache (the stuff in the middle of posh chocolates) as well as creamy, chocolatey custard. This pud is so sexy that if it was a girlfriend you wouldn't take it home to meet your parents! Speaking of which —the banana loaf recipe is my mom's and is brilliant sliced and buttered on its own. Thanks, mom.

1 First make the ganache. Put the chocolate and butter in a bowl. Pour the cream into a pan, add the sugar and bring to a boil, then pour over the chocolate and butter and stir to melt. Cover and chill for at least 4 hours.

2 Preheat the oven to 350°F. Grease a 2lb loaf tin. To make the banana loaf, dissolve the bicarbonate of soda in the milk, then add the bananas. Sift the baking powder and flour together in a large bowl, then fold in the banana mixture. Stir in the butter, sugars, and the eggs. Spoon the mixture into the loaf pan and bake for about 1 hour, until set. Allow to cool.

3 To make the custard, put the chocolate, coffee, and butter into a bowl. In a separate bowl, whisk together the eggs, egg yolks, and sugar. Put the cream and milk into a saucepan, bring to a boil, then pour over the chocolate and coffee mixture and stir to melt. Then pour this over the whisked eggs and sugar and stir to combine.

4 Trim the edges of the banana loaf and cut the loaf into 1inch cubes. Put the cubes in a large bowl, pour enough chocolate custard over to cover them, and leave to stand for 30 minutes.

5 Preheat the oven to 400°F. Butter four rings, 3inch ideally, and stand them on waxed paper. Pack each halfway with some of the custardy cake. Roll a ball of ganache and pop it onto the middle of the cake, top with more cake and a little more custard. Bake for 15 minutes and serve immediately with the remaining custard or cream. When you cut open the pud the melted ganache will ooze out.

For the banana loaf

1 tsp bicarbonate of soda

2 tbsp milk

3 mashed bananas

1 tsp baking powder

1¾ cups all-purpose flour

1 stick + 1 tbsp (9 tbsp) unsalted butter, softened

⅓ cup brown sugar

½ cup granulated sugar

2 eggs, beaten

For the custard

9oz best-quality dark chocolate (not unsweetened), broken into pieces

a shot of strong espresso coffee

½ stick (4 tbsp) unsalted butter

3 eggs and 2 yolks

¾ cup brown sugar

1¼ cups heavy cream

¾ cup milk

For the ganache

9oz best-quality dark chocolate (not unsweetened), broken into pieces

1 tbsp butter

1 cup heavy cream

2 tbsp superfine sugar

Chocolate brownies
with marshmallow sauce

Feeds 4

Are they a cake or a cookie? I can never decide, so I constantly eat them to try and make up my mind. These fellas are really rich and the melty, marshmallow sauce is like eating liquid fluffy clouds.

1 Preheat the oven to 350ºF. Put the eggs and sugar in a bowl and beat until pale and creamy, then add the butter.

2 Sift the flour and cocoa into the egg mixture, then add the melted choccy and the nuts and mix well.

3 Spoon the mixture into a greased 8inch baking dish and bake in the oven for about 35 minutes. Allow to cool.

4 To make the sauce, bring the cream and vanilla to a boil, then simmer for 5 minutes to thicken. Now stir in the marshmallows. The sauce is ready when the marshmallows are half melted.

5 Cut a decent chunk of brownie and pour over the liquid clouds!

4 eggs

1 cup superfine sugar

2 stick (1 cup) unsalted butter, melted, plus extra for greasing

⅔ cup all-purpose flour

¾ cup cocoa powder

8oz best-quality dark chocolate (not unsweetened), melted

1 cup chopped skinned hazelnuts

For the sauce

¾ cup heavy cream

seeds of 1 vanilla pod

4oz pink marshmallows

Hot choccy and churros

This makes me think of Spain—Valencia in particular. After a particularly heavy night, which ended up in an open-air salsa club by the marina, I struggled round the corner to get a sugary fix of churros, the sweet donut-like icons, together with the sweetest, bestest hot chocolate in the history of the world (it was that big a hangover). So mark this page under "hangover cure" and enjoy.

1 To make the churros, sift the flour, bicarbonate of soda, and salt into a bowl. Make a well in the center, add the water and whisk hard to combine and get rid of any lumps. Let the batter rest for 1 hour.

2 Heat the oil until a piece of bread sizzles when dropped in. Put the batter in a pastry bag and squeeze down into the oil, cutting off after each 4inches of batter. Fry until golden brown, then drain on paper towels and roll the churros in sugar.

3 To make the hot choccy, put the chocolate in a bowl over barely simmering water (make sure the water doesn't touch the bottom of the bowl), and leave until melted.

4 Put the milk and cinnamon stick in a pan and warm for about 10 minutes. Meanwhile, whip the cream. Remove the cinnamon stick and whisk in the melted chocolate and the condensed milk until smooth. Pour into a mug, top with the whipped cream and drink with the churros.

For the churros

3¼ cups all-purpose flour

1 tsp bicarbonate of soda

pinch of salt

1¾ cups boiling water

vegetable oil for deep-frying

superfine sugar for dusting

For the hot choccy

9oz best-quality dark chocolate (not unsweetened), broken into pieces

1¾ cups milk

1 cinnamon stick

1 cup sweetened condensed milk

1 cup whipping cream

Chocolate and red wine pots with donuts

Feeds 8

Even though we've got donuts with them, this is quite a grown-up taste, because of the wine in the choccy pots. The dessert is very rich, so don't serve these after a hugely stodgy meal, but if you do maybe make 16 mini pots and loads of tiny donuts.

1 First make the donuts. Cream the butter and sugar together in a bowl, add the eggs and beat well, then add a dash of vanilla extract and the milk.

2 In a separate bowl, mix the flour, polenta, baking powder, and a pinch of salt. Add to the creamed ingredients and mix well. Sprinkle with flour, cover and chill for at least 8 hours.

3 To make the choccy pots, pour the wine into a pan, add ½ cup of the sugar and bring to a boil. Simmer and reduce by two-thirds, then let it cool.

4 Melt the chocolate in a bowl over simmering water, then whisk in the wine syrup followed by the egg yolks.

5 Heat the milk, cream, and remaining sugar in a pan to scalding point, then whisk into the chocolate mixture. Whisk in the butter, pour into eight ramekins and chill until set.

6 Turn out the donut dough onto a floured surface and roll out to ½inch thickness. Using a 5cm/2inch cutter, cut out loads of rounds. Put onto a board, sprinkle with flour and chill for 30 minutes.

7 Heat the oil and deep-fry the donuts until golden brown. Drain on paper towels, then roll them in sugar. Serve alongside the choccy pots with a quenelle of whipped cream, if you like.

For the donuts

¾ stick (6 tbsp) unsalted butter, softened

6 tbsp superfine sugar, plus extra to roll the donuts in

4 eggs

vanilla extract

2 tbsp milk

6 cups all-purpose flour, plus extra for dusting

¾ cup dry polenta

2 tbsp baking powder

salt

vegetable oil for frying

For the choccy pots

1 cup red wine, medium bodied and fruity

⅔ cup superfine sugar

1lb 2oz best-quality dark chocolate (not unsweetened), broken into pieces

8 egg yolks

1 cup + 1–2 tbsp, if necessary, milk

1 cup heavy cream

1 tbsp unsalted butter

whipped cream, to serve (optional)

Strawberry samosas

Feeds 6

These are good fun and great to serve after a curry. You can use any soft fruit for the filling—mango also works particularly well. If you don't fancy them with yogurt, just drizzle with some honey.

1 To make the pastry, sift the flour and salt into a bowl, then "cut" the butter into it until combined. Add the milk and form into a dough, then cover and chill for 20 minutes.

2 For the filling, put the strawberries into a bowl, add the lemon zest, sugar, and cinnamon and stir to combine.

3 Roll out the pastry on a lightly floured surface and cut into six circles. Cut each circle in half and place a little of the strawberry mixture in one corner then fold over the opposite corner to make a tight triangle. Press down the edges to seal and brush with a little butter.

4 Heat the oil and shallow-fry the samosas until crisp and golden on all sides.

5 To make the yogurt dressing, simply combine the yogurt and mint in a bowl.

6 For the basil syrup, put the sugar, water and vanilla in a pan and heat until the sugar has dissolved. Allow to cool, then put in a food processor with the basil and blitz, then pass through a very fine strainer.

7 Serve a couple of samosas with a dollop of yogurt dressing and a swirl of basil syrup.

1¾ cups all-purpose flour, plus extra for dusting

pinch of salt

2 tbsp unsalted butter, plus extra for brushing

2 tbsp warm milk

vegetable oil for shallow frying

For the filling

8oz strawberries, hulled and chopped

zest of ½ lemon

⅓ cup soft light brown sugar

pinch of cinnamon

For the yogurt dressing

¾ cup Greek yogurt

lots of freshly chopped mint

For the basil syrup

1 cup superfine sugar

⅔ cup water

splash of vanilla extract

lots of fresh basil leaves

Bounty profiteroles

Feeds 6–8

I like to serve one large profiterole, which is probably really a choux bun, but you can do lots of little ones if you like. Oh, before you start this, you have to make the custard for the filling a day in advance—so none until tomorrow, then.

1 First make the filling. Whisk the egg yolks and sugar in a bowl until pale and fluffy, then sift in the flour and mix well. Pour the coconut milk into a pan and bring to a boil. As soon as it boils, pour it onto the egg mixture and stir well. Pour it back into the pan and bring back to a boil, then turn down the heat and cook for another 5 minutes until it thickens. Spoon it back into a bowl and fold in the desiccated coconut, then cover and chill overnight. Make sure the plastic wrap is resting on the surface so you don't get a skin.

2 The next day, whip the cream and fold into the custard.

3 To make the choux buns, preheat the oven to 400°F. Put the butter and water into a pan, bring to a boil and heat until the butter melts. Take the pan off the heat, tip in all the flour and mix well. Using a wooden spoon, beat in the eggs, one at a time. Add a pinch of salt.

4 Transfer the dough to a pastry bag and allow to cool for a few minutes. Now pipe 'blobs' of pastry onto a floured baking sheet. You'll get about 8 squash or golfball size dollops, or as many little ones as you like. The thing to remember is that the pastry will at least double in size, so give them plenty of space on the sheet to expand.

5 Bake in the oven for 30–40 minutes. You want them golden and firm on the outside and dry in the middle. I quite often put them on the bottom shelf for another 5–10 minutes to make sure.

6 To make the sauce, simply heat the ingredients together in a pan until combined.

7 Make a small hole in the base of each profiterole and pipe in some custard. Then sit it in the middle of a plate and pour over some warm choccy sauce. I think this is where I say it's a taste of paradise.

1¼ sticks + 1 tbsp (11 tbsp) unsalted butter
1 cup water
1¾ cups all-purpose flour, plus extra for dusting
6 eggs
pinch of salt

For the filling

6 egg yolks
¾ cup superfine sugar
5 tbsp all-purpose flour
1¾ cups canned coconut milk
⅔ cup desiccated coconut
¾ cup heavy cream

For the sauce

7oz best-quality dark chocolate (not unsweetened), broken into pieces
½ stick (4 tbsp) unsalted butter
⅔ cup water

Winter fruit clafoutis

Feeds 6

Sometimes winter fruits can be a bit temperamental, which is why crisps and pies are good options. Another option is this clafoutis, which is basically fruit soaked in booze, topped with a sweet batter and baked. Of course, you can use summer fruits as well.

1 Put the fruit into a bowl, sprinkle the Malibu over and leave for 30 minutes.

2 Preheat the oven to 400°F. Put the milk, cream, and vanilla seeds in a pan and bring to a boil. Take off the heat and cool slightly.

3 Put the sugar and eggs into a bowl and beat well, then add the flour and salt and stir to mix.

4 Strain in the milk mixture and beat well.

5 Butter a 9 x 10inch dish and sprinkle with sugar. Add the fruit, then pour the batter over.

6 Bake in the oven for 25 minutes, then leave to cool. Serve with lightly whipped cream.

1lb prepared winter fruits, such as cranberry, pear, apple

4 tbsp Malibu coconut liqueur

½ cup milk

⅔ cup whipping cream, plus extra to serve

seeds from 1 vanilla bean

¾ cup superfine sugar, plus extra for sprinkling

4 eggs

3½ tbsp all-purpose flour

pinch of salt

butter for greasing

Blueberry pancakes

Feeds 4–6

Now the cottage cheese in the mixture is wonderful. I started using it because one of my fave authors, Robert Crais, has a detective character called Elvis Cole, who uses cottage cheese in his pancake mix, so I tried it and it works—see what you learn from books.

1 Mix the flour, bicarbonate of soda, and sugar together in a bowl.

2 In a separate bowl, combine the egg, melted butter, milk, and cottage cheese, then stir into the flour mix. Stir in the blueberries and lemon zest.

3 Spoon some of the mixture into a lightly oiled warm skillet and cook for 1 minute on each side, until golden. Continue to make pancakes in the same way with the remaining mixture.

4 Sit a few pancakes in a stack and drizzle maple syrup over the top.

1½ cups self-rising flour

1 tsp bicarbonate of soda

4 tbsp superfine sugar

1 egg

½ stick (4 tbsp) unsalted butter, melted

1 cup milk

½ cup cottage cheese

8oz blueberries

zest of 1 small lemon

vegetable oil for frying

maple syrup, to serve

Banana tarte tatin

Feeds 6

I remember sitting in a café in Paris eating warm apple tatin and drinking a brandy with Ali, my wife, and thinking all was right with the world. That's how tatin makes you feel; it's warming, comforting and scrummy—but I prefer dark rum to brandy and bananas go better with my tipple, so I wait for the day when it's banana tatin and rum in a café in Jamaica—or pour my own!

1 Preheat the oven to 375°F. Pour the water into a heavy-bottomed pan, sprinkle over the sugar and heat, without stirring, until the sugar dissolves, then simmer gently until the sugar turns golden. Stir in the butter, then pour into a 7inch round baking pan.

2 Pack the banana pieces tightly into the pan.

3 Press the pastry over the top of the bananas and trim, then bake for about 20 minutes, until the pastry is crisp and golden.

4 Allow to cool until just warm, then turn out and serve with whipped cream.

3½ tbsp water
½ cup superfine sugar
2 tbsp unsalted butter
12 bananas, peeled and cut into 2inch pieces
7oz ready-rolled puff pastry
whipped cream, to serve

Rosemary and olive oil cake with honeyed figs

Feeds 8

You know when you fancy a bit of cake with your tea or coffee in the afternoon, but you don't want a sticky gooey beast? Well, this Italian cake hits the spot. It's sweet enough to give a boost and a treat, but doesn't overface you. However, if you serve it with the honeyed figs and black pepper ricotta, you're asking for trouble.

1 Preheat the oven to 325°F. Put the eggs and sugar into a food processor and whiz until pale and fluffy.

2 Keep the motor running and drizzle in the oil, then with the mixer on slow add the flour, baking powder, and salt and pulse to incorporate. Turn out into a bowl and fold in the rosemary.

3 Pour into a 10inch greased loaf pan and bake in the oven for 45–50 minutes. Cool, then turn out.

4 For the figs, put the marsala and honey in a small pan and bring to a boil, then quickly coat the figs.

5 For the ricotta, put all the ingredients into a bowl and stir to mix.

6 Serve slices of the cake with the figs, ricotta, and a glass of vin santo or sweet wine.

4 eggs

¾ cup superfine sugar

½ cup extra-virgin olive oil

2½ cups all-purpose flour

1 tbsp baking powder

pinch of salt

finely chopped fresh rosemary, to taste

butter for greasing

For the honeyed figs

3½ tbsp marsala wine

2 tbsp honey

6 figs, halved

For the ricotta

½ cup ricotta cheese

½ cup whipped cream

2 tbsp superfine sugar

black pepper

Lemon, lime, and orange polenta cake

Feeds 10–12

I don't know why this is so gorgeous. I'm not a huge fan of polenta and I'm not a huge fan of "plain" cakes, but this little number with a cup of tea or coffee is divine. It's so moist—traditionally it's done with just lemon, but I love that fruit candy effect of all three citrus fruits. It's also the kind of cake that cake pans were invented for.

1 Preheat the oven to 350ºF. Cream the butter and sugar in a bowl until pale and fluffy, then stir in the almonds.

2 Add the eggs, one at a time, then the vanilla.

3 Stir in the zests and juices, then mix in the polenta, salt, and baking powder.

4 Spoon the mixture into a 12inch greased and floured cake pan and bake for 45–55 minutes until golden and firm. Leave to cool in the pan.

5 Serve on its own or with some mascarpone—and tea or coffee.

4 sticks (2 cups) unsalted butter, plus extra for greasing

2⅓ cups superfine sugar

4½ cups ground almonds

6 eggs

good dash of vanilla extract

zest of 2 lemons, 1 orange and 1 lime

juice of ½ lemon and ½ lime

a quick squeeze of orange juice

1⅓ cups polenta

pinch of salt

1½ tsp baking powder

flour for dusting

Index

arancini 16, 85
Arugula, fig & pecan salad with creamy blue
    cheese 36
asparagus
    Asparagus, potato & fennel salad with Italian
      dressing 30, 31
    Rendang shallot & asparagus curry 84
    Stilton, asparagus & caramelized shallot roulade
      with spicy chutney 95
avocado, Santa Fe Caesar salad 24

banana leaf, Coconut rice in 107
bananas
    Banana dhal 49
    Banana loaf 128
    Banana tarte tatin 138, 139
    Steamed suet pudding with banana & toffee 127
Basic tomato sauce 107
Basil roulade with goat's cheese & sun-blushed
    tomatoes 96, 97
Basil syrup 133
beans
    Black bean & eggplant chili 88
    Italian bean casserole 85
    Pumpkin enchilladas with mole sauce 47
    Santa Fe Caesar salad 24
    see also fava beans; fine green beans
beets
    Beet tart 56, 57
    caviar 96, 97
    Spicy beet & coconut soup 60, 61
    Sprouts with beet 103
bell peppers
    Blinis with sour cream & roasted bell peppers 11
    coleslaw 41
    Fattoush 33
    Gruyère-filled beefsteak tomatoes 50, 51
    Lentils with lemon 102
    Panzanella 26, 27
    red bell pepper sauce 69
    Roasted red bell peppers with fennel 52
    salsa 64
    Savory Paris-Brest 65
    Spicy red bell pepper hummus 12, 13
    Stuffed pimentos with thyme & basil 104, 105
    Sweet potato & pineapple sandwich 70, 71
Black bean & eggplant chili 88
Blinis with sour cream & roasted bell peppers 11
Blueberry pancakes 136, 137
Bounty profiteroles 134
bread
    Coriander seed flat bread 12, 13
    Feta cheese bread 10
    pizza bases 46
bread (as ingredient)
    Cheese sausages 72
    Eggplant "stack" with pesto 42
    Fattoush 33
    Goat's cheese & mango 43
    Mushroom "rarebit" on brioche toast 44, 45
    Panzanella 26, 27
broccoli, Beet tart 56, 57
brownies, Chocolate, with marshmallow sauce 129

Bubble & squeak 100
butternut squash see pumpkin

cabbage, coleslaws 32, 41
Caesar salad, Santa Fe 24
cakes
    Banana loaf 128
    Lemon, lime, & orange polenta 141
    Rosemary & olive oil, with honeyed figs 140
cannelloni, Goat's cheese, with cherry tomatoes 78
Caramelized onion & mustard tart 92, 93
carrots
    Glazed, with caraway seeds 103
    Italian bean casserole 85
    Peas & carrots 53
    spicy coleslaw 32
caviar, beet 96, 97
Celeriac & potato dauphinoise 104
cheese
    Arugula, fig & pecan salad with creamy blue cheese 36
    Blueberry pancakes 136, 137
    Celeriac & potato dauphinoise 104
    Four-cheese & zucchini penne 82
    Fried halloumi with lemon & capers 14
    Gruyère-filled beefsteak tomatoes 50, 51
    Hazelnut & mushroom parcels 69
    Leek & potato rosti with "rarebit" topping 55
    Linguine with potato & pesto 75
    Macaroni cheese 74
    Mushroom "rarebit" on brioche toast 44, 45
    Pan haggerty 100, 101
    Parmesan-roasted parsnips 106
    Phyllo strudel with port wine sauce 66, 67
    Rosemary & olive oil cake with honeyed figs 140
    sauce 74
    sausages 72
    Stilton, asparagus & caramelized shallot roulade
      with spicy chutney 95
    Stuffed pimentos with thyme & basil 104, 105
    Wild mushroom pancakes 68
    see also cheesecakes; feta cheese; goat's cheese;
      mascarpone; mozzarella
cheesecakes
    Cherry tiramisu 115
    Goat's cheese & lemon 122
    Litchi & toasted coconut 119
    More chocolate than is good for you 120, 121
    Peanut butter & jelly 118
Cheese sausages with mustard mash & onion gravy 72
chickpeas (garbanzo beans)
    Coronation chickpeas & potato salad 29
    Moroccan spaghetti 80, 81
    Oriental pie 91
    Spicy red bell pepper hummus 12, 13
chili, Black bean & eggplant 88
Chinese mushroom pancakes 48
chocolate
    Black bean & eggplant chili 88
    Cherry tiramisu cheesecake 115
    Chocolate & prune tart with Earl Grey tea custard 126
    Chocolate & red wine pots with donuts 132
    Chocolate brownies with marshmallow sauce 129
    ganache 128
    Hot choccy & churros 130, 131
    Melting chocolate pudding 128
    mole sauce 47

    More chocolate than is good for you 120, 121
    Pecan & white chocolate pie 123
    sauces 115, 120, 128, 134
    Zucotto 116, 117
choux pastry 65, 134
churros 130, 131
chutneys 56, 95
clafoutis, Winter fruit 135
coconut & coconut milk
    Bounty profiteroles 134
    Coconut rice in banana leaf 107
    Curry sauce 70, 71
    Jerk-spiced pumpkin pie 94
    Litchi & toasted coconut cheesecake 119
    Red Thai bean curry 86, 87
    Rendang shallot & asparagus curry 84
    Spicy beet & coconut soup 60, 61
    Strawberry & coconut trifle 114
coleslaw 32, 41
Coriander seed flat bread 12, 13
Coronation chickpeas & potato salad 29
cucumber
    Chinese mushroom pancakes 48
    Fattoush 33
    Pickled cucumber salad 30
    Tzatziki 21
    Watermelon salad 36
curry
    Eggplant tikka masala 83
    pastes 84, 86
    Plantain & mango 90
    Red Thai bean 86, 87
    Rendang shallot & asparagus 84
    sauces 70, 83, 94
custard sauces 114, 126, 127, 128

dauphinoise, Celeriac & potato 104
dhal, Banana 49
Dolmades 21
donuts 132
    churros 130, 131
dressings 14, 24, 32, 33, 36, 50, 53, 54
    Italian 25
    nuoc cham 34, 35

eggplant
    Black bean & eggplant chili 88
    Eggplant "roll-mops" 40
    Eggplant "stack" with pesto 42
    Eggplant tikka 41
    Eggplant tikka masala 83
    Griddled eggplant salad with nuoc cham 34, 35
    Savory Paris-Brest 65
eggs
    Huevos rancheros 64
    Ojja with sweet potato & okra 89
    Sun-blush Niçoise 25
    see also recipes normally made with eggs
      (eg custard sauces)

Fattoush 33
fava beans
    Favetta 15
    Ojja with sweet potato & okra 89
    Red Thai bean curry 86, 87
Favetta 15

fennel
Arugula, fig & pecan salad with creamy blue cheese 36
Asparagus, potato & fennel salad with
Italian dressing 30, 31
Lemon, fennel & oyster mushroom salad 37
Roasted red bell peppers with fennel 52
feta cheese
Feta cheese bread 10
Warm stack of Greek salad with parsley pesto 28
Watermelon salad 36
figs
Arugula, fig & pecan salad with creamy blue cheese 36
Rosemary & olive oil cake with honeyed figs 140
fine green beans
Fine green beans with garlic & tomato sauce 106
Green papaya salad 37
Red Thai bean curry 86, 87
Sun-blush Niçoise 25
Four-cheese & zucchini penne 82
Fried halloumi with lemon & capers 14
fruit
Winter fruit clafoutis 135
see also specific fruits (eg strawberries)

ganache, chocolate 128
garbanzo beans see chickpeas
Glazed carrots with caraway seeds 103
Gnocchi with wild mushroom & rosemary ragu 76, 77
goat's cheese
Basil roulade with goat's cheese & sun-blushed
tomatoes 96, 97
Beet tart 56, 57
Goat's cheese & lemon cheesecake 122
Goat's cheese & mango 43
Goat's cheese cannelloni with cherry tomatoes 78
Savory Paris-Brest 65
granita, Strawberry, vodka & black pepper 112
grape leaves, Dolmades 21
gravy, Onion 72
Greek salad, Warm stack of, with parsley pesto 28
green beans see fava beans; fine green beans
Green papaya salad 37
Griddled eggplant salad with nuoc cham 34, 35
Gruyère-filled beefsteak tomatoes 50, 51

halloumi, Fried, with lemon & capers 14
Hazelnut & mushroom parcels 69
Honeycomb ice cream 111
Hot choccy & churros 130, 131
Huevos rancheros (ranch eggs) 64
hummus, Spicy red bell pepper 12, 13

ice cream, Honeycomb 111
Italian bean casserole 85
Italian dressing 25

Jerk-spiced pumpkin pie 94

kiwi fruit, Strawberry & coconut trifle 114

leeks
Leek & potato rosti with "rarebit" topping 55
Leeks wrapped in phyllo 54
Phyllo strudel with port wine sauce 66, 67
Lemon, fennel & oyster mushroom salad 37
Lemon grass risotto with lime leaf tapenade 79

Lemon, lime & orange polenta cake 141
lentils
Banana dhal 49
Lentils with lemon 102
lettuce
Fattoush 33
Santa Fe Caesar salad 24
Sun-blush Niçoise 25
Lime leaf tapenade 79
Linguine with potato & pesto 75
Litchi & toasted coconut cheesecake 119

Macaroni cheese 74
mango
Goat's cheese & mango 43
Plantain & mango curry 90
marshmallow sauce 129
mascarpone
Cherry tiramisu cheesecake 115
Four-cheese & zucchini penne 82
Goat's cheese & lemon cheesecake 122
Linguine with potato & pesto 75
Strawberry & coconut trifle 114
Strawberry soup 112, 113
Melting chocolate pudding 128
mole sauce 47
Moroccan spaghetti 80, 81
mozzarella
arancini 16, 85
Eggplant "stack" with pesto 42
Proper pizza 46
Roasted red bell peppers with fennel 52
Sun-dried tomato, mozzarella & basil tart 59
Tomato & mozzarella cakes 16
Wild mushroom pancakes 68
mushrooms
Chinese mushroom pancakes 48
Gnocchi with wild mushroom & rosemary ragu 76, 77
Gruyère-filled beefsteak tomatoes 50, 51
Hazelnut & mushroom parcels 69
Lemon, fennel & oyster mushroom salad 37
Mushroom "rarebit" on brioche toast 44, 45
Oriental pie 91
Phyllo strudel with port wine sauce 66, 67
Wild mushroom pancakes 68

nectarines, Strawberry soup 112, 113
Norimaki sushi rolls 18, 19
nuoc cham 34, 35

okra
Ojja with sweet potato & okra 89
Sweet potato & pineapple sandwich 70, 71
onions
Caramelized onion & mustard tart 92, 93
chutney 56
Onion gravy 72
Pickled 40
Oriental pie 91
oyster mushrooms
Chinese mushroom pancakes 48
Lemon, fennel & oyster mushroom salad 37

Pan haggerty 100, 101
pancakes
Blinis with sour cream & roasted bell peppers 11

Blueberry 136, 137
Chinese mushroom 48
Wild mushroom 68
Panzanella 26, 27
papaya salad, Green 37
Parmesan-roasted parsnips 106
parsley pesto 28
parsnips, Parmesan-roasted 106
passion fruit
Passion fruit tart 124, 125
Strawberry soup 112, 113
pasta
Four-cheese & zucchini penne 82
Goat's cheese cannelloni with cherry tomatoes 78
Linguine with potato & pesto 75
Macaroni cheese 74
Moroccan spaghetti 80, 81
Penne all'arabiata 73
pastes, curry 84, 86
pastry
choux 65, 134
shortcrust 56, 92
sweet shortcrust 124
pastry dishes
Bounty profiteroles 134
Hazelnut & mushroom parcels 69
Jerk-spiced pumpkin pie 94
Leeks wrapped in phyllo 54
Phyllo strudel with port wine sauce 66, 67
Savory Paris-Brest 65
Strawberry samosas 133
see also tarts
Patatas bravas 20
peanut balls, Sticky rice & 15
Peanut butter & jelly cheesecake 118
pears
chutney 95
Winter fruit clafoutis 135
Peas & carrots 53
pecans
Arugula, fig & pecan salad with creamy blue cheese 36
Pecan & white chocolate pie 123
Wild mushroom pancakes 68
penne
Four-cheese & zucchini penne 82
Penne all'arabiata 73
pesto 42, 75
parsley pesto 28
Phyllo
Leeks wrapped in phyllo 54
Phyllo strudel with port wine sauce 66, 67
Pickled cucumber salad 30
Pickled onions 40
pies
Jerk-spiced pumpkin 94
Oriental 91
Pecan & white chocolate 123
pimentos see bell peppers
pineapple sandwich, Sweet potato & 70, 71
pizza, Proper 46
plantain
Jerk-spiced pumpkin pie 94
Plantain & mango curry 90
plum sauce 48
polenta
donuts 132

Lemon, lime & orange polenta cake 141
popsicles 110
port wine sauce 66, 67
potatoes
    Asparagus, potato & fennel salad with
        Italian dressing 30, 31
    Bubble & squeak 100
    Celeriac & potato dauphinoise 104
    Coronation chickpeas & potato salad 29
    Gnocchi with wild mushroom &
        rosemary ragu 76, 77
    Leek & potato rosti with "rarebit" topping 55
    Linguine with potato & pesto 75
    Oriental pie 91
    Pan haggerty 100, 101
    Patatas bravas 20
    Smoky roasties 102
    Sun-blush Niçoise 25
    Thai spiced potato cakes with spicy coleslaw 17
profiteroles, Bounty 134
Proper pizza 46
prunes, Chocolate & prune tart with Earl Grey tea
    custard 126
pumpkin
    Jerk-spiced pumpkin pie 94
    Pumpkin enchilladas with mole sauce 47

ragu, Rosemary 76, 77
Ranch eggs (huevos rancheros) 64
"rarebit"
    Leek & potato rosti with "rarebit" topping 55
    Mushroom "rarebit" on brioche toast 44, 45
raspberries, Strawberry soup 112, 113
red cabbage, spicy coleslaw 32
red peppers see bell peppers
Red Thai bean curry 86, 87
Rendang shallot & asparagus curry 84
rice
    arancini 16, 85
    Coconut rice in banana leaf 107
    Dolmades 21
    Lemon grass risotto with lime leaf tapenade 79
    Norimaki sushi rolls 18, 19
    Ojja with sweet potato & okra 89
    Sticky rice & peanut balls 15
    Tomato & mozzarella cakes 16
Roasted red bell peppers with fennel 52
"roll-mops", Eggplant 40
Rosemary & olive oil cake with honeyed figs 140
Rosemary ragu 76, 77
roulades
    Basil, with goat's cheese & sun-blushed
        tomatoes 96, 97
    Stilton, asparagus & caramelized shallot, with spicy
        chutney 95

salads
    Arugula, fig & pecan, with creamy blue cheese 36
    Asparagus, potato & fennel, with Italian dressing 30, 31
    coleslaws 32, 41
    Coronation chickpeas & potato 29
    Fattoush 33
    Green papaya 37
    Griddled eggplant, with nuoc cham 34, 35
    Lemon, fennel & oyster mushroom 37

Panzanella 26, 27
Pickled cucumber 30
Santa Fe Caesar salad 24
Sun-blush Niçoise 25
Sweet potato 32
Warm stack of Greek salad with parsley pesto 28
Watermelon 36
salsa 64
samosas, Strawberry 133
Santa Fe Caesar salad 24
sauces
    cheese 74
    chocolate 115, 120, 128, 134
    curry 70, 83, 94
    custard 114, 126, 127, 128
    marshmallow 129
    mole 47
    onion gravy 72
    plum 48
    port wine 66, 67
    red bell pepper 69
    toffee 127
    tomato 107
sausages, cheese 72
Savory Paris-Brest 65
shallot & asparagus curry, Rendang 84
shortcrust pastry 56, 92
    sweet 124
Simple tomato tart 58
Smoky roasties 102
soups
    Spicy beet & coconut 60, 61
    Strawberry 112, 113
spaghetti, Moroccan 80, 81
Spicy beet & coconut soup 60, 61
spicy coleslaw 32
Spicy red bell pepper hummus with coriander seed
    flat bread 12, 13
spinach
    Goat's cheese cannelloni with cherry tomatoes 78
    Jerk-spiced pumpkin pie 94
Steamed suet pudding with banana & toffee 127
sprouts
    Bubble & squeak 100
    Sprouts with beet 103
squash see pumpkin
Sticky rice & peanut balls 15
Stilton, asparagus & caramelized shallot roulade with
    spicy chutney 95
strawberries
    Strawberry & black pepper popsicle 110
    Strawberry & coconut trifle 114
    Strawberry samosas 133
    Strawberry soup 112, 113
    Strawberry, vodka & black pepper granita 112
strudel with port wine sauce, Phyllo 66, 67
Stuffed pimentos with thyme & basil 104, 105
Sun-blush Niçoise 25
Sun-dried tomato, mozzarella & basil tart 59
sushi rolls, Norimaki 18, 19
sweet potatoes
    Ojja with sweet potato & okra 89
    Oriental pie 91
    Sweet potato & pineapple sandwich 70, 71
    Sweet potato salad 32

tapenade, Lime leaf 79
tarts
    Banana tarte tatin 138, 139
    Beet 56, 57
    Caramelized onion & mustard 92, 93
    Chocolate & prune, with Earl Grey tea custard 126
    Passion fruit 124, 125
    Pecan & white chocolate pie 123
    Simple tomato 58
    Sun-dried tomato, mozzarella & basil 59
Thai spiced potato cakes with spicy coleslaw 17
tiramisu cheesecake, Cherry 115
toffee sauce 127
tomatoes
    Basic tomato sauce 107
    Basil roulade with goat's cheese & sun-blushed
        tomatoes 96, 97
    Beet tart 56, 57
    Black bean & eggplant chili 88
    Eggplant "stack" with pesto 42
    Eggplant tikka masala 83
    Fattoush 33
    Fine green beans with garlic & tomato sauce 106
    Gnocchi with wild mushroom &
        rosemary ragu 76, 77
    Goat's cheese cannelloni with cherry tomatoes 78
    Green papaya salad 37
    Gruyère-filled beefsteak tomatoes 50, 51
    Italian bean casserole 85
    Macaroni cheese 74
    mole sauce 47
    Moroccan spaghetti 80, 81
    Ojja with sweet potato & okra 89
    Panzanella 26, 27
    Patatas bravas 20
    Penne all'arabiata 73
    Phyllo strudel with port wine sauce 66, 67
    Proper pizza 46
    Red Thai bean curry 86, 87
    Roasted red bell peppers with fennel 52
    salsa 64
    Savory Paris-Brest 65
    Simple tomato tart 58
    Sun-blush Niçoise 25
    Sun-dried tomato, mozzarella & basil tart 59
    Tomato & mozzarella cakes 16
    Warm stack of Greek salad with parsley pesto 28
Tzatziki 21

Warm stack of Greek salad with parsley pesto 28
Watermelon & lime popsicles 110
Watermelon salad 36
Wild mushroom pancakes 68
Winter fruit clafoutis 135

yellow peppers see bell peppers

zucchini
    Four-cheese & zucchini penne 82
    Gruyère-filled beefsteak tomatoes 50, 51
    salsa 64
    Savory Paris-Brest 65
    Warm stack of Greek salad with parsley pesto 28
Zucotto 116, 117